*Rachel Ran Out
    and Do...
  Slippery St...*

The gate resisted her ferverish tugs, and she
wrenched at it, half hysterical in her need to
escape the tangible hatred in the little house
behind her.

A strong hand closed over hers, and she looked
up into the tempestuous eyes of Griffin
Fletcher.

He was drenched. Rainwater poured down his
face, plastering his thick, ebony-colored hair to
his head in dripping tendrils. Through his now-
translucent shirt, Rachel could see the dark
tracery of hair matting his chest.

Griffin didn't seem to notice the rain; he simply
stood there, watching Rachel's face. Then, incredibly, he brought his hands to rest on her
shoulders.

I want him, Rachel thought with horror. *Dear
Heaven, I want him.*

Books by Linda Lael Miller

Knights
Pirates
Princess Annie
The Legacy
Taming Charlotte
Yankee Wife
Daniel's Bride
Caroline and the Raider
Emma and the Outlaw
Lily and the Major
My Darling Melissa
Angelfire
Moonfire
Wanton Angel
Lauralee
Memory's Embrace
Corbin's Fancy
Willow
Banner O'Brien
Desire and Destiny
Fletcher's Woman

Published by POCKET BOOKS

Linda Lael Miller

FLETCHER'S WOMAN

POCKET BOOKS

New York London Toronto Sydney Tokyo Singapore

An *Original* Publication of POCKET BOOKS

POCKET BOOKS, a division of Simon & Schuster Inc.
1230 Avenue of the Americas, New York, NY 10020

Copyright © 1983 by Linda Lael Miller

ISBN: 0-671-01004-2

First Pocket Books printing August 1983

15 14 13 12 11 10 9 8 7

POCKET and colophon are registered trademarks of Simon & Schuster Inc.

Cover art by Danilo Ducak

Printed in the U.S.A.

*For Rick—lover, husband, friend.
We've sailed many a stormy sea,
my love, but never run aground.*

Prologue

Providence, Washington Territory
May 21, 1889

Rebecca McKinnon sank back on her satin pillows as the pain intensified. With fingers that seemed to bear little regard for the orders of her mind, she took the letter from the table beside her bed and read it for perhaps the hundredth time since its arrival the day before.

Anguish filled her, mingled with a dizzying, hopeful wonder. *Ezra. At last, Ezra had found her. And that meant that Rachel probably would, too.*

Tears of frustration and pain burned in her eyes. *Would he tell Rachel what he knew? Would he set up some kind of mother-daughter confrontation?*

Rebecca shuddered. Her head began to throb, and she flung back the red velvet comforter that covered her and struggled out of bed. She crossed the room on thin, shaky legs, her once voluptuous body gaunt and bony beneath the gossamer beige silk of her nightdress.

On the dresser top, the liquor awaited—amber comfort confined to a crystal decanter.

A chill ran through Rebecca's soul as she unstopped the bottle and poured a generous dose of its contents into a glass, then replaced the stopper and returned the brandy to its place.

The already dim room darkened; the storm blowing in from the sea was almost upon the town of Providence. The bitter winds announcing its arrival were already screaming around the clapboard corners of Rebecca's business establishment and creeping across the bare wooden floors to sting her naked feet.

She raised the glass high, in a mock toast—to Ezra. To the mouthy sailor who had betrayed her whereabouts in a Seattle saloon. To her own vanished youth.

Rebecca glared at her shadowy reflection in the dingy, rippled mirror over the dresser, and a sigh escaped her.

Her long, ebony hair was threaded through with gray now, and the fire had long since left the wide, amethyst eyes, rendering them flat and dull and vacant. Her cheeks were hollow and void of all color, her once full and mobile lips were thinned by years of degradation and regret.

Where was that other Rebecca now? Where was the vibrant, spirited woman who had smiled back at her from so many kinder looking glasses?

"Dead," Rebecca said aloud, in answer. She tossed back the glass of brandy in a jerky, painful motion. "Dead, dead, dead."

The muscles in her shoulders and in the nape of her neck relaxed with a suddenness that was almost convulsive as the brandy burned its way into her system. A sob rose in her throat, lodging there and hurting more than the vicious disease that gnawed at her vitals and tore at her bones and muscles.

The door of the bedroom opened with a cautious creak— *when would that impossible Mamie see that the hinges were oiled?*

"Becky," challenged a gentle, masculine voice. "What in the hell are you doing?"

Rebecca turned, inclining her head toward the man entering her room. Soft relief whispered through her, like a summer breeze rustling the leaves of an elm tree.

"Griffin."

The young man took her arm in a firm, almost imperious, grasp and ushered her back to the bed, where he tucked her under the covers with the quick, impatient motions of a disapproving father. His dark hair caught what light the gray skies outside would permit, and the strong, aristocratic lines of his face were taut with affectionate annoyance. His eyes, like his hair, were almost black, and they avoided her face for a moment, while he subdued the pity Rebecca suspected was there.

She admired the supple, animal grace of his body and wished fervently to be young and well again. With a veined hand, she reached up and touched the smooth gray silk of his vest. "Where is your suit coat, Dr. Fletcher?"

A smile twisted one corner of the firm, impatient lips. "Downstairs, behind the bar. I trust your worthy employees will keep their fingers out of my wallet?"

Rebecca settled back, soothed momentarily by the brandy and the presence of her taciturn, intolerant friend. "Anybody steals from you, and I'll have them horsewhipped. Besides, I run an honest house, Griffin Fletcher."

Griffin laughed softly, and the sound warmed the chilly,

2

lavender-scented room. "The good citizens of Providence might find that debatable, Becky." He sat down on the edge of the bed and folded his skilled, strong hands around one knee. "Now. Why did you send for me? Is the pain getting worse?"

Rebecca fixed weary eyes on the gilded woodwork edging the ceiling of her room and spoke cautiously. "You said you owed me, Griff, after I helped out in Tent Town last winter. Did you mean it?"

"I meant it."

Rebecca drew a burning breath and dared to meet the doctor's eyes. "It's about my kid, Griffin. It's about Rachel."

No reaction showed in Griffin's face. "What about her?"

Tears glimmered on Rebecca's lashes now, and she made no effort to hide them. It was too late for that. "Ezra's bringing her here, to Providence," she managed, fumbling once again for the crumpled letter on the nightstand.

Dr. Fletcher accepted the offered missive, unfolded it, and scanned its message quickly. Still, there was no change in his expression, nothing to indicate whether or not he would be an ally. "According to this, they'll be here sometime tonight," he said.

Rebecca nodded. When she spoke again, her words were tinged with hysteria, and it was hard to make them come out in proper and sensible order. "Griff, she'll be living in Tent Town—and there's Jonas—good God, there's Jonas. . . ."

Griffin sighed, but no recognizable emotion flickered in the dark eyes. Rebecca knew he understood the singular threat Jonas Wilkes represented, knew he hated the man fiercely. If anyone had reason, he did.

"Calm down," he ordered sharply.

Rebecca forced herself to remain still, though she wanted, even needed, to clamor out of that bed and do something—*anything*—to stop Ezra from bringing Rachel to Providence. "Rachel is a pretty girl, Griffin," she said finally, measuring the words cautiously, so that they could not escape her control and stream out in a river of shame and panic. "I know she is. She was a beautiful child. And if she catches Jonas's eye—"

A muscle knotted in Griffin's jaw, then relaxed again. "You're afraid he'll add her to his collection."

Rebecca could only nod, and a tense, thundering silence fell. At last, she went on. "That's happened to more than one young girl, hasn't it, Griff?"

Griffin bolted to his feet, and stood with his back to Rebecca,

3

his hands on his hips. Something violent and primitive seemed to enclose him; Rebecca could sense his inward struggle even though it was being waged in the darkest recesses of his mind and heart.

She smoothed the velvet comforter. "I'm sorry."

Griffin's shoulders were taut under his white linen shirt. He lowered his head, and Rebecca heard a deep, raspy breath enter his lungs, come out again. Finally, he turned around to face her. "What is it that you want me to do?" he asked, in a voice that was barely more than a labored whisper.

Rebecca's throat worked painfully, and a small eternity passed before she could make herself say, "Marry her. Griffin, will you marry Rachel?"

The request struck him with a visible and unsettling impact. *"What?"*

A desperate momentum carried Rebecca forward. "I'll pay you! I have a thousand dollars saved, Griffin, and there's the deed to my business—"

A humorless laugh erupted from his throat, and he flung his arms outward, in some kind of outraged mockery. "You're asking me to marry a woman I've never even seen? And in return, I get a thousand dollars and a whorehouse?"

Rebecca bounded out of the bed now, to face him. The pain and weakness were forgotten, blown away by the winds of fear raging within her. "Griffin Fletcher, you listen to me, you arrogant bastard! I might be a whore—by God, I *am* a whore—but my daughter—*my daughter*—is a lady! Do you hear me? A lady!"

Cool respect glimmered in the dark eyes, and Griffin's face softened a little. "I'm sure Rachel is everything any man could want," he said evenly. "But I have no intention of marrying anybody—not your daughter or anyone else."

Grim finality echoed in the words, and Rebecca sighed and lowered her head. "All right," she said. "All right."

Griffin took a new hold on Rebecca's thin shoulders now, and guided her back to the bed.

She made no protest as he took a syringe from his battered black bag, filled it with morphine, and inspected it for deadly bubbles of air.

"I don't want my little girl to know I run a whorehouse," she whispered, in ragged tones.

"I know," replied Griffin, as he administered the injection and drew the needle gently from Rebecca's arm.

4

The pain hammered and raged inside her, in a savage crescendo. It was always like this after an injection, the pain would grow suddenly and immeasurably worse, as though it somehow knew it would be forced into submission for a little while. "Dear God," she muttered. "Oh, Dear God. Griffin—what as I going to do?"

"For the time being, relax," Griffin suggested. He lifted the painted china globe from a kerosene lamp on Rebecca's bedtable and struck a wooden match to light the wick. The brave, flickering light, unhampered by the decorative globe, pushed back a little of the gathering darkness.

It was harder—so much harder—to stay awake. But the terrible pain was ebbing, just like the tide flowing two hundred yards beyond Rebecca's window, on the shores of Puget Sound.

"We helped you," she pressed, single-mindedly. "When there was so much pneumonia and grippe in Tent Town last winter, me and my girls helped you. You owe me, Griffin Fletcher. You owe me."

Griffin drew a long, slender cigar from the pocket of his shirt, gripped it between his white, even teeth, and bent to light it from the flame dancing on the wick of Rebecca's lamp. The end of the cheroot glowed red-gold in the dim, trembling light, and the china globe made a clinking sound as he replaced it. "I know that," he said.

"Will you talk to Ezra? Will you tell him what could happen to Rachel if Jonas fancies her?"

Grimly, Griffin nodded. There was a weary, faraway look in his eyes.

Rebecca struggled to go on, before the blessed, soothing respite of sleep overtook her completely. "And if Ezra won't listen to you, Griffin, you give Rachel that thousand dollars—Mamie will show you where it is—you give her that money and you put her on board the first steamboat that ties up in Providence—"

"What if she doesn't want to go, Becky? What do I do then? Bind her wrists and throw her on board?"

"If necessary. You're my friend, aren't you?"

Griffin's chuckle sounded hoarse. "That isn't friendship, Becky. It's kidnapping."

Rebecca's eyelids seemed to be weighted, and her vision blurred. She felt like a small, smooth stone, gliding soundlessly to the bottom of a dark pond and resting there. Settling into the silt. "You owe me, Griffin Fletcher," she called, toward the rippling surface of consciousness. "You owe me."

Chapter One

Rachel McKinnon lay very still in the small island of warmth her body had created and kept her eyes closed.

For several wild, insensible moments, she actually made herself believe that she didn't live in this wretched, rain-sodden place at all, but in a fine house in Seattle, a house overlooking Elliott Bay.

Yes. Yes, she could stand at the gleaming windows of her own spacious parlor, with its delicate lace curtains and its polished oaken floors, and she could look out and see the big steamboats and clipper ships moving in and out of the harbor. Dapples of sunlight would dance, like flames of silver, on the blue, blue water. . . .

It was the stench that brought Rachel plummeting back to reality—the dreadful, piercing stench.

It forced her to remember everything.

A groan escaped her, and she squeezed her eyes even more tightly shut. Still, the grim images remained.

An acre of tents, standing like a shabby regiment of gray ghosts in the night. Rats, their eyes gleaming scarlet, darting between rivulets of rainwater. Children, whimpering and fretting behind walls of canvas.

Tent Town.

Rachel shuddered, tried to fight off the despairing panic that came with wakefulness and with knowing. She tried to summon the fantasy house back into her mind, but it would not come. She opened her eyes, and then closed them again.

But the truth was there, behind her lids, painted in sad colors on the walls of her mind. She was going to have to live in this dreadful place for as long as there was work for her father to do in Mr. Wilkes's lumber camps.

A hand clasped her shoulder, gave it a gentle, reluctant shake. "Daughter?"

Anger burned in Rachel's throat and hammered through her veins, but only briefly. She loved her father, and she knew that the suffering and the poverty pained him far more deeply than they did her. His dreams and hopes for his only child were great indeed.

"I'm awake," she said softly, smiling up at the dim outline etched against the dank roof of the tent.

A soft rain tapped out a mournful cadence on the worn canvas tent top, and Rachel could hear people talking in hushed, sleepy voices. The two sounds made her feel wretchedly lonely, for some reason.

Ezra McKinnon turned his broad back, so that his daughter could rise from her cot in relative privacy. A short, stocky man with unruly gray hair, a full beard, and mischievous blue eyes, he stooped to take up his bedroll and said, "There's a dining hall, Rachel. You go there, and have some breakfast."

Trying to ignore the numbing cold, Rachel straightened her rumpled calico dress and rummaged through the wicker satchel that contained most of her personal belongings. Finding her hairbrush, she began grooming her sable brown hair with fierce energy.

"I don't have any money, Pa. Suppose I get to this dining hall and they expect me to have money?"

Ezra cleared his throat, pulled back the tent flap, and spat into the rainy dawn. Damp, frigid air rushed into the tent. "I asked Mr. Wilkes about meals when I signed on," he replied, with gentle impatience. "He told me that mine is included, and yours will be drawn from my wages."

Deftly Rachel braided her glossy hair, wound it into a chignon, and secured it with tiny tortoiseshell combs. "You'll be in the woods until next Sunday?" she asked, already knowing that he would. She was seventeen years old, and a woman grown, but she felt like a frightened little girl just then—a little girl about to be abandoned, with no friends or money, in a town where it never seemed to stop raining.

"Yes, Daughter. Until Sunday."

Even as Rachel searched her mind for a dignified way to beg him not to go, she heard a wagon and horses splashing through the rain and mud outside, heard the snorts of the team and the creak of leather harnesses.

Ezra kissed her forehead gently, and then he said something strange. "Things will be different here, Rachel. Better."

Before she could ask what he meant, her father went off to join the other workers. There were shouts and bursts of laughter and profanity as the men of that humble canvas community met at the crew wagon and found their places inside.

Soon, they would be high on the mountain, these husbands and fathers and sons, cutting and felling timber for Mr. Jonas Wilkes. To Rachel, arriving in the night, by wagon, that mountain had seemed a looming and monstrous thing, set apart somehow from the other mountains of her experience.

She pulled her blue woolen shawl from the satchel and wrapped it around her head and shoulders. As she stepped outside the tent, into the incessant drizzle and the half light of a struggling dawn, the stench sharpened. Human waste, probably in open trenches dug too near the camp.

Rachel's revulsion was like acid in her throat and nostrils; she longed to run back to the tent—as crude as it was, it was the only refuge she had—and hide.

But there was no hiding from the desperate hunger that gnawed at her even as she tried not to retch. She raised her chin, silently defying the tears that pressed behind her eyes and ached in her throat.

All around her, other women left other tents, herding listless, silent children toward the center of the odd village. Rachel followed them, her shawl drawn tightly around her slender figure.

The dining hall was, Rachel soon discovered, just another tent. It was large, though, and adequately lit by kerosene lanterns that flickered and smoked on the long, rough-hewn wood tables. There was sawdust on the floor; it was damp and pungently fragrant and it stuck to Rachel's scuffed black shoes as she walked.

The delicious warmth radiating from the big black cookstove at one end of the tent seemed to reach out and caress Rachel's frozen bones, and the comforting smell of sizzling bacon came to meet her like a welcoming friend. She forgot the hideous odor waiting beyond the tent walls and allowed herself a deep breath.

Hunger impelled Rachel toward the table where the food was being distributed. She took a blue enamel plate and a tin fork and gave her name to a reedy, wheezing woman who recorded it carefully into a ruled account book.

A small, chattering Chinaman wrenched Rachel's plate from her hand, graced it with three slices of bacon, one egg, and a piece of toasted bread, then surrendered it again. She helped herself to a mug and coffee from the large pot sitting at the far end of the serving table.

Long benches lined the other tables, and Rachel found a place within the radius of the stove's warmth and sat down.

Looking at the meal before her, she trembled with mingled guilt and anticipation. Her father hadn't eaten the day before, nor had she, but now he was on his way up the mountain to work a full day. Would Mr. Wilkes see that his men had food to eat before they began their tasks?

The splintery benches began to fill with severe, wary-eyed women and fussy children. Rachel forced herself to believe that her father would soon enjoy an even better meal, and then she began to eat. She chewed slowly, savoring the food.

Now and then, at some other table, a defiant spirited giggle would erupt, dispelling a little of the gloom. Covertly, Rachel scanned the sallow faces of the other women, looking for the person who could live in Tent Town and still laugh like that. She longed to find her and somehow become her friend.

Involuntarily, Rachel sighed. It had been a long, long time since she'd been in one place long enough to make a friend.

When Rachel had finished eating, she took her empty plate back to the Chinaman. He snatched it from her and hurled it into a large tin washtub at his feet, obviously outraged by her ignorance of the rules. Then he railed at her in his odd, quick language.

Rachel blushed with embarrassment, all too aware that the other sounds, those of eating and muted conversation, had ceased. Everyone was probably staring, thinking what a fool the new woman was. She tried to say that she was sorry, that she hadn't known what to do, but the Chinaman gave her no opportunity. Rather, he raged on, like a tiny, furious bird.

Rachel's chagrin gave way to righteous wrath. Surely such a modest infraction as not knowing where to discard one's dinner plate didn't justify the creation of such a terrible scene!

Before she could frame a retort, however, a chill draft swept into the tent, stinging Rachel's flesh through her thin dress and shawl. The silence among the women and children still sitting at the tables deepened, and the cook swallowed his invective in one convulsive gulp.

"Is there some sort of problem here, Chang?" asked a wry, gentlemanly voice.

Rachel turned to see a lithe, good-looking man standing just behind her. He had cherubic brown eyes, she noticed, and a boyish, clean-shaven face. His tailored suit, somehow very much out of place among so much calico and poplin, was made of a fine, dark woolen and was beaded with little sparkling droplets of rain.

"Well?" pressed the man, in even, ominous tones.

The Chinaman swallowed again, and his slanted eyes were downcast.

Rachel felt both empathy and remorse; there were many who enjoyed baiting the Chinese, and she wondered if this finely dressed man numbered among them. "There is no problem," she dared to say.

The gentleman assessed her, an unsettling mixture of appreciation and suppressed amusement flashing in his velvety eyes. "Is that so? Considering the fact that I could hear Chang raving even before I got out of my carriage, I find that difficult to accept."

The hapless Chang was visibly shaken now, and he abandoned his dialect for a halting, awkward form of English. "Missy not put dish!" he cried, trembling in his shapeless black trousers and shirt. "Please, Mr. Wilkes, Missy not put dish!"

Mr. Wilkes. *Jonas* Wilkes? Rachel bit her lower lip, surprised and a little awed. From the things her father had told her about Mr. Wilkes—how he had sweeping power and almost unlimited wealth—she had expected him to be much older.

Instead, he appeared to be somewhere in his early thirties. He had soft, glossy hair the color of new wheat, and his wide eyes and small, straight nose gave him an innocent look.

Rachel had already surmised that he was no angel.

"Mr. Chang is quite correct," she said, squaring her shoulders and meeting Mr. Wilkes's amused gaze directly. "I did not put my plate in the proper place."

Mr. Wilkes drew in a sharp breath and an expression of mock stupefaction played in his face. "That, my dear, is an abominable sin if I've ever heard one. What is your name?"

She hesitated, finally said, "Miss Rachel McKinnon."

The mischievous eyes swept over her, lingering almost imperceptibly at her breasts and her narrow waist. But when they came back to her face, there was a disconcerting look of

10

recognition in them. "Rachel McKinnon," he repeated, thoughtfully.

Rachel felt swift, fierce color surge into her face, though she couldn't have said why. "I'm sorry that I've caused so much trouble," she said.

To her utter amazement, Mr. Wilkes cupped his right hand under her chin and made her look at him. His skin was smooth and fragrant from some spicy cologne, but his touch was not gentle. "I'm sure you cause a great deal of excitement wherever you go, Urchin. Those violet eyes insure it."

Rachel was stung by the word "urchin," even though Mr. Wilkes had spoken it with a peculiar note of affection in his voice. She was proud, and this obvious reference to her tattered clothing rankled. She turned her head, pulling free of his touch. "I'm very sorry that you don't find me presentable, Mr. Wilkes."

Jonas Wilkes laughed softly. "Oh, Urchin, you are more than presentable. Why, with a hot bath and some decent clothing—"

She reacted without thinking, without considering the possible consequences, without considering anything beyond the fact that she had been gravely insulted. She raised her hand and slapped Mr. Jonas Wilkes with such force that the mark of her fingers blazed, crimson, on his face.

The tense silence in the tent seemed to vibrate.

There was a frightening expression in Jonas Wilkes's eyes as he surveyed the trembling, furious girl before him. A thin, white line encircled his lips, and he clenched and unclenched his fists. "Miss McKinnon, if you ever do that again, you will bitterly regret it."

Rachel was terrified, but she was too proud and too stubborn to let anyone, especially this man, know that. She stood her ground. "Mr. Wilkes, if you ever demean my garments again, or imply that I am unclean, you will bitterly regret it."

Some intrepid soul laughed aloud just then, but if Mr. Wilkes heard the sound, he dismissed it. His eyes moved over Rachel's body with dispatch, then returned to her face. "Your father would be Ezra McKinnon—the sawyer I hired last week in Seattle. Am I correct?"

A lump throbbed, raw, in Rachel's throat as she remembered that she and her father depended upon this man for their livelihood. "Yes," she admitted.

He took a small, leather book from the inside pocket of his suit coat and made a flourishing notation on the first page.

It was all Rachel could do to keep from craning her neck to read what he'd written. She swallowed miserably. "Are you going to dismiss my father?" she asked, after an awkward, painful pause.

Mr. Wilkes smiled generously. "Of course not, Miss McKinnon. That would be a spiteful thing to do, wouldn't it?"

Rachel searched her mind for a diplomatic, dignified reply and found nothing she dared say beyond, "Thank you."

Once more, the impudent gaze swept over her. "Think nothing of it, Urchin," he said. And then, abruptly, Mr. Jonas Wilkes was striding across the sawdust floor and out of the tent.

The moment he was gone, the stunned populace of Tent Town dared to breathe again.

A thin woman with wide, fearful blue eyes approached Rachel first. There was surprise in the narrow, careworn face, but there was respect, too, and no small measure of admiration. "You *slapped* Jonas Wilkes!" she breathed.

Rachel stiffened, though she secretly enjoyed being the center of attention. "He brought it on himself," she said, with bravado.

The splendid, defiant giggle Rachel had heard before rose above the excited chatter, and she saw that it came from a slender Indian girl standing nearby. She had beautiful, nut-brown skin and wore a slim, beaded headband and a buckskin shift trimmed with twisted fringe. "I hope the gods are fond of you, Purple Eyes," she said, tossing her long, glossy black hair back over one shoulder. "You're going to need all the help you can get."

The woman who had spoken first shot an impatient glance in the girl's direction and frowned. "Don't pay Fawn any mind, Rachel. She's been traipsing all over the territory with Buck Jimson's Wild West Show these past few months, and she got into the habit of carrying on like an Indian."

"I *am* an Indian!" cried Fawn, with spirit. "You'd better remember it, too, Mary Louisa Clifford, or I'll creep into your tent some dark, rainy night and scalp you bald!"

Mary Louisa shook her head and smiled at Rachel. "It is wise to be careful, where Mr. Wilkes is concerned. He can be vindictive."

Rachel shivered. "My father—will he lose his job?"

Mary Louisa patted Rachel's hands in reassurance. "If he's a good, hard worker, he won't be discharged."

Fawn pressed closer, her dark, sparkling eyes wide with

12

foreboding. "No woman strikes Jonas Wilkes like that and gets away with it. Mark my words, Rachel McKinnon. He's making plans for some kind of revenge right now."

Small, sharp needles of dread prickled Rachel's spine. Should she run after Mr. Wilkes, beg him to forgive her for slapping him? She knew that the Indian girl was probably right; a man with that kind of power at his command would not tolerate such an affront without reprisal.

For herself, Rachel felt no fear. But suppose the retribution, which could be harsh indeed, was dealt to her father who had done nothing to deserve it? Nothing beyond siring a hot-tempered and unladylike daughter, she thought, with bitter resignation.

Jonas Wilkes frowned and, in a vain effort to shut out some of the rain, pulled his collar up around his neck. This was no day to be out and about; a man should be in his own house on such a day, sleeping late. Reading a fine book. Sipping brandy.

Or bedding a woman.

Jonas smiled as the girl, Rachel McKinnon, filled his mind, flowing into it like water into a tide pool. He felt an odd mixture of rage and desire as he relived the indignity of being slapped, and his face still smarted where her hand had made contact.

He strode on, sidestepping the worst of the mud, zigzagging between the tattered tents that housed his workers' wives and children. The stench came at him, a pungent reminder of all his sins, on the changing wind.

Damn Tent Town, he thought, pressing a clean, white handkerchief to his mouth and nose and holding it there. Damn Griffin Fletcher for practically ordering him to come here to talk to him, and damn that orchid-eyed urchin and her ridiculous calico dress and her impossible high-button shoes.

Suddenly, he stopped cold. The suspicion he'd harbored became a certainty.

Rachel McKinnon. She had to be Becky's daughter! Oh, the last name could have been coincidental, but not those purple eyes, that rich, sable hair, that proud, almost arrogant, carriage.

Jonas laughed aloud, and then walked on.

He crossed one mucky, rutted road, climbed an embankment verdant with quack grass to another road. He was approaching the cottages now, and the sight of Griffin Fletcher's buggy did nothing to spoil his good spirits.

Imagine it. Rebecca McKinnon's daughter living in Tent Town, with those dreary, slothful wretches and their brats.

Once again, Jonas laughed.

But other thoughts dogged him as he opened the gate in Fanny Harper's whitewashed picket fence and started up the walk. Rachel had slapped him, after all, and in front of the workers' wives.

That was a transgression he could not overlook. He would make it painfully, unforgettably clear that no one treated Jonas Wilkes in that manner without suffering for it. No one.

But it was odd, the way she made him feel. Helpless. By God, she made him feel helpless, like a climber sliding down the face of a cliff, unable to catch hold and break the fall.

The pit of Jonas's stomach convulsed suddenly; he saw again the wide, amethyst eyes darkening with fury, remembered the lustrous, raven hair held precariously in place by small, simple combs.

And he wanted her.

His fingers flexed as he recalled the delightful, delicious promise of her breasts.

Jonas sighed, adjusted his collar again, and tapped at the door of Fanny's cottage. All in good time, he promised himself. All in good time.

He would answer Griffin's summons first, and then he would send word up the mountain that Ezra McKinnon was to be promoted to a position of responsibility.

Chapter Two

The rain had slackened to a chilly mist by the time Rachel left the dining tent and paused, in the first grim, faltering light of day, to peer in one direction and then the other. Ragged children scuffled and played between the canvas houses, their tentative laughter blending with the cries of quarrelsome birds and the shrill whistle of a steamboat passing on the Sound.

Mr. Wilkes was nowhere to be seen.

Rachel looked up, and saw that patches of golden sunlight were seeping through the slate gray skies to shimmer among the evergreens and giant ponderosa pines that crowded the mountain. In the other direction, beyond the waters of Puget Sound, beyond Seattle, Mt. Rainier jutted toward the heavens, her snowy slopes clad in a sheer, glowing cloak of apricot and gold.

Rachel drew strength from the sight.

A stiff, sudden wind struck the small community, and canvas snapped all around her, in a startling chorus. Chang trotted out of the big tent, through a sideflap, and emptied a basin brimming with table scraps onto the ground. He glanced in Rachel's direction, but said nothing.

Above, sea gulls circled and plunged, loudly berating the Chinaman for his late arrival. He cursed them in clipped gibberish and went back inside the tent.

Rachel squared her shoulders. She mustn't delay too long, or she would lose her firm resolve to face Mr. Wilkes and seek his pardon. Again, she looked around, hoping to see him nearby.

The neigh of a horse drew her attention to the carriage. Drawn by a matched team of coal black geldings, its leather and varnish and brass gleaming even in the sparse, glowering light, the coach surely belonged to Mr. Wilkes.

She approached warily, afraid to touch the splendid vehicle. "Excuse me," she said, smiling up at the sullen driver hunched in the box. "Excuse me, but is this Mr. Jonas Wilkes's carriage, please?"

The driver studied Rachel with mingled derision and appetite, and his voice was a surly rumble, "Well, it don't belong to no flea-bitten lumberjack, Sweetness."

Rachel stiffened and retreated a step, revolted by this man and the very mention of the beastly bugs that were the bane of every lumber camp within hundreds of miles. "Could you tell me where to find Mr. Wilkes—please?"

The insolent, leering man removed his soggy bowler hat with a flourish. He was unshaven, and several of his teeth were missing. Those that remained were twisted and brown with rot. "Last I seen of the boss, he was heading out of this stinkhole and off toward them cottages of his."

Cottages?

Rachel turned and noticed the beautiful little houses for the first time. There were four of the small, brick structures, each

15

boasting its own whitewashed picket fence, narrow green lawn, and cozy porch. Gray smoke curled from the chimneys, and sturdy, cedar-shingled roofs kept out the rain. The Indian girl, Fawn, could be seen entering the one on the far right.

For just a moment, Rachel stood spellbound. Then, envy twisted, snakelike, in the pit of her stomach. Oh, to live in a real house, with wooden floors and a fire blazing on the hearth and a bed with sheets and blankets . . .

She caught herself, shut off the silly dreams that were flowing through her mind and heart like a sparkling mountain stream. She was the daughter of a poor man, she reminded herself, and she would eventually be the wife of yet another poor man. It was unlikely that she would ever live in any place so fine as those brick cottages.

"Pretty sight, ain't they?" drawled the driver.

"Yes," Rachel answered tightly without looking back at him. Then, because she knew that she would run into her tent and hide there for the rest of the day if she didn't plunge straight ahead, she lifted her shabby skirts and started off at a brisk walk.

She would find Mr. Wilkes and apologize for the scene in the dining tent. That done, she would explore beyond Tent Town.

She would fix the town of Providence firmly in her mind, and walk along the shoreline, too. Perhaps she would find oysters and clams there, as she had along Seattle's beaches and tide flats.

Rachel missed Seattle, with its wood-frame buildings and its cow pastures, its orchards and its majestic view of mountains and sea. In the six weeks she and her father had lived there, boarded in the drafty home of Miss Flora Cunningham, the rambunctious country town had carved its image into her mind and heart. Leaving had been painful in every sense of the word, but one went where there was work to be had, and her father had been anxious to move on again. He'd met Mr. Wilkes in a Skid Road saloon one night, and signed on as one of his sawyers.

They had arrived in Providence during the darkest hours of the night, after jostling their way around the edges of Puget Sound in the back of one of Jonas Wilkes's supply wagons, and had seen almost nothing of the town itself or the salt waters that ebbed and flowed at its feet.

Rachel sighed inwardly and made herself walk faster. Ex-

16

ploring Providence proper suddenly had lost much of its appeal.

After all, she reminded herself, one lumber town was pretty much the same as another; she knew that from long and bitter experience, for she had lived in virtually every one that lay between California and the Canadian border.

Ezra McKinnon was a hardworking, decent man, but he always seemed to get restless when they'd been in one place longer than a month or so. The drinking would start then, soon to be followed by the gambling and the fighting.

Rachel reached the lower road and crossed it, sinking to her instep in mud.

She made her way cautiously up the green, slippery hill, and her thoughts shifted, as they often did, to her mother. In her mind, she saw a flash of dark hair and lavender eyes and a pinched, frantic face.

Rebecca McKinnon had abandoned her daughter and husband more than ten years before, and Rachel seldom permitted herself to recollect that fact. When she did, it was with pain and confusion, but with understanding, too. It was hard, living in shacks and wagons and second-rate boardinghouses and never having anything pretty to wear.

Rachel reached the upper road. There was a mud-splattered buggy there, hitched to a patient-looking sorrel mare.

She paused to pat the drenched animal's muzzle in sympathy and to gather up her courage. She had no way of knowing which of the four houses Mr. Wilkes had entered, so there was nothing to do but knock at each door, if necessary, until she found him. Her heart swelling into her throat, she turned from the horse, unlatched the gate leading to the first cottage, and started up the walk.

In her mind, Rachel rehearsed one feverish apology, and then another. She had just reached the porch steps when the cottage's front door sprang open with an alarming crash and Mr. Wilkes came storming out, his face as dark as a tempestuous night sky.

Instinctively, Rachel stepped aside, and when she did, her left foot twisted beneath her, throwing her off balance and plunging her sideways into a rain-beaded sweetbrier bush.

Jonas Wilkes stopped, and the awesome anger drained out of his face. He smiled and extended a hand.

Mortified, Rachel accepted the assistance offered and let her

17

father's employer draw her to her feet. Color throbbed in her cheeks, and tears brimmed in her eyes, poised to slide down her muddied, thorn-scratched face. Her dress was downright filthy now, and the fabric had been snagged by the fierce nettles of the budding rosebush. Her shawl, too, was ruined.

Amusement flickered in Mr. Wilkes's shrewd, topaz eyes. "At the risk of being slapped a second time, Miss McKinnon, I must say that you are sadly in need of a hot bath."

Rachel swallowed her tears, but her humiliation remained, causing her cheeks to flame and her eyes to deepen from orchid to purple. She forgot the planned apology and turned swiftly, to flee in embarassment.

But Mr. Wilkes caught her arm in a quick, tight grasp, and stopping her, turned her to face him. "May I call you Rachel?" he asked.

The question so surprised Rachel that she gaped at him, too stunned to speak.

He laughed, and it was a sound that reminded her of a beverage she'd tasted on a rare, prosperous Christmas—brandy mixed with thick cream and sugar.

Rachel stumbled back a step, gasping softly as Jonas Wilkes's gloved hands caught her shoulders and held them firmly.

"It was my fault that you fell and got yourself covered in mud," he said, in a voice that was remote and yet somehow intimate, too. "Won't you come along to my house and have a bath?"

Rachel's face went scarlet, and words failed her. Had she been able to move, she would have raised her hand and, without regard for the repercussions, slapped Mr. Wilkes again.

Jonas smiled, and his eyes sparkled. Clearly, her outrage and shock amused him. "I'm not trying to seduce you, Urchin," he said reasonably. "My housekeeper will be there, to defend your innocence."

Rachel dared to dream of a hot bath, perhaps with scented soap and soft, fluffy towels. . . .

And then, suddenly, the slight drizzle became a pounding downpour again.

Rachel was chilled to the bone, and she was dirty and she was, of course, wet. Despite considerable qualms about going anywhere with this particular man, especially to his house, she simply could not endure the thought of trudging back to that miserable, flea-ridden tent and shivering there, wrapped in a thin blanket, while she waited for her dress to dry. Her only other gown was a somber, ill-fitting affair made of scratchy brown wool, and wearing that seemed, at the moment, even less appealing than draping herself in a blanket.

"I promise you will be perfectly safe," Mr. Wilkes prodded smoothly. And, in spite of the circumstances, the expression in his eyes was warm and inviting. All around them, rain dashed at the ground and danced in brimming brown puddles and made a sound like fire on the roofs of the brick cottages.

Certain that she'd gone quite mad—and just since breakfast, too—Rachel took the arm Mr. Wilkes offered and the two of them hurried down the grassy embankment to the main road. There, the magnificent carriage waited, like something stolen from someone else's sweet dream.

Mr. Wilkes wrenched open one gleaming door and helped her inside. When he sank into the cushioned leather seat across from Rachel, she thought she saw a look of veiled exasperation in his eyes.

She set aside the sodden blue shawl and trembled slightly. "This isn't proper," she said.

Jonas Wilkes sat back, folded his arms, and extended his booted feet. "No, Urchin, I'm sure it isn't. But why should Rebecca McKinnon's daughter be bound by such a fatuous concept as propriety?"

Rachel's mouth fell open, and blood pounded in her ears, drowning out all other sounds. After a long time, she managed to rasp, "You know my mother?"

Jonas chuckled, but a note of contempt rang in his answer. "We're partners, Becky and I. Perhaps I should say, we were partners; we've had several serious disagreements in the past few years."

Rachel forgot that her skirts were clinging, like clammy hands, to her thighs and ankles. She forgot that her shoes were full of water and most likely ruined. She even forgot that she had gotten into a carriage with a man she barely knew. "My mother lives here—in Tent Town?"

A look of indulgence curved the seraphic lips. "Urchin, Rebecca McKinnon would never stoop to living in a place like Tent Town. She runs a highly—er—respected establishment on the outskirts of Providence."

Rachel's heart was flailing against her rib cage, and her mouth felt dry. "Please—take me there!"

Calmly, Jonas Wilkes shook his head and surveyed Rachel's

19

dripping hair and muddy dress pointedly. "Surely you don't want to be reunited with your mother looking like that, Urchin."

Rachel felt real despair. "No."

"Soon enough," remarked Mr. Wilkes, half to himself and half to Rachel, as the carriage made its rattling, splashing way through the mud and rain. "Soon enough."

Rachel was full of questions, but she could not, for the moment, articulate them. She felt gratitude when Mr. Wilkes removed his suit coat and draped it over her shoulders, and she huddled inside its soft, dampened folds. The fabric smelled pleasantly of pipe tobacco and rain and that spicy cologne she'd first noticed during the confrontation in the dining tent.

"This," he said, gesturing toward the open carriage window on their left, "is the main street of Providence."

Rachel looked out, and even though her mind and heart were filled to overflowing with the knowledge that her mother was somewhere nearby, she took note of the trim, painted saltbox houses facing the angry green waters of the Sound.

They had neat lawns and picket fences and lamplight glowing in the windows, and for some reason she couldn't quite fathom, they deepened the wretched loneliness she felt. She fixed her eyes on the junglelike foliage and tall trees that edged the inlet on the other side of the water. "Does my mother live in one of those houses?" she asked, as the carriage rolled on.

Jonas Wilkes did not spare so much as a glance for the lovely little structures. He drew a cheroot from his shirt pocket and struck a wooden match to light it. "No," he said, after a discomforting delay. "No, Urchin, your mother lives more grandly than the steady, diligent sorts along Main Street. You don't mind my smoking, I hope?"

Benumbed, Rachel shook her head that she didn't. She could not imagine living more grandly than these people did. After all, they had real roofs over their heads and real floors under their feet. Rosebushes were budding in their yards, and wooden sidewalks lined the street. Most had small garden plots, where tender sprouts were beginning to break ground.

She swallowed. "What kind of woman is my mother?"

Mr. Wilkes sighed and drew thoughtfully on his cheroot. The smoke curled in the cool, misty air inside the carriage. "Rebecca is a businesswoman," he allowed, finally.

Rachel sat back in the seat, confused and more than a little stricken to know that her mother had been prospering—even "living grandly"—all this time, while she and her father had struggled, sometimes desperately, just to survive. "You are saying, Mr. Wilkes, that my mother is rich," she ventured.

He smiled. "Not rich. Rebecca is merely well-to-do."

Merely well-to-do. Rachel looked down at the pointed, cramping toes of her sodden shoes. She had been wearing them for two full years already, and they pinched, and they hadn't been new in the first place. She'd bought them second-hand, from a street peddler. Her throat worked, but no words would pass it.

Unexpectedly, Mr. Wilkes reached out and closed his hand over both of hers. "I gather that you and your father haven't been quite so prosperous," he said softly.

Tears trembled in Rachel's eyes as she looked at him. "No," she answered brokenly. "No, we haven't."

He tossed the cheroot out, through the open window. "Your fortunes are about to change, Urchin. Believe me."

Rachel stared at him, all too aware of the hopelessness of her situation in life. "I hardly think so, Mr. Wilkes," she replied. "My father is a lumberjack and my husband, when I find one, will no doubt be a lumberjack, too."

The brown eyes were speculative now, and slightly guarded. "Perhaps not," he said.

But Rachel's mind had shifted back, to the misery and lacks she'd experienced in Tent Town and all its many counterparts in all the other timber towns. Once, she had viewed such places with resignation; now, knowing how different her life might have been, had her mother cared for her, she felt aching resentment.

She pulled Mr. Wilkes's coat more tightly around her shoulders and sank into a corner of the carriage seat, closing her eyes. A sudden desire to sleep overwhelmed her, and she gave in.

Jonas forced himself to concentrate on the passing country-side, even though he knew every inch of it. The coach had left Providence behind, and there were open fields on both sides of the road, choked with the green-and-yellow violence of Scotch broom.

There was within him a need to stare openly at the bedraggled waif huddled across from him, to memorize the delicate shape of her neck, the curve of her breasts, the gentle rounding of her thighs. He dared not touch her—not yet, not after the scene with Griffin Fletcher that morning, in Fanny Harper's cottage—but he was consumed by the need to possess her. If he allowed himself to look too closely, or for too long, his resolve to keep his distance and win her trust might not hold against the oceanic onrush of hunger he felt whenever his eyes touched her.

The soft meter of her breathing told him that she had fallen asleep, and he smiled. Something very much like tenderness welled up inside him, and he braced himself against it.

Rachel was different from all the others; he had known that from the first moment. And because she was different, she was dangerous; she could so easily seize power over him, even enslave him.

No other woman—ever—had presented such a threat.

The carriage made a sharp and sudden turn, jolting Jonas out of his pensive mood. Wheels rattled on the cobblestone drive leading up to the main house, and after a moment of intense preparation, he dared to glance in Rachel's direction. She stirred, groaned softly.

The sound made Jonas's groin ache.

When the clatter ceased and the carriage lurched to a stop, he rose from the seat and opened the door. With a soft, half-smile on his face, he lifted Rachel McKinnon into his arms and carried her, like a child, across the sweeping, marble-pillared porch and through the great double doors the driver had opened.

Rachel awakened just as they crossed the threshhold, her marvelous orchid eyes wide and dazed and sleepy. After a moment, the realization of improper intimacy struck her with a visible impact. She stiffened in Jonas's arms and cried, "Put me down!"

Jonas did not want to release her, ever. Just holding her in that innocent, awkward fashion had stirred depths of need and desire in him far beyond what he had feared. It was all he could do to keep from carrying her up the sweeping staircase to his bedroom and losing himself, without regard for the consequences, in her sweetness and fire.

And there was fire inside her, all right. Jonas could feel it searing the edges of his soul even as he set her back on her feet and executed a courtly half-bow.

She was more than dangerous. She was deadly.

"As you wish," he said, in a voice he didn't even recognize.

Rachel looked like an exotic bird, half-drowned, feathers ruffled. "Just because I came here to take a bath, Mr. Wilkes," she sputtered, "Well—t-that doesn't mean that I'm—that I—"

Jonas was still struggling against the wild, agonizing desire that possessed him, but he smiled. "Of course," he said.

She relaxed a little, did not clutch his coat so tightly around herself. Slowly, her eyes darkened by awe, she began to take in her surroundings—the entry hall, with its black-and-white marble floor, cathedral ceilings, and carved teakwood walls. The dancing pastel colors cast by the crystal chandelier flashed, like sparks, in the dark purple depths of her gaze.

Jonas was entirely bewitched, and might have remained frozen in the spell if his housekeeper, Mrs. Hammond, hadn't appeared in the parlor doorway and stared at Rachel in surprise.

With a flourish, Jonas gestured toward his rain-soaked guest. "As you can see, the young lady is in desperate need of a bath. See that she has one, please."

The housekeeper's mouth tightened, grew white around the lips. "Jonas Wilkes—"

But Jonas was already striding out of the house again. He sprinted across the wide porch and stepped out into the roaring deluge.

Then, laughing, he thrust his arms out wide and lifted his face to the rain.

Chapter Three

Fanny Harper writhed wildly on the bed, tossing her head back and forth, pleading incoherently for the mercy of God.

Griffin Fletcher sighed and rolled up the sleeves of his shirt as Fanny's terrified husband brought scalding water to pour from a tin bucket into the china basin on the washstand.

Fanny screamed again, once more begged the intercession of heaven.

Purposely, Griffin dismissed the most recent confrontation with Jonas from his mind, turning his concentration to the task at hand.

"Can't you make her quit hurtin' like that, Doc?" Sam Harper whispered hoarsely, paling beneath the patchy brown and white stubble of his beard. Sam was a young man, by rights—maybe thirty-five at most—but he looked old, stooped. It was the grueling work in the woods and the lack of proper food; together, they robbed men of their youth and stamina.

Griffin shook his head and began to scrub his hands and forearms with the harsh lye soap he carried in his bag.

Harper drew nearer, his eyes reflecting the same savage pain that tore at his wife. "You could give her laudanum!" he challenged, in a raspy undertone.

Griffin stopped scouring his hands and glared at the man beside him. He was careful to keep his voice low and even, so Fanny wouldn't hear. "If I do that, the baby could fall asleep in the birth canal and smother. Besides, you know damned well I wouldn't let her suffer like that if I had a choice!"

Fanny shrieked again, and doom thundered in the sound. Overhead, the endless rain hammered at the roof.

Subdued now to a state of mute horror, Sam Harper fled the room, pulling the door shut behind him. A moment later, another door slammed in the distance.

Griffin approached the bed and tossed back the gnarled, sweat-dampened blankets that covered Fanny. Gently, by the flickering light of a kerosene lantern burning on the bedside table, he examined her.

Tears coursed down the woman's face, but she did her best to lie still, to endure. But the dignity was gone from her bearing and, with it, the delicate, flowerlike beauty that had probably gotten her into this situation in the first place.

"Soon?" she pleaded, biting back another scream.

"Soon," Griffin promised, in a soft voice.

The pain seized Fanny again; this time, Griffin guided her groping hands to the iron bedstead over her head. She gripped it, knuckles white, as the twisting, protruding knot that was her stomach convulsed violently.

Griffin waited with her, breathed in rhythm with her, wishing there were some way to ease the pain.

"I wisht I could die," she said. Her pale blue eyes were wild, glazed with effort and agony.

Under other circumstances, Griffin would have been insulted by the statement, even outraged. To him, death was a relentless enemy, a monster to be battled tirelessly but never courted. "No," he said, gently.

The baby boy was born five minutes later, and like all the Harper infants before it, the child was dead before it slipped from Fanny's exhausted body into Griffin's hands. The breath he forced into its tiny lungs did not revive it.

Still, he washed the child gently and wrapped it in a blanket. Rage hammered at the back of his throat as he set the small body aside, and he struggled against a primitive need to overturn furniture and hurl books and bric-a-brac in every direction.

"This one?" asked Fanny, with a sort of hopeless desperation rattling in her voice.

Griffin ached in every tissue and fiber of his being. The rage had passed, leaving helpless, unspeakable grief in its wake. "I'm sorry, Fanny," he answered.

"The babe weren't Sam's," the woman confessed, her feverish eyes fixed sightlessly on the ceiling. Her thick, reddish brown hair lay in twisted strands on the pillow, and damp tendrils clung to her waxen cheeks.

Griffin again washed his hands in the small supply of fresh, lukewarm water that remained and dried them on a thin, scratchy towel. Then he poured laudanum into a tablespoon and held it to Fanny's taut lips.

She swallowed the medicine gratefully, in several doses, and then turned her head away, toward the wall. Above, the incessant rain beat out a melancholy refrain on the shingled roof. "It's God's vengeance," she mourned. "God made my baby die because I'm bad."

Griffin examined Fanny again, frowning distractedly. There was too much bleeding. "You're not 'bad,' Fanny, and I doubt that God had anything to do with this, one way or the other."

Fanny became calm—frighteningly calm. "It's my sin what made Him wrathful."

Griffin took a steel needle from his bag and held it to the dancing flame in the lamp. When it had cooled, he threaded it with catgut and began to repair the tear in Fanny's flesh.

God. They always talked about God, lauding Him when things went right, bemoaning their own human nature when things went wrong. If there was a God—and, secretly, because of the order and symmetry apparent in the universe itself, Griffin suspected that there was—He was totally disinterested in mankind. He'd long since gone on to more promising enterprises, probably tossing a benevolent "You're on your own!" over His shoulder as He went.

"Just rest, Fanny," Griffin said.

But Fanny began to weep softly, even though she could not

feel the bite of the steel needle. "The baby weren't Sam's!" she insisted.

Griffin glanced at the pitiable bundle lying on the chest at the foot of the bed. His heart twisted for the undersized infant boy who would never play tag with a sparkling tide or feel the sun on his face.

"I'm a doctor, Fanny," he snapped. "Not a priest."

"T-that man—he's a devil. We all think that he's a man, but he ain't! He's the devil's own."

Griffin had even less interest in the devil than he did in God. "Jonas?" he sighed, as he tied off the stitches and permitted himself to recall the resemblance in the child's still little face.

Fanny nodded, and her sniffling became a soft, hideous wail. "Damn him—damn that man!"

Griffin, keeping his peace, felt profound relief as his patient slipped into a fitful, restless sleep. Even that, he thought, was preferable to her reality.

Griffin half-stumbled from the room to find hot water steaming on the cookstove in the kitchen and once again washed his hands. The flesh between his fingers and on his palms was raw from the biting strength of the special soap, and the water stung.

He helped himself to a mug of coffee from the blue enamel pot brewing at the rear of the stove and went back to the small, neat parlor, where a hopeful little fire blazed, crimson and orange, on the stone hearth.

Jonas. Always Jonas.

One shoulder braced against the sturdy mantle, Griffin sipped the strong, stale coffee thoughtfully. He wondered whether the warning he'd given Jonas—to stay away from Becky's daughter—had found its mark.

With Jonas, it was always hard to tell.

Fanny's labor had demanded all his attention then, and there had been no time to impress Jonas with his sincerity in the matter. There was never enough time.

Griffin drank the last of his coffee and took the cup back to the kitchen. There, he set it in the cast iron sink and pumped clear water into it until it overflowed.

All the conveniences, he thought. Jonas provided his women with all the conveniences.

His mind, snagged on the child in the other room, thrust him into a swirling current of hatred and frustration. He swore under his breath.

The cottage door opened as Griffin was reaching for his coat.

Sam Harper stood just inside the house, rainwater pooling silver around his worn boots. He stared at Griffin, trying to read his face. Beside him, the Reverend Winfield Hollister waited in calm silence, a tall, spare man with gentle eyes and an even, unblemished complexion.

Griffin's voice sounded hoarse and unsteady in his own ears. He'd seen death so many times; why couldn't he learn to accept it?

"The baby died," he said.

Field Hollister laid one hand on Harper's shoulder, but he didn't speak. That was one of the things Griffin liked best about his friend, that he knew when to talk and when to keep still. Usually.

"And Fanny?" pleaded Harper. "What about Fanny?"

Griffin searched the ceiling for a moment, wishing that he could lie or even just evade the truth somehow. "She's alive," he said, at last. "But she's lost too much blood, and she's weak."

The lumberman stumbled blindly across the room and into the small bedroom. The place of his betrayal.

"You did your best," ventured Field.

Griffin's sigh was ragged. "Yeah."

The minister folded his hands. "Fanny isn't going to survive this, is she?"

Griffin shook his head, and tension clasped the nape of his neck in a steel grip. Because he needed something to do, he consulted the watch he carried in his vest pocket. It seemed incredible that it was only nine o'clock in the morning.

Field cleared his throat diplomatically. "Well, she's in the hands of the Lord," he said, as though that settled every question, made everything all right.

The look Griffin turned to his best friend was scathing and fierce. "Damn it, Field, save that for your sheep, will you?"

Hollister slipped out of his shabby overcoat and drew a worn, much-used Bible from its pocket. Griffin could see some inner preparation taking place; it was a familiar look that never failed to nettle him.

An awkward silence fell, broken only by the pounding of the rain overhead and the soft sound of Sam Harper's grief.

Griffin folded his arms, lowered his dark head. "I'm sorry," he said.

There was compassion in Field's face, and more understanding than Griffin was prepared to encounter just then. "Nonsense," he said, somewhat gruffly. Then a wariness came into Field's features, a remembering. Again, he cleared his throat.

Griffin knew the look. "Out with it, Field," he prodded impatiently.

"Just promise you'll stay calm."

Griffin felt everything within him tense. "What is it, Field? Is Becky dying?"

Field was moving toward Fanny's room, where he was needed. "No. But Fawn Nighthorse just told me that Jonas has the girl. She saw Rachel get into the carriage and leave about half an hour ago."

Griffin felt something terrible erupting inside him. "Rachel? She was sure it was Rachel?"

"She said it was the girl with purple eyes."

Griffin grasped his coat and bag in two savage motions and bolted toward the door. "I'll be back," he growled. And then he bounded out into the rain.

Rachel felt warm color pound in her cheeks as the plump, matronly housekeeper studied her.

"Would you like a cup of tea?" the woman asked, after an agonizing moment. "It will take awhile to heat your bathwater."

Tea. Rachel couldn't remember the last time she'd enjoyed such a luxury. She nodded, trying not to seem too eager. "Please."

"This way, then," sighed the housekeeper, with noble resignation.

Rachel followed her through a great, arched doorway and across a magnificent dining room. Here, there were costly, colorful rugs on the floors and real paintings on the tastefully papered walls. A massive chandelier hung, its many prisms gleaming like bits of a shattered rainbow, over a polished oak table. Six floor-to-ceiling windows looked out on a garden of budding roses and a three-tiered marble fountain.

She thought of the tent where she'd taken her breakfast, and a small, rueful smile curved her lips.

"I'm Mrs. Hammond," the housekeeper announced brusquely, as she led the way through a swinging door and into the largest, cleanest kitchen Rachel had ever seen.

She stared at the gleaming copper kettles hanging on the

yellow walls, at the glass-fronted cupboards filled with exquisite china. "My name is Rachel. Rachel McKinnon."

Mrs. Hammond turned. There was a quickening in her expression, and her thick hands tugged at the full-length apron protecting her dark, rustling dress. "McKinnon," she mused, seeming to taste the name. "McKinnon. Now that name is right familiar to me."

Rachel shrugged offhandedly. "It's common enough, I suppose."

"McKinnon?" Mrs. Hammond shook her neatly groomed gray head. "You don't hear that often, like you do 'Smith' or 'Jones.'"

Rachel was intimidated—by her surroundings, by Mr. Jonas Wilkes, and by this stern-faced, disapproving housekeeper. Nervously, she ran her hands down the skirts of her ruined, icy dress. "Y-You're very kind—to go to all this trouble, I mean."

Mrs. Hammond took a steaming teakettle from the cook-stove, poured water into a bright yellow china pot, and measured in several generous scoops of tea. Her expression softened slightly as she looked at Rachel, and there was a note of unexpected kindness in her voice when she spoke again. "No trouble. Here—come and stand by the stove while I find you something warm and dry to wear."

Rachel approached the great, gleaming monster of a stove. It's nickel scrollwork glinted and shone, even in the dim light of a stormy day, and the warmth was wonderful. "Thank you."

"And don't be worrying about your poor, spoiled dress," the woman called, as she marched off toward the swinging door leading back to the dining room. "We've got a thing or two around here that will probably fit you."

Rachel trembled, huddled close to the stove. Her eyes fell with longing on the yellow teapot, and the curling steam from its spout brought a tantalizing scent to her nostrils.

She drew a deep breath and waited.

After perhaps five minutes, Mrs. Hammond returned, bustling and pink-cheeked, a long, flannel nightgown clutched to her rounded bosom. "There's a little dressing room right around the corner," she said. "Why don't you get out of those wet clothes while I pour us some tea?"

Rachel took the soft gown in eager fingers, her eyes downcast, and obeyed.

The dressing room sported a huge enamel bathtub, soft

chairs, and an exquisite painted silk screen to disrobe behind. Awed, Rachel stepped around it and peeled off the hateful calico dress and the sodden cotton drawers and camisole beneath it. The flannel gown felt wonderfully smooth and warm as it fell against her skin.

What would it be like to wear such things as a matter of course and take baths in a room apparently reserved exclusively for the purpose? Did her mother live this way?

Rachel smiled to herself. At Miss Cunningham's, in Seattle, she'd taken her baths in the middle of the kitchen floor, scrubbing furtively, ever fearing that one of the other tenants might wander in.

She drew a deep breath and hurried back to the kitchen, where Mrs. Hammond graciously poured tea.

It was almost like being a lady.

Rachel drank one cup of strong, fragrant tea and longed for another, but demurred when Mrs. Hammond offered it. She'd behaved scandalously enough, arriving as she had, sopping wet and in the carriage of a relative stranger. It wouldn't do to add gluttony to her sins.

Half an hour later, she sank, awe-stricken and delighted, into the hot, scented water she and Mrs. Hammond had heated and carried into the dressing room, to the bathtub. She soaked for a few glorious minutes, and then began to scrub her pinkened flesh and disheveled hair with soap that smelled of wild flowers.

Clean at last, and truly warm for the first time in weeks, Rachel wrapped her hair in a towel, turban style, and sank to her chin in liquid luxury. Beneath the scented water, she could just barely see the small, diamond-shaped birthmark beside the nipple of her left breast.

It was then that she first heard the quarreling voices. She could not make out the words, but two men were shouting at each other, and Mrs. Hammond put in an occasional shrill remark.

Rachel trembled, tried to think what she should do. Before anything workable occurred to her, the dressing room door burst open with a force that threatened to rip it from its hinges and a glowering, dark-haired man appeared in the doorway.

"Get dressed!" he snapped.

Horrified, Rachel covered her breasts with her arms and sank deeper into the water.

"Now!" the man yelled.

Speech failed Rachel; she could only nod frantically.

But the man was apparently satisfied. He gave Rachel an impatient look that scraped the edges of her soul, and then closed the door.

Rachel scrambled out of the bathtub and huddled behind the silk screen, wrenching the towel from her head and drying herself in quick, desperate motions. Her heart jammed in her throat when she heard the door open again.

But it was Mrs. Hammond who peered around the edge of the screen and extended a tangle of clothing: silken underthings, stockings, a lavender dress made of some soft, rustling fabric.

Mrs. Hammond volunteered no information whatsoever, and Rachel was fully dressed before she could manage to say anything at all. "Who is that man?" she whispered. "What does he want?"

The housekeeper sighed, but her eyes were kind. "That, my dear, is Dr. Griffin Fletcher. And I'm afraid he wants you."

Rachel was terrified. "Why?"

Mrs. Hammond shrugged. "Lord knows. He's a gruff sort, Child, but he won't hurt you."

"H-He has no right—"

"Right or no right, we'll all have hell to pay if you don't do as he says," Mrs. Hammond said. And then she was striding out of the room, closing the door behind her.

Rachel bit her lower lip, scanning the room. There was only one window, and it was firmly shut.

She wrenched at it hopelessly until she realized that someone had painted over the lock, sealing the one avenue of escape available.

Hot tears brimmed in her eyes as she pulled at the window twice more, out of sheer terror.

Again, the door opened. And the man with the dark, stormy eyes was standing there, watching her. He held out her battered, mud-caked shoes. "Put these on."

Rachel lifted her chin and walked toward him.

Jonas's wrath was bitter and vicious, but he had held it in check as his old enemy thrust Rachel through the kitchen and the dining room and out through the front doors.

He'd been afraid to challenge Griffin, and that fear lingered, further souring the defeat.

Mrs. Hammond stood in stubborn silence, at the stove, stirring something into the soup.

"Send McKay for the Indian," Jonas said, after several seconds of charged silence.

"But, Jonas—"

"The *Indian*," Jonas breathed. "Fawn Nighthorse."

Disapproval flashed in Mrs. Hammond's eyes as she dared, at last, to meet his gaze. "But it's the middle of the day. What's Tom supposed to tell her?"

Jonas whirled, pushed open the swinging door with a crash of his right palm. "That her rent is due," he answered.

Chapter Four

When she felt it was safe, Rachel risked a fleeting glance at the man sitting in the buggy seat beside her. The muscles in his jawline were tight with disapproval, as were his firm, aristocratic lips.

Dr. Griffin Fletcher. Rachel was grateful that Mrs. Hammond had volunteered his name: *he* certainly hadn't had the good manners to do so.

"Why are you doing this?" she ventured, painfully conscious of her wet, unbrushed hair and borrowed clothes.

Dr. Fletcher turned dark, intolerant eyes to her face. His voice was a low rumble, a sound like two thunder clouds colliding in a distant sky. "What did Jonas offer you?" he countered coldly.

Rachel felt crimson blood flaming in her cheeks. "I beg your pardon?" she gasped, nearly choking on the words.

"Never mind," the doctor growled, turning his attention back to the buggy reins and the horse and the rutted, muddy road at the base of Mr. Wilkes's stone driveway.

Rachel sat back on the cushioned seat, her heart in her throat, and prayed silently for a speedy and miraculous rescue.

As if to reflect the storm of emotions raging within her, the rain became a torrent, thumping at the roof of the buggy and flinging itself inside to sting Rachel's face and drench the pretty amethyst dress.

Dr. Fletcher seemed to have forgotten that she existed at all, and she found that idea oddly disturbing. She disliked the man intensely—had on sight—and yet something within her craved his notice.

"I demand to know where you are taking me," she said firmly, over the din of the worsening rain.

Now, he looked at her. The dark light in his eyes was scathing as his glance passed over the half-sodden dress and then returned to her face. "You're cold," he said almost accusingly. And then, deftly, he removed his dark suit coat and thrust it at her.

Rachel draped the coat around her shoulders and glared at him. "I insist that you tell me—"

The stern lips curled in a humorless grin. "You insist, do you?" He laughed, and the sound made Rachel ache to the marrow of her frozen bones. "That is interesting."

"Are you always nasty and impossible, Dr. Fletcher?"

"Only on my good days," he retorted. "Do you always go home with men like Jonas Wilkes?"

Shattering humiliation closed Rachel's throat for a long moment. When words were possible, she forced herself to speak in the measured, dignified tones of a lady. "Mr. Wilkes was very kind to me."

Grim amusement danced in the dark depths of his gaze. "Oh, he's a fine fellow," Dr. Fletcher drawled, with sardonic relish. Again, his eyes moved to the now nearly transparent fabric of her dress. The bitter mirth in his look faded away suddenly, and another emotion flared up, savage and unreadable, in its place. "Nice dress," he said.

Rachel was not naive enough to believe that she had been complimented, and she swallowed the automatic "thank you" that rose in her throat.

The pitiable horse trudged on, its hooves sticking now and then in the deep mud, its breath forming little clouds even in the driving rain. Rachel pretended a compelling interest in the lush foliage choking the roadside.

Presently, they reached Providence again, but the beleaguered buggy did not stop at any one of the snug, neatly painted houses Rachel so admired. It labored on and finally came to a halt in front of the very cottage where she had encountered Mr. Wilkes such a short time before.

"You might as well come inside and dry off," Dr. Fletcher

allowed tersely, springing from the buggy seat and taking an ancient black medical bag from the floor.

Rachel glanced warily in the direction of Tent Town. It was vaguely visible in the downpour, and still singularly uninviting.

She suppressed the instinct urging her to flee this officious man while she had the opportunity, and to cower, shivering, inside the questionable sanction of her own tent.

Dr. Fletcher didn't seem particularly concerned, one way or the other. He was already striding up the neat little walk leading to the cottage door.

Rachel scrambled to close the distance between herself and this arrogant, confusing man. As she fell into step beside him, she was reminded of the castles she'd read about in books. He was like one of those grim, forbidding structures, this man— cold and aloof and surrounded by a moat as real and impassable as any made up of crocodiles and water. She wondered if he had ever allowed anyone—man, woman, or child—to climb the high, thick walls of his fortress and venture into the passageways of his heart.

Rachel realized that she was being fanciful, but she didn't care. It was her affinity with the world of whimsy that made the real one bearable.

The inside of the cottage was clean and warm, but very dimly lit. The specter of death was lurking in that pleasant house; Rachel sensed its presence and drew the doctor's coat closer to her body.

A thin, exhausted man stood near the crackling fire on the hearth, his shoulders stooped, his features hidden in shadow. Rachel's lower lip trembled as she realized that he was weeping; the soft, ragged sound said too much about life in and around the lumber camps.

Dr. Fletcher moved across the room silently, disappearing through a doorway and leaving the shattered man and Rachel alone.

After just a moment, though, another man, tall and pleasant-looking, came out of the room Dr. Fletcher had entered. His smile was sad as it touched Rachel. "Hello," he said, walking toward her. He extended a hand, and she found that it was hard and calloused.

She took in his worn, clerical collar with confusion. In her experience, preachers talked a lot, and they talked loud; but they seldom did real work. Yet the skin on his hands belied that idea. Here was a man who had swung an ax times without number and probably had strained on one side of a crosscut saw, too.

The gentle eyes smiled at Rachel, even though the mouth was sad. "I'm Reverend Hollister," he said. And then, without waiting for Rachel's name, he left the room, only to return a moment later with a warm blanket and a hairbrush.

Rachel remembered her tangled, still-wet hair and blushed, but she accepted the items gratefully, with a whispered, "Thank you."

The man beside the fireplace stopped weeping, braced himself with visible determination, and went out of the house, leaving the door open behind him. He seemed heedless of the rain as Rachel watched him hurry down the walk and bolt over the gate.

Reverend Hollister explained softly as he closed the door. "Sam's baby was stillborn," he said, his kind face contorted with shared pain. "A few minutes ago, we lost his wife, too."

Rachel felt stricken tears gather in her eyes. "Oh, no," she said, feeling the loss of this strange woman and her child as keenly as if she'd known them.

There was a short, dismal silence. Then Rachel turned away, hung the doctor's suit coat on a wooden peg near the fireplace, and wrapped herself in the woolen blanket Reverend Hollister had provided. Standing beside the fire, she began to brush her hair with fierce, determined strokes choreographed by her grief.

It seemed like a very long time before Dr. Fletcher came out of the death room and stood close beside her, before the fire. In a sidelong glance, Rachel saw that his shoulders were taut under his sodden white shirt and that his magnificent, ferocious eyes were haunted.

"I'm sorry," she said.

For just a moment, she thought she saw a weakening in the immense walls that enclosed him; but he seemed to feel her scrutiny, and he stiffened. There was no emotion whatsoever in the look Griffin Fletcher gave her, and though his throat worked, no words passed his lips.

A horrible thought swept over Rachel, weakening her knees. "W-Was it because you had to leave? D-did they die because of me?"

The doctor allowed himself a look of exasperation. "You exaggerate your own importance, Miss McKinnon. There was nothing that could have been done, whether I'd been here or not."

Rachel was too stung to respond, but the Reverend Hollister rasped, "Griffin!"

Some of the awesome tension seemed to drain from Dr. Fletcher's taut body, but he said nothing. The crimson and orange light of the fire danced on his stony features as he turned his attention to the flames.

Rachel drew a deep, shaky breath and managed. "I think I'd better go now. I-I don't want to get in anybody's way. . . ."

She'd thought that this man couldn't surprise her any more than he already had, but now he grabbed her arm and wrenched her close, so close that she could feel the hard, lean length of his thigh through her skirts.

"Don't you want to explore your new home, Rachel?" he asked, in a voice that at once terrified and enraged her. "There is a vacancy now, you know. One word to your good friend Jonas, and you, too, can live in splendor!"

Having no idea what he was talking about, Rachel tried to draw back and found herself hopelessly imprisoned in his grasp. Her heart sprouted wings and flew into her throat, struggling there, cutting off her breath. Had Reverend Hollister not broken Dr. Fletcher's hold so swiftly, she was certain she would have fainted.

"Griffin," the minister bit out, restraining his friend with a glower. *"That is enough!"*

For a moment, the two men glared at each other, and the already intolerable tension in the room grew to alarming proportions. A small, strangled sob escaped Rachel's aching throat, and she whirled, frantic, to run out of the house and down the slippery stone walk.

The gate resisted her quick, feverish tugs, and she wrenched at it, half hysterical in her need to escape the tangible hatred throbbing in the little house behind her.

But a strong hand closed over hers, forestalling the battle with the rusted gate latch. She looked up into the tempestuous, condemning eyes of Dr. Griffin Fletcher.

He was drenched to the skin. Rainwater poured down his face, plastering his thick, ebony-colored hair to his head in dripping tendrils. Through his now-translucent shirt, Rachel could see the dark tracery of hair matting his chest, and the sensations the sight aroused within her were more terrifying than any she'd experienced that day.

She was too stricken to move or speak. She could only stare at him, and wonder about all the mad, conflicting emotions that were raging inside her, more violent than any storm the sea and sky could produce.

Dr. Fletcher didn't seem to notice the rain; he simply stood there, watching Rachel's face for a long time. Then, incredibly, he brought his hands to rest on her shoulders.

I want him, Rachel thought with horror and conviction. *Dear Heaven, after the way he's treated me, I want him.*

In desperation, she raised her chin and shouted over the incessant patter of the rain. "I'm going home!"

Without a word, Griffin Fletcher released her.

Wanting more than anything to stay near him, Rachel turned on her heel and strode away, toward the grassy embankment sloping down to the boundaries of Tent Town. She looked back only once, and involuntarily at that. When she did, she saw him standing at the end of the walk, watching her.

Fawn Nighthorse trembled inwardly when the summons came, but she was careful not to reveal her reluctance. If McKay thought she was scared, he'd be pleased—and there was no way she was going to let the slug have the satisfaction.

She followed Jonas's coachman and right-hand man down the cottage walk and through the gate, raising her face, once or twice, to the cleansing rain. Out of the corner of her eye, she saw Griffin Fletcher's horse and buggy at Fanny's gate.

For a second, she considered running to him. He would defend her—she knew that—but in the end, she decided against seeking his help. Griffin had enough trouble as it was, and Fawn had other, deeper reasons for not wanting to call attention to the situation.

McKay had brought an extra horse, and Fawn swung deftly up onto its broad back, clinging to the reins with white-knuckled hands. McKay's saddle creaked as he turned to grin at her.

Fawn grinned back. *Bastard,* she thought.

They rode swiftly, avoiding the main road and galloping along the path leading through the dense woods to the east of Tent Town. After about fifteen minutes, the two riders emerged from a stand of silvery-leaved cottonwood trees and cut across the narrow dirt road.

Fawn allowed herself one glance back, over her shoulder, at the large, gray stone house where Griffin Fletcher lived. If she reined in the mare she was riding sharply enough and rode hard, she might be able to reach Griffin's front door, the sanctuary within his house, before McKay caught up with her.

She swallowed hard. What about tomorrow and the day after that? She couldn't hide from Jonas forever, and Griffin, the magnificent fool, wouldn't even try.

The rain was easing up; Fawn lamented that. Just then, she wished that the skies would open and drown Jonas Wilkes in a torrential downpour.

He can probably swim, she thought, bitterly.

McKay rode up a steep, rocky sidehill, and Fawn followed. When they reached the crest, they both paused, their mounts dancing impatiently, to survey Jonas's kingdom.

McKay took in the palatial brick house and surrounding land with an obvious, vicarious sort of pride, while Fawn viewed it with dread.

I shouldn't have told Field Hollister that I saw Jonas carrying off the Fair Maiden, she reflected wryly. *Damn it! Ten to one, Field told Griffin and Griffin went busting in there to save Becky's kid from shame and degradation!*

Fawn stiffened in the saddle, stood up in the stirrups to stretch her legs. *Before this day's out, I'm going to wish I'd never been born.*

McKay tossed a smug look over his shoulder; it was almost as though he'd read Fawn's thoughts and found them profoundly amusing. "Come on, Injun. The boss has plans for you."

"Did I ever tell you what my people do with snakes like you, McKay?" Fawn shot back.

McKay paled. "Shut up."

Fawn raised her voice as the horses started down the other side of the hill. "First, we let the old ladies peel your hide off—"

McKay spurred his mangy stallion to a run, and Fawn's laughter rang to the mountain and back again.

In the privacy of her tent, Rachel removed her wet clothes and wrapped herself in a blanket. Tears gathered behind her eyes, burning, but she would not let them fall.

She lay down on her cot, a torrent of confusion storming inside her. Because the anger kept her warm, she tried to stir it into full flame by remembering the rude things Dr. Fletcher had said and implied.

But the anger kept ebbing away. Instead, she found herself wondering what it would be like to surrender herself to him.

Where the rites of men and women were concerned, she had a firm grasp of the basics, though she had never experienced them. Her father had warned her repeatedly that if she laid down with a man, she would be sullied.

Rachel had known a girl in Oregon who had been sullied by a storekeeper's son. Wilma had ended up with a very big stomach, good food to eat, and a sturdy roof over her head.

Rachel considered getting herself sullied, then set the thought wearily aside.

It had been such a confusing, worrisome day. First, there had been that unfortunate scene with Mr. Wilkes in the dining tent and then that encounter with him at the cottage. On top of that, she'd found out that her mother lived nearby, had ventured into Mr. Wilkes's grand house for tea and a real bath, and been dragged off by that insufferable Griffin Fletcher in the bargain.

He seemed to delight in hurling veiled insults at her, to hate her even. But why?

The burning tears brimmed in her orchid eyes and slid down her cheeks. *I don't like him either,* she mourned, knowing all the while that she did.

Rachel wept, tossing and turning inside the thin blanket until she finally fell into an exhausted, fitful sleep.

Griffin paused at the door of the tent Chang had pointed out to him, drawing one deep breath and running his hand through his damp hair. He was insane to go near the girl at all, considering the effect she'd had on him almost from the first moment he'd seen her.

Still, he couldn't very well leave her in Tent Town—she was too vulnerable to Jonas now. And Becky was counting on him to keep her safe.

Griffin swore. Rachel hadn't exactly been glad to be rescued from Jonas's luxurious den, it seemed to him. For all he knew, she liked the bastard.

"Rachel?" he said, quietly.

There was no answer, and a sudden and boundless fear overtook him. Suppose Jonas had already found her again and taken her back? Suppose, even now, he was caressing those delightful breasts or—

Griffin stepped inside the tent.

Nothing could have prepared him for the impact of seeing her there, asleep on that narrow cot, her thin blanket askew. The curve of one slender thigh glowed in the lamplight, and her left breast was revealed entirely. Beside the rosy nipple, a small, diamond-shaped marking caught the light.

A miniature eternity passed before Griffin could move or even breathe. Never, at any time in his life, had he wanted any woman the way he wanted this purple-eyed, quarrelsome snippet of a girl.

He tried to be impersonal about the matter; after all, there wasn't anything on that delectable little body he hadn't seen before.

I am a doctor, he reminded himself.

But Rachel was no patient.

He turned away, and inside him, different facets of his complex nature did battle. The part of him that cherished honor prevailed at last, after a struggle, and he bent and gently covered the naked breast, the appealing thigh.

There would be another time; he knew that. And he looked forward to it with both yearning and despair.

Chapter Five

Pausing outside the great double doors of Jonas's parlor, Fawn drew a deep breath. Perhaps it wouldn't be as bad as she'd thought; perhaps the dramatic scenarios she had imagined had never taken place at all.

She had only mentioned Rachel McKinnon's departure from Tent Town, in Jonas's company, in passing. For all she knew, Field hadn't even bothered to repeat the conversation to Griffin. And even if he had, there was every chance that Griffin wouldn't make the connection in his harried mind, wouldn't realize that the new resident was Becky McKinnon's kid.

But if he had . . . Oh, Lord, if he had . . . And if he'd told Jonas, in anger, that the warning had come from Fawn . . .

Fawn let her head rest against the polished mahogany framework of the French doors. Not for the first time in her eventful life, she found herself wishing that she had never separated herself from her people, never tried to stay with the Hollisters and go to school, never tried to make a place for herself in the white world.

She laughed, ruefully, under her breath. There was no place

for her in that world, even though she could read and write and figure as well as any of them. She was Jonas Wilkes's woman—and nothing else.

Fawn lifted her head. All right. She was Jonas's woman, and only one of many at that. But there was no point in standing around sniveling about it; she could not go back to her tribe now, and her pride would not allow her to return to Buck Jimson's show to be stared at like a freak.

Somehow, she would have to find a way to live between the two worlds, between the Indian ways and the ways of the whites. And if she could be neither Indian nor white, she would still be Fawn Nighthorse. She could still dream.

She was startled when the parlor doors swung open, and her fears were deepened by the glint of savage annoyance in Jonas's tawny eyes.

"How kind of you to accept my last minute invitation, Miss Nighthorse," he said.

Fawn suppressed a shudder. Jonas was a good-looking man and more skilled than most as a lover, yet the thought of his hands touching her made her skin crawl. "I dropped everything and rushed right over," she said, tempering her surrender with as much sarcasm as she dared.

A slight, mocking smile curved Jonas's lips. "Come in," he said, making a suave gesture of his right hand. In his left, he held a brandy snifter.

Fawn edged past him, into the sumptuous room, much as she would skirt a mountain lion or a bear. Tension twisted her insides into straining coils.

She whirled to face him, her right hand locked over her left, her head bloodless and light—much too light. "Jonas, I didn't mean—" she blurted, "I shouldn't have told—"

The impeccable white of Jonas's shirt collar seemed to seep into his face, pushing all color before it. His eyes were like golden fires, and his grip on the brandy snifter tightened visibly. "You!" he rasped.

Infinite horror settled over Fawn like a weight, crushing her. All her suspicions had been correct; she knew that now. Field had gone straight to Griffin with the news and Griffin had probably stormed out here and collected Rachel McKinnon before Jonas could maneuver her seduction. Too late, she realized that Griffin hadn't betrayed her—she had done that herself.

She retreated a step. "Jonas, I—"

41

But Jonas crossed the room in just a few strides, the brandy roiling, amber, in the snifter he carried. "I should have known," he growled, in an undertone more terrifying than any shout could have been. "You saw Rachel leave with me and you went straight to Griffin!"

Fawn's head was shaking back and forth of its own volition. "No—no, Jonas. I-I told Field. I'm sorry."

Jonas turned from her suddenly, and for one wild moment, she hoped for a reprieve.

But the brandy snifter sailed across the room and shattered against the ivory marble of the fireplace, sending out a shower of tiny, crystal shards. The fire roared as it caught the contents of the splintered glass and consumed them.

Just as Fawn would be consumed.

Jonas's eyes were flat, expressionless, as he turned his gaze back to her. It was going to be bad.

"Take off your clothes," he said.

Fawn trembled as she reached back to untie the leather strings at the back of her neck, but then a strange calm came over her, a detachment that always carried her through the worst times. The deerskin dress fell to the floor, revealing the nut-brown perfection of Fawn Nighthorse's body.

For a moment, Jonas seemed to be frozen in time and space. She felt his eyes slide over her body, knew that the flickering firelight danced on her cinnamon skin and worked an old and changeless magic, stirring primitive responses in the man before her.

But the spell was soon broken. Jonas thrust her down, roughly, to the massive bearskin rug at her feet. He was upon her in only a moment.

Other times, there had been a degree of gentleness in Jonas's insatiable need; it had allowed her to survive by pretending that he was the one her spirit cried out for. But this time was different.

Jonas's teeth were sharp on the edges of her nipples, his hands harsh where they ventured. Fawn closed her eyes and her mind against the inevitable entry.

It did not happen. Jonas's member, so insistent only seconds before, faded to nothing, resting soft against the cool, dry skin of her thigh.

And Fawn Nighthorse made her third disastrous mistake of the day. "The white warrior has no spear to throw," she said.

Instantly she regretted the foolish, impulsive words, but it was too late.

With both hands, Jonas grabbed her hair, wrenched her head upward, and then thrust it down again, hard, against the floor. His left fist, always the most dangerous, pummeled into the middle of her face. She felt staggering pain, and tasted blood in her mouth.

There was another blow, and then another. The pain was hideous, blinding. But Fawn Nighthorse did not utter a single sound, not even as her consciousness slipped away.

Before she opened her eyes, Rachel sensed that she wasn't alone in the tent. Someone was there, watching her.

Primitive terror surged into her throat, cutting off her wind, blocking any sound she might have made. Instinct caused her to lie very still.

There was exasperation in the voice that shattered the eerie silence. "It's all right, Miss McKinnon; I'm not here to ravage you."

It couldn't be! Drained of that first instinctive rush of fear, Rachel turned her head, squinted at the man sitting casually on the cot across from hers. "Griffin Fletcher!" she gasped, remembering all the secret things she'd imagined doing with him and blushing in response.

He didn't seem to notice her embarrassment; he simply stood up and turned his muscular back. "Get dressed. You can't stay here any longer."

Outrage roared through Rachel's being like a forest fire consuming trees and bushes. "I beg your pardon!" she snapped, sitting up on the cot and pulling the inadequate blanket closer to her tingling skin.

"You heard me," Griffin Fletcher intoned without turning around. "Put your clothes on, or I'll do it for you."

Having no doubt that he would do just that, if challenged, Rachel scrambled off the cot, still cowering in her blanket, and pulled the hated brown woolen dress—the only dry garment she possessed—from her wicker satchel.

The dress was rumpled and musty, but Rachel put it on anyway, and in record time. "Who do you think you are?" she raged, as she frantically brushed her hair and pinned it into place. "My father is going to hear about this, I assure you! He is a very strong man and he is not going to be pleased when I tell him how you've been harassing me! Why, he'll—"

Rachel's tirade was interrupted by a low, intrepid laugh. Color rushed into her cheeks as Dr. Fletcher turned, at last, to face her.

"He'll what?" he asked, grinning.

"He'll—he'll—" Rachel wasn't quite sure what he'd do, so she made something up. "He'll skin you alive and throw your insides to the gulls!"

The irritating grin broadened. "I'm terrified, Miss McKinnon," he said.

Rachel was deflated now, and frightened. "If I'm not to stay here, where am I going?" she asked, raising her chin and forcing herself to meet the dark, amused gaze of her tormentor.

"That, my dear, is your mother's problem, not mine. And you will never know how grateful I am for that one, shining fact."

All of Rachel's conflicting emotions were displaced by her curious feelings toward her mother. On the one hand, she hated the woman, wished never to see her, never to speak to her or hear her voice. On the other, she wondered about so many things, harbored so many searching questions that only Rebecca McKinnon could answer.

"You'll take me to her?" she asked evenly.

"With pleasure and relief," said Dr. Fletcher, executing a mocking half-bow and gesturing grandly toward the door of the tent.

Rachel preceded him outside with dignity.

In a gentlemanly manner, Dr. Fletcher helped her into the rain-dampened seat of his buggy. The storm had passed, though only temporarily if the angry, sullen afternoon sky meant anything.

The air was cool, but somehow oppressive, too, and Rachel mourned her lost shawl. After the embarrassing events of the morning, she couldn't very well present herself at Mr. Jonas Wilkes's door and request its return.

Dr. Fletcher swung deftly into the seat beside her and took up the reins. In a few moments, the exhausted little horse was drawing them out of Tent Town and onto the main road.

Once again, the saltbox houses along Main Street slipped by, one by one. The lamps behind the polished windows had been extinguished, and well-fed housewives were venturing out into their yards to inspect their infant gardens or just breathe the freshly washed air. Several waved spiritedly at the doctor, who responded with a slight smile and a nod of his head. Rachel could feel curious stares following her.

At the end of the street, just past the white frame church that must certainly be Field Hollister's domain, Dr. Fletcher forsook the road for a wide path leading down toward the water.

Rachel searched his face, but saw nothing there that could possibly have prepared her.

The establishment stood, tall and brazen, in the midst of a tangle of fir trees, cedars, and adolescent elms. A garish, gilded sign proclaimed it to be Becky's Place, and Rachel did not miss the meaning of the swinging doors or the tinny piano music coming from inside.

"A saloon," she breathed, stunned.

Something almost like compassion flashed in the doctor's eyes. "Yes," he said hesitantly. Then he sighed heavily, and the mocking formality was gone from his voice when he went on. "Rachel, your mother is very sick. I want you to remember that."

Rachel could only nod.

When the doctor lifted her down from the buggy seat and offered his arm, Rachel accepted. She was not accustomed to leaning on anyone, the harsh realities of her life had precluded that almost from the first, but she felt the need of this man's boundless, grudging strength now.

The inside of the saloon was far fancier than any Rachel had ever seen before. It had a real wooden floor, rather than the scattered sawdust of the boisterous establishments from which she'd sometimes dragged her good-natured father; and the walls were embossed with something that resembled red velvet. The bar was elaborately carved and polished to a high shine, and there was a long, glistening mirror affixed to the wall behind it.

Rachel caught sight of her reflection in that bottle-edged mirror and winced. She looked like a waif, lost inside a full-bodied woman's dress.

Just when she thought she was adjusting to the shock of it all, two women burst, laughing, through a fringed doorway to the left of where Rachel stood. Both had brassy, unlikely-looking hair piled on top of their heads in stiff curls, and their dresses were so scant that their robust breasts threatened to burst free.

Rachel blushed to the roots of her hair and turned her eyes, in desperation, to Griffin Fletcher's face. She saw mingled sympathy and amusement in his gaze and stiffened. "Dancing girls," she whispered.

"At the very least," replied the doctor, crisply, tightening his grasp on Rachel's arm and ushering her toward a steep, wooden stairway.

The shattering truth dawned on Rachel midway between the first floor and the second. She froze where she stood and swallowed the aching lump that had risen in her throat. "This place—this place is a—"

"Brothel," said Dr. Fletcher bluntly. But his eyes were gentle on her face now and calmly insistent.

Tears of stunned confusion gathered in Rachel's thick eyelashes, making them spiky. For one terrible moment, she thought she was going to be violently ill.

"You could have told me!" she croaked.

Griffin Fletcher's impressive shoulders moved in a sigh. "How?" he asked, reasonably.

Rachel had no answer for that, and though she wanted nothing more than to turn and run, she permitted the doctor to lead her up the stairs and into a long, dim hallway.

He tapped lightly at the last door on the left, turning the doorknob with resolution when a thin voice commanded, "Come in."

Rachel would have remained behind, in the hallway if he hadn't dragged her inside with an effectively disguised show of force.

After a long moment, he released her and moved across the shadowy room to stand beside a disheveled bed. "Hello, Becky."

Rachel could barely make out the thin frame resting beneath the tangled bedclothes, but she knew that this wraith, with its mussed hair and waxen face, was her mother. She recoiled—from the sickness, from all she had learned in the past few minutes.

The ghost-woman's voice was a vicious rasp, and her eyes were fierce on the doctor's face. "You bastard, Griffin—you brought her here!"

The doctor seemed unruffled by the challenge. "I'm fond of you, too, Becky. And yes—this is Rachel."

The comforter moved with a rustling sound as the woman raised herself from her prone position and snapped, "Light a lamp, for God's sake! What's done is done. Let's have a look at her."

The lamp light was bravely inadequate against the sullen glower of the day, but it was bright enough to reveal one woman to the other.

Griffin Fletcher scanned Rebecca's face once, with detached interest, and then quietly left the room.

"Come over here," Rebecca said, and the words constituted both an order and a plea.

Knees weak, Rachel drew closer to the bed. In spite of the ravages of the illness, the beauty and grace she remembered were still there in that wondrous face, in those compelling violet eyes.

A sudden and disconcerting laugh tore itself from Rebecca's gaunt, hollow throat. "If that isn't the ugliest dress I've ever seen!"

Rachel could not stand up any longer, could not bother with matters so mundane as her brown woolen dress. She dropped to her knees beside the bed and cried out, "Why?"

Rebecca sighed and relaxed against the pillows propped behind her. "Why what? Why did I leave? Why do I live in this place? I left because I wasn't happy, Rachel."

Rachel's anger and hurt were combining forces to choke her, but she managed a terse, "*This* makes you happy? Happier than living with Pa and me?"

"No," replied Rebecca with wounding honesty. "No, but once I'd found that out, it was too late. I wouldn't leave you, Rachel, if I had it to do over again."

"Why did you?"

"Because I couldn't be sure there would be food, among other things. I knew your father could provide the necessities, knew he would see that you had schooling. And he did, didn't he?"

Rachel lowered her head. She had been wrenched from one miserable schoolhouse to another, but she was educated. She could write a neat hand and read any book written in the English language. "Yes," she said, after a long time.

Rebecca changed the subject rapidly. "You've got to leave Providence, Rachel. And leave it now."

"Where would I go?" Rachel asked, and she was surprised by the reason in her voice, for she did not feel at all reasonable.

"Anywhere. San Francisco, Denver—even New York. Rachel, just go away."

Slowly, cautiously, Rachel raised herself to her feet. "If you're worried that I'll disrupt your life here—"

Pain shadowed the sunken amethyst eyes. "My life doesn't matter anymore, but yours does. I'll give you the money I've saved, and you can start again somewhere else. My friends will sell the business when the time comes, settle my debts, and forward the proceeds to you."

Rachel was at once appalled and touched. "I couldn't," she whispered.

"But you will," insisted her mother. "Rachel, you are a woman now, not a little girl. It is time you lived a decent, settled life."

Rachel could not absorb the things she was hearing. "You're dying, aren't you?" she asked at last.

Rebecca seemed fitful now; she was beginning to writhe from the pain she had tried so hard to hide. "That's what Griffin tells me, and it can't happen too soon, as far as I'm concerned."

Tears slipped, unnoticed, down Rachel's cheeks. She forgot her resentment and pain, forgot that this woman ran a notorious brothel. Rebecca was her mother, and she loved her.

"Come here, Child," Rebecca said, reaching out for one of Rachel's hands, drawing her into an embrace.

Rachel allowed herself to be held, and when the spate of weeping had passed, she dried her face, straightened her impossible dress, and went downstairs in search of Dr. Fletcher.

Rebecca had weakened significantly during Rachel's brief absence, and she seemed almost to welcome the decline. Her eyes strayed from Rachel's face only once, when she heard the doctor opening his medical bag.

She shook her head as he drew out a vial and a syringe. "No, Griffin. I want every moment—every moment."

Griffin dropped the items back into his bag without speaking and went to stand at a far window, looking out.

A last burst of fiery light came into Rebecca's hollow eyes as she clutched both Rachel's hands in her own. "You must go—promise me you'll go. There's a man, a terrible man—"

Rachel nodded, unable to speak.

Just minutes later, Rebecca McKinnon died.

Chapter Six

Rachel was devastated. She stood, trembling, in a shadowed corner of her mother's room as Dr. Fletcher closed Rebecca's staring eyes and covered her face with the bedsheet.

A peculiar silence filled the room for a long time; muted sunshine crept across the bare floor, only to be blotted out again by some dark, distant cloud.

"I'm sorry," the doctor muttered, as Rachel dried her eyes and raised her quivering chin.

But Rachel was hearing another voice, her mother's. *"There's a man, a terrible man—"*

She remembered the angry, almost hateful way Rebecca had greeted Dr. Fletcher, the mean things he'd said and done from the first moment she'd met him. Perhaps the man of her mother's warnings was this one.

But Rachel couldn't be certain; in spite of outward appearance, she had sensed a sort of gruff, irreverent affection between the two of them. And there was, at the moment, no room inside her for any emotion other than the boundless, tearing grief she was feeling. *I lost you twice,* she raged inwardly, gazing at the thin form lying so still beneath the bedclothes.

Rachel grappled with the knowledge that there was no shining hope to cling to now, no chance that Rebecca would reappear in her life, repentant and prepared to be her mother again. Somehow, she felt even more bereft than she had at seven years of age, and more alone, too.

Griffin knew that Becky's death was a mercy, but still, he mourned her. He would miss her boundless friendship, her blunt honesty, her magnificent wit.

Yet he would have laughed aloud, had it not been for the shattered girl huddling in a corner. *Damn it, Becky,* he thought. *You managed it after all, didn't you? You're gone and Ezra is on the mountain and I'm stuck with the kid!*

Griffin allowed himself a heavy, audible sigh. He reviewed the facts in his mind and came up with the same disturbing result every time: he could not leave Rachel there, at the brothel; places like that had a way of absorbing the bewildered and making them their own. Of course, she couldn't be dropped off at Tent Town and forgotten, either; he might as well hand her over to Jonas himself as abandon her there.

"Damn it!" he said, and the words startled him as well as Rachel.

The girl came bursting out of the shadows suddenly, her amethyst eyes clouded with shimmering tears, her perfect skin pale with outrage. The grief she felt was so tangible that Griffin could feel it mingling with his own.

"How dare you swear like that—here, now?"

He started to apologize, but before he could even frame the words, Rachel raised her hand and slapped him, hard. He swayed slightly and stared down into the pinched, furious face, stunned.

But, then, Griffin understood. He drew the girl into his arms and held her close as she sobbed into his shoulder.

Something hard and cold within Griffin Fletcher began to thaw. He nearly thrust Rachel away from him, the sensation was so alarmingly familiar; but his need to shelter and comfort her prevailed.

Jonas paced the inlaid hearth in front of his parlor fireplace, heedless of the shattered crystal grinding beneath the soles of his boots. He'd beaten the Indian too well; her bruises and cuts were visible, and the sleep that encompassed her now was not a natural one. There were too many catches in her breathing, and when she stirred on the brocade sofa, frightening, guttural sounds came from her swollen lips.

The slut could die. The thought stalked Jonas like a snarling beast; he could not outdistance it, no matter how much he paced.

He paused, resting his elbows on the ornate, gilded mantelpiece, and caught a glimpse of his own face in the mirror gleaming above it. He turned from the sight and glared at the woman groaning on the sofa.

Jonas was a man of almost limitless influence, but if this girl died, he would undoubtedly stand trial for her murder. He might even hang.

The parlor doors opened with a hesitant creak, and Jonas

looked up to see Mrs. Hammond standing there, her full face etched with furious worry as she studied the girl. "I'll send for the doctor," she said, after a long, stiff silence.

Jonas averted his eyes and walked to the liquor cabinet on the other side of the room to pour himself a generous dose of brandy. "I think that would be a good idea," he said.

All the while, Mrs. Hammond's condemning gaze dug into his shoulder blades like invisible claws.

"You are a monster, Jonas Wilkes," the woman breathed, fearless in her long tenure. "A brutal monster!"

Jonas flinched slightly, but did not turn around to face the woman who had raised him. Hammond would forgive him, as she always had. "That will be all," he said, with an authority he didn't feel.

Griffin strode up Jonas's walk, the medical bag swinging in his right hand. He remembered his earlier visit, that morning, and in spite of everything, he smiled. The animosity between himself and Jonas Wilkes went back a long way and was so fathomless that either man would have been wholly changed without it.

Jonas answered the crisp knock himself, and his bearing was that of a concerned, distracted friend. He led Griffin across the wide hallway and into the parlor.

The summons had been a brief one, delivered tersely by the henchman, McKay. Griffin had been told only that he was badly needed at Mr. Wilkes's house.

Now, as his gaze scanned the massive room and caught on Fawn Nighthorse's prone, unconscious form, a stunned hiss escaped him. "Jesus," he muttered, approaching Fawn swiftly and checking the pulse point beneath her left ear. "What did you do to her?"

Jonas shrugged as Griffin felt the girl's rib cage with deft, discerning hands. "Didn't McKay tell you? She fell down the stairs."

Griffin suppressed a killing rage as he lifted one of Fawn's eyelids and then the other. There could easily be internal injuries, and she would need stitches beneath her lower lip. "You bastard," he breathed, without looking up.

Jonas stood at the foot of the sofa now, his voice an irritating drone in the throbbing tension of the room. "Indians are a disciplinary problem, you know."

Griffin brought a bottle of alcohol from his bag and began to

51

clean the wounds on Fawn's battered face. "Shut up, you son of a bitch, and get me some hot water and a clean cloth."

Jonas did not stir from his post at Fawn's feet. "Now, now, Griffin, I thought we were friends."

Mrs. Hammond entered the room, shamefaced and stricken, bearing a basin of steaming water and several towels. The flow of the conversation was not interrupted by her presence.

"Friends, hell," Griffin growled, making use of the materials Mrs. Hammond had provided—it was annoying, he thought, how she'd spared Jonas even that small effort—and then dipping a steel needle into carbolic acid and threading it with catgut. Fawn flinched as the sharp point of the needle pierced her flesh, then stirred and opened her wide, brown eyes as he tied off the last stitch.

Soft jubilance soared in Griffin's weary spirit. It was a valid thing to be happy about, he supposed, a good friend regaining consciousness; and after three deaths and the inheritance of a troublesome, grief-stricken girl named Rachel, Griffin was especially grateful. "How do you feel?" he asked gently.

Fawn shook her head slowly back and forth. "Not good, Griffin. And no lectures, please."

"No lectures," he promised.

Fawn smiled, and the effort was obviously costly. "How do you feel, Griffin?"

"I'll show you," he replied. And then he raised himself to his full height, turned to Jonas, and aimed all the terrible pain and anger he felt at him. The thud his fist made as it landed, full-force in Jonas's midsection, was a satisfying sound.

Jonas doubled over with a windless grunt, and Mrs. Hammond cried out as though she'd been struck herself.

Slowly, Jonas straightened up again. There was hatred in his eyes as he surveyed Griffin's taut features, his shoulders, his half-clenched fists.

Then, incredibly, Jonas laughed. "Beating the hell out of me won't exorcise your demons, Griffin. Nothing will do that. By the way, Rachel was a fetching sight today, wasn't she? I ought to give her the rest of Athena's clothes."

Blood pounded in Griffin's temples, aching savagery flexed and unflexed the muscles in his hands. Athena's name fell at his feet like a burning tree, the flames flaring up to sear him in the deepest recesses of his mind and soul. A cry of brutal, murderous fury tore at his throat, and he lunged toward Jonas, blinded by his despair and his rage.

But Jonas was prepared. A thin, silvery blade flashed in his left hand; the fingers of his right beckoned calmly. "Come on, Griff. Let's settle it all, right here, right now."

Fawn's cry echoed in the room, and her words were distorted, washing over Griffin's mind like a low, tepid tide. "No, Griffin—please. Don't do it. . . ."

But Griffin could not restrain himself; there seemed to be no reason in all the universe, no sanity. All that mattered was the hatred, the hurt, the betrayal. He relieved Jonas of the knife with one swing of his arm, saw the glimmer of the steel blade as it coursed through the thick air and fell soundlessly to the rug.

The next few moments were forever lost to Griffin Fletcher; when he came back inside himself, Jonas was lying on the floor in a crumpled, groaning heap, his hands sheltering his groin, blood streaming from the corner of his mouth.

Bile roiled in Griffin's stomach and burned in his throat, but he felt no conscious remorse, no pity.

Mrs. Hammond fell to her knees at Jonas's side, her considerable bulk quivering with fear and anger. She turned a scathing gaze to Griffin's face and spat, "You're no better than he is, Griffin Fletcher!"

Griffin turned away, caught the handle of his medical bag in one hand, lifted the wide-eyed Fawn into his arms, and walked out.

"You can't leave him like this!" Mrs. Hammond cried out.

Griffin kicked the front door shut behind him in an answering crash.

Rachel could not bear to remain in her mother's bedroom after the undertaker came, so she crept down the wooden steps, through the now-quiet saloon, and outside. The rain was back, but it was a light, cool drizzle; and Rachel welcomed the bracing touch of it on her upturned face.

Dr. Fletcher had ordered her to remain inside the building until his return, just before rushing off to answer some distress call. In Rachel's opinion, that was as good a reason to leave as any.

Tent Town held as little appeal as ever, though, and she had no friends to go to, so she walked around the weathered walls of her mother's establishment and down a path curving through the thick woods.

The sound and scent of the sea came to meet her long before she rounded the last bend and found herself on the rocky shores of Puget Sound. The tide was rising, and it sounded angry as it hammered at the shoreline and battered the great brown boulders within its reach.

Out on the water, hundreds of rough-barked logs bobbed, bound together by cables. Rachel turned her head toward the mountain rising just to the north and willed her father to know she needed him now and to come home.

In her mind, she could see him working in the misty depths of the woods. Often he bound himself loosely to the trunk of some massive pine tree, climbing at least ten feet up its side to bore, with an auger, two holes: one straight into the heart of the tree, and one at an angle. That done, he would climb down, only to climb back up again, carrying several glowing coals in metal tongs. Carefully, he would press the coals into the straight cavity, to burn there while the slanted perforation provided ventilation.

Soon, the giant tree would fall, shaking the earth as it struck.

Rachel had watched her father work many times, held her breath as he placed the coals expertly, or sawed, winced as he untied himself and jumped clear of the tree's treacherous trunk. His mortality had never come home to her as it did now, on this day of three deaths.

Staring sightlessly at the incoming tide, she hugged herself. What would she do if he was killed? Where would she go?

Rachel bent, took up a smooth, green-gray stone, and flung it into the tide. A stiff wind blew, salty and cold, and pressed her hated brown woolen dress to her bare skin.

Her mother had been so insistent that Rachel go away from Providence, start a new life in some other place. Now, facing the inland sea, she knew she would not, could not leave.

She turned; through the treetops she could see a corner of the saloon's tar-paper roof. She was going to have a little money of her own—she doubted that her mother had saved much—and a perfectly good building.

No, she would not leave Providence. With the money, she would turn the brothel-saloon into a respectable boardinghouse and a real home. Surely such wealth would ease the curious wanderlust in her father's heart; they could stay here always, and live happy, settled lives.

Rachel would have friends, attend church, buy the books and pretty clothes she hungered for. In time, she would become an accepted member of the community. *I might even marry,* she thought, and blushed with chagrined pleasure as the image of Dr. Griffin Fletcher invaded her mind.

Not him! she vowed, in silence. But, still, his reflection was stuck fast to the bruised walls of her heart.

Presently, she heard the snap of a twig behind her, then the rattle of pebbles rolling down the slight slope that separated the woods on her mother's property from the beach.

Griffin Fletcher stood still where the path and the shoreline met, watching her with weary, haunted eyes. His skin was pale beneath its deep tan, and a muscle in his jaw flexed, then relaxed again.

Rachel felt a devastating, contradictory urge to run to him, to hold him in her arms and comfort him as she would a child.

He broke the spell with a gruff, biting statement. "It's time to leave."

Rachel glared at him. "I simply can't wait to find out where you're dragging me off to this time, Doctor!"

The remark had an odd effect on him; some of the misery drained from his eyes, and a tentative smile twisted his lips. Something ancient and powerful crackled back and forth between him and Rachel, overriding all the terrible experiences of the day.

At last, he held out one hand. "You know, Rachel, when my mother first presented me to my father, I don't think she said, 'Let's call this one "Doctor"!' My name is Griffin."

Rachel held back stubbornly; suddenly, his outstretched hand seemed imperious, rather than inviting. "You are wretched and impossible," she muttered. "*Where* are you taking me?"

He raised one dark eyebrow, his hand still extended, and there was weary mockery in his tone. "The food is good and the roof keeps out the rain, so what do you care?"

"I care, Dr. Fletcher!"

"Griffin," he corrected.

"All right! Griffin!"

He relented. "You'll be spending a few days at my house— under the fierce protection of my friend and housekeeper, Molly Brady."

Curious, and knowing that a vigorous argument would be a waste of precious energy, Rachel accompanied him to his house. It was a huge structure, fashioned of natural rock; and apple trees, aflame with silken pink blossoms, seemed to encircle it. Lamplight glowed, in golden welcome, from the windows.

But Rachel was stricken by that warm light, rather than bouyed. Who but a loving, devoted wife would see that lamps were lit against the gathering twilight?

She swallowed miserably as Griffin Fletcher helped her down from the buggy seat and abandoned both the vehicle and the weary horse to the care of a huge, gangly boy. Not once had it occurred to her that he might be married, and she found the possibility distinctly unpleasant.

"I can't imagine how I overlooked this house, since I must have passed it twice today," she said, in a light, false voice, glancing back toward the familiar road that led on to Jonas Wilkes's house.

Griffin's dark eyes, calm only a moment before, were suddenly brooding and remote. "Jonas's place is pretty imposing," he said, opening an iron gate in the stone fence and half-pushing Rachel through it. "Your eyes were probably too full of all that brick and gilt and marble to notice."

There was something profoundly wounding in the way he spoke, but Rachel couldn't quite identify it. Her nerves were suddenly throbbing and raw, as though they'd all been bared to the brisk evening wind, and her voice trembled when she spoke.

"I really should go back to my tent."

Griffin laughed, but there was no humor in the sound, and no warmth. "You speak as though you have a choice, Miss McKinnon. And believe me, you don't."

Rachel was too tired to match wills with this surly man, but she did manage a flippant, "I doubt that your wife will appreciate an unexpected houseguest."

He looked away quickly, but Rachel saw the brutal annoyance in his face all the same, and something that went far, far beyond it.

"I don't have a wife," he said shortly, as they climbed the stone steps leading onto the porch.

Rachel wondered as he opened the front door and ushered her inside. She wondered why part of her wanted to kick this insufferable tyrant in the shins and part of her rejoiced that he had no wife.

The inside of Griffin Fletcher's house was as tasteful and appealing as the outside. It was a clean, spacious, well-furnished place, with high ceilings and polished wooden floors.

Rachel felt welcome in that house, even in the disconcerting presence of its taciturn owner. It was as though the structure itself had drawn her to its heart, to comfort and strengthen her.

Griffin startled her out of her fanciful thoughts by tossing his medical bag onto a table with an irritated crash and calling out, "Molly!"

A trim, strikingly pretty woman with hair the color of cinnamon and sparkling, humorous green eyes appeared in a wide doorway. She was probably somewhere in her late thirties, Rachel thought, but no matter how long she lived, she would never get old.

"Saints be praised, Griffin Fletcher!" she beamed, her tones shaped by a lilting, musical brogue. "You've brought home another one!"

Rachel found herself liking Molly Brady very much.

Chapter Seven

Jonas tried to raise himself from his pillows and failed miserably. The pain in his groin was sharpened by the motion, and sweat beaded on his forehead and along his upper lip.

Everything hurt. Everything.

Jonas lifted swollen eyes to the bedroom windows, saw the deep darkness, heard his name in the voice of the night. To distract himself, he sought the hours wandering lost in his mind, and they eluded him.

His breath burned hot in his lungs and parched his throat. *Griffin.*

Rage assuaged some of Jonas's pain as he recalled the beating he'd taken, and he swore harshly in the darkness.

Instantly, the door nearest Jonas's bed swung open, the half-hearted light of a coal-oil lamp flowed into the room. *McKay.* Jonas was revolted by the subtle stench of the man.

"Need some whiskey or anything, Boss?"

Jonas closed his eyes, swallowed. "Bring the doctor."

There was a sound—metal colliding softly with wood. He turned his head, caught sight of McKay's rifle leaning against the doorjamb. Jonas laughed inwardly; the fool had been standing guard in the hallway.

McKay brought the lamp into the room, set it down on Jonas's bedside table. "But, Boss, he's the one what did this—"

The pain was growing intolerable. "Do tell. *Bring the doctor!*"

McKay hurried out, and Jonas made the costly effort to reach out and retrieve his pocket watch from the bedside table. He opened the case, pressed the small button near the stem, heard the odd, gentle tune it played. He squinted, saw that it was nearly ten o'clock.

Jonas waited, remembering his flighty, excitable mother and the high hopes she'd had when she'd presented him with this very special watch. *Sorry, Mama,* he thought, with grim amusement.

He heard the faint, ponderous chiming of the great clock standing downstairs in the entry hall, but after that, he lost track of time. The pain swept over him in waves, leaving nausea in its wake, bearing down on him again the moment he tried to rise above it.

Finally, a lengthy shadow appeared in the open doorway. Without speaking, Griffin Fletcher tossed his medical bag onto the foot of the bed, pulled back the blankets, and began to examine Jonas with swift, deft motions of his hands.

Jonas bore it all in silence, until Griffin drew a syringe from his bag and filled it from a glass vial. "You know something, Griffin? You're an honorable man," he said, without admiration.

"I'm a damned fool," replied Griffin flatly, injecting the compound into Jonas's right arm.

"True," said Jonas.

Griffin dropped the syringe and vial back into his bag. "The swelling will go down in two or three days," he said. "In the meantime, your romantic pursuits will be severely limited."

"What about the fine mash you made of my face?"

"Only temporary, unfortunately."

Jonas laughed as the pain began to ebb a little. "It's too bad we're enemies, you and I."

Griffin raised one eyebrow and snapped the medical bag shut with a sharp motion of his right hand. "No sentiment, Jonas. There is a limit to my patience."

Jonas felt measurably better, and he eased himself into a

sitting position. "A limit? I didn't know you had any patience to set limits on. There really won't be any permanent damage?"

Griffin smiled. "Not unless you bother Fawn again. Or Rachel."

Jonas ignored the remark. "Why did you come here—after what happened?"

Griffin stood in the doorway now, poised to leave. "I had to, and you know that."

"Stay. Have a drink."

"Why? Did you poison the brandy?"

Jonas frowned. "I'm proposing a truce, Griffin. We've been at each other's throats for too long. I honestly—"

"You never did an honest thing in your life," Griffin broke in, clearly uncomfortable. "What do you really want, Jonas?"

"Rachel McKinnon."

Griffin's face hardened in the tremulous light. "I'll kill you first."

Jonas sighed, relaxing on the down pillows. "Oh, I would hate to see things go quite that far. Besides, I think I love her."

"Sure you do, Jonas. After knowing her for one day, you're ready to swear your undying loyalty and devotion."

Jonas's laugh was soft, even. "You don't believe that people can fall in love that fast? Or is it that you're not immune to her charms yourself?"

This time, Griffin laughed. It was a rough, ragged sound. "She's a child, Jonas—a child."

"She's seventeen. Thirteen years younger than you and I."

"Exactly."

"But she's a woman, Griffin."

"That's an opinion."

Jonas knew that his weakness was an advantage, for the moment, and he pressed it. "She is a beautiful *woman*, Griffin. Maybe even more beautiful than Athena."

Griffin lowered his head, closed his eyes. It was odd, Jonas thought, the power that name still held over the man. He looked as though he'd been gut-shot.

"Well, Griffin?" Jonas prodded. "Is she more beautiful than Athena?"

Griffin glared down at him, his anguish plain in his face. "Yes," he said, and then he was gone.

Jonas tossed back his blankets, eased himself out of the bed, and hobbled across the room to the bureau. There, he opened a bottle of whiskey, raised it to his lips, and drank until the last remnants of the pain didn't matter anymore.

Rachel lay perfectly still beneath the sheets and blankets of a real bed, Molly Brady's good cooking resting lightly in her stomach. A soft rain pattered on the solid roof overhead, and she was warm in her borrowed nightgown.

She did not permit herself to think of the staggering course that day had taken; she could not bear to remember it all now. But she did allow her mind to slide back over the evening.

They had eaten dinner, not in Dr. Fletcher's expansive, many-windowed dining room, but in the large, bright kitchen, around a circular oaken table.

There had been so much food, all of it hot and fresh, and to Rachel's great surprise, she had been ravenously hungry.

Molly Brady, her huge, slow-witted son, Billy; Dr. Fletcher, and herself. Reviewing the scene in her mind, Rachel knew she would relish the quiet, ordinary celebration of it always.

Molly was a spritely, direct woman with a ready laugh, and Rachel liked her, even though she wondered whether or not her relationship with Griffin Fletcher went beyond cleaning and cooking and doing wash.

Rachel sighed and drew the heavy flannel sheets up under her chin. She wondered which of the bedrooms contained Fawn Nighthorse, the Indian woman she'd met that morning— a lifetime ago—in Tent Town.

A great fuss had been made over Fawn throughout the evening; Molly carried trays up to her room, and Dr. Fletcher visited her frequently, his face grim.

Rachel didn't know whether Fawn was ill, or whether she'd been hurt somehow. She hadn't dared to ask.

Now, alone in a small, quiet bedroom, she felt a twinge of envy, followed by a deep, shattering sense of loneliness.

And Dr. Fletcher—Griffin—was out. She could feel his absence throbbing in the substantial house, as though the structure was straining to hold its breath until his return.

Then, in the distance, a door closed. The house let out its breath, drew another, and was normal again. Rachel closed her eyes and slept.

* * *

Griffin awakened reluctantly with the dawn. Another day. God, sometimes he wished that time would stop just long enough to allow him to gather his thoughts.

He threw back a tangled blanket and moved, naked, across the cool smoothness of his bedroom floor. At the washstand, he poured tepid water from a pitcher into a basin and washed. That done, he shaved, dressed in his customary black trousers and a fresh white shirt, and brushed his hair.

Though he had a number of other matters to think about, his mind kept straying back to Rachel, who was sleeping in the room directly across from his. A sudden, devastating need sprang up inside him, consuming him, thrusting aside all his good intentions.

He was free now, he reminded himself. There was no good reason why he shouldn't be attracted to her.

Fitful and unaccountably anxious, he moved to the windows, looked out on the clear, freshly washed day forming itself of sunshine and blue sky and fading mists. He drew a deep, ragged breath and searched his mind for specific fears but found only one—loving again.

Griffin braced himself inwardly, turned from the window, and left his bedroom.

In the hallway, he paused, everything within him drawn to Rachel's closed door. After several seconds, he summoned enough discipline to walk away, to open the door of the room where Fawn rested and look in.

She was gone, and the room was as neat and unchanged as if she'd never been there at all.

Griffin was both exasperated and amused, but he wasn't surprised. Even as a small child, Fawn had had trouble staying in one place for more than two hours at a time.

He descended the stairs, strode through the quiet house to the kitchen.

There, four different lamps aided the struggling dawn, and Molly stood before the enormous cookstove, stirring something in a cast-iron kettle.

Her smile was wary, and a tendril of steam-dampened, coppery hair fell over her forehead. She brushed it aside with the back of one hand. "What about the McKinnon girl?" she demanded without preamble.

Griffin bowed slightly and laughed. "And good morning to you, too, Molly Brady."

Molly shook her head good-naturedly and ladled hot oatmeal into a crockery bowl as Griffin helped himself to coffee.

"She's a pretty thing, isn't she?" Molly pressed. "Saints above, I can just imagine what those lilac-colored eyes do to a man's insides."

Griffin sat down at the round oaken table and spooned coarse brown sugar over the cereal Molly set before him. "She's only a child," he snapped, speaking as much to himself as to Molly.

Her laugh was pleasantly derisive. "Some child, that one."

"She's only seventeen," Griffin said, taking an unusual interest in the cream pitcher.

"Aye," Molly agreed cheerfully. "And at her age, I was a year married and mother to my William."

Griffin ignored the remark and ate in silence.

Molly wouldn't have it. "The poor thing—she looked so lost and confused last night! I'll be bound you didn't trouble yourself to explain matters to her, Griffin Fletcher."

Griffin sat back to finish his coffee. "Her father can explain. I'm going to find him today."

Molly raised one shapely auburn eyebrow. "Aye? And it's a day's ride up that mountain and back. What if you're needed here?"

Griffin shrugged with an indifference he didn't feel. He shouldn't go, he knew that—especially not when he could probably persuade Field to go instead. But he needed the ride, the distance, the time.

"I'll be back as soon as I can. Until I am, you keep Rachel in or near this house. Jonas is flat on his back and hurting in some crucial places, but that doesn't mean he won't try anything."

Swiftly, before he could refuse, Molly refilled his cup with coffee. "Griffin," she ventured, with gentle caution. "I know that you and Becky McKinnon were close friends. I know you promised her that you would see Rachel safely out of Jonas's reach. But what if Rachel is attracted to him? Whatever else he is, Jonas is good-looking and rich. Those qualities make a powerful combination when a girl has been poor all her life."

Griffin shoved his cup away, staining the crisp white table-cloth in the process, and rose to take his suit coat and round-brimmed hat from the peg beside the back door. "Jonas would destroy her," he said.

Squaring her shoulders Molly, extended the ever-present

black bag. "Maybe he does love her," she said doubtfully, her green eyes haunted and faraway.

"Love?" The word was bitter on Griffin's tongue. He wrenched open the door and was comforted by the resulting rush of cool air. "Jonas wouldn't know love if it did a jig on his breastbone."

Molly's strong, Irish chin lifted. "And you're a fine one to be throwing stones, Griffin Fletcher. The word practically makes you scream and run."

Griffin went out, slamming the door behind him in eloquent response.

When Rachel awakened, she was bemused to find that she felt nothing. Not grief for her mother, not anger at Griffin, not loneliness. There was, it seemed, a void inside her.

The lovely house was cool and quiet as she made her way through it, to the kitchen.

Molly Brady was there, with her quick smile and her cautious, questioning eyes. "Here, then, sit down and have a bite," she commanded, in her melodic brogue.

Rachel smiled wanly as she accepted the offered oatmeal, with muttered thanks, and sat down to eat. As she moved, the cheap wool of her dress scratched at her bare thighs and irritated her breasts, but she didn't care. Nothing mattered, nothing at all.

Molly centered a wide-brimmed straw hat atop her head. "Rachel?"

Rachel looked up, managing a soft, distracted smile. "Yes?"

"Welcome."

Tears clustered in Rachel's throat, which was odd, she decided, since she had no feelings.

Molly must have seen something in her face, for she approached swiftly, took off her hat, and sat down in the chair nearest Rachel's. "I'm thinking you're a girl in need of someone to talk to, Rachel McKinnon."

"It's very strange," Rachel confided, pushing her half-finished breakfast away. "So much has happened to me, and yet I don't feel anything."

"You will," Molly promised, one of her small, reddened hands coming to rest on Rachel's wrist.

Rachel swallowed, averting her eyes. "What kind of man is Dr. Fletcher?" she asked.

The housekeeper sighed. "He's a good man—a strong, responsible man."

"But he's arrogant and aloof, too!" Suddenly Rachel's lost emotions were streaming back, and she wasn't so sure she welcomed them. "My goodness, Molly, I was minding my own business. I went to Mr. Wilkes's house because he invited me to take a bath—"

Gentle amusement sparkled in the green, green eyes, but there was something disquieting there, too. "Yes?"

"It was all very innocent—I'd gotten muddy, you see, and there was no place *else* to bathe! In any case, Griffin—Dr. Fletcher—came storming in there and dragged me out, and he's been giving me orders and insulting me ever since!"

Molly sat back in her chair and folded her arms across her chest. "Tact has never been one of Griffin's outstanding gifts. He is a very direct man."

"What right does he have to tell me where I can stay and where I can't, to bring me here?"

"None, I suppose. But the doctor and your mother were good friends, Rachel. And he promised her that he would protect you."

"From what?" Rachel demanded, her voice sharp with frustration.

"From Mr. Jonas Wilkes," replied Molly evenly. There was a darkness in her shamrock eyes, a shadowy remembering.

Rachel heard again her mother's words. *"There's a man, a terrible man."* Had she referred to Mr. Wilkes then, rather than Dr. Fletcher? It was all too confusing. "Why would Mr. Wilkes want to hurt me?"

Molly looked distinctly uneasy, and she lowered her voice. "We don't know that he does, Rachel. From what I gather, he fancies you—and that's a dangerous thing."

Rachel sighed. Had everyone gone mad? What would a man of Jonas's wealth and power want with a sawyer's daughter? "Dr. Fletcher hates him—and I think Mama did, too."

Molly nodded. "Aye. It's my guess that Becky thought Jonas would get even with her for some differences they had by striking at you. As for Griffin, he has good reasons for what he feels, though I wish he'd forget them."

"What differences did Mama and Mr. Wilkes have?"

A patch of sunlight glimmered, square, on the table between them, and Molly's features were hidden by the brightness of it. "Jonas Wilkes is one of the most powerful, influential men in

Washington Territory, Rachel. And he was never able to control your mother, as he does so many other people. She simply didn't fear him—not until you came along, that is."

Rachel was silent for a time, her mind busy absorbing this peculiar information, but finally, she spoke again. "Is that why he hates Dr. Fletcher—because he can't control him?"

"I'm sure that's a measure of the problem," agreed Molly, as the sunlight dimmed and her features were visible again. "But there's far more between those two, and it began long before Jonas inherited the mountain."

Something in Molly's manner made Rachel frame her words carefully. "It has something to do with the pain inside Dr. Fletcher, doesn't it?"

Molly was suddenly fretful, rising from her chair, straightening her spotless apron, tying a yellow kerchief over her bright hair. The straw hat lay, forgotten, on a sideboard. "I've said too much as it is, and there's gardening to do. You're to rest quietly, but we've hundreds of books in the doctor's study, if you've a mind to read."

Rachel welcomed the prospect of losing herself in a novel or a volume of epic poetry—if, indeed, the forbidding Dr. Griffin Fletcher possessed any such flighty books.

Thoughts and feelings were swirling inside her as she made her way back through the house, toward the closed room she suspected was Griffin's study. Molly clearly knew so much more than she was willing to tell, and Rachel was frustrated by her silence.

Chapter Eight

Rachel paused in the study doorway, enchanted. Molly Brady had not exaggerated; there were, indeed, hundreds—perhaps thousands—of books here. They were packed tight on shelf after shelf, stacked precariously on chairs and tables, piled high on the massive desk occupying the center of the room.

And yet, conversely, the place had an air of austere neatness. The brass andirons in the fireplace gleamed, the two barrel-backed, black leather chairs facing the hearth smelled of saddle soap, and the surgical instruments, neatly aligned in a glass-fronted cupboard, sparkled.

Never one to hesitate for long, Rachel entered the room, approached a book-lined wall, and ran delighted fingers across rich, colorful leather bindings. Many of the titles were stamped in gold, and the works themselves ranged from one end of the literary scope to the other.

There were medical books, of course—thick, dry treatises on the working of the human anatomy—but there were classics, too, and texts on botany, astronomy, philosophy, and government. Interspersed among these tomes, as if for spice, were irreverent comedies and daring adventures. These, without exception, were inscribed, "Louisa G. Fletcher" in flourishing, ornate handwriting.

Rachel turned over the name in her mind, wondering. She would have to live with her curiosity, for she had no intention of asking Griffin who Louisa was, and Molly probably wouldn't tell if she did.

Resigned, she settled into one of the intimidating chairs facing the hearth and opened a saucy French novel. The morning passed in sweet, restful indolence; for a few hours, at least, Rachel McKinnon was able to set aside the grim realities of her life. During that glorious respite, her scratchy, ugly dress became a gown of silk, her poverty became opulent wealth, and her loneliness was swept aside by the adoration of dapper gentlemen wearing clothes so fine that she could only vaguely picture them.

Rachel's eyes were fogged with dreams and her cheeks flushed from the sheer daring of her heroine's exploits when she realized that she wasn't alone in the study and looked up into the kind face of Reverend Hollister.

"Excuse me," he said, his eyes bright with gentle amusement. "I seem to have interrupted something very absorbing."

Embarrassed, Rachel closed the book on one index finger and smiled. "Please," she said, lamenting the obvious warmth in her cheeks. "Sit down."

The reverend sank into the chair opposite Rachel's with the unthinking grace of a frequent, welcome guest. She knew, instinctively, that this man was the best—and possibly, with the exception of Molly Brady, the only—friend Griffin Fletcher had.

The silence was awkward, and Rachel broke it deliberately. "I'm afraid Dr. Fletcher is out," she said, unconsciously assum-

66

ing the gracious, educated vernacular of the well-placed young lady she'd been reading about.

He seemed quietly uncomfortable, even hesitant. "Actually, Miss McKinnon, I came to see you." The soft blue eyes were averted, and the refined voice fell away in distracted silence.

Rachel wanted to reach out and grab the man by his shabby collar and shake him. Instead, she prodded. "Yes?"

Now he seemed charged with tension. Seeing dozens of conflicting emotions battling in his manner, Rachel was startled when he stood up and turned his strong, narrow back to her. "Miss McKinnon, there is simply no delicate way to phrase this. It is most important that you leave Providence as soon as you can."

Rachel, watching in stunned silence as the preacher turned to face her, trembled at the fierce sincerity flashing in his azure eyes.

He sighed, examined the ceiling for a moment, and then went on. "Miss McKinnon—"

Rachel was suddenly very conscious of her shabby, horrible dress, her notorious mother, and her improper presence in Dr. Fletcher's house. A lump ached in her throat, and her stomach twisted painfully within her. "Rachel," she said. "Please, call me Rachel."

The reverend sat down again, his discerning eyes sad now, rather than fierce. "Rachel," he complied. "My name is Winfield, though Griffin has long since shortened that to 'Field.'"

Rachel nodded slightly. "Field," she said, testing the name, tasting strength and honor in it. "I-I'm not like my mother, if that's why you want me to go away," she said.

Compassion played in his face like silent music, and his voice carried a gentle reprimand. "Rachel, your mother was admirable in many ways. While I certainly didn't approve of her—vocation—I did regard her as a valued friend."

Rachel lowered her eyes for a moment, then forced them back to Field's face. "You know, I don't feel very welcome here. All anyone ever talks about is how fast I should be sent away."

Field's hand crossed the narrow space between the two chairs to grasp Rachel's. "Please, don't feel shunned." Suddenly, he bolted to his feet again, pacing back and forth along the edge of the hearth in his agitation. "I probably shouldn't have come here, shouldn't have said anything. . . ."

Rachel sat up very straight, the book forgotten in her lap. "Field, what *did* you come here to say?"

The tall man ceased his furious movement and looked down at Rachel with what appeared to be sincere concern. "You've met Mr. Wilkes," he stated. "And, of course, you've made Griffin's acquaintance. Rachel, in the name of heaven, don't get caught between those two!"

Rachel's astonishment was equaled only by her confusion. "Between them?" she echoed.

Field was pacing again. "I've made a disaster of this, I can see that!" he muttered, shaking his head in such comical frustration that Rachel laughed.

"You make me sound like an irresistible prize, Field! Are you actually saying that Jonas and Griffin might come to blows over me?"

Hollister seemed to relax a little, in the face of Rachel's explosive amusement, even though high color surged from his neck to his cheekbones. He sat down once again, and when he met Rachel's slightly blurred gaze, his face was suddenly stern.

"It might be more tragic than that, Rachel. Jonas Wilkes wants you—that is an established fact. And my very practiced intuition tells me that Griffin finds you just as appealing."

Rachel looked down at her oversized dress and her second-hand shoes and gave way to the burst of wild amusement this prospect inspired.

Field sighed impatiently and fell back into his chair, clearly waiting for the unsettling laughter to stop. When it ebbed, he snapped, "Believe me, Rachel, if you knew just how delicate the peace between those two men really is, you wouldn't laugh."

Rachel was sobered by the force of his sincerity, outwardly at least. Inwardly, some part of her went on laughing. "Reverend Hollister—Field—I really think—"

"You'd *best* think!" interrupted Field Hollister, his knuckles whitening on the arms of the leather chair he sat in. "You are a very lovely young woman. Neither Jonas or Griffin lacks the wit to see that."

Rachel was certain that she'd never heard anything more ridiculous in her life, but the high romance of the idea was too delicious to thrust quickly aside. For a long moment, she savored it.

When she spoke again, her voice was dignified. "I have no intention of leaving Providence," she said. "My mother left me

68

some money and her building, and I intend to make full use of both."

Field gaped, his face suddenly as white as his immaculate clerical collar.

Valiantly, Rachel suppressed another bout of unrestrained laughter. Except for a slight twitch at the corner of her mouth, her face was composed. "I gave you an unfortunate impression," she said, borrowing more of the lofty words she'd read in the novel. "I don't mean to follow my mother's craft—I'm starting a boardinghouse. My father and I will live there and, I imagine, a lot of the women from Tent Town, too."

Field Hollister recovered himself with admirable grace. "I see," he said, and then he cleared his throat and blushed to his ears.

He was a dear man, and Rachel wanted to reassure him. "Field, please don't worry about Mr. Wilkes and Dr. Fletcher anymore. Why, look at me! I'm a sawyer's daughter. I don't have nice clothes, or a fine education, or a beautiful face. What would men like that see in me?"

Field Hollister was gazing off into space, seeing something awesome, it seemed, at a great distance. He stood up, at last, and visibly wrenched himself back to the spacious, book-crammed study. "God save the innocent," he muttered.

Rachel opened the book she'd been reading and traced the inscription on the flyleaf with one finger. "Field, who is Louisa G. Fletcher?" she dared.

He sighed. "She was Griffin's mother," he answered, distractedly.

Wild relief swept through Rachel's heart. "What was she like?"

Field smiled, remembering. "She was beautiful, practical and, like her son, not inclined toward idle conversation." Then, after adding a cordial, if somewhat crisp, farewell, he left.

Rachel opened the book that had so fascinated her before the reverend's visit and read the same paragraph three times in succession. The words wafted into her mind, and then dissipated, like so much smoke.

In frustration, she closed the book and set it sharply aside. Suddenly, her own life was much more absorbing.

The midday sun was bright in the sky as Griffin rode into Jonas's base camp. A few men were straggling in and out of the mess shack but most, he knew, were hard at work farther up the mountain.

Griffin's throat tightened against a persistent memory as he dismounted and tethered his horse to a railing in front of the cookhouse. The scent of pitch, the whistling, deadly fall of a giant tree, his father's broken body being carried into camp—all of it came back to him, as it always did.

Jack Swenson, the cook, appeared in the shack's doorway, clasping a mottled pot in the crook of one arm and stirring his concoction with determined motions. "What in hell brings you way up here, Doc? Ain't been no accidents today."

Perversely, Griffin allowed himself a quick glance at the contents of Swenson's cooking kettle. He regretted the indulgence immediately. "I understand you have a man named McKinnon in camp—a sawyer."

Swenson hooted with disdain and spat a stream of tobacco into the dirt. "McKinnon ain't no sawyer now, Doc. He's givin' orders as of this mornin'."

The thought made Griffin uneasy. Why would Jonas hire the man as a sawyer, and then promote him after only one day?

"Where is he?"

"Can't think what you'd want with him," Swenson countered, watching Griffin with open contempt. "He ain't sick."

Griffin sighed, removed his hat, and ran the sleeve of his sweat-dampened shirt across his gritty forehead. The old man had never forgiven him for choosing medical school over his father's timber interests, he suspected. Maybe, in some ways he'd never forgiven himself. "Where's McKinnon?" he pressed.

Swenson's stubborn, stubbly jaw jutted out a little. "Ain't seen him."

Griffin swore under his breath.

Swenson's grizzled face cracked in an unnerving grin. "Maybe you got some o' Fletch in you after all, Boy. Been some of us wonderin' if you was really who your mama claimed you was."

Griffin closed his eyes, counted methodically. When his reason returned, he spoke in careful, measured tones. "Unless you want a throat full of that pig slop you're stirring, Swenson, you'd better shut up."

The old man shoved the kettle and accompanying wooden spoon into the arms of a bewildered lumberjack and hobbled across the porch, bristling. "You think you can take old Swen, Little Fletch?"

Griffin rolled his eyes. "You know damned well I can, you stupid old bastard."

Swenson edged cautiously down the sagging cookhouse steps, into the glaring sun. "You just roll up them linen sleeves, then, and give it a try!"

"Oh, shit," groaned Griffin.

"You scared of me, Little Fletch?"

A snicker rose from the small, gathering crowd of lumberjacks drawn by the discussion.

Griffin removed one of his cuff links, and then the other. Then, playing the game, he rolled up his sleeves. *Are you watching, Pa?* he thought. *After all these years, I still can't set foot on this mountain without some old-timer forcing me to prove I'm your son.*

"Okay, Swenson," he said aloud. "Who stands in for you this time?"

Right on schedule, one of the new men stepped forward. The others had seen the ritual before, but they did an admirable job of keeping straight faces.

The rube was a head taller than Griffin, with a barrel chest and a look of outraged honor in his eyes.

Griffin nearly laughed aloud. "You fighting the old man's battles these days?"

Sunlight caught in the lumberman's fiery red hair. He searched the faces of the other men with affronted disbelief. "I sure as hell ain't gonna stand around and watch a man half his age kick shit out of him!" he vowed, heroically.

Griffin beckoned with the fingers of both hands. "Come on, Greenhorn. Swen isn't going to let it rest until it happens."

The man looked uneasy and more than a little stung. "Who you callin' 'Greenhorn,' anyway?"

"You," Griffin replied, grinning.

To the delight of the onlookers, Greenhorn advanced ominously. His first blow landed in Griffin's midsection like the kick of an ox, knocking the wind out of his lungs. He was outmatched, but then, that was part of the ceremony.

The second blow was as obvious as an arriving train, and Griffin sidestepped it. He debated letting the spectacle go on for a while; God knew the life in camp was dull and the men needed the entertainment.

The digression had been a mistake. Greenhorn's right fist made bone-grinding contact with Griffin's jaw, sending explosive pain through his head, down his neck, into his shoulder blades. His mind went blank, and the deadly dance began.

Suddenly, Griffin Fletcher was not a man, but a boy. He was not in a lumber camp, but on board one of the ships in which his father owned an interest, sailing the run between San Francisco and Seattle.

There, on the slippery, shifting deck, La Ferrier urged him on, chanting the deadly principles, taunting him until his body and spirit became one force. And Griffin Fletcher's booted feet became weapons more formidable than his hands could ever have been.

When Griffin came back inside himself, the victim of Swenson's lust for diversion was lying still on the ground, one side of his head glistening with congealing blood. Only the motion of his enormous chest indicated that he was alive.

Griffin staggered a little, and a bucketful of ice-cold water plunged into his face, dispelling the last of his dazed confusion.

The bucket wielder had young eyes, but his beard and hair were gray. "Son of a bitch," he breathed, "Where did you learn to fight like a Frenchie?"

Griffin couldn't answer. Instead, he took a fresh look at what he'd done to Swenson's innocent rescuer and reeled, stumbling, around the side of a tool wagon. There, he retched convulsively long after his stomach was empty.

The bearded man watched him the whole time. When it was over, he shoved a bucketful of water into Griffin's hands.

Griffin filled his mouth, spat, and poured the remainder of the well water over his pounding head. His voice was hoarse when he spoke. "Thanks."

The blue eyes were watchful, but not wary. A calloused hand was extended. "Name's McKinnon."

Griffin's laugh burned in his throat. It began as a rumbling, tortured chuckle and grew to an anguished roar. "Fletcher," he managed, after a long time. "Griffin Fletcher."

It was dark outside, and Rachel didn't like the way Molly Brady kept leaving the table to stand at the kitchen window and peer out toward the barn. Who was she watching for? Dr. Fletcher? Or was it the vanished Indian woman, Fawn Nighthorse?

The latter's disappearance had been a disappointment to Rachel; she'd wanted to know her, to ask her questions about so many things, so many people.

72

"Saints be praised!" Molly cried out, suddenly, startling both Rachel and the silent, vacant-eyed boy who ate at the table beside her.

The kitchen door opened, and Dr. Fletcher appeared in the space. Rachel was so perplexed, and stricken, by the bruised, swollen state of his jaw that she bounded to her feet.

Dr. Fletcher did not so much as glance in her direction, and she was still smarting from the unaccountable pain that caused her when her father walked in.

"Pa!" she shrieked, flinging herself into his strong, ready arms.

Ezra McKinnon smiled down at his daughter with amused tenderness. "Now that's a greeting if I ever saw one," he said.

It was then that Rachel remembered. She felt the color drain from her face, the tears gather in her eyes.

Ezra held her close. "It's all right, Little One," he said. "I know your mama's gone."

Rachel allowed herself the broken, defenseless weeping she needed. By the time the storm had passed, she and her father weathering it together, she was so weary that she could hardly stand.

Ezra settled her into a chair at the oaken table and sat down nearby. For the first time, she noticed that they were alone in the spacious room.

"We'll put this place behind us," Ezra promised, his voice gruff with suppressed emotion. "There's no point in staying now."

Rachel swallowed hard, wondering how her father would take the news. Then, bravely she explained that Rebecca had left her an inheritance, that they could have a home now, that there was no need to move from town to tiresome town anymore.

She was stunned by the fierce set of her father's face, by his terse words. "We'll do no such thing, Daughter. After what Griffin Fletcher told me today, I wouldn't stay here for anything."

Disappointment and frustration made Rachel stiffen obstinately in her chair. "What did he tell you that was so terrible, Pa?"

"You just never mind what he told me. Soon as Becky's been buried proper and we've paid our respects, we're moving on. And that's all there is to it, Rachel."

And so it was, Rachel thought, with a sinking heart.

Chapter Nine

The messenger stood awkwardly beside the parlor fireplace, burly in his rough-spun trousers and worn flannel shirt.

Jonas, clad in a brocade robe, poured brandy for himself and then for the visitor. "Well, Peterson," he demanded sharply. "What now?"

Peterson's eyes kept straying to the grandeur surrounding him, and his Adam's apple bobbed up and down in his thick neck. "Swenson said you'd want to know that McKinnon's gone. He turned in his time today."

Jonas absorbed the information calmly. "After a long talk with Griffin Fletcher, by any chance?"

An irritating grin split Peterson's otherwise unremarkable face. "You ever seen Fletcher fight, Boss?"

A bitter, rueful chuckle escaped Jonas. The grinding, ceaseless pain in his genitals was answer enough to that question, for him if not for Peterson. "So Griffin was there. Who did he kick hell out of this time?"

Peterson twisted an already shapeless hat in his massive hands. "That redheaded toolsmith that hired on last month—Dobson."

Jonas shook his head. The irony of it was exquisite. Would Griffin make another trip up the mountain tomorrow, to undo today's damage? "Is the man all right?"

Peterson nodded, putting aside his hat to accept the offered drink. "Swenson had to stitch up his head, and he's off his feed, but other than that, he's fine."

Jonas took a drink of his brandy. "Swenson's food would put anybody off. Did McKinnon say why he didn't want to stay on?"

"Didn't explain nothin'—just said he wanted whatever money he had comin' and left with the doc."

"I see," muttered Jonas. And then he sank gingerly into his favorite chair, wincing at the resulting ache between his legs.

74

"Finish your brandy and get out of here, Peterson. And tell Swenson thanks."

Mrs. Hammond came in as Peterson went out. She fixed an annoyed gaze on Jonas and demanded, "What are you doing downstairs? You're in no condition—"

Jonas closed his eyes. "Where's McKay?" he asked sharply.

"Probably under the nearest rock," replied the woman.

Jonas grinned and opened his eyes again. "Well, overturn it. I want to see him—*now.*"

The quiet outrage playing in Hammond's face was delightful. For the millionth time, Jonas wondered why she stayed, year after year, when she disapproved of almost everything he did.

"If you think for one minute that you're going to send for a woman at this hour—"

Jonas laughed. A woman! It would be days before he could contemplate that. "Rest assured, Mrs. Hammond. Thanks to Griffin Fletcher, that sweet prospect is out of the question. You'll have no cause for moral outrage tonight."

Scowling, Mrs. Hammond left the room.

Jonas had no doubt that McKay would appear shortly. He refilled his glass from the bottle standing on the table beside his chair and thought.

So Griffin had gone to McKinnon and warned him that his daughter was in grave danger of losing her virtue to the monstrous Jonas Wilkes. He swore harshly, and the sound echoed in the empty room.

He closed his eyes, thought of Rachel. He should let McKinnon take her away, he knew that. But even the thought of her absence filled him with a shattering, insufferable void.

Good God, what had she done to him? What magic had she worked, to make him feel things he'd sworn he never would?

Jonas opened his eyes to see McKay standing in the doorway, watching him.

"What is it, Boss?"

Quietly Jonas gave the order.

Ezra McKinnon stood on the doctor's front porch, staring up at the star-strewn sky, dealing with his own grief. How could Becky be dead?

He grasped the painted porch railing for support. What a fool he was, letting this second, final loss of her shatter him the way it did. What reason did he have for mourning her? She'd half-killed him, leaving that way—leaving him, leaving her own child.

A ragged sob tore itself from McKinnon's throat, echoed in the night. There were other sobs wanting to follow, but he pressed them back.

A drink would be just the thing. Yes, a drink and a willing woman.

Squaring his shoulders, McKinnon swung over the porch railing and walked around the house, across the moon-shadowed yard and into the barn. There, he saddled a horse, the bay he'd borrowed back at the lumber camp.

In the half-light of the barnyard, he traced the Wilkes brand with the tip of one finger, turned his head, and spat. *Over my dead body, you bastard,* he vowed, addressing the words to the timber baron who thought he could use a good man's daughter like she was nothing.

The familiar remedy worked as well as it ever had. Becky'd done all right for herself, McKinnon thought, two hours later, as he left the saloon. He remembered Rachel's high-flown idea about turning the place into a boardinghouse and chuckled to himself.

McKinnon mounted the bay and rode out, following the dark road. They'd spend this one night in Griffin Fletcher's house, he and Rachel, and in the morning, they would say a proper and respectful good-bye to Becky and get out of Wilkes's reach. He'd heard there was work further north, in Canada.

The riders surrounded him suddenly, no sound having warned of their approach. There were six of them, as near as he could tell, and their faces were covered. McKinnon cursed the damp ground that had muffled the hoofbeats of their horses.

Rachel awakened with tears on her face.

This day would hold too many good-byes: one to her mother, one to her dreams of having a real home, one to Griffin Fletcher. The idea of rebellion turned, shining, in her mind.

Suppose she simply refused to leave? What would happen then?

The morning sun glimmered in the guest-room window, and Rachel hated it, hated herself, hated her father. She was helpless against his authority, according to laws both moral and civil.

Eventually that control would shift to an as-yet-unknown

husband, bypassing Rachel completely. She would never be able to make real choices for herself, and the knowledge filled her with rage.

For the first time, Rachel understood why her mother had run away.

She drew a deep breath, flung back the covers, and got out of bed. At least there would be money now, she wasn't going to leave without that no matter what. And there would be more later, when the saloon was sold. Life would be easier. She would buy a few books, and a new wardrobe and maybe—just maybe—she would find a man who would allow her at least a semblance of freedom.

There was a light tap at the bedroom door as Rachel finished dressing and began brushing her hair. "Come in," she said, with resignation.

The reflection of Molly Brady's face and shoulders appeared in the mirror beside her own.

A consuming, unfounded dread twisted in Rachel's heart. "Molly—what is it?"

Some of the color returned to Molly's uncommonly pale cheeks. "Rachel, have you seen your father this morning?"

The room was thick with foreboding. Unable to speak, Rachel shook her head in reply.

Molly was making an admirable effort to hide her misgivings. "Well, I'm sure it's nothing to worry about. The doctor and Billy have gone to look for him."

Rachel laid aside the hairbrush Molly had given her and sat down, dazed, on the bed.

Molly sat beside her, taking one of Rachel's icy hands in her own. "Now, don't be worrying. He wouldn't leave without you, would he now? And it isn't likely that he's changed his mind and gone back up the mountain."

In spite of her earlier yearning for independence, Rachel was frightened. She loved her father, whatever their differences. "I-I thought he was spending the night here. . . ."

Molly's voice was soothing. "We all did, Rachel. But the truth is, his bed hasn't been slept in, and the horse he was riding is gone."

Rachel swallowed hard. "He's left me. I know he has."

Molly slipped a motherly arm around Rachel's shoulders, but said nothing.

Lost in her brown dress and her own confused emotions,

Rachel endured the funeral at her mother's grave side. There were many mourners there, listening grimly to Field Hollister's gentle, compassionate words, but Ezra McKinnon wasn't among them.

When all the words had been said, Molly and Dr. Fletcher led Rachel away, past the new, mounded graves of the Tent Town woman and her tiny baby.

I should be crying, Rachel thought wildly. Wondering why she couldn't release the tears that hammered behind her eyes and throbbed in her throat, she turned her head, looked back, and saw the simple pine coffin being lowered into the ground.

A scream pierced the air, and Rachel's knees trembled beneath her, then went slack. Dr. Fletcher was lifting her into his arms when she realized that the scream had been her own and gave in to the black fog rising around her.

Griffin sat back in the chair behind his desk, closed one hand around the drink he'd just poured, and endured. Pain swept over him—his own, Rachel's.

What was happening to him? Why couldn't he separate his feelings from hers?

"Griffin?"

He looked up to see Field standing in the study doorway, watching him. "Have they found McKinnon?" he asked, in a low, gruff voice.

Field's gaze touched the double shot of straight whiskey sheltered in Griffin's hand as he removed three books from a chair and sat down. "Not a trace. And you can't afford to drown your sorrows, old friend," he observed patiently.

Griffin took a deliberate swallow, tilting his head back as the whiskey burned its way down his throat and warmed his stomach. "Something is wrong, Field. McKinnon wouldn't have disappeared like that—not without his daughter."

Field sighed. "Isn't it possible that he just didn't want the responsibility anymore?"

Griffin drained his glass in one gulp. "No, damn it, it *isn't* possible. He loved her very much."

There was a short, tense silence. Field broke it briskly. "It isn't what you think, Griffin. If McKinnon was dead, somebody would have found his body, or the horse, at least."

Griffin glared at his friend. "Jonas is one hell of a lot smarter than that, Field."

78

Field Hollister was no friend of Jonas's, but he slammed one fist down on Griffin's desk, all the same, and shouted, "All the problems in this world do not begin and end with Jonas Wilkes, Griffin! You're obsessed with the man!"

"He killed McKinnon."

"Griffin, listen to reason for once! He couldn't have. Thanks to you, he hasn't left his house in two days!"

Griffin started to reach for the whiskey bottle, and then thought better of it. He had trouble meeting his friend's steady gaze. "You heard about that, then?"

"Of course I did; Mrs. Hammond made a point of telling me. And I know about that lumberjack, too."

Griffin ignored the reference to the incident in Jonas's base camp, the day before, and snapped, "Did Mrs. Hammond tell you what Jonas did to Fawn Nighthorse?"

The color drained from Field's open face, and his throat worked fruitlessly.

"I thought that would take the righteous indignation out of you, old friend."

Field was on his feet now, his hands gripping the edge of Griffin's desk. "Tell me!"

"Believe me, Field, you don't want to know. I brought her here, but she must not have been hurt as badly as I thought she was, because she left."

"She *left*? But where—"

Griffin shrugged with an indifference he didn't feel. "Who knows?"

Field turned away quickly, but Griffin saw the old grief in the set of his shoulders. The room darkened as a cloud passed overhead, and then it was light again.

Field gathered enough composure to return to his chair. "What now, Griffin? What are you going to do about Rachel?"

A brutal headache grasped the back of Griffin's neck, throbbed in his temples. "I haven't had a chance to give that a lot of thought," he said, again avoiding Field's eyes. "She's in no condition to leave right now."

"Nonsense. Have Molly pack her things, and I'll take her to Seattle myself and see her settled there."

"Seattle?" Griffin rasped. "Why don't you just set her down on Jonas's front doorstep and be done with it?"

Field sighed in frustration. "I'm beginning to wonder if you aren't just as obsessed with her as he is."

79

Griffin felt impossibly restless, all of a sudden. He raised himself out of his chair and went to stand facing the fireplace, his back to his friend. "I can't let him touch her, Field. I can't."

"Then listen to reason, Griffin! Let me take her away, where she'll be safe!"

Clasping the mantelpiece with both hands, Griffin lowered his head. "In a few days, Field. She needs the time."

Field's voice was low, forceful. "Does she, Griffin? Or do you?"

The words landed on Griffin's mind like blows. He tried to answer and failed.

Field was suddenly beside him, searching his face, seeing, Griffin feared, all the things that should be hidden.

"Dear God, Griffin—it's true, isn't it? You want her yourself!"

Griffin closed his eyes, swallowed. "Yes," he whispered, after a long, long time.

Field's voice was gentle. "Be careful, my friend. Be very, very careful!"

Griffin released his hold on the mantelpiece and straightened his weary, aching shoulders. "I will."

"And be certain that you're not using her. You know as well as I do that anything Jonas wants has infinite appeal for you as well."

Griffin looked away. "This is different."

One of Field's hands came to rest on his shoulder. "If you care about Rachel, you have two choices. You can ask her to marry you, or you can see that she starts over in some other town. But make the decision carefully, Griffin, and make it fast."

Griffin nodded, then listened as Field turned and walked out. The decision had already been made. When Rachel was composed enough to travel, he would take her to Seattle himself, and buy her passage on the first outbound ship he could find.

Saturday morning found Jonas largely recovered from the unfortunate tangle with Griffin and in very high spirits. He enjoyed the look of shocked outrage in Molly Brady's face when she opened the front door and found him standing there.

"Good day," he said, touching the brim of his hat.

Flushed with fury, Molly tried to close the door again, only to find it blocked by Jonas's left boot.

"I want to see Rachel," he said smoothly. "Right now."

Molly's chin shot up, and it was clear that she was going to resist him fiercely. At least she didn't try to convince him that Griffin was around, he had to give her credit for that. "I'll not let you near her, Jonas Wilkes. Aye, and the poor thing has troubles enough as it is!"

Jonas resisted a need to close his left hand around Molly's proud, flawless throat and kept a smile fixed on his lips. "Now, Molly—"

The small, firm voice broke in then, startling both Jonas and Molly. "It's all right," Rachel said. "Please—let Mr. Wilkes come in."

Jonas recovered sooner than Molly did and caught her off balance. He brushed her aside graciously as he strode into the wide hallway and approached Rachel.

What a wondrous sight she was, even in that infernal brown woolen dress. Again, Jonas withstood the violent, savage need of her. "I'm sorry about your mother," he said softly.

Tears rose in the brave, violet eyes. "Thank you."

Jonas was devastated by the sight and suddenly he felt a new desire for this woman, a wish to shield her and cause her to smile again. "Rachel, come for a carriage ride with me. You need some fresh air."

A slow, sweet smile spread across her pale, pinched little face. "Oh, that would be wonderful, Mr. Wilkes!"

"My name is Jonas," he corrected, smiling.

A fetching blush rose in her finely sculpted cheeks. "Jonas," she repeated, shyly.

"Now just a minute!" Molly burst out, finding her voice at last. "You're not taking her anywhere, Jonas Wilkes!"

There was a warning in the gaze he turned to Molly, however pleasantly it was delivered. "I promise to be a gentleman, Mrs. Brady. And I think you and the doctor have kept Rachel a prisoner long enough."

Molly's green eyes shot to Rachel, frantic. "Don't go, Rachel—please. . . ."

Rachel's rebellion was dignified. She raised her chin and met Molly's shamrock gaze with one of dark orchid. "I can look after myself, Molly Brady. And I intend to have that carriage ride."

Molly subsided, pale with frustration and anger. "The doctor won't like it," she warned.

Rachel took the arm Jonas offered, but her eyes were still

fixed on Molly's face. "Perhaps he won't," she said. And then she allowed Jonas to lead her out of the house and down the front walk.

But at the gate, Rachel hesitated. "Maybe I shouldn't go. They've been kind to me, and . . ."

Jonas was careful not to press his advantage; it was too delicate, at the moment, and far too precious. "Another time, then?" he asked evenly, prepared to walk away affably if necessary.

The words were exactly right. A daring smile flashed on the soft, mobile lips, danced in the magical eyes. "No, Jonas. If I have to stay in that house any longer, I'll perish."

He tilted his head to one side. "We can't have that, can we, Urchin?"

Rachel's face brightened. "You did promise to be a gentleman," she reminded him.

"And I will," he said, helping Rachel calmly into the carriage even though a shout of delight was clamoring at the back of his throat. "I'm not the monster Griffin believes me to be, Rachel."

She studied him with wide, stricken eyes. "Why does he feel that way, Jonas?"

He settled into the seat across from hers, removed his hat. "The truth is, Rachel, we've never gotten along well. I admire Griffin, actually—he's a brilliant man—but he's just not fond of me."

The sympathy in her face made Jonas want to laugh with triumph; he would have to think of more nice things to say about Griffin Fletcher. Still, he must be very careful not to move too rapidly and frighten her. If he did, she might fly away, like a terrified bird, and disappear forever.

Chapter Ten

It was not until the carriage was moving, until she heard the slight creak of leather and the clomp-clomp of the horses' hooves that Field Hollister's words came back to her. "*Jonas Wilkes wants you. That is an established fact.*" Behind Field's remembered voice came the echo of Molly's. "*From what I gather, he fancies you.*"

Rachel raised her chin and returned Jonas's calm, appealing smile. Suppose Field and Molly were right? What would be so terrible about that?

An image of Griffin Fletcher surged, unbidden, into her mind. Unaccountably, achingly, she wanted him. Even as his gruff, unfeeling sarcasm repelled her, his arrogant strength drew her.

She shifted uncomfortably on the carriage seat and looked out the window.

Jonas Wilkes spoke gently. "What is it, Rachel? Are you having second thoughts?"

She was remembering Griffin Fletcher, standing in front of that small Tent Town cottage, his shirt plastered to his chest by the rain. Hot color flowed into her cheeks as she met Jonas's eyes. "It's my father. Mr. Wilkes, he's gone away without me, and that's very strange."

The cherubic face sobered with concerned sympathy. "Perhaps he had something important to do, and he plans to return."

Rachel lowered her eyes. "No," she whispered, as the knowledge broke over her like a small, brutal storm. "No, he won't be back."

When Jonas's hand touched her chin and gently raised it, Rachel did not resist. "What makes you so sure of that?" he asked softly.

Rachel's throat closed, opened again. "I know he wouldn't have left without telling me. He was very determined to go, even though I begged him to stay here and live with me, in Mother's building."

One of Jonas's dark gold eyebrows lifted just the slightest bit. "So you do want to stay in Providence?"

Rachel nodded.

She heard caution in the even voice. "And live in a brothel?"

Rachel suspected that this man's reaction to an affirmative answer would be interesting indeed, but she couldn't bring herself to offer one. "I planned to convert the establishment into a boardinghouse," she said.

"Planned? Have your plans changed?"

Glumly, Rachel nodded again. "Yes. Dr. Fletcher and Molly are most anxious to see me go away, and well, it just wouldn't be the same here without my father. As soon as I can collect the money my mother left and arrange for her business to be sold, I'm going to Seattle."

Jonas's eyes darkened to an unsettling shade of topaz, and his smile appeared oddly fixed. "What will you do in Seattle, Rachel?"

"I mean to find a job, Mr. Wilkes. And ask after my father, of course."

The topaz eyes slid politely over Rachel's rumpled brown dress, and the conversation veered off in an entirely unexpected direction. "Where is that lovely lavender dress you were wearing when you left my house?"

Rachel, coloring at the memory of Griffin's stormy invasion of Jonas's home, was freshly wounded to recall the way he'd taken such a dark view of the pretty dress. "I-I suppose it's still in Tent Town," she answered. "It—it was very wet, you see, and Dr. Fletcher never gave me a chance to go back for it. . . ."

Even as she marked the swift, veiled annoyance rising in Jonas's eyes and the sudden hardness of his jawline, Rachel mourned the soft, wispy beauty of that pale purple gown.

"You looked incredibly lovely in it," Jonas remarked, after a throbbing, uncomfortable silence. But his eyes were far away now, as though he were seeing some painful, tragic scene.

Rachel felt an unaccountable need to say something that would bring him back. "If we could stop at Tent Town, I could get the gown and wash it and return it to you."

The distance in Jonas's eyes faded, and he smiled at her. "Of course we'll stop. But there is no need for you to return the dress, Rachel. It looks far better on you than it ever would on me."

A medicinal burst of laughter rose in Rachel's throat, coupled with the first real joy she'd felt in a long, long time. The wonderful dress was to be hers! "Thank you."

"There are other dresses, Rachel. Will you take those, too?"

Rachel was unaware of the way her orchid eyes widened at the prospect. "I couldn't—"

"Of course you could. And you would be doing me a great favor in the bargain. The dresses take up too much space and they're—er—a painful reminder."

Rachel was ecstatic, even though a vague, disturbing question pulsed in the back of her mind. To whom had the dresses belonged in the first place? "A painful reminder?" she echoed.

Jonas sighed bravely. "Yes. But to see you wearing those splendid clothes would be a delight."

"Really?" she whispered, enchanted.

"Oh, yes. Say you'll take them, Rachel."

Feeling eager and magnanimous and wildly expectant, Rachel nodded.

And so it happened that she returned to Griffin Fletcher's house, two hours later, in possession of trunk after trunk full of billowing gowns, satiny underthings, lace-trimmed nightgowns, delicate silk blouses, and crisp, flattering skirts.

Jonas's coachman, McKay, carried each trunk past a stunned Molly Brady and up the stairs to the room Rachel had specified.

Rachel's joy sparkled within her, and she had already forgotten Molly's original opposition to the carriage ride with Jonas. "Oh, Molly," she beamed, "I've got such beautiful, beautiful clothes! Just wait until you see!"

Molly's eyes darkened to an ominous shade of emerald. "Saints preserve us!" she breathed, thrusting her hands out in a gesture of hopelessness.

Rachel was on the stairs, gripping the banister so that she wouldn't float away. "And there is a picnic tomorrow, after church—"

"Is there, now? And what has that to do with you, Rachel McKinnon?" Molly Brady's hands came to rest on her small, trim hips.

"Oh, everything!" cried Rachel, smiling down at Griffin Fletcher's housekeeper. "I'm going to have a wonderful time there! Mrs. Hammond is packing a basket for us; there'll be chicken and chocolate cake and—"

"And trouble," said Molly Brady, just before she turned and strode away, skirts swishing with fury as she went toward the

85

kitchen. "More trouble than you've seen in your young life, Miss Rachel McKinnon!"

Rachel shrugged and then dashed the rest of the way up the stairs and into the hallway. She would wear a white silk blouse tomorrow, she decided, with a crisp, black sateen skirt. . . .

Exhausted, Griffin fell into the chair at his desk and bent forward to fill a glass with whiskey. Well, he'd seen Fawn; at least he wouldn't have to worry about her for a while. She was staying at Becky's and under the quiet care of the black cook, Mamie, she was recovering nicely.

Griffin kicked one booted foot, and the other, up onto the desk's surface. His tired legs throbbed in momentary protest, and then began to feel better as the blood flowed back toward his knees and thighs. He closed his eyes and reviewed the day's cases methodically.

"Griffin?" ventured Molly's voice, from the doorway.

Griffin opened his weary eyes, forcing them to focus on the agitated frame of his housekeeper. "Hello, Molly," he said companionably.

She was wringing her hands, and her eyes were snapping. Both bad signs.

"What now?" Griffin sighed.

"It's Rachel. . . ."

Griffin felt a sudden need for a lot more whiskey. "Yes?"

Molly crept into the room, as though she was approaching a bonfire laid with dynamite. "I tried to stop her, Griffin, I swear I did."

Griffin closed his eyes again, braced himself. "Go on," he snapped after a long, tense moment.

The answering words came in a burst, like bullets flung from a Gatling gun. "Jonas Wilkes took her for a carriage ride, and she came back with trunkloads of clothes. Tomorrow, she tells me, Jonas will escort her to a church picnic!"

Griffin absorbed the news calmly, for Molly's sake. Obviously, she hadn't exactly been looking forward to telling him. "Is she here now?" he asked, with consummate reason.

"Aye. She's upstairs, trying on all her new clothes."

Griffin spoke in carefully modulated, nonexplosive tones. "Send her in here immediately. And Molly?"

"Yes?"

"If you hear her scream, rush in here and throw cold water in my face or something."

Molly laughed with soft, constricted amusement, and her skirts rustled as she hurried out.

Griffin refilled his empty glass and went to a window to wait. The darkness outside seemed to be seeping into his spirit, gathering there for God knew what disastrous purpose. A carriage ride, a few clothes, a picnic—what did he care?

But something writhed within him. *Not again*, it vowed. *Not again.*

She spoke his name cautiously, softly. "Dr. Fletcher?"

Griffin forced himself to turn slowly; it was a moment before he allowed his brain to absorb what he saw. When it had, he felt as though he'd just intercepted ten of the lumberjack Greenhorn's best gut punches.

Rage pounded in Griffin's throat and twisted in his taut stomach as he looked at her, looked at the too-familiar lines of her rose-colored taffeta dress. A savage word tore itself free of his throat and hissed past his lips.

The open, torturously lovely face paled and Rachel retreated a step. It was the dazed confusion in her eyes that stayed him from striding across the room and ripping the dress from her body.

"Jonas gave you that?" he rumbled, and the sentence was at once a question and an accusation.

Purple eyes bright, Rachel nodded quickly. "I didn't think it would matter—the clothes were going to waste. He said they were a painful reminder—"

"Yes, I imagine he did. Take it off."

The fine, fierce little chin lifted. "I will *not!* It's my dress and I'll wear it if I please!"

Griffin closed his eyes against the sight of her—the sight of the dress—drew one raspy breath, and then another. A blonde, laughing wraith played in his mind, wearing that rose taffeta gown. *"Don't be such a goose, Griffin,"* it taunted, in a distant, musical, and devastatingly well-remembered voice. *"I only love you . . . you know I only love you."*

"Whore," breathed Griffin, speaking not to Rachel, but to the bewitching sorceress laughing in his memory.

There was an outcry, and a small, frantic fist made numbing contact with his face, another battered at his chest. Choking on an old and fathomless fury, Griffin opened his eyes, grasped Rachel's thin wrists in one hand, and stayed the attack.

She glared up at him, her orchid eyes dark with wounded rage. "I hate you!" she gasped.

"Don't say that." It was a plea, and it was an order.

Rachel struggled; he held her fast. "You called me a whore!" she whispered, incredulously.

"No," he said, closing his eyes.

"Liar! I heard you!"

He opened his eyes, forced them to focus on her pinched face. "What you heard had nothing to do with you," he said. And everything sensible within Griffin demanded that he thrust her away and escape from the deadly magic of her nearness, but he couldn't. He wrenched her close, felt the sweet, soft press of her breasts against his chest, the shattering promise of her thighs and stomach against his hips. Grasping her face in both hands, he bent his head and kissed her.

She resisted only briefly, then he felt something powerful course from her body into his. She was pliant against him, her lips soft and searching under his own.

He released her so swiftly that she stumbled a little before catching herself. "Is that how you got to Jonas?" he drawled, in a voice that was purposely cruel.

Tears sparkled in her thick, dark eyelashes and trickled down a proud, defiant face. "Griffin Fletcher, you—you *bastard!* You wicked, lecherous—"

Griffin smiled brittlely. "Don't forget 'arrogant'," he urged.

She was retreating backward, her fists clenched. "I hate you, I *despise* you. I hope you burn in hell!"

Griffin let his hands rest on his hips, his eyes travel over her with deliberate insolence. "If I see you wearing that dress again, Miss McKinnon," he said. "I'll tear it off you. Is that clear?"

Horror filled the rounded violet eyes. Rachel turned to run and collided hard with Field Hollister.

Field kept her from falling by grasping her trembling shoulders. "Rachel, what is it . . . ?" His eyes scanned her face, lifted, and came to rest scorchingly on Griffin's. "You," he breathed, his beloved brimstone crackling in his voice.

Griffin executed a courtly, mocking bow. Then, for emphasis, he strode to the desk, poured more whiskey, and offered a brisk, vicious toast. "Here's to Becky McKinnon's daughter."

Rachel cried out suddenly; it was a tortured sound that flooded Griffin with wild, boundless anguish. He wanted to say he was sorry, but for some reason, he couldn't. He glared at her when she turned, slowly, in Field's gentle grasp.

"I *am* Becky McKinnon's daughter," she said, in a proud, ragged voice. "And you may take that however you wish."

With that, Rachel moved around Field and fled. Griffin closed his eyes against the sound of her footsteps on the stairs.

Field's tone was volcanic, starting as a low, rumbling sound, rising to threaten mayhem. "Have you gone mad, Griffin?"

Griffin opened his eyes again, sighed. "Maybe."

"Apologize to her."

But Griffin shook his head. "No. It's better that she hates me. It will make everything easier."

Field was outraged. "For you perhaps!" he growled. "But what about her? Griffin, she didn't deserve that kind of vicious treatment, and you know it!"

"Have her show you all the clothes Jonas gave her. Athena's clothes."

Hollister's jaw looked rock-hard, stubborn. "So that was it. Griffin, she has no way of knowing."

Griffin went to the cabinet where his medical supplies and instruments were kept, opened the glass doors. Then, methodically, he began to sort items that were already in perfect order.

Rachel had not known that it was possible to bear such pain and still live. She sat stiffly on the edge of the guest-room bed, tears stinging her face, her breath coming in short, searing gasps.

"*Whore*," he'd said. "*Here's to Becky McKinnon's daughter.*"

Bile rose in Rachel's throat, and she felt the first real hatred she had ever known—for herself, for her mother, and most of all, for Dr. Griffin Fletcher.

There was a cautious knock at the soundly locked door.

"Go away," Rachel said flatly.

"I won't be doing that," replied Molly Brady in brisk tones. "And I've a key if I need it."

Rachel's legs trembled treacherously beneath her as she made her way across the room and slowly opened the door.

Molly's kindly composure was reassuring. "It wasn't you he was raging at, Rachel."

The very mention of Griffin's savage tirade rankled her anew, prodded the raw wounds within her. "Who then?" she bit out.

"That's not important, and it's not my place to discuss it anyway. I tried to warn you, Rachel, and you wouldn't listen to me. God knows what will happen now."

"I'll tell you what is going to happen!" Rachel retorted. "I'm going to pack my things and leave this house!"

"You ignored my first warning, Rachel. Now listen, please, to my second. Don't go."

Frustration displaced the blood in Rachel's veins and coursed through her in its stead. "Surely you don't expect me to stay now!"

Molly arched one eyebrow. "Where is there for you to go?" she asked, with shattering logic. "There are no steamers at this hour, and if you turn to Jonas Wilkes, the results will be tragic."

There was Tent Town, for one place; she could go there. And the saloon, for another.

Frantically, Rachel surveyed the stacks of rich clothing billowing all around the room. For the first time in her life, she knew the burden treasured possessions could be.

"Well?" prodded Molly.

"I don't know," lied Rachel.

But hours later, when at last the house was quiet, Rachel gathered as many clothes as she could carry and crept out into the cool, welcoming night.

Because Mrs. Hammond had gone to bed early, Jonas answered the door himself. The set of Griffin Fletcher's face put him instantly on guard, but the day had been a rewarding one and the triumph of it sustained him.

"Hello, Griffin," he said affably.

Griffin brushed past him and stood, glowering, seeming to darken the entry hall with his rage. "Where is she, Jonas?"

Jonas smiled cautiously. "Where is whom?" he asked.

Swiftly, Griffin's hands grasped the lapels of Jonas's smoking jacket. A muscle constricted in his jaw, relaxed again. Then, slowly, Griffin released his hold and stepped back.

Jonas's laugh was dangerous, and he knew it. It was also involuntary, born of his hatred and his need to see Griffin Fletcher brought to his knees. "Rachel!" he said. "You think Rachel is tucked into my bed, don't you, Griffin?"

The torment in Griffin's dark eyes was a source of immense satisfaction. "If she is, I'll kill you."

"Then I can draw my next breath without worrying. She isn't here."

Griffin's stormy gaze swung to the stairway, and a second later, he followed it, taking the gleaming marble stairs three at a time.

Jonas gripped the newel post at the base of the stairs and breathed a silent, unlikely prayer of gratitude. Then he laughed and shouted with relish, "You're making a fool of yourself, Griffin—again!"

Overhead, he heard doors being thrust—or kicked—open. The sound brought back bittersweet memories. *You won't find Rachel here*, Jonas thought, with relief. *And that's fortunate, by the looks of things.*

Presently, Griffin came downstairs again. He didn't have the grace to look sheepish. "Jonas, if you have any idea where she is, you'd better tell me. Now."

Jonas knew the mind of his enemy; formidable as it was, it was also plagued with a sort of noble naiveté. Griffin would consider the obvious possibility briefly, and then dismiss it in disbelief.

Acting on instinct, Jonas offered it aloud, in ingenuous, helpful tones. "I think she might be at Becky's."

Griffin's conjecture was clear in his eyes, and so was the doubt that displaced it. Jonas had a hard time hiding his gratification as he said a cordial good-night, but once he'd closed and locked the door, it broke through in a shout of laughter.

Chapter Eleven

Rachel lay, tense and sleepless, in the bed that had so recently been her mother's. The room was locked, and there was a sturdy chair propped beneath the doorknob; but the terrible, consuming fear still snarled at the edges of Rachel's mind.

It was very late, but the raucous piano music and coarse laughter coming from downstairs showed no signs of waning. Worse, seductive feminine giggles and the tread of heavy boots sounded in the hallway, and bedsprings creaked constantly in the room next door.

Rachel was totally miserable. In fact, if she hadn't been mortally afraid of encountering a drunken, amorous lumberjack in the hallway or on the stairs, she would have scampered back to Griffin Fletcher's house and babbled whatever apologies were necessary.

She blushed hotly in the darkness. Why was it that his kiss was so fresh and clear in her mind, while his savage cruelty was fading? Why had her body been so drawn to his, even as her proud spirit was repelled?

Rachel allowed herself to imagine his hands touching her breasts and stomach, his hard, fierce frame pressing down on hers. Desperate, aching need rose in response.

Had Griffin Fletcher been there with her in that dark, haunted room, she would have surrendered to him willingly, even eagerly. Assuming he wanted her.

She turned, punching the goosedown pillows angrily. Damn him! Damn his condemnation and his insults!

He'd made his brutal opinions clear enough, and the raw desire she'd sensed in him stemmed from those false ideas, rather than any worthy, human feeling.

Tears slid down Rachel's cheeks as she closed her eyes, burrowed down in the bed, and let tomorrow's picnic absorb all her thoughts. Eventually she slept.

The brothel did not seem nearly so intimidating in the bright light of morning. The lumberjacks were apparently gone, the piano music was stilled, and the "girls" were asleep behind closed doors.

Rachel washed, put on the planned white silk blouse and black sateen skirt, and took special pains arranging her hair. She was humming when she walked purposefully into the tiny kitchen tucked away at the back of the first floor.

She glanced at the door and smiled. To think she'd been cowering there only the night before, humbly seeking sanction in her own building!

The gentle black woman, Mamie, came in as Rachel was pouring a cup of coffee.

"Don't you look nice, Miss Rachel!"

Rachel smiled. She'd never felt so good about the way she looked or the person she was. "Thank you," she said.

Mamie began to gather pots and pans, making a great, cheerful clatter in the sunny warmth of the kitchen. Soon eggs were frying in a cast-iron skillet, and bread was toasting in the oven.

Rachel felt ravenous. She was eating with as much restraint and decorum as she could manage when Fawn Nighthorse, the Indian girl she remembered from Tent Town, came shuffling in, clad in an oversized flannel nightgown, and stared, open-mouthed, at the newest resident of Becky's Place.

"Good morning!" chimed Rachel, pleased.

Fawn peered at her, squinting her bright brown eyes and then widening them again. "Rachel?" she whispered at last.

Rachel nodded, then giggled at the wild disbelief playing in Fawn's swollen face.

Fawn crept to the first available chair and fell into it, shaking her head. Her midnight-colored hair glimmered on her shoulders, trailed over her breasts and past her elbows. "Does Griffin know you're here?" she asked, in a soft, awe-stricken voice.

Rachel bristled. "No. It's none of his business!"

Fawn tossed a grateful look in Mamie's direction as the enormous, suddenly anxious woman set a mug of hot coffee before her. When her eyes linked with Rachel's again, however, they snapped with warning. "If Griff finds you here, he'll blister your bustle!"

The very thought stirred depths of outrage Rachel had never experienced before.

But Fawn held up a slender brown hand before she could protest. "Don't even say it—I know what you're thinking. But if anybody *would* dare, Griffin would. You'd better not test the theory, Rachel."

Even though Rachel smiled with unshakable confidence, the certainty in Fawn's tone had found its mark. Before she could frame an answer, however, the kitchen door swung open and Jonas Wilkes appeared, splendidly dressed in a tailored gray suit.

As his golden eyes connected with Fawn's dark brown gaze, an intangible, soundless explosion seemed to rock the room. In its shuddering aftermath, Jonas's charged glance slid to Rachel's face and was instantly genial. "So my guess was correct, Urchin. You were hiding here all the time. Ready?"

Rachel was so anxious to escape the taut hostility in that kitchen that she scrambled to her feet without answering, nearly overturning her half-filled coffee cup in the process. Her toes and arches ached inside the soft velvet slippers she'd found among her mother's things.

Fawn rose slowly to her feet, her eyes on Jonas's composed, admiring face. "Now, just a minute, Jonas . . ."

He surveyed Fawn's flannel-covered frame with polite disinterest. "It's good to see that you're recovering so rapidly, Miss Nighthorse," he said. And then, frowning, he touched the neat row of stitches in her lower lip. "I hope your progress continues."

Fawn paled—Rachel would have sworn to it—beneath the cinnamon smoothness of her skin. Then she sank silently back into her chair.

Jonas nodded slightly, with an air of distracted chivalry, as though he were confirming something the Indian woman had said.

Rachel was unnerved by the whole situation, sensing that it held meanings as deep as Puget Sound itself, but when Jonas offered his arm and smiled at her, she thrust aside the vague misgivings she felt and accompanied him out of the kitchen, through the deserted saloon, and into the bright, fragrant glow of the morning.

"How did you guess that I was here?" she asked, as she settled herself into the carriage seat across from Jonas.

He shrugged. "No one can remain in the same house with Griffin Fletcher for long, Urchin. He's fundamentally obnoxious, you know."

"I do know," she said, ruefully. "I was wearing one of the dresses you gave me—a beautiful pink taffeta—and he exploded."

For a moment, Jonas looked as though he might laugh, but then a guarded look came into his face. "What did he say?"

Just the memory made Rachel blush profusely. "He—he implied that I was following my mother's trade," she said, leaving out an account of the bruising, hungry kiss.

Jonas shook his head sadly. "Don't let that upset you, Rachel. Griffin sees most women in pretty much the same way."

Rachel was still digesting this information when Jonas's carriage drew to a stop in front of the stark, white-frame church. Horses, some standing alone and others hitched to buggies or wagons, were tethered to the sturdy picket fence, and men and women stood in small groups, chatting in subdued, Sabbath Day voices.

Rachel noticed immediately—and with singular annoyance—that the stylish ladies of the community had separated themselves from the calico-clad women of Tent Town. Subtle glances swept in her direction from the privileged; frank stares came from the others.

Rachel lifted her chin and smiled winningly at the dapper man whose arm she held.

The interior of the church was rustic, but spotlessly clean.

There was an organ, and there were leather-bound hymnals resting neatly, at two-foot intervals, on the rough-hewn pine-board pews.

Jonas guided Rachel into a seat near the door and took his place beside her. With a wicked and quite endearing grin, he whispered, "If it's one of his hellfire and damnation days, we can make a run for it."

Rachel smiled at the image that suggestion brought to her mind, but she was looking forward to hearing Field Hollister preach, knowing instinctively that the experience would be memorable.

A plump, elderly woman began to labor over the organ keys, and as the parishioners straggled in from the churchyard, the canvas-dwellers, as well as those who boasted solid houses, continued to stare at Rachel.

But when a fearsome glower formed in Jonas's features, the scrutiny came to a swift, if petulant, halt.

The organist's fervent, if slightly discordant, voice rose in a rousing rendition of a normally somber hymn, and the congregation joined in shyly. Some knew the words, while others riffled quickly through their songbooks in search.

Field Hollister rose as the last self-conscious notes fell away, looking quietly magnificent in his neat, shabby suit and spotless collar. His eyes swept over the congregation, catching only briefly on Jonas's slightly upturned face, but pausing with disconcerting amazement on Rachel's.

There was a slight catch in his voice as he wrenched his attention away and began the fine, sensitive sermon Rachel had expected.

Rachel was moved by his gentle, compelling words, but she was also relieved when the service ended. Field's eyes had strayed to her face several times during the sermon, and each time she had seen a scolding look in their azure depths.

Now, to her profound discomfort, Field was standing at the church's open doors, greeting his congregation warmly as they passed.

Rachel would have given anything to slip by him unnoticed, but that was impossible. Jonas had stopped in the aisle to converse with a portly, gray-haired man, and all the other worshipers had departed in the interim.

"Where have you been?" Field asked directly, in a sharp whisper. "Griffin is half crazy with worry!"

95

"Griffin is more than half crazy," Rachel retorted, desperate to defuse the confrontation.

Field's gaze found Jonas and glinted with sky-blue fury, and his voice was still low. "Rachel, you weren't—you didn't—"

Rachel blushed so hard that it hurt. "Of course I didn't!" she hissed.

The minister, averting his eyes for a moment, sighed. "I'm sorry. It's just that we looked everywhere—"

"Except my mother's saloon," interrupted Rachel, impatient and self-conscious.

Field touched her arm gently. "You're all right, that's the important thing. I'm glad—"

"Of what?" demanded Jonas, suddenly.

Something terrible gleamed in Field's eyes. "Did you enjoy my sermon, Jonas?" he countered. "If I'd known you were going to be here, I would have chosen a different text entirely."

Jonas's smile again seemed fixed. "You did fine, Reverend. Now, if you'll excuse us . . ."

Field shook his head in some deep frustration and turned away, and Jonas's grasp on Rachel's arm, almost painful a moment before, slackened as he led her graciously outside.

Preparations for the picnic were well under way in the spacious, grassy lot behind the church and the tiny cottage Rachel knew was the parsonage.

Small children played the quiet, restrained games that were deemed suitable for the sabbath, while well-dressed women in broad-brimmed bonnets spread colored tablecloths on the warm soft ground. The men smoked and clung together in tight little groups, as though they were braced for some violent invasion. The subdued, shabby populace of Tent Town gathered at a suitable distance.

Across the breach, ragged children watched the prosperous ladies take pies and cakes and chicken and ham from their baskets, and their small, scrubbed faces were bewildered and full of yearning.

Rachel knew, even as she folded her crisp sateen skirts to sit on the blanket Jonas had spread for her, that she would have no appetite.

Jonas's voice severed her thoughts gently. "What is it, Rachel?"

Rachel lowered her head, pretending great interest in the folds of her skirt. "Those children over there," she whispered brokenly, knowing full-well the gnawing emptiness they endured, an emptiness that had little, if anything, to do with food. "We have so much, and they have nothing."

Jonas, who was lying on his side on the blanket, his head propped up on one hand, reached out to lift her chin with the other. "Suppose we remedy the situation, Urchin? Will you enjoy the day then?"

Bewildered and hopeful, Rachel nodded.

Jonas bounded to his feet and moved from one bright picnic blanket to another, speaking in charming undertones to the occupants. Almost magically, the bounty began to move from one side of society to the other. Blushing matrons carried generous shares of their food to the startled, somewhat suspicious recipients, and while the two groups did not really blend, they did draw closer together.

Rachel's step was light as she thrust most of Mrs. Hammond's fried chicken into the fray, along with a cherry pie and half a chocolate cake.

Field Hollister intercepted her as she walked back to rejoin an amused Jonas.

"Did I really see this happen?" he asked, smiling in amazement.

Rachel shrugged. "It was Jonas's idea, Field."

Field looked pleasantly skeptical. "I think you have a remarkable effect on our Jonas Wilkes, my dear."

Rachel laughed warmly and shook her head, but the words she was planning to say died suddenly in her throat. Griffin Fletcher was striding toward her, his face pale and stiff with rage.

Hoping to find a defender, she looked imploringly to Field. But his arms were folded and his kind eyes seemed to be saying, "I told you so." Rachel turned, in desperation, to appeal to Jonas.

The blanket where he'd lain, only moments before, was empty. Jonas was nowhere in sight.

Rachel drew closer to Field, frightened and all too conscious of the hush that had fallen over the picnic grounds.

"Don't you dare make a scene here!" she hissed with bravado, as Griffin came to a forbidding halt approximately two feet away.

Griffin reached out and took Rachel in a painless but inescapable grasp. His voice was ominously low. "Fair enough," he said. "Might I suggest a little conference over by that willow tree?"

Rachel, following his gaze, thought the tree in question was rather too far away, situated, as it was, on the far side of a murky, moss-strewn pond. "Well—"

"It's that or a drama this town will never forget," he said reasonably, a false smile twisting his lips.

Rachel tried to look calm as Dr. Fletcher half-dragged her through the deep grass, around the edge of the pond, and behind the sheltering branches of the willow.

There, he suddenly took her shoulders in a hard grip and thrust her backward, so that she could feel the rough bark of the tree through her blouse and thin camisole.

"Where the hell have you been?" he demanded.

Rachel was terrified, but she did her very best not to reveal that. She met his eyes and fired back bright purple malice from her own. "I don't have to explain anything to you!"

A mockery of a smile lingered on his lips for a moment. "No. No, Rachel, maybe you don't. Maybe the fact that you're here with Jonas explains everything."

Rachel was outraged. "You're as bad as Field! I spent the night in my mother's room!"

The scornful amusement in Griffin Fletcher's eyes was so expressive that he didn't have to voice his contempt, didn't have to speak at all.

And Rachel was wounded to the quick. She lifted her black skirt, to reveal the velvet slippers she'd taken from her mother's wardrobe. "Look!" she pleaded, foolishly, hating herself all the while for wanting so desperately to prove her innocence. "These are my mother's shoes. . . ."

Jonas was rounding the edge of the pond now, and approaching fast. Griffin watched him advance with frightening relish. "You seem to be filling Becky's shoes, all right," he said.

Rachel, reeling under the brutal impact of his words, nearly fell as Griffin released her and strode away.

Jonas and Griffin met in the middle of the path that encircled the small pond, but if they spoke to each other, the interchange was too low-pitched to reach Rachel's ears.

The day was spoiled. As Griffin went around Jonas and exchanged inaudible, wildly gestured words with a red-faced Field Hollister, Rachel whirled blindly to escape.

The slick bank of the pond shifted beneath her feet. Just before she fell, Rachel heard a hoarse, hurried voice shouting

Dr. Fletcher's name. The sound died as the shallow, stagnant waters of the pond closed over her head.

Rachel struggled, sputtering, to her feet. Her silk blouse and wispy camisole were drenched and clinging, and musky leaves hung in her hair.

The rapt expression on Jonas Wilke's face made her look down. Her breasts, her nipples, even the small, distinctive birthmark—they were all as clearly visible as if she'd been stark naked.

Shivering with cold and embarrassment, Rachel covered herself with her arms and stood there, stubbornly, until Jonas laughed softly and turned his back.

"Wait here," he said, his voice trembling with suppressed amusement and something indefinable. "I'll bring a blanket."

As Jonas walked away, Rachel struggled out of the water and stood with her forehead resting against the rough bark of the willow tree. Desolate, muted sobs racked her. Griffin had struck out at her again, in senseless ferocity. And now she'd fallen into that nasty pond and spoiled the nicest clothes she'd ever owned.

She hadn't heard his approach, and his words startled her.

"Rachel, I'm sorry."

Rachel turned, sniffling miserably, her arms still shielding her breasts, and looked up into the familiar dark eyes.

Griffin laughed tenderly as he plucked a soggy leaf from her hair. "You are so beautiful," he said. "Even with moss on your head. Come on; we're going for a wagon ride."

Rachel's mouth worked, but no words came.

His arm was strong around her sodden shoulders. "Hurry up, will you? I'm needed on the mountain, and if Jonas gets back here before we can get away, he and I will have a nasty disagreement."

Numbly, Rachel allowed Griffin Fletcher to lead her through a tangle of blackberry vines, giant ferns, and hazelnut bushes. Beyond that was a sun-dappled clearing, where two horses, a buckboard, and one anxious driver waited.

It was wrong to leave Jonas like this, without even offering an explanation, but Rachel had no inclination, and no voice, to resist.

They were well up the rutted ox trail that led to the lumber camps before Rachel found her voice again. Wrapped in a smelly horse blanket, she bent toward the contradictory man sitting on the seat beside her. "Why did you bring me?" she asked, hoping that the driver, who sat on her left, wouldn't hear.

Griffin looked down at her, smiled, and plucked yet another leaf from her hopelessly mussed hair. "I wasn't about to leave you there, Sprite. You would either have drowned or gotten youself ravaged before the day was out."

She raised one eyebrow. "Of course, I'm safe *now*."

He laughed, shrugged, and looked away.

Rachel shook her head, and looked down at her ruined shoes, fervently hoping that the sun would penetrate that horse blanket and dry her blouse before they reached the lumber camp.

Chapter Twelve

Time, coupled with the brightness of the summer sun, made it safe for Rachel to toss the horse blanket into the back of the wagon without fear of revealing her womanly charms to all and sundry. It was about four o'clock, she guessed, when the wagon jolted into camp; she might have asked the doctor the time, but she'd suspected that it would be wiser to maintain her silence. Words seemed to threaten the tentative, cautious peace they had established.

The camp was like many others Rachel had seen—a cluster of weathered shacks, wagons, and tents. The ramshackle cookhouse stood in the center, wispy gray smoke wafting from its crooked tin chimney.

An almost imperceptible grimace tightened Griffin Fletcher's jaw as the driver pulled the brake lever up and simultaneously reined in the team of horses. Clearly, Griffin hated this place, and Rachel wondered about that as the buckboard lurched to a stop. The camp was shoddy and, like most of its counterparts, extremely isolated, but still, it seemed that he should have been used to it.

The doctor jumped deftly from the wagon and reached up to aid Rachel. A primitive jolt went through her as his hands gripped her waist. As their eyes met, she saw an unmistakable warning snapping in the stormy depths of his gaze. She blushed.

Griffin set her firmly on her feet, beside the wagon, and released her to take his medical bag from the wagon bed. "Stay close to me," he ordered, in a terse undertone. And then he turned to stride toward the cookshack.

Rachel tarried only momentarily—her pride demanded that much—then scurried to catch up with Griffin. The eager, bluntly speculative glances coming from several of the men still in camp gave weight to his demand.

The inside of the cookhouse was dimly lit, and it smelled of stale bacon grease, kerosene, and sweat. A grizzled, wiry old man lay prone on the long, rough-hewn table in the center of the room.

"What's the matter?" Griffin snapped, setting his bag down with an unsympathetic thud.

"I've got this here fearsome ache in my belly, Little Fletch. It's like I'm gonna die."

Griffin's response was a hoarse chuckle. His hands began to prod the old man's middle, causing him to cry out.

Rachel turned her back and stood stiffly at the murky, grease-coated window, looking out. There weren't many workers in camp, since it was Sunday—only those who tended tools or horses or saws. The great oxen, used to drag mammoth logs to the inevitable 'skid road' slanting down the mountainside to the sound, were nowhere in sight.

The old man was groaning. "Stop that pokin' and pushin' afore you kill me!"

Rachel closed her eyes.

"Shut up," Griffin said.

"What's the matter with me, Doc?" There was a whiny, pleading note to the words.

"You're a greedy old bastard, that's what's the matter. You've been eating too much of your own lousy food."

"I ain't got a ruptured bendix?"

"Your appendix is fine."

When Rachel turned from the window, the old man was sitting up, looking deeply disappointed. But then his eyes caught at her shoes and traveled the distance to her face with frank appreciation.

"Damn," he breathed. "You got anything in that bag that'll take twenty or thirty years off me, Doc?"

Griffin's eyes touched Rachel's face with an amusement that

101

was almost tender. "This is Rachel McKinnon, Jack. Rachel, Jack Swenson—the worst cook in the Pacific Northwest."

Rachel's name gave the old man obvious pause. "McKinnon, you say? Any relation to Ezra?"

"His daughter," Griffin said, and something in his bearing cautioned Rachel to silence.

There was a guarded look in Swenson's eyes, and they swept swiftly away from Rachel. "Oh. Well, I ain't seen McKinnon around here."

Griffin leaned back against another table, and folded his arms. "Nobody asked if you had," he pointed out.

Swift alarm quivered in the pit of Rachel's stomach, though she couldn't have said why. It had more to do with Griffin's quiet restraint than the old man's remarks. Before she could say anything, however, the dark eyes stayed her tongue with a sharp, flashing admonishment.

"Is there anybody around here who is *really* sick?" Griffin asked the old man, in a gruff, taunting challenge.

Swenson looked properly affronted, then answered the question grudgingly. "Dobson ain't feelin' real chipper. That's that redheaded feller that you tangled with last time."

Rachel's eyes shot to Griffin's face, and she watched in wonder as his expression hardened and then became completely unreadable.

"Where is he?" Griffin bit out.

Swenson gave terse directions to a certain bunkhouse, and Griffin set out for the place in strides so long that Rachel nearly had to run to keep up with him.

The bunkhouse was a crude structure, composed of four leaning walls and a sawdust floor. The man, Dobson, lay still on a cot in a far corner, just out of reach of the dust-speckled sunshine shafting in through one grimy window.

Dobson's crop of unkempt red hair was matted to his flesh, and awkward black stitches glared, garish and misshapen, against the paleness of his forehead. The knuckles on his great hands looked raw, and there was a filthy, ragged cloth binding his massive rib cage.

Griffin shot a dangerous look backward, to Swenson. "Why didn't you send for me?"

Swenson shrugged, glanced once more at Rachel, and walked out.

Pity ached in Rachel's throat as she surveyed the half-dead

102

man stretched out on the skimpy cot. "You did this?" she whispered, appalled.

Griffin was already bending over the man, examining him with swift hands, undoing the makeshift bandages, scowling at the ugly stitches above Dobson's eye. "Go back to the cookhouse and get me some hot, clean water," he ordered.

Too stricken and sick to argue, Rachel turned and stumbled out. She returned, minutes later, with a basin full of steaming water and the one clean cloth Swenson had been able to find.

Griffin took the items and began cleaning the man's wounds with a gentleness that belied what he'd done. "If you're wearing a petticoat," he said, without looking at Rachel at all, "I need it."

After a fleeting, self-conscious glance at the window and the open door, Rachel reached up under her skirt and removed the requested garment.

With no word of thanks, Griffin tore the magnificent, hand-embroidered taffeta into wide strips and began to rebind Dobson's ribs with them. That done, he examined the jagged stitches again, and cursed.

"What is it?" Rachel dared to whisper.

"Silk," he snapped. "Those idiots used silk."

Rachel swallowed, feeling unaccountably guilty—as though she'd put the offending sutures into Dobson's flesh herself. "That was wrong?" she ventured, as Griffin plundered his medical bag, took out a brown glass bottle, and began dabbing something on the crudely mended gash.

"Yes, it was wrong," he replied impatiently, intent on the task at hand. "Silk is unsanitary."

Unwittingly, Rachel touched the soft, deliciously smooth fabric of her wrinkled blouse. "I think silk is wonderful," she said.

At last, Griffin spared her a quick, surprisingly tender glance. "For clothes, it's fine. But wounds call for catgut, Sprite."

The lumberjack stirred on the narrow cot and groaned, low in his throat, the way an injured animal will.

"I—I think I need to go outside," Rachel muttered, feeling sick.

"Go ahead," Griffin said shortly, all his attention focused on his patient again. "Just don't wander off."

Just don't wander off. The order made Rachel blush hotly; he'd spoken as if she were a child. But there was no use calling him on it; he would only become even more nasty and impossible than usual.

The sun was moving imperceptibly westward when Rachel scanned the blue sky. What time was it? Five o'clock, six? If they didn't start down the mountain soon, it would be dark.

She leaned back against the dirty, unpainted wall of the bunkhouse and breathed in the soothingly familiar, pungent scent of the pine trees towering around the camp. Half a dozen lumberjacks were gathered nearby, perched on stumps and tool crates and embroiled in a card game of some sort.

Rachel deliberated carefully before she approached them and bluntly demanded, "Have any of you seen a man called McKinnon in the past few days?"

There was an unnerving silence. Several of the men surveyed Rachel with insulting questions in their eyes.

"Who's askin'?" countered an older man, with massive shoulders and arms so thick that the muscles strained at the worn flannel of his shirt.

Rachel lifted her chin. "I'm his daughter."

A blond man with gaps between his teeth rolled languidly to his feet. "What do you say we go off somewheres private and talk about it, Sugar?"

The burly man who had spoken first glared at him in warning. "Didn't you learn nothin' by what happened to Dobson, Wilbur?"

Wilbur sat down again, reluctantly. "You Fletcher's woman?" he asked, spitting out the words as though they tasted bad.

Warm color surged into Rachel's face, but she stood her ground. "Yes," she lied, exuding ominous confidence. "And you'd better be polite to me."

Wilbur paled and turned his attention back to the cards in his hand.

With great dignity, Rachel turned and walked in the direction of the cookhouse. *Fletcher's woman. Now that was an interesting thought.*

At the cookshack, an eager Swenson served her rancid coffee and regaled her with boisterous tales about life in the lumber camps. He'd been working in the woods for almost forty years, he claimed, first with Big Mike Fletcher, and then for Jonas Wilkes.

Rachel's interest was peaked by the mention of Griffin's surname. "Was Big Mike the doctor's father?"

104

Swenson nodded, and scorn played in the worn expanse of his face. "He was a gentleman, Mike Fletcher was, but he was no dandy like that high-falutin' son of his, no sir. He had ships, and he sailed 'em—felled timber on this mountain, too. Damn near broke his heart when his own flesh and blood turned on him."

"Turned on him?" Rachel prodded, with caution.

"Little Fletch sailed off to Scotland. He wanted nothin' to do with old Mike's lumber interests." Swenson shook his grizzled head sadly. "But he weren't too proud to use the money Mike sent to pay for his fancy education. When the boy got back—him and that Hollister kid—he was so full o' bein' a uppity doctor that he couldn't be bothered takin' up a saw."

Rachel absorbed the information without revealing her consuming interest. "I thought the mountain had always belonged to Mr. Wilkes," she threw out, after a long, idle pause.

Swenson was warming to the subject; he was as gossipy and ardent as any old woman. "No, sir. Wilkes—Jonas, Sr., I mean—made his money in the China trade. Some say he was a bit of a smuggler, too. He built that grand house o' his and brought his wife and baby up from San Francisco."

"Then how—" Rachel blurted the words, and then caught herself. "Shouldn't the lumber business belong to Griffin—Dr. Fletcher?"

The old man actually blushed; his rough cheeks turned flame red with righteous denial. "Griffin didn't want the business. He and his daddy had one hell of a set-to about it, right here in this camp. Old Fletch, he near beat the livin' daylights out o' that boy, but he still wasn't havin' none o' fellin' timber and workin' saws. Fletch went stormin' off into the woods to set his hand to the work his men was doin', and Griffin went after him." Sadness dimmed the flush in Swenson's avid face. "Mike was killed that day, and some say it were the boy's fault for breakin' his mind thatta way. When the will was read—Griffin's mama had already passed on while he was off learnin' his doctorin'—it said that the boy wouldn't inherit nothin' but the house and the shippin' interests if he didn't set aside that doctorin' fuss and work on the mountain like a man."

Rachel closed her eyes, secretly pitying both Griffin and the domineering old tyrant who had been his father. She was careful not to speak, not to break the flow of Swenson's feverish talk.

Sure enough, the old man put a stirring cap on the wild story. "The lumber interests went to Jonas Wilkes, him bein' the son of Mrs. Fletcher's only sister."

Rachel thought she understood the staggering hostility Jonas and Griffin felt toward each other now. It was incredible to think that they were first cousins—the sons of sisters.

Swenson watched in appreciative silence as McKinnon's girl walked out of the cookshack and past them leerin' woods rats playin' Sunday poker. Maybe he should have mentioned the woman, too—but that hadn't seemed delicate like.

Besides, Old Swen was no fool. He understood Little Fletch's murderin' temper as well as anybody. No sense stirrin' *that* up, no sir.

His eyes followed Rachel until she disappeared, and he hoped she wasn't countin' real heavy on ever seein' her daddy again.

Rachel stood in the bunkhouse doorway for a moment, her hands clasping the framework, and let her eyes rest on Griffin Fletcher. He was sitting on the cot opposite Dobson's, his dark head in his hands, his shoulders slack under the smudged white fabric of his shirt.

She understood him better now, although there was still much that puzzled her. His abject hatred for Jonas Wilkes was not such a mystery anymore, even if it was unfair.

Jonas had been kind—very kind—to her, and she liked him. She pictured him searching for her, back at the church picnic, and felt a rush of shame at her rude departure.

"If we don't leave soon, it will be too dark to travel," she said, her voice sharp with her own guilt.

Griffin stood up, stretched his arms above his head, and yawned. "I'm afraid we're spending the night here," he announced, with resignation.

Rachel's hands tightened on the framework of the doorway. "What?"

Griffin's smile was weary—and far too aware. "Sorry, Sprite. It can't be helped. This man is running a fever, and I think he has a concussion."

Rachel's sudden, delicious terror made her croak, "Thanks to you!"

He ignored the remark and approached her slowly. "Jonas can get along without you for one night, can't he?"

Rachel's hand flew up, ready to make sharp contact with Griffin's wan face, but he grasped her wrist and stayed the attack. A long, charged silence crackled in the dusty confines of the bunkhouse.

Griffin's grip loosened, but his thumb caressed the tender flesh on the underside of Rachel's wrist, sending treacherous shivers throughout her body.

"Where am I going to sleep?" she whispered finally, her heart in her throat.

Griffin's free arm encircled her waist, drew her gently against the lean, hard lines of his chest, his hips, his thighs. Suddenly, everything within Rachel cried out to be joined with this man, to become a soaring, inexorable part of him.

She gasped as his lips brushed her temple, the tender, throbbing skin beneath her ear, the hollow of her throat. His soft, rumbling groan stirred awesome depths of need inside her, made her offer herself to him in silent surrender.

But, suddenly, he held her at arm's length. She felt shattering loss at the swiftness, the decisiveness of the gesture. "Griffin—"

His index finger came to rest tenderly on the tip of her nose. "Not now, Sprite. Later, I fear—but not now."

Rachel felt such need that she changed the subject, just to keep herself from bluntly asking for his love, his touch. "I know why you don't trust Jonas now," she announced, in a shaky voice.

Griffin raised one eyebrow. "Do you?" he asked, with only moderate interest, his hands moving to her waist and resting there. "Tell me, Sprite—why don't I trust Jonas?"

Rachel swallowed a gasp as his hands rose to the space under her arms where her breasts rounded. "S-Swen told me about the w-will—"

Griffin laughed, and the dark shine of his eyes indicated that he knew what he was doing to her, and enjoyed it. "The will. Oh, yes, the Great Loss of the Lumber Empire. As far as I'm concerned, Jonas can keep it."

Beneath his palms, beneath the silk blouse and the camisole, Rachel's nipples ached. "But—if that isn't it—what—"

"The lumber interests weren't important to me, Rachel. But Jonas took something that was."

Rachel stepped back, out of his reach, and lifted her chin. "A woman?" she dared, meeting his eyes intrepidly.

But Griffin turned away, his face hardened, and didn't say another word until after they'd left the bunkhouse a long time later.

The evening was interminable.

First, there was Swenson's abominable cooking to be eaten. All during the meal, the fair-haired man, Wilbur, and some of the others, sneaked furtive glances in Rachel's direction, openly envious ones in Griffin's.

The earlier strain Rachel had glimpsed in Griffin was gone now; he ate a diplomatic portion of the dreadful salt pork and the gritty bread and listened with interest to the main topic of debate—statehood.

Washington Territory wanted to join the union and take her rightful place in the scheme of things, though there were those who maintained that statehood would be more trouble than it was worth.

Hoping for a respite from the unnerving inspection of her person, Rachel slipped away from the table and began helping Swenson with the preparation of dishwater.

At last, Griffin excused himself from the table, summoned Rachel with a courteous glance, and ushered her out into the warm, fragrant summer night.

What would happen now? she wondered.

Nothing happened, as it turned out. Griffin deposited Rachel at the door of a tumbledown shed, brushed her lips briefly with his own, and walked off toward the bunkhouse and his patient, Dobson.

Feeling wretched and wanton and brutally rejected, Rachel went inside the shed. The place had been neatened a bit, obviously, and there was a lamp burning beside the pallet of straw and blankets on the floor.

Rachel stripped to her drawers and camisole, mourned the beautiful taffeta petticoat for a moment, to keep herself from mourning other things, and lay down on the musty bedding to dream.

Through gaping cracks in the shed's roof, Rachel could see silvery stars glinting in the black sky. She blew out the oil lamp and lay motionless on the old quilt and the underbed of straw, looking up.

She felt only brief alarm when, nearly an hour later, the shed door creaked open. The silhouette filling the doorway was blessedly familiar.

Griffin's voice was very low, and carefully measured. "If you're going to say no, Rachel, say it now."

She was silent.

"Are you awake?" he asked.

Rachel laughed softly. "Wide awake," she answered.

Chapter Thirteen

Rachel was grateful that the darkness hid her flaming cheeks, that the nightsongs of the frogs and insects outside concealed the swift, sweet fearfulness of her breathing. She listened, the back of her head cupped in her hands, as Griffin undressed. The straw beneath her rustled as he stretched out beside her, all but invisible in the darkness.

Gently, cautiously, his lips parted hers. They nibbled, they tasted, they exhorted. Rachel moaned with this new, and singularly compelling, delight. She moved to lower her hands from the back of her head and entangle her fingers in his hair, but one of his hands closed around her wrists, imprisoning her.

And all the while, his lips were moving down, over her chin, onto her neck, to the pulse point beneath her ear. He tugged downward on the delicate camisole until one throbbing breast felt the cool touch of the night air.

Griffin's thumb roused the bared nipple to a hard, pulsing peak. When his lips closed around it, Rachel gasped with pleasure. And still, his hand held her wrists.

Presently, he bared her other breast, teased it ruthlessly, and then suckled.

Rachel writhed with the commanding, primitive need of him. Surely, he would take her soon. . . .

But there were more wonders to come. He released her wrists to slide her drawers down and toss them aside. His hand caressed the silky, secret place, and then his fingers parted it.

Rachel arched her back and gasped in a spasm of delight as

the warm demands of his mouth sent searing flames of need throughout her system. As his hands pressed downward on the insides of her knees, a series of shattering, soundless explosions burst inside her.

She cried out lustily in release and then lay perfectly still.

Unbelievably, Griffin chuckled. "That ought to keep them talking for a while," he teased.

Rachel didn't care if the lumberjacks had heard the outcry. At the moment, she didn't care about anything beyond finishing the wondrous ritual, carrying it to its natural completion.

Understanding, Griffin lowered himself onto her and entered her gently. There was only the slightest, briefest pain before the throbbing enchantment began again.

It grew with each motion of their bodies, with each muted gasp, until they were both lost together in a sparkling storm of complete release.

She was asleep.

Griffin listened to the soft, winsome meter of her breathing and hated himself for using her as he had. He'd been so sure that she wasn't a virgin—so damned sure.

But she had been, and the knowledge made him feel like a skulking thief. He had no right to want her, nothing substantial to offer her.

A stray shaft of silver moonlight illuminated her face, and Griffin drew in a sharp, aching breath.

What could he give her? Fidelity, surely—just the thought of coming to her whenever he needed her precluded turning to any other woman—a comfortable home, money, lust. Definitely lust.

But she deserved more, so much more. She deserved love, and Griffin Fletcher no longer had that shining, noble element to offer. He was incapable of it.

Even as he reaffirmed an earlier, very painful decision, that he would send Rachel as far from Providence as could be managed, Griffin again felt the staggering, hungry need of her. When he reached out, she awakened, came to him eager and sleepy and warm.

The birth of the new day held no interest for Jonas Wilkes; his nerves were still raw from the slow passage of the night, his vision was slightly blurred from lack of sleep.

Where was Rachel? The question dogged him as dauntlessly

now as it had during the long, torturous night. He'd searched the saloon and Tent Town himself, while his men had questioned Field and Molly and even the Chinese cook, Chang.

Wherever she was, she was with Griffin. For the thousandth time since Rachel's disappearance from the picnic, Jonas closed his eyes and let the full, crushing anguish of that pass over him.

Mrs. Hammond startled him by appearing suddenly at his side and setting a plateful of fried eggs and sausage before him. "Land, you haven't slept a wink, have you?"

Jonas pushed the plate away. "I'll kill him. If he's touched her, I'll kill him."

Jonas's former nanny and present housekeeper took the liberty of sitting down at the great, polished dining table. "What on earth are you talking about?"

He drew a cheroot from the inside pocket of his suit coat and clamped it between his teeth. The light of the match was warm on his face. "I'm talking, Mrs. Hammond, about Griffin Fletcher."

"And Rachel," guessed the woman.

Suddenly, Jonas's weary mind caught onto something he'd overlooked before. Just as Rachel had fallen so unceremoniously into the parish pond, someone had shouted Griffin's name.

Of course. The mountain. Griffin had been summoned to the mountain, and he'd taken Rachel with him. And Jonas had been so distraught that the obvious answer had eluded him.

Perhaps she hadn't even gone willingly.

Rage surged through Jonas, searing the last remnants of fatigue and then consuming them. He stood up so fast that his chair overturned with a resounding crash and then he strode out of the house, leaving Mrs. Hammond and calm reason behind.

McKay was just riding up, his face haggard in the glowing dawn. "Me and Wilson been keeping watch all night, Boss. Ain't nobody over there at the Fletcher place besides Molly Brady and her kid."

"Well, get Wilson and Riley and whoever else you can round up," Jonas ordered evenly. "I know where they are. When Griffin rides down off the mountain, we'll be there to have a few—words—with him."

McKay shifted in the saddle, uneasy. "What about the girl?" he muttered.

Jonas ached at the mention of her, but he wasn't about to

111

reveal the things he was feeling to a slug like McKay. He kept his face under rigid control. "I don't want her hurt, under any circumstances. The man that lays a hand on her will have his back laid open with my whip. Is that understood?"

McKay nodded, looking even more uneasy. "I ain't so sure it's such a good idea, tangling with Fletcher, I mean."

"How about keeping your job?" Jonas shot back. "Is that a good idea?"

"I'll get your horse," replied McKay, reining his own mount toward the wooden stables behind the house.

Calmly, Jonas looked up, scanning the blue, cloudless sky. It was a good day for repaying debts, old ones and new alike.

An image of Rachel writhing in Griffin's arms sprang, unbidden, into his mind. He put the picture aside; it was better to think about the beating he'd taken over Fawn Nighthorse.

And much less painful.

When Rachel woke up, Griffin was not beside her. For the merest portion of a moment, she was panic-stricken, bolting upright on the itchy straw bed, ready to cry out.

Dobson. Griffin was surely in the bunkhouse, looking after Dobson.

Rachel scrambled into her clothes and straightened her hair as best she could. Memories of the night before made her cheeks burn. *Rachel McKinnon*, boomed a thundering voice within her. *You have been sullied.*

She smiled to herself and quietly opened the shed's thin door.

The camp was virtually deserted. From higher up the mountain, Rachel could hear the rasping squeak of saws, the shouts of the workmen, the bawling of the oxen.

After a brief visit to the woods, Rachel drew water from the well near the cookhouse and splashed her face repeatedly.

"Mornin', Miss," beamed Swenson, from the shack's sagging porch. "Fine day, ain't it?"

Ignoring the lewd knowledge in the old man's eyes, Rachel agreed that it was, indeed, a fine day.

Griffin was in the bunkhouse, but the situation there had improved considerably. As Rachel came in, she saw that Dobson was not only awake, but laughing at some story Griffin was telling.

She felt distinctly uneasy. Was it her shameless surrender they found so amusing?

Griffin rose from his seat on the cot next to Dobson's and turned to smile at her. And in spite of the smile, his face bore the same tight, grim look she'd seen when they arrived.

Wounded, Rachel lowered her eyes and clasped her hands together. "Are we leaving soon?" she asked, hating herself for the tremor in her voice.

The side of Griffin's index finger lifted her chin. "Can you swallow another of Swenson's meals first?" he countered, gently.

His touch and the reassuring approval she saw in his eyes made her feel much better. "I can if you can," she said briskly.

Minutes later, Rachel and Griffin sat across from each other, at Swenson's table, and exchanged silent laughter as they choked down soggy oatmeal.

Later, Griffin commandeered two horses from the camp remuda, hitched them to the same buckboard they had brought up the mountain, and gallantly lifted Rachel into the wagon seat.

The trip down was long and treacherous, even by daylight. At the halfway point, they could look out over a breathtaking expanse of Puget Sound's Hood Canal, pine trees interspersed with shimmering cottonwoods, tall cedars, and squat firs, even Providence itself.

"Look," Rachel whispered. "I can see Field's church."

Griffin was looking in the same direction, but his expression was suddenly very intense. "Did you see that?" he asked, after an ominous pause.

Rachel stared hard at the church and, as she did, she saw a flash of silver light. "A mirror?" she asked.

Griffin secured the brake lever and sprang to the ground without answering. Quickly, he unhitched the horses.

"What are you doing?" demanded Rachel, her wonder turning rapidly to dismay.

"Can you ride?" Griffin snapped, swinging onto the bare back of one of the geldings that had been drawing the wagon.

"I guess I'll have to," retorted Rachel, who had never been on a horse's back in her life.

Grasping the mane of the remaining horse, Griffin guided it to within easy reach of Rachel's perch in the wagon box. "Get on," he said.

Rachel lowered herself onto the animal's sweaty back, stretching her skirt to nearly disastrous limits. "What—"

But Griffin had somehow prodded his mount into the thick

underbrush that carpeted the mountain. Rachel's followed, with no urging from her.

The descent was slow, but hair-raising. They'd been traveling for at least a half an hour before Rachel's frustration made her call out, "Griffin Fletcher, if you don't tell me what's going on—"

He turned, grinned at her over his broad shoulder. "It's a long, involved story, Miss McKinnon. Suffice it to say that Field once used that same trick to warn me that my father was on his way up the mountain with a razor strap in his hand and blood in his eye."

Rachel wrinkled her nose. "He couldn't have said all that with a mirror!" she scoffed.

"He didn't. My father caught up with me and beat the hell out of me. It was *after* that that Field explained the signal."

Rachel's laughter bubbled into her throat and escaped in a delighted burst. "What did you do that was so terrible?"

Griffin grinned again. "I wrote a composition for school—all about how my dear old grandmother came over from the old sod, got a job as a housemaid, and broke up the master's marriage."

Rachel laughed once more. "Did she?"

"Yes, but I wasn't supposed to tell," Griffin answered, and then he turned his attention back to the steep incline before them.

They saw the flash of the mirror twice more before they reached the base of the mountain and rode slowly into the woods behind Field Hollister's churchyard.

He came bounding out of the parsonage as the horses paused to drink from the pond, his face red with annoyance and relief. "Confound it all, Griffin—" he sputtered.

Griffin laughed as he swung one leg over his horse's neck and slid to the ground. "Relax, Field. I got your message. *This time.*"

In spite of himself, Field laughed, too.

Inside the parsonage, Griffin's friend politely pointed out a room where Rachel could freshen up. The moment the door had closed behind her, Griffin folded his arms and leaned back against the kitchen wall.

"Where were they waiting, Field?"

Field shook his head and gestured toward the tiny parlor at

the front of the house. There, he spoke in normal tones. "Probably at the base of the mountain," he replied. "Molly's boy brought me a note this morning. According to her, Jonas's men had been posted outside your house all night. That bore some looking into, so I rode by Jonas's place and happened to notice that he was assembling a small army. I guessed the rest."

"You probably saved my neck." Griffin said, even as memories of the wondrous night just past flooded his mind. He turned away, pretending a great interest in Field's perfectly ordinary brick fireplace in an effort to keep the sordid facts from shining in his face.

He hadn't been quick enough. "Damn it, Griffin," Field hissed, circling Griffin to stand in front of him. "You did it, didn't you? You compromised that girl!"

The shame Griffin already felt was beyond anything Field could engender in him. "I didn't think she was a virgin!" he snapped.

Field's soft answer was hoarse with outrage. "You idiot, Griffin—you thick-headed *idiot*. You were trying to spite Jonas!"

Griffin shrugged, carefully avoiding his friend's eyes. "And I succeeded," he said, with a lightness he didn't feel.

Rachel stood, frozen, in the middle of Field Hollister's small, spotless kitchen. *You compromised that girl. You were trying to spite Jonas.* The words echoed cruelly in her mind, but not so cruelly as Griffin's response.

And I succeeded.

After what seemed like an eternity, Rachel was able to move again. Bearing her outrage and her pain in silence, she crept out of Field's back door and ran until she reached the sanction of the saloon's kitchen. During the flight, she noticed that the steamer, *Statehood*, was in port.

"Mamie!" she cried, leaning, trembling and exhausted, against the inside of the back door. "Oh, Mamie, where are you?"

The kindly woman bustled in from another room, her round face perplexed and worried. "Why, Rachel, what in heaven's name . . . ?"

Rachel's breath came in short, frantic gasps. "I—there's a steamer in port—I need my money—"

"Well, my goodness—"

Rachel was bounding across the kitchen floor, now, tears pouring down her face. "Please, Mamie, there's no time—there's no time. . . ."

She scrambled up the stairs, ignoring the questioning looks of the idle dancing girls and the few Monday-morning drinkers lounging in the saloon. In her mother's room, she found a sizable suitcase and began crumpling the clothes she'd brought from Griffin's house into it.

The level, unruffled voice went through her like a sword. "You don't have to hurry, Rachel. The steamer doesn't sail for an hour."

Slowly, a blue muslin camisole crushed in her hands, Rachel turned to face Griffin Fletcher. Just the sight of him caused her fathomless, raging pain. "You—" she began, "You—"

But her voice fell away. There were simply no words terrible enough, wounding enough. She forced herself to turn back to the soothing mechanics of packing her clothing.

"I'll see that the trunks you left at my place are on board in plenty of time," he said rationally.

And then he was gone.

Rachel sat down on a bench upholstered in red velvet, covered her face with her hands, and cried until there were no more tears inside her.

When the steamer made its way out of Providence harbor, Rachel McKinnon was aboard it. She stood gripping the railing with both hands, memorizing the wharf, the saltbox houses, and the graveyard at the top of the green knoll overlooking Tent Town.

"Good-bye," she said softly.

Mamie Jenkins didn't think she'd ever seen more misery in a single face than she saw now, in Griffin Fletcher's. He looked broken, somehow, sitting there at Becky's table and pretending to drink the coffee she'd set before him.

My Lord, she thought, *He loves that girl.*

"Why don't you go after her, instead of sitting there like a fool?" Mamie burst out, running her huge, workworn hands down the front of her apron in agitation, remembering the anguish in Miss Rachel's face when she'd given her the money Becky left.

Griffin shook his head, but his eyes didn't quite meet Mamie's. "It's better to let her go, Mamie. Believe me."

"Mule," rumbled Mamie, as she turned to pluck gnarled

116

potatoes from a bin and drop them, with resounding thuds, into her colander. "Damned, cussed, thick-headed mule!"

"Thank you."

Mamie began to pare the potatoes with savage motions. "How many times do you think love's going to happen to you, Griffin Fletcher?"

He took a draught of his coffee, made a face that fell far short of the nonchalance he was probably aiming for. "If I'm lucky, it will never happen again," he said. And then he drained the coffee cup and left.

It was dark outside. Billy Brady didn't like the dark; it was too full of unfriendly things. Just like the town was full of unfriendly people.

He was grateful for the light glowing in Field Hollister's parlor window. If it hadn't been for that, he might have been afraid to knock on the door.

Field answered quickly, so quickly that Billy wondered if God told him things that were going to happen, right out loud. He even had his coat in his hand, and he only said one word. "Griffin?"

Billy nodded. "Ma says please come quick, 'cause we can't manage him."

"Nobody can," Field said, sighing like Billy's ma did when her bread didn't rise right. But then he set right out to do it anyway.

Chapter Fourteen

None of it had any substance for Rachel—not the deck of the *Statehood*, slick beneath her feet, not the white, painted handrail she leaned against, not the lush, tree-choked beauty of the verdant shorelines.

The sternwheeler made two stops: one at Kingston, another at Bainbridge Island. Rachel paid no attention to the ports themselves, or to the people who boarded and disembarked.

Instead, she fixed her eyes on the snowy, unconquerable

slopes of Mount Rainier. It rose like a bastion in the eastern skies, its descents traced with pearlescent purple shadows and aglow with the gold and crimson rage of the retiring sun opposite it. Nothing else in Rachel's world, besides that magnificent, cloud-crowned peak, seemed larger and more profound than the pain and shame tangled within her.

The dazzling fierceness of the late afternoon sun was interspersed with the first shadows of twilight by the time the vessel steamed into Elliott Bay and progressed confidently toward Seattle.

Some of Rachel's remembered fondness for this rousing, adolescent city came to the fore. She looked away from Rainier, at last, and allowed her burning, aching eyes to focus on the rambunctious town that would now be her home.

Except for a limited area along the waterfront, Seattle was a hillside city. Its wood frame buildings, interspersed only here and there with structures of brick, clung to the landscape like bold children playing king-of-the-hill. On the western side of the shoreline, the tents and shacks that housed Skid Road brothels and saloons stood precariously on their tide flats, almost arrogant in their determination to exist as a part of Seattle proper. The raucous voices of their customers and employees already echoed out, past the gray warehouses and the creaking wharfs, over the water.

Rachel closed her eyes for a moment, against the many memories she had of venturing there, to the Skid Road, to fetch her father and bring him home. Was he there, even now, swilling whiskey and regaling other lumberjacks with his tall stories?

Rachel drew a deep breath, a breath filled with the scents of salt and kelp and kerosene, then opened her eyes resolutely. She would see Miss Cunningham first, and secure a room in that lady's boardinghouse if she could. She would eat, no matter how repugnant the prospect now seemed, and hide the thick roll of bills Mamie had turned over to her in Providence.

After that, she would summon up what strength she had left and invade the imposing Skid Road. Even if her father wasn't there now, the chances were good that someone in one of those notorious establishments would have word of him.

As the *Statehood* drew neatly alongside a wharf and was made fast to the pilings by adroit, loud-voiced crewmen, Rachel steeled herself for the new life that awaited her here.

Other passengers were met by smiling families with buckboards and buggies, and Rachel felt a deep, stabbing sense of loneliness as she made her way up the wharf. Her suitcase was heavy, and her ancient high-button shoes pinched her toes beneath the hem of her smart, gray linen traveling suit. Not for the first time, she wondered about the lady, surely a friend of Jonas's, who had worn this clothing before.

Where the land and the groaning wooden wharf converged, an outrageously ugly Indian woman offered to read Rachel's fortune from an array of colored clam shells. Rachel shook her head and, with a rueful smile, pressed on, crossing the wide plank street and advancing up the hill, toward the modest residential section where Miss Flora Cunningham rented rooms.

She had forgotten the boisterous song Seattle sang, with its steam whistles shrilling from the lumber mills and from the harbor, the clanging bells of horse-drawn trolley cars, the raucous debauchery of the Skid Road.

Setting aside all the sweet fantasies she'd entertained of living in this city, Rachel longed inconsolably for the peaceful, sauntering pace of Providence. There, the saws in Jonas Wilkes's mill were only a distant hum, and the whistles of steamers passing on the canal had seemed hauntingly melodic.

Rachel raised her chin and continued the climb, wishing that the pain in her heart would turn to numbness, as had the pounding ache in her feet.

She'd been a joke in Providence, she reminded herself sternly—the lumberman's daughter daring to dally with the likes of Jonas Wilkes and Griffin Fletcher. What wicked merriment she must have provided, not only for those two worldly men, but for the women who poured tea in cozy parlors and tended soft pink roses in fenced gardens.

Tears burned in Rachel's eyes. *Fool!* she chided herself, with a cruelty she would not have leveled at any other living creature, *Now you know why Pa warned you about laying down with a man—now you know. And you'll be tainted by what you've done for the rest of your life; no good man will want you.*

But beneath the stylish lines of her traveling suit, Rachel's breasts remembered the sheer delight of Griffin Fletcher's touch, the ecstasy of his mouth tugging at her hardened nipples. The ghost of his passion, still entwined with her own, throbbed in her midsection.

The hand-painted sign hanging from the cherry tree in Flora

119

Cunningham's dooryard brought Rachel's mind back to practical matters. Rooms to Let, it read. F. Cunningham, Prop.

Rachel opened the whitewashed wooden gate and marched purposefully up the pine-board walk to turn the bell knob. There were lilies etched in the oval glass window of the front door, and Rachel admired their intricacy anew as she waited.

Miss Cunningham, a small, nervous woman with wispy gray hair and quick blue eyes, opened the door herself. "Why, Rachel McKinnon!" she chimed, frankly assessing the girl's upgraded wardrobe, suitcase, and beaded handbag.

She's wondering what I've been up to, Rachel thought with wistful humor. *And she'd perish if she knew.* "I've come to take a room," she said out loud.

Miss Cunningham looked like a delighted little wren, peering out of its nest. Then, suddenly, an almost comical shadow of disappointment fell across the avid, narrow face. "There's just you, is there? And where is your father?"

Rachel was tired, miserable, and more than a little irritated by the mention of Ezra McKinnon. "My pa and I have parted ways," she said simply. "But I have money, and I mean to find a position as soon as I can."

The spinister eyed Rachel's costly garments once more and stepped back to admit her.

The quarters she offered Rachel consisted of a dim, hastily constructed nook under the stairway. It contained a narrow, lumpy-looking bed, a washstand with a cracked toilet set on its warped wooden surface, and a series of pegs, aligned along the inside of the door, to serve as a wardrobe.

The alarm in Miss Cunningham's eyes was a source of carefully subdued amusement to Rachel. *She thinks I'll be too grand now, in my fine clothes, for such a room as this.*

"Is this the only room you have?" she asked aloud, knowing full well that the enterprising lady would have offered the finest room in the house if it had been available.

Anxiously, the woman nodded. "The whole upper floor's been taken by a single gentleman—Captain Douglas Frazier of the *China Drifter.*"

Rachel summoned a look of imperious discontent to her face, though she actually cared nothing about Captain Frazier or his ship. She only longed to pull off her shoes, wash her face and hands, and collapse for an hour or two on that singularly uninviting cot stretched beneath the slant of the stairway. "I do hope he's quiet and well mannered," she said, because something within her required that she be contrary.

Miss Cunningham was nodding again; this time, the motion was almost feverish with sincerity. "Oh, yes, he's a gentleman —no question about that. And, of course, once the *Drifter* sails, you may have your choice of the upstairs rooms."

Rachel offered the smallest bill she had in payment of two weeks' board and room, and was, once again, mildly amused by her landlady's surprise.

"I can't make change for that!" cried Miss Cunningham, her thin hands flexing and unflexing in their need to grasp the strip of currency.

"Then surely you won't mind if I pay you tomorrow, after I've been to the bank?" asked Rachel, with the air of one who has conducted many lofty transactions.

You're going to look a fool, taunted a practical voice in her mind, *if you can't find work and all that money gets spent. Then you won't be carrying on like you're something more than a lumber brat.*

After great deliberation, Miss Cunningham agreed to be paid in the morning, scrounged up a bulky brass key, and left Rachel to settle in.

She did not settle in—at least, not immediately. Once the door was locked behind her, Rachel pried off the hateful shoes—whatever other pleasures she might forego, she would buy new shoes first thing in the morning—and began to scour the cramped little room for a sensible place to hide her money.

After an extensive search, she chose an open nook in the framework of the wall behind her bed. Any accomplished thief would find it in minutes, simply by lifting the faded patchwork quilt and looking beneath the bed, but Rachel was too tired and heartsick to lend the project further effort. Her feet were sore and swollen, now that she'd freed them from the horrible confines of her shoes, and she doubted that she would be able to manage the walk downtown to the Skid Road that evening.

She took off her bonnet, the beloved linen suit, and the soft lawn blouse beneath it, and washed fiercely in the tepid water awaiting her on the washstand. Then, clad only in her muslin drawers and camisole, she lay down on the cot and closed her eyes. Immediately, the face of Griffin Fletcher filled the dark void behind her lids.

Rachel wrenched her eyes open, determined not to think of

him, and the way he'd used her, until she felt strong enough to withstand the inevitable onslaught of contradictory emotions.

Oh, but she was tired—dismally tired. Soon her eyes would close of their own accord. Stubbornly, she stared up at the slanted ceiling inches above her head and waited.

After a while, she slept and dreams overtook her. She was back on that musty straw bed, high on the mountain looming above Providence, and Griffin Fletcher was making love to her.

When the hammering of boots climbing the stairs above her ceiling awakened Rachel with a cruel start, the little room in Flora Cunningham's house was pitch-dark. All the same, Rachel dashed the tears from her face, in fierce pride, and ordered herself to be strong.

She might have hidden there, alone and broken, like a wounded creature cowering in its den, if Miss Cunningham hadn't rapped on her door and chirped companionably that supper was getting cold.

Stricken though she was, Rachel was hungry. And she knew that she would need strength in the hours and days and weeks ahead, she would need all her faculties if she was to find work, seek out her father—or at least some word of him—and gather the scattered pieces of her hopes.

Captain Douglas Frazier rose from his chair at the dining-room table with accomplished grace when the sea nymph entered the room. She wore a pretty gown of sprigged cambric, along with a brave, if slightly dazed, smile. Her hair, brushed to a high, sable shine and plaited into a single thick braid, lay like a beautiful rope on her right shoulder.

He'd never seen, in all his years on land and sea, a more enchanting creature than this one. And if she was wearing her broken heart like a banner, well, there were things that could be done to improve matters.

"How do you do?" he asked, in what he hoped was a steady voice. "I'm Captain Douglas Frazier."

The stricken, purple eyes assessed him frankly, but the captain wasn't worried by that. He was, at thirty-seven, a fine figure of a man, with auburn hair aplenty, a stylish and manly mustache, and blue eyes that laughed even when his mouth didn't. "This is Miss Rachel McKinnon," chattered Flora Cunningham, in a pleased, motherly fashion.

Douglas nodded politely. "Miss McKinnon."

The girl blushed and sat down in the chair assigned to her. "Captain Frazier," she acknowledged, before turning her attention to the bowl of oyster stew steaming on the crocheted tablecloth before her.

Broken heart or none, in Douglas Frazier's opinion that one had the appetite of a deckhand. He wondered, as he sank back into his own chair, who the wastrel was who had crushed her spirit in such a way that there were wild, writhing shadows in her eyes.

Douglas sat down again. He would take Miss Rachel McKinnon to the finest restaurant this bumbling frontier town had to offer, and soon, he decided. After that, they would see a performance at the Opera House.

Yes. A little fun might mend her, and make her fit for the purpose he had in mind.

Rachel liked Captain Frazier well enough, though she had no wish to know him any better. She volunteered nothing about herself during dinner, even though he plied her with skillfully framed, refined questions.

Undaunted, the handsome, redheaded man began telling stories of his experiences at sea and in foreign ports. He spoke of faraway, mystical China and of the natives of Hawaii, who dressed themselves in the multicolored feathers of tropical birds when they celebrated their pagan holidays.

In spite of her weariness and her heartbreak and the nagging suspicion that she would never see her father again, no matter how much she searched, Rachel was enthralled. Captain Frazier's words were vivid and softly spoken; it was as though she were seeing the beautiful, brown-skinned people of Hawaii, bedecked in their feathered finery, with her own eyes.

"Surely there are cities there," she said in wonder, as she ladled a second helping of stew into her bowl.

"Villages," allowed the suave sea captain. "But one day there will be cities, more's the pity. The islanders will become strangers in their own land, just as the red man has here."

Rachel thought of the spirited, beautiful Fawn Nighthorse, and ached. "I hope not," she mourned.

"It is inevitable, my dear," replied the captain, succinctly.

Rachel supposed that he was right, and the conviction saddened her further. She could empathize with those who lived between two worlds, fitting into neither.

* * *

Jonas and his men waited more than two hours, by his watch, at the base of the mountain. Someone, somehow, had warned Griffin—that was clear.

Jonas's rage was a searing, tearing thing, but he kept it to himself. There was no need to let the men know.

"What do you think, Boss?" McKay asked, clasping his saddle horn with both hands and leaning forward to study Jonas's carefully masked expression.

"I think we'll have to take this matter up with Dr. Fletcher another time," he said, couching his fury in a tone of weary resignation. "Perhaps after dark."

McKay smiled his foolish, rotted smile.

He likes doing this kind of work in the dark, thought Jonas, with only slight disgust. Griffin would be expecting that; retaliation shrouded in the night.

He raised one hand to signal a retreat and smiled to himself. Mustn't be too predictable.

Boldly, McKay brought his horse into step with Jonas's Arabian gelding, while the other men followed behind. "We can't take him if he stays holed up in that house—can we?"

"That's the advantage of dealing with a man like Griffin Fletcher, McKay," Jonas answered. "He's too proud and too stubborn to 'hole up' anywhere. No, he'll ride right out into the open, once he's sure we won't catch him with the girl."

McKay ruminated for a while. "We gonna kill him?" he asked finally.

Jonas glanced heavenward in impatience and shot a fierce, quelling look in McKay's direction. "Hell, no, we're not going to kill him."

"Why not?"

"Because I want him to stay alive, McKay—for a number of reasons. He's the only doctor within miles, for one thing, and he is my cousin, for another." *I want him to see Rachel's belly round with my babies. I want him to crawl.*

McKay was clearly disappointed, but to Jonas's relief, he stopped talking.

And a picture sprang full-blown into Jonas's tortured mind—Rachel, heavy with child. His child.

The image had nothing to do with revenge against Griffin; no, that would be only a minor pleasure, compared to seeing Rachel bear his children, to having her surrender her sweet softness to him whenever he desired her. And that would be often.

Jonas smiled. With rueful certainty, he admitted to himself that he'd fallen in love.

After that, his plans were easier to make.

Field Hollister expected to find wholesale destruction when he strode into Griffin's study that night, and he was not disappointed.

The great oak desk had been overturned, its drawers askew like flailing limbs. Books littered the floor, and the heavy velvet draperies had been torn from their rods and flung in every direction.

Teetering in the middle of the wreckage was Griffin Fletcher.

Field had seen his friend through other rages—when Louisa Fletcher had died, after Athena's betrayal—but none that even remotely rivaled this one. "Give me the bottle, Griff," he said evenly.

Griffin smiled, lifted the bottle to his lips, and drank copiously.

Field sighed, caught Molly Brady's eyes, and nodded to her to leave the room.

She shot one reluctant, distraught glance in Griffin's direction and did as she was bidden. Mute with fear, Billy tagged after her and closed the study doors behind him.

Field knew better than to try to reason with his friend at this point; it was too late for that. There was little to do but wait and stand by until the storm passed. He knelt and began gathering up the scattered books.

Griffin's voice was a low, wretched drawl. "You know what you are, Field? You're a mender."

Field did not look up. "Is that so?"

There was a long pause. "Do you know how long I know Rachel, Field? Six days."

Field examined the broken binding of a volume of Greek philosophy, unruffled. "God made the world in six days, Griffin. Obviously, a lot can be accomplished in that length of time."

Griffin's laugh came in a broken rasp. "It's fitting, don't you think, that it takes the same amount of time to tear it down again?"

Field gathered Chaucer and Shakespeare and Ben Johnson in reverent hands. "Everything is going to be all right, Griffin," he said quietly.

Griffin growled, low in his throat, and flung the bottle across

125

the room. It shattered against the sturdy doors of the study, bathing them in a sheet of alcohol.

Field ignored the violence of the action. "That's a start," he said.

Chapter Fifteen

Miss Cunningham was clearly displeased by Rachel's request that hot water and a bathtub be brought to her room, but she complied, nonetheless, after informing her tenant that such favors cost extra and weren't to be expected more often than once a week.

As Rachel lowered her aching body into the water, after the old woman had gone and the door was locked again, she couldn't help remembering another bath, in another, much grander house.

How Griffin had frightened her that day, standing in the doorway like a solidified storm cloud, ordering her to get dressed.

Something ached in Rachel's throat, and she glanced toward the sturdy door of the stairway room. If only he would appear in this doorway, now, and say that it had all been a terrible mistake, that he had done all those beautiful things to her that night in the lumber camp because he loved her.

Rachel sat bolt upright in the steaming water and berated herself in a sharp undertone. "Ninny!"

Then, fueled by her own self-scorn, she scrubbed her body until it was pinkened and squeaky. Her hair, bound atop her head by combs and pins she'd taken from her mother's vanity table just before her departure from Providence, would have to be washed in the evening. There was no time, now, to sit toweling it dry.

Quickly, she rose out of the water and reached for the scratchy white towel Miss Cunningham had so grudgingly provided. She would put the bulk of her money into the bank first, keeping back enough to buy new shoes; perhaps she would even splurge and purchase a pair made of kid leather—

with shiny patent toes. Of course, she would pay Miss Cunningham, too.

It was only as she went through her clothes, in search of something suitable for seeking work, that she remembered the trunks of other garments left behind at Griffin Fletcher's house. He had promised to put them on board the steamer before it sailed—but had he?

In an instant, Rachel knew that he had. Except where romantic escapades were concerned, he was a man of his word. She would ask after the trunks at the shed near the wharfs, where passage was paid and baggage was stored.

Hoping that the treasured garments were not lost, Rachel put on clean underthings, then a simple, navy blue skirt of crisp sateen, and a shirtwaist of azure silk. She braided her hair, pinning it securely into a very businesslike coronet. Then, after one final inspection before the mirror she'd cajoled from Miss Cunningham that morning, she went out.

When she made her entrance, Captain Frazier was sitting at the dining-room table, reading a crumpled copy of the *Seattle Times.* She did not miss the look of polite speculation in his eyes as he smiled at her.

"Good morning, Miss McKinnon," he said.

Buoyed, as always, by the possibilities of a brand new day, Rachel curtsied slightly and smiled. It was a combination she had practiced many times in private, but had never had occasion to execute in public.

Captain Frazier seemed charmed. "Tell me you're not lowering yourself to join the work-a-day world, Rachel!"

Rachel allowed his improper use of her first name to pass unchallenged and sat down at her place, where eggs and toasted bread awaited her. "I must work, Captain Frazier," she said lightly. "I don't have a choice."

"Poppycock!" he said, a smile dancing in his eyes. "You should have a husband. A rich husband."

Rachel suddenly felt again all the wretched loneliness she'd endured during the endless night. Her appetite fled, and she bounded out of her chair, her breakfast untouched, to take her handbag and her bonnet from the sideboard and rush toward the door.

But Captain Frazier's strong, sun-browned hand detained her in the hallway. "Rachel, forgive me. I didn't mean to upset you."

Her voice trembled, though she willed it to be steady. It was all she could do to meet the captain's sea blue eyes. "You didn't upset me—"

"Nonsense. I *did* upset you by making that insensitive remark about your needing a husband. It was rude behavior on my part, and I'm sorry."

Rachel raised her chin and managed a soft, half-smile. "You simply insist on taking the blame for my bad manners, don't you? I shouldn't have bolted like that; it was silly. Now, if you'll excuse me, I have so many things to attend to."

Captain Frazier offered his arm. "Allow me, then."

Rachel raised one eyebrow and withdrew a little. "Allow you to what?" she demanded.

The captain laughed uproariously. "Oh, Rachel, Rachel. Just when I decide you must surely have been educated in some prestigious eastern school, you ask such a question as that!"

Rachel looked into his mirth-crinkled face warily. "Are you making fun of me?"

Douglas Frazier brought himself skillfully under control. "Oh, no, my dear—never that. But tell me, if you are truly a lumberjack's daughter, as Miss Cunningham confides that you are, why are you so well-spoken?"

Rachel's tremendous pride made her bridle. "In the first place, Captain, there is nothing wrong with being a lumberjack's daughter! In the second, if I speak well, it is because I read well!"

"I see," said the captain evenly, the humor still dancing in his eyes. "I've been a bore. Again, I apologize."

Rachel was exasperated and ashamed of her outburst. "I really must leave—"

"As I must." Captain Frazier executed a slight, courtly bow. "My carriage is here now, Rachel. Let me give you a ride down to the world of commerce and excitement."

Rachel laughed, but at the same time, she was wondering if he was testing her, if he wanted to see whether or not she understood sophisticated words like "commerce."

She shouldn't allow him to cart her off in his carriage; it wasn't proper. But her shoes did pinch so, even just standing there in the hallway. The thought of walking down that hill in them gave her pause.

"I would like very much to ride in your carriage, Captain," she said loftily.

His chuckle was a low, rich sound, and his blue eyes twinkled as he offered a gentlemanly arm. "Leave us expatriate," he said.

"That means we're going now," Rachel said, accepting the arm he offered.

His chuckle grew to a warm laugh. "Of course it does," he said.

The morning was bright, and Miss Cunningham's cherry tree was a puff of pink, translucent blossoms. In the distance, Elliott Bay sparkled like a huge sapphire dappled with silver and gold.

Captain Frazier's carriage, probably hired, was a splendid sight, too. It glistened in the sunshine, and it was drawn by four coal black horses.

Rachel's spirits lifted as the fine carriage rumbled and jolted over Seattle's questionable streets, toward the waterfront, and she allowed them to carry her high, knowing that the night would bring less enjoyable emotions.

That morning the noisy bustle of the city seemed cheerful, rather than intimidating. After all, she was going to buy new shoes—and perhaps, a book to read.

But the first order of business, even before opening an account at the bank, was to find out whether or not her trunks were being held at the steamboat office.

They were. Rachel was delighted and relieved, but she felt a remnant of the sadness that had plagued her during the night, too. She shook off the image of Griffin Fletcher carrying those trunks aboard the *Statehood* and smiled up at Captain Frazier, who had offered to have his driver deliver the cumbersome trunks to the Cunningham house.

She thanked him.

Boldly, Captain Frazier took both her hands in his. "Will you be all right, now?"

Rachel nodded, thinking with pleasure of the money in her handbag, of the kid leather shoes she was going to buy, of the job she would surely find.

"Good," said the captain, gently. And then he turned and strode away, along the waterfront.

Rachel found the shoes for which she'd been longing in a Front Street shop, and she bought them proudly. They like felt gentle hands caressing her feet as she walked along the wooden sidewalk, full of the certainty that today would be a good day.

Because it seemed like a fortunate omen, Rachel deposited most of her money in the Commerce Bank. The memory of her silly exchange with Captain Frazier, in the boardinghouse hallway, made her smile.

From the bank, she proceeded to a well-stocked general store, where she purchased a novel, scented soap, and a packet of hair pins. At the last minute, she added writing paper, a pen, and ink to her other things. Perhaps, after a decent length of time, she would write to Jonas, thank him properly for his kindness in giving her so many lovely clothes, and apologize for leaving the picnic without an explanation. She would write to Molly, too, she decided, because Molly was, after a fashion, a friend.

The search for work, as it turned out, was far less enjoyable than the shopping expedition had been. In fact, it was downright discouraging.

In the very bank where she had been such a welcome depositor, she was crisply turned away because she could not typewrite. At the mattress factory, it was decided that she was far too delicate to do such work. In a seedy tearoom, where a sign indicated that a girl was wanted to wait tables, the proprietor was too forward and implied that a plainer young woman was required to keep his female customers happy.

By noon, Rachel was feeling patently desperate. It seemed that she didn't know how to do anything worthwhile, and though she was educated, she couldn't claim formal schooling beyond the eighth grade. She had learned her letters in one place and her numbers in another, and when a crate of musty old books had come temporarily into her possession by the good graces of a kindly schoolmaster, she had pieced the letters together until they made words. By knowing the meanings of just a few, she had discerned the definitions of others.

But she had no specific trade.

Rachel was standing in the middle of the sidewalk, near tears, when it occurred to her that she had been very rash in thinking that there would be a job waiting for her here.

"Rachel?"

She looked up and saw, with abject delight, the smiling, concerned face of Captain Frazier. "Douglas!" she cried out, so relieved to see him that she forgot he hadn't given her permission to use his first name.

He took her arm and deftly squired her out of the mainstream of passersby and into a clean, brightly decorated restaurant. "I am relieved," he said jovially, as they sat down at a table covered with a floral cloth. "I feared you intended to call me 'Captain' all my days. Tell me, does that ominous little frown mean that you haven't found work?"

Rachel nodded miserably. "I've asked everywhere, it seems. Either they want me to typewrite, or they want me to be bigger and stronger. In a tearoom on Marion Street, they wanted me to be uglier!"

There was sympathy in Douglas's laugh, and one of his hands reached out to shelter both of hers and still the nervous motion of her fingers. "What kind of work would you like to do, Rachel?"

Coffee was served, and Rachel laced hers with generous helpings of sugar and cream. "Anything."

Douglas raised one auburn eyebrow. "Surely not *anything.*"

Rachel's cheeks flamed. "Well," she replied, "Anything that isn't wrong."

Again, the cerulean eyes smiled at her. "Many things would be wrong for you, Rachel, simply because they are menial. You were born to be the the mistress of a fine house and the mother of a great man's children."

Now, it was Rachel who laughed. But, in her mind, she saw Jonas Wilkes, stretched out on a picnic blanket, smiling up at her. The memory was oddly sobering. "I am, as you said this morning, a lumberjack's daughter."

There was a serious quality in his smiling eyes, belying their merriment. "Many wealthy men would be happy to take you as a bride, Rachel, and I could arrange for you to meet several."

The words were vaguely frightening. "I couldn't marry a man I didn't love," she said lamely, after a long, disturbing silence.

A muscle in Douglas's jaw tightened almost imperceptibly. "Love," he said, turning the word disdainfully from his mouth. "That is something you read about in silly books. The world is a hard, practical place, Rachel."

Indeed, the world was a hard, practical place. Rachel had rarely known it to be anything *other* than hard and practical. But love existed outside the covers of books, all right, she had discovered that in a most unfortunate way.

She swallowed, suddenly remembering that girl in Oregon who had made love with the storekeeper's son and gotten herself into trouble. Dear heaven, was Griffin Fletcher's baby growing inside her, even now? If it was, Rachel's life would progress from "hard and practical" to downright grim, and in a hurry, too. She would not be so fortunate as that chubby Oregon bride. . . .

"Rachel?" Douglas's voice brought her back abruptly. "You looked so pale—what were you thinking?"

Rachel had to struggle to keep back tears of panic. "I'm all right, Douglas. Just a little discouraged, that's all." *And perhaps a little pregnant.*

He reached out gently to touch her face. "If it means that much to you, I'll speak with some of my friends. I know a number of merchants."

Hope surged through Rachel, immediately followed by embarassment. "That would be wrong," she mourned.

"Wrong? For a friend to help a friend? Why would that be wrong?"

"I would be obligated to you," she said.

Douglas laughed. "Yes, my dear, you would. I would insist that you let me buy your supper tonight and escort you to the Opera House."

Rachel's eyes widened. "The Opera House? What would we see?"

Douglas surveyed her with gentle amusement. "In this city, who knows? Perhaps a trained bear or a lumberjack who plays tunes on a crosscut saw."

After a second's pause, Rachel realized that he was teasing and laughed. "I'll have you know, sir," she said archly, "that Seattle has witnessed far stranger performances."

Douglas raised his coffee cup in a dashing salute. "I have absolutely no doubt of that, my dear," he agreed. And then he summoned a waiter and ordered their lunch.

Directly after eating, they went to call on a storekeeper Douglas knew. Rachel was introduced and then left to examine ribbons and bolts of brightly colored cloth while the two men disappeared into the back room.

Five minute later, Rachel had a job. She was to serve as a "notions girl," selling thread and buttons and other dressmaking supplies to the female clientele.

She should have been happier than she was, but she suspected that Douglas had somehow coerced her new employer into hiring her. The thought left a distinctly bad taste in her mouth, but she couldn't afford to turn down the position, so she accepted it graciously.

Mr. Turnbull, who had a slack jaw and a part through the exact middle of his thinning chestnut hair, instructed her to report for work at eight o'clock the next morning.

Back at Miss Cunningham's, in the comforting silence of her room, Rachel fought down her misgivings and took out her paper and pen. "Dear Molly," she began, in her small, rounded hand. "Today I found a job. . . ."

The letter was quite fat by the time she signed it and slipped it carefully into a matching blue envelope. She had never written a letter before, and for a moment, the idea of parting with it seemed very unappealing.

In the end, however, hoping that there would be an answer some time, she addressed it simply, "Mrs. Molly Brady, Providence, Washington Territory" and tucked it into her handbag. Tonight, when she went to Skid Road to look for her father, she would stop off at the steamboat office and see that her message was on board the *Statehood* the next time it sailed.

Rachel was halfway down the hill before she remembered her promise to have supper with the captain and see whatever performance the Opera House had to offer. She stood still for almost a minute, debating silently while looking up the hill toward Miss Cunningham's, then down the hill toward the harbor.

In the end, she chose the harbor and the Skid Road. Until she understood her father's abrupt and puzzling disappearance, there would be a part of her that never rested. Surely Douglas would understand, once she had explained.

The *Statehood* was in port, her deck lanterns spilling golden light onto the twilight-darkened waters of the bay, her big paddles still as she rested. The captain, a husky, middle-aged man with mischievous eyes, like her father's, was lounging in the shack on shore, his coat unbuttoned and his hat, limp with long use, resting on the corner of a cluttered desk.

Rachel gave him the letter, paid him the fee for its freight, and turned to leave. There was still the Skid Road to be braved, and it was getting dark.

As an afterthought, she turned in the doorway. "Captain," she ventured, shyly, "I wonder if you know many of your passengers by name?"

The aging seaman smiled. "Not all of them, else I'd surely know yours. And I remember your being aboard yesterday."

Encouraged by his friendly attitude, Rachel described Ezra McKinnon to him and asked if he remembered such a passenger.

To her disappointment, if not her surprise, the steamboat

pilot recalled neither the name nor the man himself. He promised to keep an eye out, however, and to pass on whatever pertinent "scuttlebutt" he might hear.

Rachel thanked him and walked steadily toward Skid Road. Along the dusky wharfs, ship rats scurried on whispering feet, and whiskey barrels and shipping crates loomed like specters. Ahead was the light, laughter, and bawdy music peculiar to this notorious section of town.

The heels of Rachel's new shoes made a lonely, clicking sound on the plank walkway edging the road, and once or twice, a sailor or woodsman paused, reeling, to stare at her. She walked faster, keeping well away from the shadows along the walls of the warehouses lining the waterfront.

The first saloon was housed in a shack with walls so haphazardly erected that the light showed through in golden strips. Beneath it, under the sawdust floor, was the tide flat. The stench of rotten seaweed and dead clams blended with those of sweat, cheap whiskey, cigar smoke, and the kind of perfume that was sold in quart jars.

It took all Rachel's considerable courage to push open the swinging doors and walk inside.

Chapter Sixteen

The sawdust on the saloon floor was dampened by the seeping tidewater beneath it and stained with tobacco juice. Rachel thought of her beautiful new leather shoes and groaned inwardly.

Then she sighed and reminded herself that her father had to be found. If he was tired of being burdened with a grown daughter, that was all right, because now she had a life independent of him anyway, and certainly she had no wish to traipse after him to yet another timber town.

All the same, Rachel longed for a decent and honest parting—and an explanation. After all the years of his rough devotion and fierce concern, it seemed odd indeed that he would leave her behind without a word.

One sweeping glance told Rachel that she would not find Ezra McKinnon in this particular place, but there were people there—people who might know where he was working now.

Rachel was about to approach a group of burly lumberjacks when a thin, somewhat grubby hand grasped her arm. She paused, then turned to see a plump blond woman standing beside her, wearing a sleazy yellow dress and a decidedly unfriendly look.

"Honey," the woman began, patting her stiff, false-looking curls with one hand. "If you got a husband here, it wouldn't be smart to face off with him in public. Men got mean pride when it comes to things like that."

Rachel lifted her chin. "I'm here to ask about a man named Ezra McKinnon. Do you know him?"

The blonde's painted eyelids descended slightly. "What if I do?"

Exasperation nettled Rachel, as did the stench and the noise of that place. "He's my father," she said tersely. "And it is very important that I find him."

The prostitute studied her own uneven fingernails and rough, pale hands. "Ezra ain't been on the Skid Road since Jonas Wilkes hired him to come over to Providence—if he had, I'd know it. He used to say to me, 'Candice, Darlin', you're too good for a place like this. You ought to go independent.'"

Rachel made a concentrated effort not to roll her eyes. Thinking of her father and this disgusting woman coupling on some filthy pallet made her feel ill, but she drew herself up short. She certainly had no room to criticize, not after that magical, tragic night with Griffin Fletcher. "Your career plans don't interest me," she said coolly. "But my father does. If you see him, or even hear something about him, send word to Miss Flora Cunningham's, on Cedar Street."

Candice tossed her head and leveled a petulant, defensive look at Rachel's trim, costly clothes. The question was so clear between them that it didn't need to be spoken aloud. *Why should I?*

Rachel was out of her element in these surroundings, and her courage was ebbing fast. Again, she raised her chin. "I'll pay you ten dollars if you contact me," she said, in answer to the silent question.

And then she turned, with quiet dignity, and walked out into the cool sanction of the night.

There was no point in searching the other saloons that night;

135

Rachel knew instinctively that Candice was telling the truth. Besides, she'd felt the curious, speculative glances of the patrons in that saloon. If she stayed, it was inevitable that one or even several of them would approach her, and discouraging them might not be an easy task.

Rachel started back along the waterfront, avoiding shadows that lurked in the darkness, beyond the reach of the timorous light the kerosene streetlamps gave off. She'd been a fool to venture onto the Skid Road alone, and at night no less, but even as she made that pragmatic admission, she knew that she would be back.

Griffin Fletcher awakened in his own bed, his head thick and throbbing, his stomach turning inside him. Molly was there, looking down at him with sharp green disapproval in her eyes.

"Aye, and it's time you came to, Griffin Fletcher. Time and past. 'Tis a whole day gone and wasted."

Griffin groaned. "What day is it?"

Molly bent to set an ominous-looking tray on the bedside table. "It's Wednesday," she volunteered testily. "May twenty-ninth, eighteen eighty—"

Griffin uttered a coarse word and struggled into a sitting position. "Good Lord," he snapped, "I know what year it is!"

"Do you, now?" retorted Molly. "Well, that's something then. It's just by the grace of our Lord that no one needed you, Griffin Fletcher."

Griffin glanced at the breakfast she'd assembled on the tray—fried eggs and riced potatoes and pork sausage—and looked away again. Even his housekeeper's well-justified scorn was preferable to the sight of food. "Maybe I'm not so necessary to this town as you and I like to think, Molly."

Molly Brady drew herself up to her full and unremarkable height. "Perhaps not," she said curtly. And then, in a rustle of sateen skirts and outrage, she walked out of Griffin's bedroom, pulling the door shut behind her with a force that jarred his fogged, aching head.

The scent of coffee made him risk another look at the tray. He reached out for the mug of steaming brew and drank from it slowly as he reviewed his fall from grace.

Rachel was gone—he faced that dark reality staunchly, though there was still jagged, wrenching pain in the knowledge. If only he hadn't had to hurt her like that, to let her leave thinking that he'd used her without love.

For there had been love—love like nothing Griffin Fletcher had ever felt before. Almost from the first moment when he'd seen her cowering in Jonas's bathtub, he had felt it, but it was only now that he could stop denying the emotion and face it squarely.

He would suffer the consuming need of her all his life, he expected. But it would be cruel to bring her back, as he longed to do, within the deadly reach of Jonas's passion.

Griffin finished his coffee, set the mug aside with a thump, and scrambled out of bed. There were, as always, rounds to make.

He dressed quickly, only to pause at his bedroom window for a time. The sky was dark with the promise of rain, and the air felt heavy and still, even with the window closed. Jonas's mountain towered toward the sky, looking ominous in the impending gloom.

Shaking off an uneasy feeling, Griffin left his bedroom and went down the back stairway, to the kitchen. There, he accepted his coat, hat, and medical bag from a grim, speechless Molly, and went out.

In the barn, he found his horse, Tempest, saddled and waiting. He led the stallion out and then swung deftly onto its back. "Billy?" he called, halfheartedly, meaning to thank the boy for guessing that he would want to ride today, instead of driving the buggy. "Hey, Bill!"

There was no answer. Griffin shrugged and raised his collar against the gray drizzle of the morning. The boy was probably in the woods somewhere, playing the strange and lonely games his limited mind suggested to him.

The close silence of those woods appealed to Griffin that bleak morning, too, but for more practical reasons. He could save time by taking the narrow path leading through them and avoiding the main road, and it was unlikely that he would meet anyone there. He needed the brief isolation to assemble the expression and bearing his patients would expect to see.

Griffin's horse neighed with obvious impatience as they rounded the hidden pond Billy loved to explore and approached the two giant boulders just beyond it.

Griffin smiled, remembering that the boy saw soldiers inside those giant rocks and believed that they guarded the path. Instead, rising on both sides of it as they did, they made it barely passable for a man on horseback.

The men were upon him the moment he passed between the

137

boulders into a small, sunless clearing. He cursed as the damp, leaf-matted ground came up to meet him.

Dazed, Griffin raised himself to his knees. Just as he did so, a rifle butt caught him hard in the side of his head.

The blow blurred his vision, and the impact of it echoed, throbbing, through his skull. He raised himself from the ground again, conscious of the rain falling on his neck.

How many were there? He couldn't see clearly, but he guessed, from the shifting shadows, that there were six or seven men crowded around him.

"Watch those feet of his," ordered a cold, calm voice.

Griffin reeled, unsteady. A boot landed in the center of his rib cage and brought him back to his knees. He spat a curse, tasted blood in his mouth. "Is this what you did to McKinnon, Jonas?" he rasped.

Hands grasped Griffin's arms, wrenched him to a standing position, held him fast. A thick, gray fog settled around him and the commands he gave his feet came to nothing. He sensed, rather than saw, Jonas's approach, but he did catch the blue-black gleam of a rifle barrel.

"Good morning, Griffin," Jonas said affably.

The excruciating pain in Griffin's head and rib cage made speech impossible for the moment. He managed nothing more than an outraged groan. Somewhere behind him Tempest danced, bridle jingling, and whinnied in agitation.

Something hard—probably the butt of Jonas's rifle—smashed into his face suddenly. Pain exploded in Griffin's head, and he felt his knees give way again.

"Get him on his feet!" Jonas hissed.

Griffin tried to struggle as his ambushers wrenched him upright, but the effort was hopeless. He fought down the vomit that burned in his throat.

Jonas's rage surged toward him like an invisible wall, immediately followed by a fist. But he was beyond pain now, beyond any feeling at all.

He laughed, and his words came out in a soft rush. "You bastard, Jonas. You're too late—you're too goddamned late."

"Let him go," Jonas ordered, from somewhere in the throbbing void.

Griffin's knees buckled as his arms were released, but some of his vision came back as he slid part way to the ground, and he felt rage as Jonas's hand entwined itself in his hair and wrenched his head back.

Jonas bent, to smile into Griffin's battered face. "I'll find her, Griffin—I promise you that. Seattle isn't big enough to hide her. But Rachel is another topic, for another day. This little set-to was my payment for the beating you gave me last week."

Griffin flailed one leaden, aching arm, to knock Jonas's hand from his head. The swearword he uttered was lost in the dismal drone of the rain.

Jonas was standing up straight now, smiling with satisfaction. "Now, my old friend, I have a little scripture for you. 'As ye sow, so shall ye reap.'"

An instant later, the toe of Jonas's boot slammed into Griffin's groin. The pain burst in his genitals like an explosion, and radiated into every fiber of his being. He fell forward, half-conscious, into the mud.

When the bad men were gone, Billy crept from his hiding place in the thick trees and scrambled toward Dr. Fletcher's motionless body. Kneeling, he dashed tears of fright from his face and whispered, "Doctor?"

Griffin groaned, stirring on the wet ground.

Billy pulled off his own coat, crumpled it, and, with gentle, trembling hands, placed it under Griffin's head for a pillow. He didn't know what else to do.

"H-horse," the man muttered, the rain mingling with the blood that gleamed in his dark hair and coursed from his face.

Billy looked around for the stallion with frantic eyes. When he whistled, the animal ambled out of the underbrush, the reins of his bridle dangling in the mud. Billy moved cautiously toward the horse, crooning soft words as he went.

Tempest balked when he grasped the bridle near the bit, and then settled down with a frightened nicker. "Easy, boy," Billy breathed. "Real easy. The bad men are gone."

As Billy turned, he saw Griffin raise himself to his hands and knees and then fall again.

He was shattered by the sight, by his own helplessness and fear. "I'll go get Ma—or Field," he sniffled. "I could get Field—"

Griffin shook his bloody, rain-drenched head and tried again to stand. "No. Help me up."

The boy obeyed, feeling the doctor's pain in his own body as he brought him to his feet.

Griffin raised his face to the rain, groped until he found the horn of Tempest's saddle, and held onto it. After a moment, he forced himself to endure the increased pain in his rib cage long enough to grasp one of the reins in his right hand. With quick, costly movements, he bound his left hand to the saddle horn. "Lead him home, Billy."

It was a long, agonizing process, stumbling back to the house beside Tempest. But Molly was there, sensible and calm, the rain plastering her copper-colored hair to her forehead and her neck.

"Saints in heaven," she breathed, "What happened?"

"Jonas," Griffin whispered, flinching as Molly untied his hand and positioned herself under his right arm.

Because of Griffin's size, Molly, even with the help of her son, could bring him no farther than the study. At Field's insistence, the room was still a fine mess of overturned furniture and scattered draperies.

While Molly trembled under the leaden weight of Griffin Fletcher's inert frame, Billy put the sofa right. Then, together, they dragged their burden toward it.

After depositing him there and covering him with the first thing that came to hand—a drapery—Molly took firm command. "Run and fetch Field Hollister, Billy. Don't stop looking until you find him."

Tearfully, Billy ambled off to obey, casting an occasional wounded glance backward, at the still form stretched out on the leather sofa.

Molly went to the cupboard where supplies and instruments were kept. It had been untouched by the doctor's rampage, and not by accident, she thought.

From its shelves, Molly took a bottle of alcohol, clean cloths, tape, and a roll of gauze. These supplies secured, she placed them carefully on a corner of Griffin's upended desk and hurried into the kitchen for hot water.

It was only after she'd tended Dr. Fletcher's wounds that Molly Brady permitted herself to cry.

Rachel began her first day of work in a bustle of brave enthusiasm, even though she felt foolish and inept and, somehow, imposed upon Mr. Turnbull like a troublesome relation.

By noon, she had sold only a length of satin ribbon and a card of pearl buttons. No matter how friendly she was, her feminine customers seemed affronted by her presence, asking petulantly after someone named Poor Marie.

More than once, during the morning, Rachel had raised her

eyes to the grim, rainy bay and regretted her hasty flight from Providence. The dream of turning the saloon her mother had left her into a respectable boardinghouse still ached in a corner of her heart.

For a few minutes, as she drank her solitary noon-time tea in the cluttered storeroom behind the dry goods counter, Rachel dared to imagine herself buying passage on the steamboat, *Statehood*, and returning to the small town on Hood Canal.

Of course, she couldn't—not for the time being, at least. She needed time to heal, and to reassemble her broken pride. Until she had done these things, she could not reasonably expect to encounter Griffin Fletcher time and time again, as she undoubtedly would, and still retain her dignity.

Suddenly, as she munched dispiritedly on a lettuce sandwich snatched from Miss Cunningham's kitchen that morning, Jonas Wilkes loomed in her mind. Rachel again felt tremendous guilt for the way she'd left him behind at the picnic. How on earth would she apologize, when and if she ever saw him again?

I'm so sorry, she imagined herself saying. *I didn't mean to abandon you like that, but I had to go up onto the mountain and lose my virginity, you see.*

Rachel meant to laugh, but hot tears came to her eyes instead.

She turned her mind to memories of the night before. The trip to Skid Road had been fruitless, and dangerous in the bargain. There had been footsteps echoing behind her as she hurried along the waterfront, and she'd been mute with terror when a sleek carriage had rattled to a stop beside her and disgorged a lividly angry Captain Douglas Frazier.

He had shouted at her in the street, shouted at her in the carriage, shouted at her in Miss Cunningham's dooryard. And he'd still been angry at breakfast.

This is not my decade, Rachel thought.

Jonas Wilkes felt a disturbing sense of disquiet as he rode onto his own property, his men straggling, single file, behind him, their horses nickering in the rain.

Griffin Fletcher's words echoed in his mind. *"You're too late. You're too damned late."*

Suppose it was true? Suppose Rachel had not remained in Seattle, after taking the hasty steamboat ride Fawn had finally recounted to him this morning? If she had boarded another ship, she would be lost to him, perhaps forever.

Jonas stiffened in the saddle, his muscles still aching with the satisfaction and release of bringing Griffin to his knees.

Dismounting at the door of his barn, Jonas considered the element of time with cold logic. Today—he would begin the search today.

Striding toward the house, Jonas allowed his thoughts to shift to Griffin. He was badly hurt, Griffin was, but he wouldn't be laid up long. Two days—maybe three—and he would be as formidable as ever. That was all the more reason, as far as Jonas was concerned, to act with haste.

Chapter Seventeen

Griffin made a strangled, soblike sound, deep in his throat, as Field grasped him beneath the arms and lifted him into a nearly upright position.

"Hold him there, then," breathed Molly, as she cut away the muddy suit coat and blood-soaked shirt. Then, tossing the garments aside, she gently washed Griffin's swollen, horribly bruised ribs and began binding them tightly with strips of cloth torn from a bedsheet.

Field watched her swift, capable hands with distraught admiration. She'd learned much, it was clear, helping Griffin with the patients who were so often brought, virtually in pieces, to his door. "Molly, you are a fine nurse," he remarked wearily, as she finished her task and nodded to Field to lay his friend down again.

Molly didn't answer; her eyes swept Griffin's face with a gentle, wounded look, and she brushed the dampened, blood-crusted hair back from his forehead. Her lips formed the plea soundlessly. *Don't die.*

"He won't, Molly," Field said, out loud.

On the sofa, Griffin writhed in an anguish that was shattering to see. Molly reached out to touch his face and, when she did, his twisting frame grew still beneath her hand. Her eyes were like polished emeralds, gleaming in the sun, when she raised them to Field's face. "This is the work of Jonas Wilkes."

Field put his hands into his trouser pockets and sighed. "I'd guessed that," he said. He did not add that, while it was vicious, the attack had not been entirely unprovoked. When would it stop, this ceaseless, mindless violence?

There was a long, terrible silence, broken only by the grating rasp of Griffin's breathing.

Finally, her eyes dark with misery, Molly drew herself up, squared her small, straight shoulders, and lifted her chin. "This will be a long night, I'm thinking. You'd best build a fire, Field Hollister, while I'm making tea."

Glad of something practical to do, Field crossed the room and placed crumpled newspaper inside the fireplace. Then, kneeling, he took splintery sticks of kindling from the brass bin beside him and stacked them, teepee fashion, around the paper. Into this structure, he tossed a lighted match.

As the flames crackled and popped in response, Field laid a pine log in their midst, closed his eyes, and prayed devoutly that Griffin would not die.

Behind him, Griffin moaned in delirium and cried out. Thunder, relatively rare on Puget Sound, rumbled in the night skies overhead, and Field looked heavenward as he turned from the newly laid fire.

"I hope you're not saying no," he muttered.

Presently, Molly came in carrying a tray. Field righted a small table and two chairs, and they sat down, facing each other.

Molly's eyes were oddly distant as she poured tea for Field, and then for herself. When her hands were free again, she brought a pale blue envelope from her apron pocket and laid it on the table. "I've gotten a letter from Rachel herself," she said, in a tone that suggested awe.

"What did she say?" Field asked evenly, not really caring.

Molly shook her head, and the firelight danced, crimson, on the strong planes of her face. "I've had no chance to read it; all I know is that someone gave it to Billy while he was looking for you."

Field averted his eyes from the neat, childish, and somehow hopeful handwriting on the face of the blue envelope. "She's gone, Molly—she's gone, and still it isn't over."

Again Molly's gaze was fixed on something far, far away, and her head was inclined to one side, as though she might be listening to a sound only her Celtic ears could hear. "No," she agreed, at last. "No, Field, it isn't over."

Restless, Field gulped the bracing tea Molly had given him

143

and surveyed the colorful shambles that was Griffin's study. *What a ridiculous sight we must be,* he thought. *Two sentinels drinking tea in the rubble. And the war is just beginning.*

High overhead, two massive air fronts collided with a reverberating crash. Field listened soberly, his eyes on the shadowed ceiling. *Complete with cannon fire,* he remarked to himself.

As far as Rachel was concerned, the afternoon was no better than the morning had been; indeed, it was worse. The store's front windows were sheeted with rain, and the atmosphere inside was dreary.

Shortly before it was time to close the store, Mrs. Turnbull bustled in, her face a study in petulant rebellion, her voluminous poplin skirts drenched with rain and muddy at the hem. Her small eyes were like black beads, gleaming in the pasty corpulence of her face, as she hurled a suspicious glance in Rachel's direction and then flounced into the back room, where her husband was totaling receipts.

Rachel sighed. The woman hadn't looked any happier than she had an hour earlier, when she had come into the store for the express purpose of being introduced to "the new clerk who was taking Poor Marie's place."

In the back room, the Turnbulls' voices rose and fell in a spate of polite bickering, and only the occasional phrase was distinct enough to understand. "I don't *care* what the Captain said— you've always had an *eye* for the pretty ones—what could *she* know about business?"

What indeed? Rachel closed her eyes and gripped the edge of the ribbon counter.

It was no surprise when Mr. Turnbull came out, mumbled that he was sorry she couldn't work for him anymore, and paid her the day's pay she'd earned.

Outside, the rainy wind bit into Rachel's flesh with icy teeth, even through her navy woolen cloak. Her despair ached in her throat, and stung behind her eyes. She would not have noticed the carriage at all if Captain Frazier hadn't gotten out of it and caught her arm as she passed.

"The life of a shop girl is not what you thought it was?" he asked, in a surprisingly gentle voice, as seconds later, Rachel sank into the carriage seat across from his.

Rachel did not dare to speak; if she did, she would burst into tears. She fixed her eyes on the tufted leather ceiling of the carriage instead and wished that she had never left Providence.

Unruffled, Douglas Frazier pressed a clean linen handkerchief into her hands. "There's no shame in crying, Rachel. It cleanses the soul, they say."

Still, she did not speak. Words could not possibly contain all the misery she felt; once freed by even the simplest utterance, it would come in torrents.

Gracefully Douglas shifted his sizable frame from his side of the carriage to hers. His arm slid around her shoulders in a brotherly fashion, and his voice was warm, almost tender. "Rachel, Rachel," he muttered. "Poor, brave little Rachel. When will you see that you can have everything—*everything*— if you'll only reach out for it!"

Everything. But not Griffin Fletcher, who personified that sweeping term. "How wrong you are," she whispered. And then, as she had feared, her composure was shattered. She allowed Douglas Frazier to press her head to his shoulder and hold her close as she wept.

She was a mystery, this one. Douglas Frazier felt both rage and tenderness as she huddled against him, broken by the loss of a paltry, wretched position in a common shop.

Rachel dressed like a lady, and she certainly spoke like one. And yet she wandered in places like the Skid Road—after dark, no less—without an escort.

Was she, after all, nothing more than a trollop?

Douglas pried his handkerchief from her clenched hands and used it to dab at the ceaseless tears streaking down her face. If she was a tart, she was a devastatingly lovely one, even when she cried.

Yes, Douglas assured himself, Ramirez would want her— volatile nature, scandalous tendencies, and all. Her amethyst eyes and the sweet invitation of her body would bind the bargain.

The wheels of the carriage clattered on the plank street beneath them, and Rachel's sobs subsided a little, leaving sniffles in their wake. Was she a virgin, he wondered? Surely, she was.

Ramirez definitely wanted a virgin.

Inwardly Jonas cursed the rain as he strode, hatless, along the waterfront, flanked by McKay and one of the other men. Ahead were the shacks and sheds and tents of Skid Road.

Jonas did not expect to find Rachel here, not for a moment. But little transpired in Seattle that wasn't common knowledge in these disreputable environs; vital information could often be had for the price of a drink.

Instinctively Jonas selected the saloon where he'd met and hired McKinnon, just over a week before—though it seemed like a century—as the starting point of his search. He knew, when he saw the slut McKinnon had been drinking with that first night, that the capricious element of luck was with him.

It was so easy that Jonas was almost disappointed; while he was desperate to find Rachel, he enjoyed a challenge, too. And he wasn't exactly pleased to hear that a violet-eyed young woman claiming to be McKinnon's daughter had come into the saloon alone, only the night before, asking questions.

"I know where she lives, too," volunteered the whore, with a smug grin.

Jonas was annoyed, relieved, and stricken to know that Rachel hoped to find her father. "Where?" he snapped.

"What's it worth?" countered the prostitute.

Bitch, Jonas thought, but he drew out his wallet and produced an impressive bill. "Tell me."

She snatched the money from his fingers with an eagerness that, coupled with the stench of her, sickened Jonas on some primary, half-discerned level of awareness. "She's stayin' at Cunningham's, on Cedar Street."

Jonas turned abruptly, almost colliding with McKay and the other man who stood gaping just inside the saloon doors. "Get me a buggy," he ordered, in a tone that tightened their slack jaws and sent them scrambling to obey.

Stubby, eager fingers came to rest on Jonas's sleeve. "I could offer some entertainment while you wait," drawled the prostitute he'd just paid.

Wrenching his arm free, Jonas inspected the fabric of his suit coat with revulsion. "I would rather eat slug stew," he said. And then he strode outside, to wait in the misty drizzle.

The slattern howled an obscene word after him and followed that up with a shrill invective concerning fancy gents who don't know a real woman when they see one.

Jonas bore the tirade with uncharacteristic patience. There was only one woman he wanted; and she was "real," all right—real as the rain that beaded in his hair and crept down his neck to saturate his collar.

McKay and his sidekick returned with a hired horse and buggy in record time and were plainly delighted when Jonas freed them to spend the evening as they saw fit. They half-killed each other in their eagerness to get inside that stinking saloon.

As Jonas got into the buggy and took up the reins, he smiled. Perhaps the prostitute would ply her trade this evening after all.

Cedar Street was easy to find, and so was the Cunningham house. It was marked by a prominent sign, dangling from one limb of a blossoming cherry tree.

Jonas drew the buggy to a halt behind a carriage as impressive as the one he'd left behind in Providence. The presence of such a vehicle disturbed him, though he couldn't have said why; but the sensation was only momentary, and he had forgotten it by the time he'd abandoned his horse and buggy and sprinted up the pine-board walk.

He turned the bell knob briskly, and clasped his hands behind his back, wondering how he would bear even the briefest delay.

But the luck of the day was holding. When the door opened, Rachel herself was standing there, staring at him with puffy, red-rimmed eyes.

Jonas's hands ached for the feel of her, but he knew better than to betray the true depths of his passion before the time came. His voice was deceptively light and more than a little mischievous. "Hello, Urchin. The picnic was marvelous; you should have stayed."

Rachel's throat worked for a moment, and beguiling shame darkened her lavender eyes, deepening the worrisome shadows beneath them. Then, unbelievably, she cried out softly and flung her arms around Jonas's neck.

If there had ever been any doubt that she held him captive, it was dispelled in that instant. Jonas's emotions churned within him as he drew her close and held her.

Presently, she fell away and drew Jonas into the house with both hands. Her splendid chin quivered in the half-light of the hallway. "Oh, Jonas," she whispered, "Will you forgive me for abandoning you like that? It was thoughtless. . . ."

Jonas cupped her chin in a hand he hoped was more steady than his voice. "Forgiven. And why have you been crying?"

The answer came in a surprising rush of soft words and sniffles. She had found a job, only to lose it again the same day. She despaired of ever finding her father, and she wasn't sure she should have come to Seattle at all.

Jonas listened, his eyes gentle on her wan face, but some-

147

thing inside him seethed all the while. At the core of her misery was Griffin Fletcher; she bore the mark of him on her face and along every enchanting curve of her body.

If Griffin hadn't possessed her, it wasn't because she hadn't wanted him.

Purposely, Jonas sustained the light, undemanding tone he sensed was vital. "Wash your face, Urchin, and change your dress. We'll have supper at the Seattle Hotel and make plans for tomorrow."

The uncertainty in her face was maddening. "Hotel?"

Deliberately, Jonas smiled. "In the *restaurant,* Urchin—not the bridal suite."

A smile flashed in her eyes and brought the faintest color to her too-pale cheeks. "I'll be ready in a few minutes. In the meantime, please come in and meet Miss Cunningham and Captain Frazier."

Captain Frazier? The name struck Jonas with a spinning, gut-jarring impact, thrusting all thoughts of Griffin Fletcher from his mind. *Good God,* he thought, his smile aching on his face. *It can't be.*

But it was. Inside Miss Cunningham's prim parlor, his massive frame at ease before a crackling fire, was Douglas Frazier himself. It was all Jonas could do to keep from thrusting Rachel behind him, ordering her to run.

"Douglas," he said instead, with a cordial nod.

The sea blue eyes flashed with recognition, and the parody of a smile played beneath the familiar red-gold mustache. "Jonas," the captain marveled, rising from the flimsy chair beside the fireplace.

Rachel dispensed with an obviously unnecessary introduction and looked puzzled. "You know each other?"

"Oh, indeed," smiled the captain.

Jonas gave her a slight push, rasping, "Change—we'll be late."

For once, Rachel obeyed, leaving Douglas Frazier and Jonas Wilkes to square off in a primitive, wordless confrontation.

Jonas swallowed the bile rising in his throat and let the rythmic *tick-tock* of the clock on the mantle lead him through the silence.

Finally Frazier spoke. "So you're the unfeeling bastard who broke that young girl's heart," he said affably enough.

The words compounded Jonas's suspicions about Rachel

148

and Griffin, but he was careful not to let the inevitable reaction show. "She's mine, Frazier. I plan to marry her."

Frazier raised an auburn eyebrow. "Do you?" he asked, skeptically. "That surprises me, Jonas, knowing your illustrious history as I do."

Jonas closed his eyes. Why hadn't he seen the *China Drifter* riding at anchor on the bay, among the other ships? He swallowed again and met Frazier's even gaze. "And knowing yours, Douglas, I'm warning you—don't get any ideas."

Frazier laughed, though there was a certain wariness in his bearing. "She would bring double the usual price," he said.

Jonas's voice was a harsh, rasping rumble. "How much?"

The captain appeared to deliberate. "Well, that depends, since it's you I'm dealing with."

"On what?"

"On whether or not she's a virgin. My people will beat any offer you make if she is."

Jonas shivered inwardly, but he knew that he appeared as calm and detached as Frazier. At least, he hoped he did. The lie—and he prayed it *was* a lie—came easily to his lips. "Better luck next time, Frazier. She's not as innocent as she looks."

Frazier was watching him closely. "I don't believe you, Wilkes. In any case, it's something my people can prove or disprove easily enough."

Jonas felt sick. *"How much?"* he repeated.

The captain named a staggering sum.

"You'll have my draft in the morning," replied Jonas, just as Rachel swept into the room like a fresh breeze. "Is it a bargain?"

Frazier smiled fondly. "It's a bargain."

Jonas grasped Rachel's arm and hustled her out of that house at such a brisk pace that she stumbled beside him, barely able to keep pace.

"What on earth did you buy from Captain Frazier?" she asked, wide-eyed, as Jonas helped her into his waiting buggy and then climbed in beside her to take the reins.

His smile felt as though it had been tacked to his face. "Something I want very much. Now—what would you like for dinner?"

In spite of the dismal events of the day and the curious sensation that she was coming down with something dreadful,

149

Rachel had a fine time that evening. She hardly touched the magnificent dinner of fresh cod, green peas, and rice that Jonas bought for her, but she did enjoy the new experience of watching a traveling theater troupe grope through a production of *Hamlet* at the Frye Opera House.

Once or twice during the performance, Rachel felt Jonas's eyes touch her and turned to look at him. It was very dark, and his expression was unreadable, though the angle of his head confirmed that he was, indeed, watching her.

When the play had ended, and gaslights flared on the walls of the theater, his golden eyes were carefully averted. He ushered her almost roughly up the center aisle and through the plush lobby, where other weekday theatergoers were expounding on the quality of the performance just past.

Outside, the storm was waning, riding away on a westbound wind. Reaching the buggy, Jonas grasped Rachel by the waist and hoisted her unceremoniously into the seat. Then, glowering up at her, his hands on his hips, his tawny hair glistening with rain, he said, "You're staying at my hotel tonight."

Rachel's heart scrambled into her throat. "What?"

Jonas was striding around to the other side of the buggy, climbing up beside her, bringing the reins down on the horse's back with a decided *thwack*. "You heard me," he said.

Rachel stiffened, folding her arms under the navy blue cloak. She had an unreal feeling, and her chest ached. "Jonas Wilkes, don't you *dare* take me to that hotel."

His face was grim and set in the faint glow of the kerosene street lamps lining the street. Too soon, they came to a stop in front of a plain, two-story board structure.

"I'll scream," Rachel threatened.

Jonas's jaw tightened as he secured the brake lever. "You do, Rachel McKinnon, and I'll turn you over my knee, right here on this street!"

Chapter Eighteen

Rachel knew that Jonas meant exactly what he said, but she wasn't about to follow him meekly into that hotel, like some mindless tart. She raised her hand to slap his face, and he caught her wrist in a grip that was torturously familiar. *Griffin,* grieved the part of her that had reveled in the gentle, demanding restraint of his hands, taken joy in the total vulnerability of her naked breasts—

What was she thinking about that for? She blushed, fearing that Jonas would read the memory in her eyes.

It almost seemed that he had. "You are not going back to that house," he informed her furiously. "Not now, or ever. I'll get your things tomorrow."

Rachel stared at him, stunned. Only minutes before, she had actually believed he was her friend. "You are insane!" she hissed finally.

He released her wrist with an abrupt motion of his hand, his golden eyes glittering. "Until the *China Drifter* sets sail, Rachel, I'm not letting you out of my sight. Now, you might as well accept that, because there is nothing you can do about it."

"I can *still* scream!" Rachel reminded him in a hoarse undertone. The pain in her lungs was worse, her head felt thick, and it was getting harder and harder to care about anything except going to sleep.

Jonas sighed in exasperation. "Screaming women are no novelty this close to the Skid Road, Rachel. Now, are you coming in with me or not?"

"I hardly think so."

His shoulders moved in an irritating, easy shrug. "Fine. Perhaps I should let Frazier sell you to one of his rich, foreign friends after all."

Rachel's mouth fell open; cold horror jiggled in the pit of her stomach, rose to fill her raw throat. She was incapable of speech.

But Jonas went on with grim matter-of-factness. "You could

end up in a Chinese court, as a concubine. If that doesn't suit you, there are always remote *ranchos* in Mexico, Brazil, Argentina. . . ."

Inwardly Rachel reeled. Captain Frazier's compliments, so pleasing when they were delivered, had an ominous ring now. *Many wealthy men would be happy to take you as a bride, Rachel, and I could arrange for you to meet several.*

But she was being silly, she decided. Surely Douglas could never do anything like that. Rachel folded her hands in her lap, and they felt cold, even cradled in the soft warmth of her cloak. "I'm not sure your motives are any purer, Jonas Wilkes," she said.

Suddenly, unexpectedly, Jonas laughed. The hard, determined set of his face softened a little. "Urchin, there is nothing I would rather do, to be perfectly honest, than carry you up to my room and ravage you shamelessly." He looked away for a moment, then back again. Some anguished emotion flickered briefly behind the laughter in his eyes. "When I take you, Rachel—and I *will* take you—you will be ready."

Rachel was scandalized by the bluntness of his declaration. "You are unspeakable!"

He laughed again and jumped out of the buggy. In a moment, he was standing on her side of the vehicle, looking up at her. "Come along, Rachel, my dear," he said, companionably.

Rachel trembled, fixed her eyes on a street lamp nearby, and refused to budge. She considered shouting for help and then thought better of it. Her throat was sore, there was no breath in her lungs, and none of the men passing by looked even remotely chivalrous.

Jonas's voice was level and laced with amusement. "You have two seconds, Urchin. And remember, if you make the wrong decision, you might be sitting on pillows for a month."

She pivoted grudgingly on the buggy's seat. "Do you promise not to—not to—"

Jonas raised one hand in a solemn vow. "I promise, Urchin."

Rash as it seemed, Rachel believed him. "All right, then," she said.

Jonas encircled her waist with his hands and lifted her down. She was trembling now, with fright and frustration and the nip of the chill night wind.

Jonas wrapped a proprietary, protective arm around her waist and steered her calmly into the austere lobby of the hotel.

The one room clerk in evidence, a thin, studious-looking young man, greeted Jonas with an almost obsequious grin. "Mr. Wilkes!"

Rachel felt as though she'd suddenly become invisible. The clerk didn't seem to see her at all.

Jonas smiled winningly. "Good evening, Herbert. How are things at the university?"

Herbert beamed. "Splendid, sir. Just splendid."

"Good. I trust that my room is available?"

"Always, Mr. Wilkes," replied the clerk, extending a brass key.

"Good," Jonas repeated. And then he strode, dragging Rachel with him, across the small, neatly kept lobby and up a flight of steep wooden stairs.

"Why would they keep a room open just for you?" Rachel asked, feeling a great many misgivings as Jonas unlocked a sturdy-looking door and pushed it inward.

He smiled. "That's simple, Urchin. I own it."

"The room?"

"The hotel."

Rachel blushed. Believing Jonas outside, in a buggy, was different from believing him at the doorway of his room. Why hadn't she tried to scream, or run away?

"Why are you doing this? Were you only friendly to me so that you could lure me here?"

Jonas silenced her by laying an index finger on her lips. "Hush. I brought you here because I don't want you sailing off as an unwilling passenger on the *Drifter*. I have no intention of making love to you—not now, at least."

Rachel was very tired, and she was sick. Could she possibly have been so wrong about Captain Frazier? He'd seemed like such a gentleman.

And what of Jonas Wilkes? Was he the rascal Molly and Griffin thought he was—or was he a rescuer?

Ruefully, Rachel faced the distinct possibility that he was both.

The interior of the room was alarmingly dark until Jonas struck a match and lit a series of kerosene lamps. The glow of soft, almost fluid light enabled Rachel to release her hold on the woodwork framing the doorway and step inside.

It was not an elegant room; like the lobby, it was so simply furnished that it seemed almost Spartan. There was a closet— its door was slightly ajar, and Rachel could see the sleeves of coats and shirts, the legs of trousers, and part of a leather valise. In one corner, under the windows, sat a desk; in another, a little round table flanked by straight-backed chairs.

The bed was gigantic, however, and its heavy, intricately carved headboard was made of some dark, oppressive wood. Rachel shifted her gaze from it, only to catch Jonas staring at her.

He had shed his rain-dampened coat and stood beside a polished bureau, a decanter of some amber liquor in one hand, a glass in the other.

"You are so incredibly beautiful," he said.

Involuntarily Rachel's eyes slid back to the bed. "Please, Jonas—take me back to Miss Cunningham's now—tonight."

"No."

"If you don't, I'm going to make so much noise that your reputation will be ruined forever."

Jonas laughed softly and raised the glass in some sort of mocking salute. "Be my guest. My reputation is already such that you could only enhance it."

Rachel's head began to ache, and she was limp with exhaustion. A soft, broken sob of frustration slipped past her lips to echo in the shadowy room. Feeling wretched, she made her way to the bed and sat down heavily on its edge.

She could not see Jonas, but she heard the rattle of glass against glass, and then the sound of his boot heels clicking on the bare floor.

When she looked up through a pounding haze of tears, she saw that he was standing before her, extending a crystal tumbler.

"This will help you sleep," he said, his voice reassuringly gentle.

Trembling, Rachel took the glass. "You promised—"

He was squatting before her now, looking up into her face. "I know, Sweetheart," he said. "And I'll keep my promise. You take the bed, and I'll sleep on the floor."

The smooth, measured meter of Jonas's words had a trance-like effect on Rachel, and she drank the mellow, warming contents of the glass. She remembered nothing after that.

Griffin stirred and immediately a jagged, explosive pain shot through his rib cage and into his groin. His stomach convulsed in rebellion.

He opened his eyes, endured the spinning dizziness that

resulted, and slowly took a mental inventory of his anatomy. Cracked ribs—four, he thought—and a possible rupture. Other than that, he was all right.

"Griffin?"

Field was somewhere just behind him, by the sound of his voice. "Damn it, come around here where I can see you."

His friend's face loomed over him suddenly, looking strained and incredibly weary. "How do you feel?"

"Like hell," replied Griffin, in a gruff whisper. "Get me a syringe from the cabinet, and some morphine."

Field looked annoyingly reluctant. "Do you think that's wise, Griffin? I mean, maybe you shouldn't—"

Griffin swore. "Damn you, Field. I'm the doctor here—remember?"

Still, Field hesitated. "Will it stop the pain?"

Griffin laughed, and it hurt. Badly. "No, it won't 'stop the pain.' It'll just make me so happy that I don't give a damn."

Field brought the requested materials from the supply cabinet, but he looked scared. "Now what?"

"Now you fill the damned thing and inject the stuff into my arm."

Field paled, staring down at the syringe and vial lying in his right palm.

Suddenly, bless her, Molly was there, her hair tangled, her eyes puffed with the lack of sleep. "Give me those!" she snapped impatiently. Field obeyed with relief.

Griffin grinned as he watched Molly fill the syringe and raise it to the dim, struggling light of dawn. She pumped it once, to force out any air bubbles that might be lingering inside, swabbed the inside of his forearm with alcohol, and injected the medicine.

Minutes later, the drug began to take effect. The shattering pain ebbed to a quiet, pulsating feeling.

But there was something wrong; Griffin had an unpleasant sensation of being outside himself, and his control, ever rigid, was slipping. He had never used morphine before, and as its full power came sweeping down on him, he vowed that he would never use it again. Walls were beginning to crumble inside him—necessary walls. God knew what he might say or do in the next few hours.

For a time, he slept, or thought he did. One moment, he was lying on his study sofa, the next, he was standing high on the mountain, in the woods, watching that massive tree fall and crush his father. Athena was beside him; then her features dissolved and reassembled themselves in Rachel's image.

Screams went through Griffin's frame like echoes in a deep cave. He wondered if they were staying inside him, where they belonged.

Rachel awakened, naked and alarmed, in the gigantic bed. To her tremendous relief, Jonas was not sleeping beside her, but on the floor as he'd promised.

Thoughts of escape played in her mind; but even as she reviewed them fuzzily, Rachel knew the task was impossible. Rolled up in a chenille bedspread, Jonas lay directly in front of the door. Whether he was keeping her in or Captain Frazier out was anybody's guess.

A window was open, letting in a stream of sunny, rain-washed air, but Rachel had no intention of dropping two stories to the alley below.

It was odd, she thought, how languid and achy she felt. How resigned. She pulled the bedclothes up under her chin and turned onto her side.

And it was then that Rachel felt the tearing pain in the lower part of her right lung. With agonizing slowness, she rolled back again, to lie flat, but the wrenching ache did not abate.

The room was too hot and then, almost immediately, too cold. She sneezed, and the involuntary motion hurt so badly that she groaned.

Jonas was standing beside the bed, shirtless and sleep-rumpled and worried. His voice came from too near, and then too far away. "Rachel . . . what is it . . . rest . . . I'll find a doctor . . . just rest."

There was darkness and then light, heat and then cold, a moment and then eternity. It was a world of opposites.

Rachel heard Jonas's voice again and one that she didn't recognize.

"The rain . . ." that strange voice droned. "State of collapse . . . too much strain . . . pleurisy . . ."

It was dark. She was slipping down a smooth, icy hillside. Only the knowledge that eternity yawned beneath made Rachel catch hold and cling to the face of the precipice with the last shreds of her strength.

Jonas was frantic. After the doctor had gone, he paced the small expanse of the hotel room, torn. Rachel's breathing was a soul-numbing rasp, and her face and hands were hot to the touch. She could die.

What if he left her alone, just long enough to take the bank draft to Frazier, and she died?

Sick fear washed over Jonas at the thought, and he paused in the center of the floor, fighting it down. He had to go; whatever happened, he had to go to Frazier and settle the debt. If he didn't, Rachel's life wouldn't be worth living if she did survive.

Jonas opened the door leading into the hallway and bellowed, "Herbert!"

In response, footsteps clattered on the stairs, but the form that burst into the hallway was not that of the night clerk. Instead, a plump, weary-looking woman appeared, her gray hair falling in wisps about her face. "My Herbert's at college in the mornings, Mr. Wilkes!" she prattled.

Jonas closed his eyes just long enough to yearn for Mrs. Hammond's nerveless, comforting presence. Then he handed the room key to the woman and barked, "Stay in this room until I get back. Lock the door, and don't let anyone in. Do you understand? *No one.*"

Herbert's mother looked distraught. "But how will I know it's you that's back?" she whined.

Jonas was already striding past her, toward the landing and the stairway. "There's another key downstairs—I'll use that."

The lobby was empty. Jonas raced through it and out into the warmth of a summer day. He glanced once in the direction of the bay and was almost blinded by the silver dazzle of the sunlight dancing on the sapphire water.

In the august chambers of his bank, Jonas snapped an order for a draft to be drawn. The amount so staggered the timorous clerk that confusion reigned.

Jonas shouted until the other patrons fled and then he shouted until the president of the bank came out of his cubicle to attend to the matter himself. The delay was intolerable.

Finally, when Jonas could bear the endless checking and rechecking, tallying and subtracting no longer, he barked, "Have it ready in five minutes!" and ran outside.

The telegraph office was next door, and Jonas debated for only a moment before he went inside and dictated two messages, both destined for Providence.

The first was very brief.

The second, which cost Jonas a great price, pridewise, was only slightly longer.

GRIFFIN. CHINA DRIFTER IN PORT. HURRY. J.W.

The draft was ready when Jonas stormed back into the bank. He snatched it from the banker's hands and darted out again.

Jonas was winded now; he forced himself to stand still and consider the fact that he had forgotten to reclaim the horse and buggy from the livery stable. But there were horses tethered all along the street, and Jonas helped himself to a pinto gelding. Ignoring the outraged shouts of its owner, he booted the stunned animal into a dead run.

Reaching Miss Cunningham's sturdy house, minutes later, he tied the stolen horse to the picket fence, vaulted onto the walk, and ran to the door. Breathless, Jonas wrenched at the bell knob.

The door opened almost immediately, and Captain Frazier filled the chasm, looking almost like a gentleman with his frock coat and gracious smile.

Bracing himself with one arm on the doorjamb, Jonas ferreted the draft from his coat pocket with his free hand and held it out. "Your word?" The question was a ragged, windless whisper.

Frazier took the draft and examined it with quick, eager eyes. "My word," he agreed, after a long time.

Jonas whirled, staggered back down the pine-board walk, and dragged himself up into the saddle.

The ride back down the hill seemed interminable, and Jonas had time enough to regret a great many things. He could have been kinder to Rachel the night before, instead of baiting her as he had, instead of letting her wonder whether or not he would take advantage of her in spite of his promise. And he could have chosen a better time to beat the hell out of Griffin Fletcher, too.

Jonas skirted a trolley car, and the bell spooked the borrowed gelding, making it rear. He brought the animal under control easily, however, and prodded it into a run again. Slow—even at its top speed, the horse was slow. *So next time steal a racehorse,* he chided himself.

A block from the hotel Jonas owned, he nearly collided with a buckboard. Minutes later, he abandoned the lathered horse where he'd found it in the first place and ran into his building.

Jonas was halfway up the hotel staircase when the sound of the woman's frantic wails reached him. For a moment, panic fused him to the wall of the stairwell, and a wordless litany of rage and fear hummed in his mind.

He wrenched himself free from the wall, bounded up to the landing and into the corridor.

The door of his room was wide open, and the cries of Herbert's mother were louder now.

Dear God, he prayed. *Don't let her be dead. Please, don't let her be dead.*

In the doorway, Jonas froze. The bed was empty.

"Where is she?" Jonas demanded, never knowing whether the question was screamed or whispered.

The blubbering woman raised herself slowly from the floor of Jonas's room. There was a gash in her forehead, and the sleeve of her shabby calico dress was torn to reveal a plump shoulder.

It took all of Jonas's forebearance to keep from wrenching her the rest of the way to her feet and then beating her back to the floor again. He closed his eyes, sank against the doorframe, and hissed, "What happened?"

Chapter Nineteen

It was so hot. So unbearably hot.

Rachel opened her eyes. A Chinese woman, eyes downcast, swayed in the void above her. A wooden spoon nudged gently at her lips.

"Drink," urged the woman.

Dear God, it was true—everthing Jonas had said was true, Rachel thought wildly. *Douglas has brought me to China!* She groaned, turning her head away from the figure sitting nearby.

"Please drink," pleaded the woman. "Make strong."

Rachel did not want to be strong. She wanted to die.

But the woman was quietly insistent. "Drink."

159

Rachel drank, tasted the unfamiliar, herb-laced broth on her tongue. How could she be in China? The journey took a long time, even on the fastest ship, and it seemed only last night that Jonas had bought her dinner and taken her to see a play—and forced her to spend the night in his hotel room.

But she had been very ill. Perhaps the sea voyage had taken place while she was fighting that strange battle on the dark cliffs of her spirit. Perhaps she had been asleep for months! Vaguely, she remembered a sense of motion.

No, that had been a clattering, jolting sort of movement. Ships glided smoothly over the water, unless they encountered rough seas.

She accepted more of the broth. "Where am I?"

"Seattle," came the toneless reply.

Seattle. If Rachel had had the strength, she would have given a shout of joy. As a healing sleep swept up to enclose her, she submitted to it, allowed it to carry her. This time, there would be no battle in the darkness.

Molly Brady stood still in the cool sanctuary of the general store, her shopping basket over one arm, her eyes bright with an intuitive, mysterious fear as they examined the folded message.

Throat dry, she opened the telegram and boldly read it, even though it was addressed to Dr. Fletcher.

GRIFFIN. CHINA DRIFTER IN PORT. HURRY. J.W.

Molly stiffened. J.W. Jonas Wilkes, of course. The gall of that man, summoning Griffin when no one knew better than he did how difficult—even dangerous—it would be for him to travel now.

Outside the store, in the morning sunlight, Molly reread the message, puzzling. Why should the presence of any particular ship interest Griffin?

Overhead, in the azure sky, gulls shrieked their constant, raucous complaint. But Molly ignored them, crossing the road slowly, wondering.

The *China Drifter*. Now, why did that name prickle the lining of her stomach the way it did?

She wandered through Tent Town, only half-hearing the friendly greetings of the women who were taking advantage of the warm weather to wash out clothes and blankets. Molly

160

smiled distractedly, and uttered a directionless "good morning" at suitable intervals. She'd lived in Tent Town herself once, and she didn't want the others thinking she considered herself above them because she worked for the doctor now.

In the woods that separated Tent Town from the Fletcher house, Molly stopped along the path and thought hard.

Griffin's main source of income came from the interests he held in half a dozen sailing ships. Heaven knew, he would have starved on what he earned as a doctor.

Molly sighed. Was the *China Drifter* one of those ships? If it was, why would Jonas Wilkes, of all people, trouble to wire Griffin that it was in port? Surely, vessels that he owned a share in came and went all the time, bringing various cargoes to Seattle and leaving with the inevitable lumber.

Molly's stomach clenched. It was a trap. Jonas was trying to lure Griffin to Seattle, where all manner of fatal accidents could befall him.

A lulling, sea-scented breeze whispered in the treetops, and Molly picked idly at the peeling bark of a madrona. Griffin was recovering now—the frightening effects of the morphine had passed—but it was still difficult and painful for him to move about. If something in this strange message drew him out of his bed and off on some wild trip to Seattle, the results could be disastrous.

Molly longed to crumple the offending wire into a ball and toss it into the woods, where it would lie forgotten until it became a part of the mossy ground, but she knew that she couldn't. There was the small matter of integrity, and Molly had more of that than she needed.

Squaring her shoulders, she lifted her skirts with one hand and marched home.

Griffin's reaction to the telegram was just what she had feared it would be. He paled when he read it, and a muscle flexed taut in his jaw. *"Frazier,"* he whispered, and his tone gave the name an ugly sound.

Molly stood by, wringing her hands, as Griffin crushed the paper and tossed it furiously against a wall. "Griffin, it's a trap of some sort—don't you see that it's a trap?"

But Griffin's right hand was white with force as he grasped the quilt that covered him. "Get out of here, Molly, unless you want to watch me dress."

Molly turned and fled the room, though she stood by in the hallway. The sound of Griffin's struggle was almost unbearable;

there were muffled groans and curses as he opened bureau drawers and pillaged through them for his clothes.

"Molly!" he demanded, after a few minutes.

Molly hurried back into the room to find her employer braced, white with pain, against the edge of the bureau. He had managed, somehow, to get into his trousers and his boots, but his shirt was hanging open, revealing the tight linen binding holding his ribs in place.

"Button this damned shirt!" he snapped, releasing his grip on the bureau to turn toward her.

Molly knew better than to reveal the pity she felt; she cloaked it in honest disapproval and unshakable reason. Closing the buttons with quick, efficient hands, she muttered, "For heaven's sake, Griffin, how do you expect to make such a journey? You can't even button your own shirt! There won't be a steamer leaving for hours, and you certainly can't ride a horse!"

The dark eyes were flashing when Molly dared to meet them. "Jonas had a good reason for sending that wire, Molly. If it's what I think it is, I have to go."

"Since when are you in league with Jonas Wilkes?"

"Since the *China Drifter* dropped anchor in Seattle," snapped Griffin, flinging himself in the direction of the bedroom doorway and groping along the corridor to the top of the stairs.

Molly took care not to reveal that she was braced to grasp Griffin should he fall. "What could be so important that you would take a chance like this?"

"Rachel," he said. And then he was at the bottom of the staircase, gripping the newel post for support. There was no color at all in his face, and Molly could see the effort he was expending just to stand.

"Will you listen to reason!" she shouted, in her fear and her affection. "This could kill you!"

The look in his eyes was terrible and desolate and absolutely unyielding. "I would rather be dead," he rasped, "than see Douglas Frazier hand-deliver Rachel to one of the slugs he does business with!"

Molly's mouth fell open, but words would not pass her throat.

Griffin was alternately thrusting and dragging himself through the house, toward the kitchen.

There, Molly managed a choked, "He sells *people?*"

"Specifically, women," Griffin replied, as he plundered a

162

kitchen drawer for the supply of cash he kept there. "Nobody has managed to prove it yet, but young ladies have a way of disappearing suddenly when Frazier is around. He's clever—he probably charms them into leaving."

"And then?"

Griffin's eyes were fierce as he stuffed currency into the pocket of his trousers. "And then they find themselves the personal property of some rich old lecher in Santiago or Hong Kong or Mexico City."

Molly felt sick. She touched Griffin's sleeve gently as he opened the back door. "Godspeed, Griffin Fletcher," she whispered.

He kissed her forehead lightly, squeezed her shoulders once in a kind of stricken reassurance, and turned to make his way down the steps and stumble toward the barn.

Molly was watching from the window when he emerged, seconds later, with Billy and the horse, Tempest. Together, exchanging words she could not hear, Billy and Griffin hitched the horse to the buggy.

Molly closed her eyes, felt warm tears gather in her lashes. The prayer shining in her heart was a fervent one.

"What happened?" Jonas repeated, marveling at his own patience.

Herbert's mother was still whimpering, still wringing her hands. "They had the key—I thought they was you—one of them hit me—"

Breathing deeply, Jonas made himself speak in moderate tones. "How many men were there—and what did they look like?"

The woman's face was woebegone, and the cut in her forehead was bleeding slightly. "There was four of them, Mr. Wilkes—big, strapping men with sunburned faces. They came busting in here and took the girl, and I said to myself, 'Marlys, there ain't nothing you can do except scream.' So I screamed, and one of them came back and hit me!"

Rage pounded in Jonas's veins and burned in his throat. He'd been had—Frazier had his fee, and he had Rachel, too. By now, he was probably back on board the *Drifter*, laughing his ass off.

And Rachel was sick—so very sick.

Jonas couldn't bear to face the possibilities; if he did, he would slip into stark, useless panic. No, he had to *think*.

163

He turned and glared at the door opposite his own. The windows of that room overlooked the street and much of the bay.

He prowled across the hall, almost as though he was stalking something, and tried the door. It was locked.

Jonas retreated a step, raised his left boot, and kicked. The lock gave way with a thundering crash and the door whined on its hinges as it swung open.

At the window, he wrenched the curtains apart and scanned the still, glistening waters of the harbor. Incredibly, the *China Drifter* was at anchor, her white sails limp in the warm, motionless air.

A harsh, jubilant laugh escaped Jonas's taut throat; *she was becalmed!*

But there were tugs to be hired, he reminded himself. The *Drifter* could be drawn out of the bay, into the Strait of Juan de Fuca. Beyond that lay the open sea, where it would probably be an easy matter to catch the wind. Once Frazier reached the coastline, there would be no hope of catching him.

Calmly Jonas left the hotel and walked toward the Skid Road.

Grim with pain, and sometimes only half-conscious, Griffin raced overland, to Kingston. There, he abandoned his horse and buggy and coerced the skipper of a small salmon boat to take him south, to Seattle.

The cost of his passage was high, and he didn't know which smelled worse—the residue of thousands of fish or the skipper himself.

None of it mattered. Griffin stood at a railing near the bow, willing the pain into submission, feeling infinite gratitude for the laboring chortles of the craft's steam engine.

It was dark when the salmon boat groaned into Elliott Bay, but light from the kerosene street lamps along Front Street lay in golden splotches on the water. Peering into the gloom, Griffin thought he made out the sleek, familiar form of the *Merrimaker,* a craft in which he owned a major share.

"Please," he said, in a half-whisper, addressing himself to whatever superior forces might be listening. Then, as the salmon boat pulled alongside a wharf, Griffin bid the skipper a grim good-bye and vaulted over the side onto the shifting, creaking dock.

As his feet made contact with the hard surface of the wharf, jarring pain shot through his testicles and exploded in his rib cage. Griffin staggered, caught himself, and started toward the shoreline.

Behind him, the salmon boat was already retreating back into the bay.

To keep his mind off the searing pain, Griffin concentrated on the click of his boot heels, the sound of the tide slapping at the pilings beneath the wharf, the familiar scents of pitch and sawdust and kerosene.

Reaching the wooden walk that edged the wharfs, Griffin turned toward the lights and spirited debauchery of the Skid Road. The shrill laughter of a prostitute echoed over the dark water and the puddles of liquid light.

He thought of the soft, warm way Rachel laughed and walked faster.

The Chinese woman was trying to feed her again; Rachel could feel the spoon prodding at her mouth. She wanted so to sleep!

A man spoke sharply, in a rapid dialect, and Rachel opened her eyes just as he lifted her head from the pillow. At the sight of his face, her mouth fell open, and the woman shrewdly grasped the opportunity to thrust the spoon in.

Rachel nearly choked on the broth, then muttered, "Chang?"

The Tent Town cook did not look at her; instead, he scolded the woman sitting on the other side of Rachel's cot. The poor creature trembled visibly, lowered her eyes, and then padded away, disappearing through a curtain of clattering beads.

Chang sighed, and his eyes were fixed on some point just above Rachel's head. "Missy in bad trouble," he said.

Even though Rachel was gaining strength moment by moment, she was still very weak. "Chang, you must help me. If you'll just find Mr. Wilkes—"

Chang's thin face hardened. "Not find Wilkes!" he spat. "He tell Chang go, not come back!"

Tears of hopelessness gathered in Rachel's eyes. "It was my fault that you lost your job, wasn't it? It was because you and I had that argument in the dining tent."

The Chinaman seemed surprised by her words, but he made no response.

Rachel groped for his arm, found it. "Oh, Chang, I beg

165

you—don't let Captain Frazier sell me—please. I'll be a stranger and a slave!"

Chang shrugged, but there was a glimmer of sadness in his eyes, a sadness that said he understood what it was to be a stranger and a slave all too well. "If Chang tell, Captain beat—maybe kill."

"No! Mr. Wilkes will protect you—and your wife! I know he will!"

The Chinaman deliberated. After a torturously long time, he asked, "Missy is Wilkes's woman?"

A lump gathered in Rachel's throat, but it did not block the desperate lie. "Yes."

Again Chang thought. He was still thinking when Rachel slipped back into the dark velvet folds of sleep.

At the base of the Skid Road, Griffin paused. Jonas was here somewhere, he was certain of that. But where? It would take all night to search every saloon, and Griffin didn't have a night to spare.

He took a cheroot and a wooden match from the inside pocket of his coat, struck the match on the sole of his right boot, and drew deeply of the smoke.

A prostitute sidled past, looked back, and paused. "Hello, Handsome," she drawled, her face in shadows. "You look sorta lonely."

Griffin was careful not to let the light of the street lamp reveal his battered face; it wouldn't do to scare the poor girl away before he found out what he wanted to know. "I'm here on business," he said, in a toneless voice.

"Well, so am I!" giggled the girl. "What can Chloe do for you, Sugar?"

Griffin pried a bill from his trouser pocket and, without bothering to look at it, held it out. "I've got some questions for you, Chloe. But tonight anyway, that's all."

The faceless Chloe snatched the bill from his fingers. "Chloe does like easy money, Handsome. Ask away."

"Do you know if the *China Drifter* is still in port?"

Again, Chloe giggled. It was a grating, affected sound, underlaid with a singular sort of misery. "She's right on the bay, Honey. I'll hate to see her sail, too; there's some big spenders on that crew."

"I imagine there are," Griffin remarked evenly. "I have another question; do you know a man named Jonas Wilkes?"

166

"Land sakes, Sweetness, everybody on the Road knows Jonas Wilkes."

"Have you seen him tonight?"

"He's in the Shanghai, buying whiskey for any swabbie who'll sit down and talk."

"Thanks," Griffin said, as he turned and walked away, toward the Shanghai Card Palace and Saloon.

Chloe's voice rang, petulant, through the night. "Hey, Sweetness, no need to rush away—"

"Another time," Griffin called back, over his shoulder.

Five minutes later, he found Jonas just where Chloe said he would—trying to get what looked like a whole damned navy roaring drunk.

At the sight of Griffin, he shot to his feet. There was a gruesome strain in his face, in the set of his shoulders, in the nervous gestures of his hands. "It's about time you got here!" he shouted.

Griffin sighed. "Where can we talk?"

Jonas dropped a sizable bill on the saloon table and left his newfound friends to drink on in prosperity. "Outside. Shit, you look bad."

Griffin grinned venomously. "Yeah. I got run over by a train."

With elaborate good manners, Jonas held open one swinging door to let Griffin pass. "Damn shame, Griff. You're normally so good-looking—or at least presentable."

Griffin pushed open the other door, and held it stubbornly. "After you, Jonas. I'm superstitious."

"Superstitious?" frowned Jonas.

Griffin nodded. "It's usually bad luck to turn my back on you."

Jonas's laugh was raw and guttural. "So it is," he said. "So it is." And then he walked out of the saloon into the starry warmth of the night, his back to his cousin.

Chapter Twenty

They walked along the waterfront, neither one speaking until the Skid Road was far behind them.

"He's got her, Griffin," Jonas said finally, in a voice that held an eerie, plaintive note. "Frazier has Rachel."

Griffin was amazed at the calmness he felt. Even the ceaseless pain in his rib cage and groin was easing, as though he had somehow shifted it to another level of his mind, to deal with later.

"Did you go to the police?"

Jonas was leaning against a wooden railing now, glaring out at the ghostly shadows of ships anchored in the bay. "Of course I did," he snapped.

"And?"

"And they boarded the *Drifter*. Rachel wasn't there."

Griffin muttered a curse. "Jonas, are you sure Frazier has her? How do you know she didn't leave on her own?"

There was a stiff silence before Jonas explained. When he did, it was all Griffin could do to keep from closing his hands around his throat and squeezing the life out of him. "I came to town to find Rachel. She was staying at a boardinghouse on Cedar, and who do you think she introduces me to? Her fellow tenant—Captain Frazier. I knew what he had in mind right away, and when I offered him a price, he took it. Like an idiot, I kept Rachel in my hotel room all night—I should have known what would happen."

Griffin's mouth was dry, and the muscles in his hands ached with restraint. "What happened?"

"I didn't make love to her, if that's what you're asking. But in the morning, while I was paying Frazier, his men broke into my room and took her. God, Griffin, if only I'd taken her back to Providence—"

"Well, you didn't."

In a spasm of furious despair, Jonas clenched his fists and

168

slammed them down, hard, on the wooden railing separating the walkway from the bay. "Griffin—that isn't all."

Griffin sighed, bracing himself. "Oh, good."

"S-She's sick. I guess it was the rain—or everything she's been through—I don't know. I found a doctor and he said she had pleurisy. Like I said, when I got back, she was gone."

"You left her alone?" The words were only whispered.

Jonas shook his head. "Of course not. I found a woman to stay with her while I was gone. To say the least, Frazier's thugs didn't have any trouble at all getting past her. Griffin, what are we going to do?"

Griffin took a few moments to sort his tangled thoughts and feelings. It all distilled down to one grim fact: if they didn't find Rachel before Frazier made his move, whatever it was, her life wouldn't be worth living even if she did survive the pleurisy.

"Get some men together, Jonas, and make sure nobody gets on or off the *Drifter* without your knowing it. If none of your—people—are around, I think I can persuade the crew of the *Merrimaker* to help."

"What about you?"

"I'm going to find out where Frazier hides his women. If she's not on board the *Drifter,* she's got to be somewhere nearby. My guess is that he'll make a run for the Pacific just before dawn."

Grimly, Jonas nodded. "He's smart, Griffin. He must know we'll be watching the *Drifter.*"

"He does."

"Do you think he might be planning to use another ship? He could sail while we were standing around watching the *Drifter.*"

Griffin shook his head. "He's a rogue, Jonas. I can't think of another captain who would be willing to drink with him, let alone cooperate in a scheme like this one. All the same, keep an eye out for anything that even looks out of line."

The two men parted then, Jonas remaining where he was, within sight of the spectral *China Drifter,* Griffin moving rapidly back toward the Skid Road.

It took more than an hour to find the captain of the *Merrimaker,* but Griffin managed it.

Standing outside a seedy crib behind the Widowmaker Saloon, he rasped, "Lindsay—get out here!"

There was a shuffling of hastily gathered clothing. "Who the hell is that?" demanded Malachi Lindsay, captain of the clipper ship, *Merrimaker.*

"It's Griffin. Will you get your ass out here?"

The rickety board door of the crib creaked open, and a muscular, middle-aged man appeared in the gap. "Shit," he said, in gruff greeting. "It is you! What the hell do you think you're doing, dragging a man from his pleasures when he's been at sea for two months?"

In the darkness behind Malachi's half-naked form, a woman whined something obscene.

"I need your help," Griffin said flatly.

Malachi cursed roundly as he wrenched on his shirt. "Damn your hide, Little Fletch, this here is the best gal in the place. Whatever it is, it had better be good."

Griffin himself was surprised by the blunt honesty of his answer. "Frazier's got the woman I love," he said, striking a match on the weathered board of the crib's outside wall and lighting another cheroot.

In the glow of the flame, Malachi's face showed every minute of the long, hard life he'd led. "Why, that seagoing skunk, I thought the sheriff of San Mateo County put him out of business two years ago when he tried to sell that San Francisco banker's daughter to a Pinkerton man!"

Griffin drew deeply on the cheroot. "You didn't see the *Drifter* riding at anchor? Your eyes are going, Malachi."

The jibe made the old seaman bristle and sputter. "I see you've still got the same smart-ass mouth you've always had! Old Mike should've tanned your hide more often and broke you of that."

"Did you see the ship or not?" snapped Griffin.

"Hell, yes, I seen the ship!" Malachi roared. "I just figured she had a new captain—high time she did. What do you say we find Frazier and slide his features around like the furniture in an old maid's front parlor?"

Griffin sighed. "Just come on, will you? I haven't got all night!"

Over the shrill and somewhat colorful objections of the prostitute he'd engaged, Malachi Lindsay righted his clothes; wrenched his ancient, billed cap onto his head; and followed Griffin out of the dirt alleyway and onto the Skid Road.

Barely twenty minutes later, the scattered crewmen of the *Merrimaker* were converging on the wharf, half-drunk and full ready to tangle with the mates from the *China Drifter*.

Malachi was warming to the project. "What do you say we just board the *Drifter* and wait?"

Jonas obviously liked the idea, but Griffin was already scanning the dark hillsides of Seattle. "I'm going to make sure he isn't planning to take her overland, to Tacoma or somewhere. Malachi, you know Frazier. Where did he hide his 'cargo' when he worked San Francisco?"

Malachi puzzled for a moment, rubbing his stubbly beard with one huge, muscular hand. "Probably in Chinatown."

"Good," said Griffin, turning to walk away. "Let's hope the bastard is consistent."

Douglas Frazier was feeling uneasy, and he was beginning to wonder if one temperamental young woman, however enticing, was worth the risks he was taking.

The carriage shuddered and creaked as it moved along the rutted dirt roads into the Chinese quarter. Frazier longed for the rolling shift of a deck beneath his feet.

Jaw tight with lingering annoyance, he remembered the night he'd found Rachel wandering along the Skid Road, completely unattended. It worried him—proper young ladies avoided such places.

Douglas closed his eyes and tilted his head back, wondering. Was she really a virgin, or had Wilkes been telling the truth? If she wasn't untouched, Ramirez would know within minutes of being alone with her. And he wouldn't pay the agreed price until he was sure the bargain was to his liking.

Douglas sighed. Chang Su could be prevailed upon to examine Rachel, to determine the true state of affairs.

The carriage rattled to a stop, and Douglas bounded out, grateful for the bracing coolness of the night air. But the doubts followed him, howling at his heels like dogs.

Rachel had spent the night in Jonas Wilkes's bed. To the delight of the men he'd sent to fetch her, she'd been completely naked.

Douglas Frazier cursed. Maybe he should have taken Wilkes's bank draft and honored the bargain. Maybe he would have been ahead. After all, the violet-eyed nymph was of questionable innocence, and she was sick, too. She might not even survive the journey.

He tapped briskly at the door of a board hut, annoyed. The stench of spoiled fish and offal stung his nostrils; he wondered how these yellow-skinned devils could bear living the way they did. They were so damned passive—

There was a whistling sound, and then an explosion of pain in the back of Frazier's skull. He cursed as his knees buckled beneath him, groaned when the side of his head struck a wooden step.

Chang Wo dragged the captain away from the step and into the shadows; he was a heavy burden, and the task took precious minutes. When it had been completed, he knelt and bound the captain's wrists behind him.

There was still the carriage driver. He hadn't heard anything, but he would become suspicious if the captain didn't reappear when expected. Chang weighed these facts in his mind as he groped for Frazier's handkerchief, wadded it, and pressed it between the captain's teeth and far back into his throat.

The man was like a great, red lion. When he awakened, his bonds would hold him only briefly, for his rage would give him much strength.

Chang crept back into the hut where Su waited, frightened and distraught. "You have killed?" she whispered, raising her lowered eyes to the face of her brother. "You have killed the sea lion?"

Change shook his head, impatient with her fear, yet all too conscious of its basis in reality. "Missy is ready?"

"She be big sick. Not walk."

Chang had gone too far now to turn back. He had struck down Frazier, who might already be stirring in the darkness. "We carry," he said.

They supported the inert girl between them and crept slowly out through the one door and into the night, taking care to keep to the shadows as they passed the captain's carriage.

Driving a dishonorably acquired horse and buggy, Griffin went uphill toward the Chinese community. Comprised of tumbledown shacks and poverty, it was not a place that inspired civic pride.

They had been so welcome once, when there were railroads to be built, these quiet, yellow-skinned people. They were lauded for their ability to hang by a rope over the side of a trestle for fourteen hours at a stretch, working industriously and without complaint; and for their placid ability to lay charges of dynamite in precarious pits where other men refused to go.

All this for a bowl of rice and a minuscule wage.

Griffin remembered the bitter uprisings against the Chinese in the middle of the decade. Once the tracks had been laid, there weren't so many jobs. Competition became fierce, and the yellow man's willingness to work for next to nothing was no longer venerated—it was despised.

Griffin spat. Such was the grateful nature of mankind. *You've served your purpose now. Go home.*

Something inside him tensed suddenly as he rounded a corner and came into another street. In the moonlight, he could see that there was a carriage up ahead, and a man was bellowing in rage—a white man, judging by the cadence of his words and the timbre of his voice.

Instinctively Griffin drew the buggy to a stop, hoping that its approach had gone unnoticed in the fuss.

Frazier. The howling maniac was Frazier himself. Griffin held his breath.

"There weren't no wagon, I'm tellin' you!" whined the dark figure in the carriage box. "Those Chinks must have sneaked past me on foot!"

Frazier was reeling in his anger and his panic. "And I'm telling you that you're a liar, Hudson! How much did Wilkes pay you?"

"Cap'n, I swear there weren't nobody by here!"

Frazier's big frame seemed charged somehow; he lumbered toward the carriage, flung himself up into the box, and hurled the trembling driver to the ground. Hudson crawled ignobly into the sanction of the thick darkness of a copse of fir trees.

The moonlight was so bright. If Frazier turned in Griffin's direction, he would surely see him, surely realize that the opposition had caught up to him. But the giant was intent on his own purposes.

Towering like a mountain in the box of the carriage, Frazier bent, took up the reins, and stood straight again. Griffin watched with a sort of hateful admiration as he brought the panicked team under control and turned the phaeton around in a broad, graceful sweep.

Everything inside Griffin screamed for Frazier's blood, but he sat still in the buggy seat, waiting. After the longest minute of his life, he brought the reins down with a light slap and followed the carriage at a discreet distance.

It was immediately apparent that Frazier was on his way back to the waterfront—probably planning to cut his losses and run. Whatever his plans were, it was highly unlikely that Rachel was a part of them.

Griffin felt mingled relief and frustration. Where was Rachel now? Was she still alive?

A cloud moved across the moon, blotting it out, and then passed by to reveal it again.

A small, queued form leaped in front of the buggy, waving frantic arms. "Dr. Fletcher? Dr. Fletcher!"

Griffin reined in the stolen horse and peered into the darkness. A shaft of silvery moonlight illuminated the Chinaman's anxious features. "*Chang?*"

He nodded vigorously. "You take Missy!" he pleaded breathlessly, disappearing into the shadows and then reappearing again, with Rachel propped between himself and a slight, terrified girl.

Rachel. Griffin jumped to the ground so quickly that the impact jarred his battered body and made his head spin. He drew a deep breath, righted himself, and lifted the unconscious Rachel into his arms.

She stirred against him, a strangled sound bubbling in her throat. "No . . ."

Griffin closed his eyes, let his forehead rest against hers. He could manage no words of comfort or reassurance.

Chang tugged hesitantly at his sleeve. "Missy say Chang get job back. Say Mr. Wilkes let Chang work again."

Griffin opened his eyes. "If he doesn't, I will. But you'd better keep out of sight until the *Drifter* sails."

"Nowhere Chang hide!" protested the distraught man, his voice rising in a thin rush of panic.

Griffin lifted Rachel gently onto the buggy seat, ferreted crumpled currency from his pocket, and extended all but a few dollars to Chang. "This might make it easier."

Change stared at the money in disbelief. "Buy horse," he breathed, finally. "Buy *wagon*."

"Come and see me as soon as you get back to Providence," Griffin said, climbing gingerly onto the footrail on the buggy's side. "And Chang? Thanks."

Chang and the woman were gone a moment later, whispering as they went.

Griffin lifted Rachel up, sat down, and then lowered her again, so that her head rested in his lap. The even meter of her breathing was like music in the night.

He touched the pulse point beneath her right ear and smiled. She needed rest and care, but she would recover. The knowledge made Griffin's spirit soar.

When Rachel was strong enough, they would talk about that night in the lumber camp, the night they'd made love, and what it had really meant to him. Perhaps she wouldn't even want him; she might leave the territory forever or even, God forbid, marry Jonas.

Whatever happened, Griffin vowed he would not pretend indifference toward her again.

Aware that the business of the night was far from finished, he deposited Rachel in the competent care of his friends, Dr. and Mrs. John O'Riley, and guided the horse and buggy toward the waterfront.

Frazier, he thought, as the sounds of a rousing, all-out brawl reached his ears. *I want a piece of you.*

The fight was everywhere—on the shoreline, on the wharfs, even on board the *Drifter.* Flailing bodies were splashing into the water from her decks, and howls of rage and grunts of pain came from every direction.

Griffin scanned the rowdy crowd of sailors and found Jonas in the center of the fray. His back to a mountain of whiskey barrels, he landed a decent punch in Frazier's mammoth midsection.

Frazier didn't even flinch.

Griffin vaulted over the railing and ran down the wharf, the magic already beginning in his feet. "Rachel is all right," he said, for Jonas's benefit.

A smile broke over Jonas's face, only to be replaced by a grimace as the captain's fist caught him squarely in the stomach.

Griffin considered letting the battle take its inevitable course, but he couldn't quite bring himself to turn away. He and Jonas would come to terms later, on their own turf.

Almost of its own accord, his right leg swung into a high, graceful arch, his foot catching the side of Frazier's head and dropping him to his knees. The wharf seemed to vibrate under the impact.

Douglas Frazier was a big man, and even though he looked stunned as he raised himself to a crouch and then his full height, Griffin knew that he was far from defeated.

He swung hard, and Griffin ducked, feeling the savage protest in his rib cage. He thrust the heel of his boot into Frazier's throat, watched without satisfaction as he crumpled back to his knees, with indifference as he struggled up again.

The captain was savagely angry now, and consequently,

175

reckless. Raising both hands, he lunged for Griffin's throat and grasped it, like a bear grasping the trunk of a tree. For a moment, Griffin was off balance; he couldn't breathe, much less move to break the hold.

Jonas's voice came from somewhere nearby, prodding him lightly. "He was going to sell Rachel, Griffin. Frazier was going to sell her to some rich bastard for a plaything."

The reminder exploded in Griffin's mind, splintering his reason. By the time it had reassembled itself, Jonas and Malachi were struggling to restrain him, and Frazier was lying motionless on the wet, shifting wharf.

Griffin shrugged free of the men at his sides, turned, and stumbled slowly toward the shore. The police were arriving, and Malachi met them with an animated account of Frazier's many sins.

Chuckling over the small irony, Griffin climbed into the stolen buggy and drove off.

Chapter Twenty-one

Rachel felt the warmth of the sun on her face, caressing her, cajoling her to open her eyes and take notice of it. Her lashes fluttered in response, but she was afraid to look.

Lying very still, she awaited the rolling sensation of a ship at sea, but it did not come. So, she was not on the ocean then, on her way to be devoured by some man she didn't know. Tears of gratitude seeped through her lashes.

Rachel's hands moved, and she knew that she was not in Chang's shanty either. There, she had lain on a narrow cot, but this was most certainly a bed, and the sheets were made of some deliciously smooth material that whispered when she moved.

Curiosity triumphed over fear, and Rachel opened her eyes. A woman sat nearby, in a rocking chair, knitting industriously and humming a soft, familiar song. Her hair was light, and the sunlight gave it hues of rose-gold and silver.

She seemed to sense Rachel's scrutiny, and looked up from the woolly red sweater she was constructing. Her face was that of a young woman, even though there were little lines, barely visible, at the corners of her dark blue eyes and the edges of her generous mouth.

"Well, good morning," she said pleasantly. "I'm Joanna O'Riley; and you're perfectly safe here, so don't be frightened."

Rachel sensed that she would not have been frightened of this woman even if she had awakened to find her standing over the bed with an upraised hatchet. "Where . . ."

Joanna O'Riley rose from her chair and dropped her knitting into the seat. As she crossed the room, the strangest thing happened—she stepped into a shaft of golden sunlight that ran straight up and down, like a pillar. The soft dazzle lent her an indescribable, otherworldly beauty.

Rachel was quite taken aback, until she looked up and saw that there was, of all things, a window right in the ceiling, a window that was round and had spokes like a wagon wheel.

Mrs. O'Riley stood beside the bed now, holding Rachel's hand. "Wouldn't you like to see Griffin now?" she asked.

This silky bed, this room bathed in light, and Griffin, too? Was she dreaming? She voiced the question aloud.

Mrs. O'Riley smiled. "No, Rachel, you're awake."

Surreptitiously, Rachel raked the side of one foot with the toenails of the other, just to make certain. This was definitely the real world. "How did I—where—"

Joanna O'Riley laughed. "My husband and I are Griffin's friends. He brought you here last night, after that terrible business with Captain Frazier was over. Now—may I please send him in before he drives us all mad with his incessant pacing and grumbling?"

Rachel blushed, and then nodded. "Thank you, Mrs. O'Riley."

"Joanna."

"Joanna," Rachel conceded, feeling very nervous and very happy, both at once.

When Griffin appeared at the foot of the bed, minutes later, Rachel was appalled. His face was so badly bruised that he hardly looked like himself, and his clothes were hopelessly disheveled. Through a gap in the buttons of his shirt, she could see that his ribs were bound.

"Griffin—what happened?"

His grin was engaging proof that this battered stranger was really Griffin Fletcher, badly in need of a shave. "That doesn't matter, Sprite. How do you feel?"

For the first time, Rachel realized that she was wearing a satiny nightgown of some kind, and she felt the sunlight touching the rounded swell of her breasts with its warmth. Blushing, she wrenched the covers up to her chin. "I feel better."

Griffin laughed and shook his head. "You're safe with me, Sprite. Which is not to say I don't find you appealing."

Rachel was confused. Was this the same man who had practically thrown her on board the steamboat only a few days before in Providence?

He grasped the carved foot railing of the bed and leaned forward, just slightly. The motion seemed stiff and cautious—probably, his injured ribs were hurting. "I have strict orders from the good Dr. O'Riley not to remain in this room for over five minutes. When you're stronger, we'll talk—with your permission, of course."

Rachel was wild with curiosity, but too weak to do anything. She relaxed against the fluffy pillows at her back. "When I'm stronger," she repeated, giving the words the tone of a promise. "Griffin?"

A crooked smile. "What?"

"I don't know what happened, but Joanna told me that you brought me here, and that I—I shouldn't be frightened because everything is over now. Captain Frazier won't come for me, will he?"

Something deadly flashed in the dark eyes and was subdued. "No, Sprite. He won't."

Rachel's gaze slide, of its own volition, to the bandages binding his ribs and then back to his face. "W-Were you hurt like that trying to help me?"

He shook his magnificent head, and some of the sunlight that seemed to bathe the room caught in his dark, rumpled hair. "Molly Brady herself did this to me. You see, she'd just scrubbed the parlor floor, and I walked across it—"

Rachel giggled. "Liar."

Griffin sighed, and his eyes caressed Rachel—or did she imagine that? "My five minutes are up," he said. "Rest." And then he was turning, walking away.

For a moment, Rachel was certain that she couldn't bear for him to go. "Griffin?"

He turned in the doorway and grimaced in mock impatience. "What?"

"Thank you."

Griffin only nodded, but somehow, it was as though he had crossed the room and touched her.

In the bright light of that early summer day, it seemed incredible that the events of the night before had taken place at all. Griffin sighed, and a half-smile caught on his lips. Rachel was safe, and she was recovering. Nothing else seemed important.

In the stables behind Dr. John O'Riley's fine brick house, Griffin collected the horse and buggy he'd stolen on the Skid Road the night before and hitched them together. He would return the rig to the place where he'd found it, meet with Jonas, and buy something for Rachel.

Elliott Bay gleamed bright blue in the distance, as though it were trying to rival the sky. Beyond it, in the west, rose the craggy, white magnificence of the Olympic Mountains. And the trees—there were so many trees. Griffin never tired of their impossible, incredible, eye-jarring green. He had to force his attention back to the rattling traffic of Friday morning.

On the Skid Road, Griffin abandoned the horse and buggy, knowing that the animal had been fed and watered and curried, and walked back in the direction of the small hotel where Jonas stayed whenever he came to Seattle.

The visit to Jonas's room would not be a social call, but it would not be an attack either. In Providence, they battled constantly—it was a habit that had probably begun when their mothers made the mistake of putting them both in the same pram—but Seattle was neutral ground.

After striding past the room clerk with an impatient wave, Griffin climbed the stairs and rapped at the familiar door. "Jonas? Let me in."

"It's open," came the toneless reply.

Griffin entered, closing the door behind him. Jonas was still in bed, and the curtains were drawn against the sun. When Griffin threw them open, he was startled to see Mrs. Hammond, Jonas's nursemaid-turned-housekeeper, sleeping bolt upright in a straight-backed chair.

"What the hell—"

"Keep your voice down!" Jonas rasped irritably, making no attempt to get out of bed. "She's tired."

Griffin nodded sagely. "Didn't she have the price of a room, Jonas?"

In spite of himself, Jonas laughed. "You bastard. She could have had any bed in the place, but she wanted to sit there and stare at me."

"No accounting for taste," shrugged Griffin, leaning back against the bureau and folding his arms.

"You ought to play the Opera House, Griffin. You're very goddamned funny."

"I got beat out by a fat lady with tassels on her tits."

Jonas laughed again and sat up in bed. "Damn it, Griffin, shut up. It's too early for that shit."

There was a short silence; then Mrs. Hammond snored and they both laughed again. The sound awakened her, and she glared at them, disgruntled and very red in the face.

Mumbling something about finding coffee, she went out.

The laughter evaporated from Jonas's eyes. "How is Rachel?"

"She'll be fine."

"Where is she?"

"With friends of mine, Jonas. That's what I came to talk about."

Jonas was visibly annoyed. He settled back on his pillows and stared up at the ceiling. "Let's hear it."

"We've got to leave her alone for a while—both of us. She needs time, and she needs rest. Jonas, I'll back off if you will."

"You know where she is, and I don't. That makes it a little hard to be sure you're practicing what you preach, Griff."

"Not if we go back to Providence together. Tonight."

Jonas swallowed, thought for a while. "All right—on one condition. That we make sure Frazier isn't going to crawl out from under some rock and carry her off."

"Agreed," Griffin said, moving across the room again, to the door. "I'll meet you at the courthouse in an hour, and we'll talk to the police."

"I'll be there."

Griffin opened the door to leave. "She's safe where she is, Jonas," he said.

"She'd better be," Jonas vowed. "And Griffin?"

"What?"

"Nothing's changed."

"I know," replied Griffin. Then he went out and closed the door behind him.

In the next half hour, Griffin visited three different stores. In the last, a tiny jewelry shop in the Pontius Building, he found what he wanted, bought it, and stuffed the tiny parcel into his shirt pocket.

Outside again, Griffin walked toward the telegraph office. It was going to be hard to leave Rachel now, even for a few days. As he dictated the wire letting Molly know that everything was all right, he worried.

What if Frazier happened to be released from jail? He might look for Rachel, just to avenge the indignities of the past night.

Half an hour later, Jonas and Griffin met outside the courthouse. Without exchanging a single word, they went inside.

Frazier wasn't going anywhere, a constable assured them. He was still unconscious, but when and if he came to, he wouldn't be released. No, sir, enough proof had been found in his boardinghouse and in his cabin aboard the *Drifter* to keep him in the territorial prison for the rest of his days.

Griffin glanced in Jonas's direction and knew that his cousin felt the same need he did. "I want to see Frazier," he said.

The constable shrugged and led them downstairs, where over a hundred prisoners were incarcerated. Frazier had his own cell, and there was a doctor examining him. John O'Riley closed his medical bag, turned, and met Griffin's gaze.

It was the worst kind of luck. Jonas knew O'Riley, knew that in spite of the vast difference in their ages, the two doctors were close friends.

Griffin risked a sidelong glance at Jonas and saw a smug light in his eyes. He'd guessed where Rachel was staying, that was clear.

"How is he, Doc?" asked the constable, unaware of the sudden tension in the air.

John rattled the cell door impatiently. "Let me out of here, Horace, and I'll tell you."

Horace hastened to comply, and led the way back upstairs and into a small, incredibly cluttered office. There, John O'Riley plucked a handkerchief from the pocket of his rumpled suit coat and wiped his brow.

"Frazier is comatose," he said finally. "Frankly, I don't think he's going to last the night, let alone stand trial."

Horace looked genuinely concerned, and Jonas's face was closed tight. Griffin wasn't sure what he, himself, felt—hatred surely, but a singular sort of shame, too. Whatever else Frazier might be, he was a human being, and if he died, it would be because of Griffin.

Dr. O'Riley cleared his throat, careful not to look in Griffin's direction. "Horace, are your people looking for the other man—the man that fought the captain last night? Maybe meaning to arrest him, too?"

Horace shook his head. "Cap'n Lindsay—he's skipper of the *Merrimaker*—he says the fight was provoked." A look of wonder played in the man's heavy-jowled, mustached face. "I'd sure have liked to see that fight, John. From what I've heard, it was like nothing you and me has ever seen."

Griffin felt sick. Without saying a word, he left the courthouse and stood staring at the ugly bell tower of the church across the street.

Presently, a hand came to rest on his arm. "Griffin," John O'Riley began in the level, sane voice that so reassured his patients. "You did what you had to do. Don't torture yourself."

"I'm a doctor," Griffin whispered.

"Before that, you're a man. And men lose their heads sometimes, Griffin—especially when there's a woman as lovely as Rachel involved."

Griffin closed his eyes, remembering. "I wanted to kill him, John."

John's sigh betrayed his weariness, his advancing age. "I guess Old Mike was trying to prepare you when he hired that Frenchman to teach you to fight special, but I think he did you a disservice by it. More than one, actually. But that old cuss was as hard-headed as they come—and he wanted you to be bull-of-the-woods."

Griffin opened his eyes, searched the face of his friend, his father's friend. "You'll do what you can for Frazier?"

"You know I will, Griffin. But if he dies, you keep in mind that none of this would have happened if Frazier hadn't been what he was. And you weigh the loss of his life against the lives of all the young girls who won't end up in the hold of his ship, on their way to hell." John paused, then added, "If it turns out that you've taken one life, Griffin, remember all the lives you've saved."

Griffin drew a deep breath, nodded. "I'm going to get some sleep. Thanks, John."

O'Riley smiled. "You do that. And make sure you eat something, too." Then, seeing Jonas's approach, the old man scowled and walked away, toward one of several buggies waiting on the road.

Jonas grinned. "Unlike you, my friend, I had the good sense to hire a rig. Shall I give you a ride to the O'Riley place, or are you dead set on walking?"

Griffin swore. "All right—Rachel is staying with John and Joanna, damn it! And Jonas, God help you if you go near her."

Jonas raised an eyebrow. "You don't trust me?"

"Why the hell should I?"

Jonas shrugged, but the look in his eyes was serious. "I guess I don't blame you—we have had our moments, you and I."

"Like now, for instance. Are you going to keep our agreement, or not?"

Jonas was striding toward a battered buggy that was hitched to an equally worn-out horse. He climbed into the seat and took the reins, smiling acidly as Griffin joined him. "I'm keeping the bargain, Griffin—but I'm doing it for Rachel, not you. Once she's well, all deals are off."

Griffin sat back, his eyes on the road. "Fair enough," he said.

Rachel had never, in all her life, known such luxury. But now, thanks to the infinite kindness of Joanna O'Riley, it surrounded her.

The first marvel was a pot of spiced tea, complete with supplies of sugar and cream, brought to Rachel's room on a tray and left on her bedside table. She was to drink as much as she wanted, Joanna informed her, for John believed that sick people needed to take a great many fluids.

With lunch came another wonder—cinnamon pears. Of course, Rachel had eaten pears on occasion, the kind that were plucked from a tree and still wearing their splotched, leathery skins. But these fruits were another matter; they had been peeled and cooked, and the sweet, cinnamon-flavored sauce they floated in was ruby red.

Joanna was amused by her delight. "Rachel, I do believe you could be maintained on pears and sweet tea alone!"

"Ummm," replied Rachel, closing her eyes in reverence as she chewed the last, sweet morsel. "I never want to eat any other kind of pear."

Joanna laughed. "That's a pity, because we have a whole pantry full of mint pears. They're in an emerald green sauce."

Rachel stared at her, wide-eyed, and the answering laughter

was still ringing in the room when Griffin came through the open doorway.

Joanna leveled a playful look at him and intoned, "Griffin, my love, if your intentions toward this young lady are serious, you'd best plant a grove of pear trees."

He looked so confused by this advice that a torrent of giggles swelled into Rachel's throat and escaped.

Griffin scratched the back of his head in comical bewilderment and muttered, "I wish you two would cheer up."

Joanna made a face at him, took Rachel's denuded lunch tray, and left the room.

She took the laughter with her.

Griffin sat down on the edge of the bed, and his face was suddenly bleak and weary. Without thinking, Rachel reached up, and caressed his cheek with her hand. "What is it?" she asked softly.

Griffin's voice was hoarse, and while he did not turn from her touch, he did avert his eyes. "Rachel, I have to go back to Providence tonight."

Slowly, Rachel lowered her hand, sank back onto the pillows. "Oh."

Griffin's index finger came to rest under her chin, raising it slightly. "My patients, Rachel. I've got to get back to them."

Rachel nodded. "Yes."

He stood up again, suddenly, and for a moment, he looked angry. But his words belied anger; they reached into her spirit like fingers and took hold, never to let go again.

"Rachel, I love you."

Rachel was speechless; her lips moved, but there was no sound. Crazy, delightful feelings whirled inside her, in kaleidoscope colors.

Griffin laid a gentle finger to her mouth. Then he took a tiny parcel from his pocket, laid it in her hand, and said, "I'll be back late next week, Rachel. Get well."

He bent, and his lips brushed hers; then he was walking away. The bedroom door closed softly behind him.

Chapter Twenty-two

Rachel stared at the door of her room for a long time, hardly daring to believe what she had heard. Griffin Fletcher *loved* her—it was incredible.

She remembered the small package he had pressed into her hand, and with trembling fingers, she opened it. Nestled in the brown paper was a delicate gold bracelet, with one golden charm dangling from it—a tiny, perfectly detailed crosscut saw.

Rachel laughed; then she cried. And then she slipped the bracelet onto her wrist and admired it, suspending her arm so that the light streaming in through the windows caught in the metal and turned it to fire. He did love her, and the night of lovemaking in the lumber camp had meant as much to him as it had to her. In this tiny, significant charm was the proof.

She slept, and when she awakened, the house was quite dark. For one terrible moment, Rachel thought she had only dreamed that Griffin had said he loved her; but then she remembered the charm and sought it with her hand, and it was there, dangling from her wrist. She traced the jagged teeth of the tiny saw.

Rachel reached out and lit the lamp beside her bed. She had Griffin's words to remember, and she had the bracelet; but he was gone. She could feel his absence echoing through the O'Riley house like the toll of a great, sad bell.

A week. He had promised to be back in a week. Rachel dried the tears that had gathered in her lashes, and when Joanna came in with a dinner tray, Rachel was very careful to smile.

Probably sensing Rachel's carefully concealed loneliness, Joanna sat down and knitted in silence while her friend ate. After that, she took a book from a shelf beneath the windows, opened it, and began to read softly from *A Midsummer Night's Dream*.

Rachel slept, and when she awakened from her own dreams, June had brought the summer. She concentrated hard on getting well.

It seemed that Griffin's love and the special bracelet had combined to work some indefinable magic. By the next day, Rachel was well enough to leave her bed for short periods of time. By the day after that, she had recovered to such an extent that Dr. O'Riley grudgingly gave permission for her to take a brief carriage ride with Joanna.

Almost immediately, Rachel's great joy at the prospect gave way to despair—she had nothing fresh to wear. In a miserable whisper, she admitted this to Joanna.

"That is certainly no problem," Joanna said, with brisk kindness. Opening a pair of doors at the far side of the bedroom, she disappeared for a few moments, into a closet. She came out carrying a lovely pink- and white-striped shirt-waist and a gray flannel skirt.

"Wear these," she said, laying the splendidly made garments over the foot of Rachel's bed.

I'll die if they don't fit, she thought, taking the beautiful clothing into her hands and delighting silently in the incredible softness of it.

"They were Athena's," said Joanna, and there was a look of sadness and distance in her dark blue eyes.

"Athena?" Rachel asked gently, not certain that she should have spoken at all.

But Joanna smiled warmly and gestured with good-natured impatience toward a folding screen near the bed. "Athena was—is—our daughter. Hurry, Rachel, before John changes his mind and forbids you to leave the house today."

Like the clothes Jonas had given Rachel, Athena's flannel skirt and gaily colored shirtwaist fit her perfectly. And even though she was relieved at that, she was vaguely discomforted, too.

There had been that peculiar look in Joanna's eyes when she'd mentioned her daughter's name. And she'd hesitated in an odd way, too, as though she wasn't certain whether Athena was a part of the past or a part of the present.

And there was something more, something that lurked in the corner of Rachel's mind like a cat cowering in the darkness beneath a bed or a table, something that she couldn't identify.

"Where is Athena now?" she dared, as she and Joanna made their way down a graceful, winding stairway to the floor below. *And why did she leave her clothes behind?*

Joanna said nothing until they reached the marble-floored

entry hall below. There was a strain in her smile, and the tiny lines around her eyes seemed deeper somehow. "Our daughter is in Europe, Rachel. I'm afraid life in Seattle is a little too raw for her. Now," Joanna patted Rachel's arm, and there was a plea in her eyes, behind the lame smile. "Why don't you wait right in there, beyond those doors, while I ask Cook what to bring back? There is a lovely view from the front windows."

Feeling sorry, and more than a little ashamed that she had pried the way she had, Rachel nodded mutely and walked off to pass through a giant set of French doors.

The window drew Rachel immediately, for through it, she could see a patch of aquamarine water.

She drew in her breath at the beauty of the sight that awaited her beyond those gauzy, white curtains. All of Elliott Bay lay spread out before her, sparkling blue in the bright sunshine. There were boats of all sizes and sorts: fast, noble clipper ships and hardworking tugs, fishing boats and steamers, specks that must surely be rowboats and canoes. Beyond all this rose the ferocious, snow-capped beauty of the Olympic Mountains. On the land lining the bay were millions of evergreen trees, standing so close together that it didn't look as though there could possibly be room for even one more.

Rachel closed her eyes for a moment, overcome. The scene was exactly like the one she'd dreamed that first miserable morning in Tent Town. How she'd longed to live forever in a house just like this one!

But now— Oh, now she would have given anything to be in plodding, unremarkable Providence again. To be near Griffin Fletcher.

She opened her eyes and turned from the window to look at the room itself.

It was magnificent, with its polished crystal chandeliers; its bright, costly rugs; its beautifully upholstered furniture. Everything seemed mammoth, in comparison to the ordinary rooms of Rachel's experience—particularly the gigantic fieldstone fireplace.

Rachel approached it in wonder, and as she raised her eyes to see whether it stretched all the way to the ceiling without narrowing, she saw the portrait for the first time.

It was a stunning work—probably the canvas was as tall as Rachel herself—framed in gilded wood.

The subject was a woman more beautiful than Rachel had

ever dreamed a mere mortal could be; blond hair, so pale that it was almost silver, billowed around an impish, hauntingly perfect face. The eyes were wide and astonishingly blue, and they seemed to be teasing the viewer somehow, as did the impertinent smile that did not quite reach the delicate lips.

But it was the dress she wore that made Rachel's breath catch, fiery, in her throat. It was the very rose taffeta dress that Jonas had given to her, the dress that had stirred such confounding madness in Griffin on that awful night when he'd spoken so cruelly and caused Rachel to flee to her mother's building and hide.

What did it mean? Feeling wretched, Rachel groped for a chair and sank into it, covering her eyes momentarily with one hand. But the portrait seemed to be exerting some mystical force, compelling her to look at it again.

Athena. Of course, this impossibly lovely creature had to be John and Joanna's daughter.

Rachel imagined that she saw challenge in the thickly lashed, mischievous indigo eyes—and a certain hint of malice, too.

By an act of will, she tore her eyes from the goddess's face and looked instead at the golden bracelet on her own wrist. And even as she turned the miniature crosscut saw in her fingers, she knew that Griffin Fletcher had loved this woman, Athena—or hated her. Either way, his emotions must have been violent, or he wouldn't have reacted the way he had to the sight of that pink taffeta dress.

Joanna was beside her chair before Rachel realized that she was back from the kitchen.

"Rachel, dear, are you—" Joanna's voice broke off as she raised her eyes to the portrait of her daughter. "Oh," she said, after a long, lame silence.

Rachel raised glistening eyes to the face of this woman who had been so unfailingly kind. "Griffin loved her, didn't he?" she whispered, in the voice of a wounded child.

Joanna perched on the arm of Rachel's chair and gently laid her hands on the girl's tear-dampened face. "Yes, Rachel," she said, very gently. "Griffin did love Athena very much at one time. They were to be married, in fact."

Rachel closed her eyes against the impact of those words, then opened them again. "What happened?"

There was pain in Joanna's beautiful face and shame, too. "I can't tell you that, Rachel—it would be unfair, and Griffin might never forgive me. You must ask him."

Brokenly, Rachel held up her wrist to display the cherished bracelet. "He said—he gave me this—"

Joanna nodded, releasing Rachel, and there was an unquestionable certainty in her voice when she spoke. "Sweetheart, if Griffin Fletcher has declared himself to you, he meant it. He and Athena parted ways two years ago, after all. And I don't mind telling you that there were no romantic farewells.

"Now—are we taking that carriage ride, or am I to forget my important business on Pike Street?"

The sound Rachel made was somewhere between a sob and a giggle. She rose from the chair and, without looking back at the portrait even once, followed Joanna out into the sunny magnificence of the day.

But the battle was only half won, for if Rachel's eyes had not betrayed her by seeking Athena's image, her mind had. All during the ride downhill, when she should have been admiring the scenery and enjoying the warm, fresh air, she thought of that beautiful woman in the portrait. Athena was certainly an apt name for her; she was the closest thing to a goddess Rachel had ever seen.

It seemed incredible that any man, constructed of bone and sinew and all the attending human failings, could love such a woman and then stop caring about her entirely. Rachel sighed.

Griffin *hadn't* stopped caring—if he had, he wouldn't have reacted so passionately, for good or ill, to that rose taffeta dress. What memories had the sight of it stirred in him?

On Pike Street, Joanna left the carriage momentarily to rush inside a shop and speak with her dressmaker. Rachel was more than content to remain behind in the shadowy insulation of the phaeton.

Three days before, in Johnstown, Pennsylvania, there had been a terrible, sweeping flood when a dam gave way. Rachel kept herself from wondering about Griffin and Athena by reviewing the tragedy in her mind.

When Joanna came back, and the driver had helped her into her seat, she smiled. "You look so sad, Dear. You're not still thinking about my daughter, are you? She's safely married, to a French banker named André Bordeau."

Rachel shook her head and said, in all honesty, that she had been considering the hideous destruction in that faraway Pennsylvania town, the loss of life and property, and the suddenness with which disaster can strike.

Joanna nodded sadly, and Rachel knew that her concern

189

went far deeper than a display of sympathy. She and her friends had been collecting food, money, and clothing for the victims ever since word of the Johnstown calamity had reached Seattle.

Both women were lost in thought when the carriage lurched to a jarring, unexpected stop. The vehicle shifted slightly as the driver jumped from the box and appeared at the window.

His voice could barely be heard over the mournful strains of a brass band. "There's a Chinese funeral procession coming, Mrs. O'Riley," he said to Joanna. "Do you want me to try and go around them?"

"Mercy, no," whispered Joanna, impatiently. "The only decent thing to do is wait."

The driver grumbled, but went back to his post in the carriage box and held the nervous horses in check.

"Come here," Joanna ordered, "And watch."

Rachel couldn't imagine how such a grim spectacle could hold appeal for anyone besides the mourners, but she slid across the seat and looked out the window, as she was told.

Sure enough, a marching band led the sad group. Behind it rolled a grimly decorous hearse, bedecked in bobbing feather plumes. A Chinaman sat beside the impervious driver of the death carriage, flinging bits of white paper into the breeze. It billowed like snow against the bright blue sky and wafted down to earth again in slow motion.

"Why is he doing that?" Rachel whispered, frowning.

Joanna smiled sadly. "It looks odd, doesn't it—all those thousands of papers flying in the air? He is trying to deceive the devil, Rachel; the idea is that the Evil One will be so busy picking up the mess that he will lose sight of the deceased and be unable to find him or her before that person is safe in the Celestial Home."

Behind the hearse carriage came an assortment of carts and buckboards, brimming with wailing mourners in dark pajamalike clothes and pointed coolie hats.

"As they progress up Pike Street, toward Lakeview Cemetery," Joanna explained, "they will turn many corners—another tactic to confuse the devil."

Rachel was grimly amused. "It is assumed, then, that the devil is both neat and poor at directions," she commented.

"Yes," said Joanna, as the end of the odd procession came into sight.

The last vehicle was a wagon, overflowing with food of every sort; Rachel could see crates of live chickens, a whole roasted pig, and huge bags that probably contained rice.

"The food is for the spirits?"

"Yes," confirmed Joanna. "Like the Indians, the Chinese believe that gifts should be left for those ancestors who will come to meet the departed and guide him homeward."

"I think it's beautiful that they care so much," said Rachel, as the driver shifted impatiently in the box, shaking the whole carriage.

Joanna nodded. "It is beautiful, Rachel. I find the Chinese fascinating. They've been sadly mistreated in this country, though. They were the darlings of labor for a long time, because they would work for such low wages. But when the railroads were completed, dearest 'John' suddenly became a fiend. To this day, there is a law that he cannot own land or a house."

Rachel clearly remembered the riots that had taken place in and around the lumber camps during the heat of the controversy. When she was twelve, and passing through Tacoma with her father, she had seen the Chinese being loaded into boxcars, like animals, to be taken away. In other places, like Seattle, Chinese people had been beaten and driven from their homes. No one seemed to know where these placid outcasts were supposed to go.

Once again, Rachel felt sad empathy for those who lived on the edges of acceptability, never really belonging anywhere, for those who tore papers and turned corners all their lives, trying to deceive the devil.

The carriage was moving again, but it soon came to another stop—a market where Joanna wanted to buy the items on a list Cook had given her.

Again, Rachel remained behind, but this time, she could not keep Griffin so easily from her mind.

He had said he loved her and had given her a token of that love to wear on her wrist. He might, by some miracle, even mean to marry her. And if he did, would she have his complete devotion, or would she merely be a replacement for the lost Athena?

In that event, Rachel would be as displaced as Chang or Fawn Nighthorse—even though she would live out the rest of her life under a sturdy roof, lacking nothing, she would have no home.

191

Rachel closed her eyes, suddenly missing her father more than ever. *Oh, Pa, where are you?* she thought.

Joanna closed gloved hands over Rachel's trembling ones, startling her. "I think today has been too much for you, Dear. I've got to get you home and into bed; if you suffer a relapse, John will have me shot!"

In spite of the tangle of painful feelings within her, Rachel looked upon her friend and smiled. "Why are you so good to me? Because Griffin brought me to you?"

Joanna shook her head and returned Rachel's smile. "I'll admit that John and I would probably never have known you if Griffin hadn't carried you to our door the other night, but we do, and we're beginning to love you very much."

Rachel blushed slightly and lowered her head.

Joanna's voice was stern. "Do you find that so difficult to believe, Rachel? That someone would care about you without being forced to?"

Rachel did not know how to answer, so she remained silent.

Joanna laughed warmly. "Well, I'm not going to tell you all the reasons why John and Griffin and I think you're splendid. They might turn your head, and we can't have that, now, can we?"

But Rachel made no answer. Again, her fingers sought and found the significant little charm on her bracelet. Somehow its magic had waned; she couldn't help comparing herself with the resplendent Athena.

Athena was beautiful, almost certainly educated in fine schools, and, surely, sophisticated, too. And she must be adventurous, as well, to live so far from her family and her country.

Rachel knew that she, herself, was a pretty woman, but in no way could her looks be put into the same Olympian category as Athena's.

Despair swirled inside her like a numbing blizzard, there in the warmth of that third day of June. The other comparisons Rachel made were woefully like the first; she had virtually educated herself, and there were a great many gaps in the result.

Rather than being sophisticated, Rachel was, she felt sure, a bumpkin, completely ignorant of such graces as dancing and proper table manners and speech befitting a lady. And as for being adventurous—well, Rachel had had her share of that during all the years of traveling from one camp to another with her father. She wanted nothing so badly as a home and a family of her very own.

She felt this last need more keenly than ever when the carriage came to a stop in front of the O'Riley's big, lovely house. They were kind—so very kind—but she did not belong here with them, any more than she had belonged in Miss Cunningham's boardinghouse, Tent Town, or the book-lined study in Griffin's home.

Indeed, she didn't really belong anywhere.

Alone, in the sunny, pleasant bedroom allotted to her, Rachel undressed. There was a fresh nightgown lying on the bed, a splendid creation of ivory silk edged in delicate lace, but Rachel could not bear the thought of wearing it. Surely, it belonged to Athena.

Suddenly, Rachel sank to the edge of her bed, rocking back and forth as a new realization washed over her in shattering waves. As the rose taffeta dress Jonas had given her was Athena's, so, undoubtedly, were all the other garments still stored at Miss Cunningham's.

Why would Jonas have Athena's clothes at his house when she had been Griffin's intended?

Rachel could not deal with the obvious answer to that question, so she thrust it aside. It was bad enough that she was Griffin's second choice, and that every stitch of clothing she owned had belonged to Athena first—as had Griffin.

Chapter Twenty-three

Douglas Frazier felt as though he'd been submersed in something black and pounding and thick as paste. He heard few sounds, and those that drifted down to him were distorted, one indecipherable from another. For an indeterminate length of time, he thought he was dead.

But there was pain. Dreadful, ceaseless pain.

Douglas clung to that anguish and exalted in its meaning. He was alive.

Sounds were becoming clearer—voices, he heard voices,

and the occasional clang of metal against metal. And the dark fog surrounding him was not so pervasive now; it was losing its unbearable density, becoming something of a mist. Calmly, deliberately, Douglas Frazier began to struggle through that strange, shifting twilight, toward the real world.

Rachel McKinnon awakened that bright morning with the certainty that something dreadful was about to happen. June fourth. She considered the date and etched it on a wall of her mind.

The weather was wonderfully warm and sunny, though, and Rachel felt the returning tide of her strength in the muscles of her arms and legs, in the rising power of her spirit. Even though she missed the undemanding refuge of her illness in some ways, there was something inside her that would not turn away from the eternal scraps and skirmishes that were life.

With a certain alacrity, she took the bath that Joanna and Cook had prepared for her in a small room downstairs, and when she sat down to breakfast in the sunny kitchen, her damp, fragrant hair toweled and combed, she found that she had her usual impressive appetite.

Of course, she had no choice but to go on wearing Athena's clothes until she could have some made for herself, but she took that in stride. Rachel was a young woman skilled in making the best of things and going on—always going on.

When she had eaten, she borrowed one of Joanna's many books and ventured out into the garden, where the sun could dry her hair.

For a time, Rachel mused over the strange undercurrent of dread flowing beneath all her ordinary, practical actions. Surely, the recent upheavals in her heretofore unremarkable life would be enough to upset anyone, she reasoned.

But there was something more, though the gentle weather and the blue skies and the sweet, fragrant unfolding of Joanna's garden belied it. Something much more.

With a sigh, Rachel opened her book and began to read a scholarly account of life in ninth-century England. Between the turning of the pages, her fingers moved often to the miniature crosscut saw suspended from her bracelet.

Athena O'Riley Bordeau left the train, bag and baggage, in Tacoma. It was a rough, clamoring town, and she hated it, but,

194

somehow, she felt she needed the twenty mile steamboat ride to prepare herself for the inevitable unpleasantries awaiting her in Seattle. Besides, she'd been rattling along in that insufferable train for well over a week, ever since she'd gotten off the ship in New York, and she didn't think she could bear the jostling lurch of it another minute.

Long accustomed to the gaping stares of workingmen and the subtle glances of coolies, Athena ignored both as she arranged for her trunks to be carried aboard the sidewheel steamer, *Olympia,* and walked up the boarding ramp.

Within herself, Athena was no longer so sure of her charms, however, no longer given to the old assumption that she was infinitely superior to almost everyone she met.

At the starboard railing edging the deck, she stood very still, chin raised, and waited. The great wheel began to revolve, flinging a glistening, prismlike spray of water upward as it turned.

Seattle. Athena could not bring herself to look toward it, even though the *Olympia* was bearing her closer and closer with every passing minute.

What would Mama and Papa say when she appeared, unannounced, at their front door? Would they turn her away?

Athena closed her dark blue eyes against the thought. They simply must welcome her; she had no money left and nowhere else to turn.

And what of Griffin? Her mother's rare letters left no doubt that he was still a friend of the family, still a frequent visitor to the gracious brick house high on the hill.

Athena sighed. That was Griffin. In this shifting, changeable world, he was that rare element, a constant. His behavior was as predictable as the course of the stars and planets in the heavens.

At one time, Athena had found this characteristic maddeningly dull. His stubborn refusal to obey his father's will and dispense with those eternal, sniveling patients of his had enraged her. Much that was Jonas's might have been his, and he had forsaken it all to battle the ills of people who simply did not matter.

Lately, however, this very quality, this implacable determination of Griffin's, had haunted her. She had felt drawn to him ever since the first humiliating evidences of André's infidelities had begun to surface.

Athena closed her eyes and gripped the steamboat's railing desperately. Griffin would never forgive her, never. And yet, somehow she must find a way to win him back.

Perhaps because she could not function without it, some of Athena's native self-confidence began to return. She was still one of the most beautiful women this miserable territory on the outskirts of nowhere had ever seen, she reminded herself. And Griffin's need of her had been a consuming, fathomless one.

Surely, by making an intelligent effort to stir those feelings in him again, she could win out over his fierce, boundless pride.

Athena drew a deep breath and opened her eyes. Believing that all beauty centered in her, she took no notice of the primitive, indomitable splendor of the land and water and trees and mountains all around her. Instead, she saw the party she would persuade her mother to give, the fine new clothes she would buy, the renewed passion she would somehow ignite in Griffin Fletcher.

The morning was almost gone when the *Olympia* docked in Seattle, and though Athena felt gritty and rumpled from the long journey, she felt hopeful, too. A bath, a change of clothes, maybe something to eat, and she would be her unconquerable self again.

On the waterfront, as they had in New York and Paris, London and Rome, Athena's silver blond hair and soul-jarring smile stood her in good stead. It was easy to secure a carriage, even in the modest rush, and to persuade the driver to hurry.

Certain now of a warm welcome, Athena was anxious for the care and comfort of her mother, the grumbling devotion of her father. Like Griffin, they were constants, and while they were probably still vastly annoyed, their love for her was fundamental to their natures, unchangeable by even the most flagrant of scandals.

Settled into the carriage seat, Athena smiled. They would be the same; Mama and Papa were always the same. Joanna, heiress to a vast fortune, would be busy with her eternal, boring charity work, unconcerned with the fact that life in San Francisco or New York was infinitely more exciting. John, the sweet, plodding darling, would still be treating his ungrateful, half-educated patients, never minding that his efforts seldom brought in anything tangible.

Constants. Again, Athena smiled. Hadn't she said it often herself, that Griffin Fletcher was so inflexible that he might as well have been carved out of granite? If he was, then the love he'd born her, the sweeping passion, was still there, inside him, in spite of his outrage and his wounded pride.

After all, the love had been there first.

In front of the stately brick house—only a cottage in comparison to the Parisian villa she had shared with André Bordeau—Athena paid the driver and then stood on the street for a moment, savoring the sturdy, practical beauty of her parents' house.

As the carriage rumbled away, its driver bent on securing her many trunks and satchels from the steamboat landing, Athena opened the gate and started up the walk.

She was never certain what drew her attention to the garden lining the eastern wall of the house. Certainly, she heard no sound beyond the buzzing of bees and the early summer songs of the birds.

No, it was a mystical pull of some sort—a feeling that tugged her off course and made her round the corner of the house and pass beneath the arbor of pink primroses to enter the sunny sanction of the garden.

Athena's first sight of the girl was alarming on some fundamental level, and worse, it was unaccountably painful.

Head bent over an open book, the girl sat on a stone bench, her feet tucked beneath her. Her sable ebony hair streamed down, gleaming, over her back and shoulders, and curled in fetching little tendrils around her face. Her eyes, Athena noted with strange apprehension, were wide and thickly lashed and just the color of wild violets. There was a look of innocent wonder about her that undoubtedly enthralled unwary men, and her skin was as perfect as Athena's own, if a little pallorous.

Athena cleared her throat in a ladylike fashion and felt oddly reassured as the nymph looked up from her book, lavender eyes widening with unmistakable horror.

"Athena?"

Athena felt a sort of sweeping triumph, as though she had been challenged to some vital struggle and then emerged the winner. "You have me at a disadvantage," she smiled, taking a seat on the stone bench facing the girl's.

"Rachel," the snippet whispered miserably. "My name is Rachel McKinnon."

With a theatrical sigh, Athena removed her bonnet to reveal the full glory of her soft, platinum hair. Jonas had always said it was like moonlight trapped in a silver dish, her hair, not meant for the look or touch of ordinary men. Griffin, on the other

197

hand, had not been so poetic; Athena doubted, even now, that he had ever really appreciated the distinctive shade of her hair.

But this girl had. Her violet eyes were taking it in, and she looked stricken.

Again, without knowing why, Athena felt a delicious sense of hard-won victory. "Do you work for Mama and Papa?" she asked, idly, even though her curiosity was a deep and wary one.

A bright peach tint glowed suddenly in the too-pale, too-thin cheeks. "I am a guest," Rachel said, with tremulous dignity.

"I see," replied Athena, settling back on the bench with another sigh, drawing her eyes over the girl's soft amethyst morning gown. "That is, I believe, my dress."

The orchid eyes were steadfast and fierce upon Athena's face. "Is it? Would you like me to take it off?"

Athena smiled a patronizing, wounding little smile. "Of course I wouldn't want to wear it—now."

Tears of outrage and pride glistened in the devastatingly beautiful eyes, gathered in the thick, dark lashes. But before Rachel could frame a retort, a third voice broke in with dry disapproval.

"Athena, that was an unconscionable thing to say. You will apologize immediately."

Athena looked up, surprised, to see her mother standing at the back gate, watching her with eyes that had, since the beginning, seen to much. "Mother!" she cried, a nervous little smile rising to her lips. She sprang from the bench, flung her arms around her mother, and babbled, "Oh, Mama, André was so terrible to me! He was so heartless and selfish."

Athena felt the usual cold distance between herself and this woman, even as they held each other.

"Heartless and selfish," Joanna repeated, thoughtfully. "Perhaps there is, after all, some justice in this wicked world."

Truly stunned, Athena drew back in her mother's stiff embrace. "I know I was terrible, Mama," she said, in a small, pleading voice that was not wholly false. "But you won't turn me away, will you? André has divorced me, and I haven't any money left, or any friends. . . ."

But her mother's weary blue eyes had moved to Rachel, and softened. "We'll talk in private, Athena. And the dress Rachel is wearing is her own, not yours."

Athena had no choice but to nod apologetically.

* * *

198

Rachel remained in the garden for a long time after Athena and her mother had gone into the house, arm in arm. Even the premonition she'd had hadn't prepared her for a disaster so sweeping as this one.

Unable to continue reading, she thrust the book aside, pulled her knees up under her chin, and let the full scope of the situation come cascading down on her in a crushing torrent.

She had seen the portrait and known that Athena was beautiful, but now she knew that the painter had not even begun to capture the splendor and grace of her. He had not caught the glow of her skin, the softness of her eyes, the incredible impact of her personality.

Rachel thought of Griffin's impending return to Seattle with almost unbearable dread, rather than the delight she had felt before her encounter with the woman who had almost become his wife.

While it was possible that Athena had no lingering interest in him, it seemed improbable. He was, for all his shortcomings, not the kind of man a woman loved and then forgot about.

Feeling desolate, Rachel looked down at the bracelet shining on her wrist. *He told me he loved me,* she reminded herself, in firm desperation. *And Joanna said his promises could be accepted as truth.*

Rachel's throat closed over a sob as she tilted her head back, closed her eyes, and remembered the sweet intensity of his lovemaking, the glorious demands his body had made of hers.

She was now completely confused.

Athena drank her tea slowly, watching her mother's face over the rim of her cup. She had recounted the horrible death pangs of her marriage, embellished the details she particularly hoped would incline Joanna toward sympathy, and shed a number of wistful tears.

"You should have written," Joanna scolded, even though there was a flash of the old, selfless love in her blue eyes.

Athena executed a rather tragic sigh. "I didn't see any point in alarming you, Mama. You were so far away—you and Papa would have worried."

Joanna shook her head. "If there is one ability you have never lacked, Athena, it is that of looking after yourself."

Stung, Athena thrust aside her cup and saucer and tried to block the angry words that were rising, like steam, within her.

She was only partially successful. "Who is that young woman, Mother? Why is she staying here?"

Joanna's voice was annoyingly fond. "Rachel is Griffin's friend. And I think he has very serious intentions toward her."

The news came as a brutal shock to Athena; while she had felt an immediate dislike for Rachel, she had never dreamed that the naive thing could be any kind of threat. "That isn't possible," she protested, in a harsh whisper, her cheeks warm with sudden color.

But Joanna was nodding. "Yes, Athena, it is possible. He's coming back for her on Thursday or Friday, in fact—in spite of Jonas Wilkes, Griffin plans to take Rachel to Providence with him."

Athena felt doubly wounded. "Why would that concern Jonas?" she dared, after a long, groping silence.

Joanna sat back in her chair and folded her arms. The brown silk of her blouse gleamed in the afternoon sunshine streaming in through the dining-room windows. "Griffin tells me that Jonas fancies himself in love with Rachel—as if Jonas Wilkes could possibly love anyone."

Athena's throat worked spasmodically for a moment, before she managed to bring herself under rigid control. "That's it, then—you know Griffin opposes anything Jonas wants. They're like oil and fire, those two. If Griffin has declared some affection for this Rachel person, it is only because he loves to nettle Jonas!"

Joanna's spoon clattered as she stirred lemon into her second cup of tea. "Nonsense. Griffin's feelings were clear to anyone who took the trouble to look. Both your father and I knew immediately that he adored Rachel."

"No," said Athena, shaking her head once in feverish denial.

But Joanna surveyed her without pity. "Don't tell me you've come all the way home from Paris just to chase after Griffin Fletcher; if you have, you're letting yourself in for a nasty shock. I do believe he hates you."

Athena grappled for the bright hopes she had nursed all these weeks just past, but they were suddenly elusive. "I want Griffin, Mother," she said, as a headache began at the nape of her neck and climbed, pounding, to her temples. "And I will have him."

Joanna raised her teacup in a toasting gesture that bordered on mockery. "So the sheep woos the raging panther. Or is it the other way around, Athena?"

Athena leaned forward, her lower lip trembling, her hands clenched together in her lap. "You hate me, don't you, Mother? You hate me because I disgraced your precious good name!"

Without warning, Joanna's hand lashed out, made sharp contact with Athena's face. The cold silence that followed found Athena reeling, inwardly, in shock. Never, even during the worst of times, had her mother struck her.

She was just recovering when Joanna went ruthlessly on. "You disgraced yourself, Athena—not your father and I, not Griffin. *Yourself.* Furthermore, you know that I do not hate you—you are my only living child and, God help me, I love you very much. All the same, it would behoove you to remember that I, unlike some people, see through your theatrics and your simpering witchery, Athena."

"Mother!"

But Joanna's face was hard, implacable. "Tread lightly, Athena. Sooner or later, we are always compensated for the things we've done, and in kind. Your compensation might be evil indeed, my dear, because Griffin Fletcher had done nothing to deserve your cruelty. Nothing but swim against the tide of your formidable will."

"Y-You almost sound as though you hope I'll be destroyed," Athena whispered, aghast.

"On the contrary, I hope you will be spared. But I don't think that's very likely. I must admit, you have met your match in Miss Rachel McKinnon, my dear."

Athena was considering this almost inconceivable possibility when Rachel herself appeared, looking small and frightened and hopelessly untutored in the ways of the world. Her bright purple eyes were fixed on Joanna's face.

"I-I think perhaps I should go back to Miss Cunningham's—"

Before her mother could speak, Athena floated to her feet, all gracious solicitude, and smiled winningly. "Of course you won't leave, Rachel! Tomorrow is my birthday, and there's bound to be a party. You wouldn't want to miss *that* would you?"

The wretch's confusion was balm to Athena's chafed spirit. *Oh, Griffin, you magnificent idiot,* she thought. *What you feel for this orchid-eyed woman-child is pity, not love.*

Joanna spoke suddenly, her tone sharp. "There will be no party, Athena."

But there would; Athena knew it for a certainty. Never, in all her life, had she ever been denied a single desire—and the party would be no exception.

Calmly, Athena turned and swept out of the room to prepare. Once people had been invited, there would be nothing her mother could do except be gracious.

Chapter Twenty-four

It was very dark outside.

Jonas looked up from the accounts spread over the surface of his desk and frowned. The lace curtains billowed at the window, and for one insane second, he thought he heard his name on the nightwind.

He stood up, strode to the window, and lowered the sill with a resounding crash. He had to stop being so superstitious, he told himself. He'd done nothing that he hadn't had to do.

But when the door of his office opened abruptly behind him, Jonas tensed.

McKay was standing there, looking as stupid as ever, and much too pleased with himself. "You got a telegraph letter here—that lawman-storekeeper just gave it to me."

Jonas was alarmed, and suddenly glad of any company—even McKay's. He held out his hand for the message, unfolded it, and read, JUNE 5 MY BIRTHDAY. COME CELEBRATE. ATHENA.

Certain that there must be some mistake, Jonas scanned the hand-copied telegram again. There was no mistake; Athena was in Seattle and, from the looks of things, up to her usual no good.

Jonas groped for his desk chair and fell back into it, stunned. He wouldn't have believed she had the audacity to come back, not after all that had happened.

But what an opportune time she had chosen! Jonas sat back in his chair, kicked his feet up onto the desk, and laughed, low in his throat. "Bring some brandy, McKay—and some extra glasses. Unless I miss my guess, we'll have company within five minutes."

McKay brought the requested items grudgingly, probably

resenting the task. Jonas dismissed him with a curt nod, cupped his hands behind his head, and waited.

He'd been wrong about the time element, but that was all. Half an hour had passed when he heard the front doors open in the distance, and then, from the stairs, the outraged approach of not one set of boots, but two.

Jonas smiled. So Field Hollister had been invited, too. Well, that was like Athena—the more the merrier.

Griffin entered the office with as much decorum as he'd bothered with downstairs, sending the heavy door crashing against the inside wall. In his right hand was the telegram, and in his face was murder.

"What the hell is going on?" he shouted.

Field flushed with embarrassment and laid a restraining hand on Griffin's shoulder. "Will you just calm down?" he hissed.

Griffin shrugged the hand away, never once averting his ominous gaze from Jonas's face. "If this is one of your tricks, Wilkes, I swear—"

Jonas smiled, brought his hands from behind his head, and folded them calmly in his lap. "I'm as surprised as you are," he said. And then he pulled his own message, which he suspected was a duplicate of the others, from his shirt pocket and tossed it onto the desk.

Griffin picked it up, consumed it in a glance, and flung it down again. He swore hoarsely, and turned his back.

"You're going, of course?" asked Jonas affably. "It will be The Event of the year, I think."

"I don't believe this," Griffin raged, in an undertone that was somehow far more threatening than a shout would have been. "I don't believe it!"

Jonas braced his thumbs beneath his chin, fingers touching at the tips and splayed. It was all he could do not to laugh aloud. "How about you, Field? Will you forsake your devoted flock for a night of intrigue?"

Field's reply was a scorching glare that just missed smelling of sulphur.

Allowing himself a cautious smirk, Jonas went on, addressing his words to Griffin's taut back. "Rachel will understand about Athena," he said reasonably. "Or have you already broken our bargain and declared your undying love?"

Griffin swung slowly around, and his eyes were glittering with an emotion Jonas wouldn't have dared to recognize. "What I have or have not said to Rachel is none of your concern," he said, in that same vicious monotone he'd used before. "But if you've had any part in this, I promise you, I'll tear you apart!"

"A distinctly unpleasant prospect," replied Jonas dispassionately. "This time, I'm innocent."

Now, it was Field who turned away in an obvious effort to control himself.

Griffin's eyes fell on the brandy waiting on the corner of Jonas's desk. Briskly, he opened the bottle and poured double shots into two glasses, one of which he shoved at Field.

To Jonas's enormous amusement, the pastor drank with unusual thirst.

But Griffin was perched on the side of the desk, swirling his own drink, untouched, in his glass. "What's keeping you, Jonas? Why aren't you on the way to Seattle to reclaim your woman?"

Jonas didn't dare smile, though he wanted to. He wanted to so much that he ached inside. "I promised not to, remember?"

Griffin scowled. "I'm talking about Athena, and you know it."

"I don't want Athena, I want Rachel."

A visible tremor moved in Griffin's wide shoulders, made the brandy rise in small, amber billows in his glass. "You don't want Athena. Now it seems to me that you once wanted her very much."

Jonas shrugged. "So did you."

Griffin downed his drink in one swallow, and a muscle tightened in his neck, creating an ominous, pulsing cord. When he looked at Jonas, there was a frightening smile twisting his features. "I've made love to Rachel," he said flatly.

The words struck Jonas in just the way Griffin had probably intended them to. He felt a knotting sickness in his stomach, an ache in his jaw. "Liar!" he spat.

"Griffin, in the name of heaven—" Field pleaded, his own anger forgotten.

But there was no stopping him. "She was a virgin, Jonas."

It wasn't true that Rachel had surrendered to this man; Jonas couldn't bear for it to be true. He fought to control his voice, his muscles, his emotions. "You're lying, you bastard. You're lying because you came back from your fancy San Francisco convention and you found your precious Athena cavorting in my bed!"

Griffin closed his eyes against the memory, but Jonas could

204

see that it had followed him into the darkness. "Shut up," he rasped.

Field broke in deftly, his voice calm. "Stop it, both of you. There is nothing to be gained by this."

Hatred pulsed in the room, like an unseen entity, seeming to pound at the walls and ceiling.

It was Field, the eternal peacemaker, who plunged into the breach. "There is a simple way to defuse this situation, you know," he offered quietly. "Both of you ignore Athena—pretend she isn't back, pretend she doesn't exist, for that matter. Stay away from the party."

Griffin shook his head. "I'll be damned if I'll stay away and let that she-wolf tear Rachel apart."

Field was clearly exasperated. "Griffin, you are assuming a great deal. It's possible that Athena returned to Seattle for reasons that have nothing to do with you—and, thus, nothing to do with Rachel."

Jonas relaxed, with considerable difficulty. "You're wasting your breath, Field. It is inconceivable to our arrogant friend here that anything other than deathless passion would bring her home again."

Griffin frowned at the glass in his hand, set it down with a crash. A moment later, he was striding through the office doorway. "I'll see you at the party, Jonas," he called, over his shoulder.

Outside, in the muggy night air, Griffin raised his face to the star-strewn sky and wished incongruously and fiercely that it would rain.

Field stormed to the hitching rail, untying his horse's reins with quick, furious motions. "That was wonderful, Griffin," he snarled. " 'I've made love to Rachel. She was a virgin, Jonas.' "

Griffin stiffened at the angry mimicry in his friend's voice. "All right. I shouldn't have said it!"

Field swung up into the saddle, his horse dancing fretfully beneath him, as though it shared its master's outrage. "How do you think Rachel is going to feel, Griffin, when she hears that from Jonas? And rest assured, she will!"

Griffin ached. There was no excuse for what he'd done, and he knew it. In return for a moment of delicious revenge, he had betrayed a woman as necessary to him as the breath in his lungs. "You know I wouldn't hurt her, Field."

Jaw tight in the moonlight, Field waited while Griffin untied Tempest and climbed gingerly into the saddle. "Be careful, Griffin. You know how you felt about Athena. If you risk facing her again, and you find out that things haven't really changed—"

Griffin spat. "I despise her."

"Do you?" retorted Field. "Well, keep in mind, my friend, that love and hate are sometimes almost impossible to untangle from each other. If you can't offer Rachel honest, undiluted devotion, then let her go."

They rode in silence for a minute or so, both listening to the steady cadence of their horse's hooves striking the cobblestones of Jonas's driveway.

But as they passed beneath the frame of the gate, and onto the road, Griffin's irritation got the best of him. "You're a hypocrite, Field," he observed. "'Honest, undiluted devotion' is it? Is that what you're giving the woman you love?"

To his credit, Field didn't curse. "I love her more than my own life, Griffin, and you know it."

"Then why don't you tell the world? Why don't you marry her?"

Field sighed, and it was a broken sound, a sound that made Griffin regret raising the subject at all. "She refuses to marry me. There doesn't seem to be much point in 'telling the world.' She would be ruined, and so would I."

With the heels of his boots, Griffin prodded his horse to a dead run. "You're insane!" he yelled, into the wind.

Field's half-wild pony caught up to Tempest easily. "Coming from you, that is praise indeed!" he shouted back.

Griffin laughed out loud. "So it is," he retorted, reining in his horse again, slowing it to a canter.

Field followed suit. "You're really going to that party, aren't you?" he asked, his eyes searching Griffin's face in the moonlight. "You're going to stumble right into Athena's trap, whatever it is."

"Don't worry, Field," Griffin returned blithely. "I'll come out with the bait."

"That's what I'm afraid of."

"I was talking about Rachel."

Field nodded. "I know. And I'm talking about Athena. Don't underestimate her, Griffin. She brought you to your knees once before, and she could do it again."

Griffin scanned the magnificent sky in exasperation and then, deftly, changed the subject. "How about a drink?" he said. "I'll bet it would liven things up over at Becky's Place if you walked in."

Field laughed. "I've got better things to do, thanks."

"Who knows, Field? You might save a few souls, or something."

Hollister shook his head, laughed again, and prodded his horse into an answering run. Griffin turned onto his own property, thinking that maybe Field could see to the saving of Athena's soul. Provided she had one.

Fawn Nighthorse lay still in the forbidden bed, waiting. Moonlight shafted in through a window, eerie and beautiful, bathing her bare skin in silver.

She sighed, then caught her breath as she heard a door open and close again. His name escaped her in a hoarse, broken whisper.

"No," he said, from the bedroom doorway, but his voice was trembling, uneven.

Patiently, Fawn patted the bed, and after an obvious, interminable struggle, he came to her, stretching out, fully clothed, on the counterpane. He groaned as she unbuttoned his shirt, slid her hands gently over the strong, warm width of his chest.

Raising herself to her hands and knees, Fawn let the nipple of one breast trail slowly across his mouth. When she felt the responding flick of his tongue, she cried out softly, pressing her breast to his lips in a gesture of pleading.

But he slid from beneath her and sat up in the darkness, watching her. On her knees beside him, Fawn waited.

He was still for an eternity, it seemed, but then he traced the outline of one of her breasts with an index finger. Still kneeling, Fawn leaned back until her shoulders touched the rough, cool wall.

He groaned and came to her. His lips explored her neck, her collarbone, the soft undersides of her breasts. His tongue came back to a nipple, worked its wicked, pleasing magic, teasing until the peak was hard and pointed with need. When it was, he suckled.

Fawn's entire body began to move to the rhythm of her pleasure, of her love. His mouth moved to the untasted breast,

207

again nibbling, teasing, tugging. The nipple was distended, and he sucked only the very end until she begged him, in hoarse, incoherent words, and then begged again.

At last, he suckled, hungrily, and his fingers caressed the throbbing nubbin between her legs lightly, drawing at it, flicking it, rubbing it.

Fawn trembled, cried out, and convulsed in the throes of her release.

Grasping his shoulders, Fawn pressed her lover backward, until he lay flat, vulnerable. Slowly, she undid his trousers. He writhed, groaning, as she freed him, knelt between his knees.

It was she who teased and tempted now, she who nibbled until he was pleading raggedly for fulfillment. Satisfied that his arousal was complete, Fawn straddled him, guided him gently inside her.

They moved in an ancient and beautiful rhythm, slowly at first, and then more rapidly. Fawn's second shattering release exploded within her just as he cried out in the naked need of his own.

There were tears on Fawn's face as she lay down beside him, her hand kneading his taut, sweaty stomach. "I love you," she said.

"No, you don't," he replied, in an undertone.

Fawn sat up quickly. "I do!" she cried out.

But she could see that he was shaking his head. "If you did, you would marry me," he reasoned, without petulance or rancor.

Desperately, Fawn dashed at her tears. "If you married me, it would be the end of everything for you!"

"It would be the beginning," he argued, implacably. "I can't stand this anymore, Fawn. I can't keep hiding what I really feel. I'm not ashamed, even if you are."

Fawn crawled over him, awkward in her haste, and lit the lamp standing on the bedside table. Staring down at his face, she saw desolation, and she wept because his desolation was her own. "Oh, Field, you can't marry an Indian!"

"Why not? I *love* an Indian."

"You'll lose your church!"

"For what—getting married? I'm a minister, not a priest."

"For marrying *me!*" she screamed.

Field turned away from her, his back taut in the soft glow of the lamplight. "This is wrong, Fawn. Our meeting like this, your 'visits' with Jonas, all of it. Marry me, so I can face God again."

Shattered, Fawn slipped to her knees, tangled the fingers of one hand in the glossy chestnut hair at the back of his head. "They will call you Squaw Man," she breathed.

He rolled back again, to face her. "I wouldn't care what they called me, Fawn."

"But our children—"

"Our children will be 'half-breeds'—is that what you were going to say?"

"Yes!"

"Fawn, don't you see that it will be their own opinion of themselves that matters, and not the opinion of some nebulous 'they'? We'll love them so much that they'll feel safe and strong and wanted, no matter what anyone else has to say."

Fawn was silent for a long time, considering. To marry Field Hollister was the dream of her life, and had been since the first time she'd laid eyes on him years before, when his mother and father had found her wandering in a Seattle street, hungry and alone, and brought her to live with them.

Field had hardly noticed her, for he was ten years older and ready to sail off to a place called Scotland, with Griffin Fletcher. When he did, Fawn had been devastated. Night after night, week after week, year after year, she had lain in her small bed, in the attic of the house that was gone now, weeping for him.

Even when he returned, an ordained minister, Fawn had still been a child in his eyes. He had suffered her endless adoration with characteristic good humor, allowed her to arrange and rearrange his multitude of lofty, theological texts, and eaten the abominable things she baked for him in Mrs. Hollister's oven.

He had even taken her along on calls sometimes; she would sit and listen to him offering counsel and compassion and she would wish that he would notice her, really notice her.

For a time, Field had shown an offhanded interest in Ruby Sheridan, the judge's daughter, taking her to the occasional social, enduring Griffin's ruthless, constant baiting with a shake of his head and a grin.

And Fawn had promised the spirits that she would never do another bad thing if only they would make Field Hollister love her as a man loves a woman.

As so often happened, the answer came in tragedy, with Griffin Fletcher's near collapse. Field's empathy for his friend had been so great that he had suffered Griffin's grief as his own.

Soon after that, the Hollisters' house burned, and both Field's parents were gone. Field and the little Indian orphan his mother and father had grimly cherished turned to each other for comfort. Gradually, a tempestuous, on-and-off love had grown between them.

Now the reckoning had come. Fawn was faced with two choices, both of which, she knew, had the power to destroy Field forever. If she married him, he would be scorned, maybe even dismissed from his church. If she did not, the results might be equally disastrous.

"I'll marry you, Field Hollister," she whispered.

Field drew her into his arms, his eyes gentle as they searched her face. "It will be good, Fawn—you'll see."

"Yes," she said, trying to sound certain that it would. "I-I'd better leave now, Field, before the light comes."

But his arms tightened around her. "No. We'll be married tomorrow, in Seattle."

Fawn smiled and silently petitioned his God to show mercy.

Rachel was desperate, that hot and glaring Wednesday morning, so desperate that she sneaked out of the O'Riley house before anyone was awake and began the long walk downtown.

She would buy clothes of her own, even though it meant dipping into the cherished cash reserves stored at the Commerce Bank. Wearing Athena's clothes was unbearable.

Rachel was nearing the business district when she realized that her bankbook was in her handbag—which she hadn't seen since the night Jonas had taken her to stay in his hotel room.

She was frightened—wildly frightened. Suppose the bank wouldn't give back her money, since she couldn't produce proof that the account was really hers? She would be penniless!

Rachel broke into an undignified run and was breathless by the time she reached the bank's doors—which were soundly locked. The establishment would not open for business for more than an hour.

Chapter Twenty-five

Fitful, Rachel paced the board sidewalk for some minutes, wondering what to do. If she pounded on the shaded glass windows in the bank's doors with her fists, would someone come and let her in?

Her heart scrambled into her throat and turned there, hurting. That money was the only security she had.

There were produce wagons lumbering over the plank streets of Seattle now, carrying early crops of lettuce and peas and rhubarb to market. Rachel raised her eyes to the pearlescent blue of the sky and felt a peculiar uneasiness—one that had nothing to do with her lost bankbook, her fear of Athena, or her love for Griffin Fletcher. *Please God,* she prayed silently, unaccountably. *Let it rain.*

But the still warmth of the air precluded rain. Rachel moved toward the waterfront, stood staring, for a long time, at the soft brightness of Elliott Bay.

Even though it was early, the harbor was busy. The salmon were striking further out; boat after boat arrived, burdened with the catch. Merchants waited on the wharfs, scrambling to pay cash money for their share.

Rachel watched for a while, still feeling unsettled, and then walked on, rounding the edge of the bay. The tideflat squished beneath her kid leather shoes as she walked, kicking an occasional stone out of her way. Tiny hermit crabs scurried in every direction, panicked at her passing.

She watched as a gull garnered a clam from the mud, swooped into the sky and hovered. The bird dropped the shell onto a pile of rocks, breaking it open, and then wafted down to eat the soft gray meat inside.

Rachel walked on, feeling as helpless and vulnerable as that denuded clam. Of its own accord, her mind shifted to the coming party.

In spite of Joanna's protests, Athena had gone ahead and invited dozens of people. Half of Seattle would probably converge on the O'Riley house, and much of the outlying regions, too.

Rachel froze suddenly, the low tide pooling around her shoes. Griffin. Had Athena, in her cool grace, had the nerve to invite him?

Rachel trembled at the prospect. While part of her yearned for Griffin's presence, another part truly feared it. He could hardly venture into the O'Riley house without coming face to face with Athena.

Knees trembling beneath her, Rachel found a huge, brown rock and sat down on it, staring sightlessly at the calm waters of the bay. She wondered about the mysterious André, who had had the temerity to divorce such a woman. If he could resist her considerable charms to such an extent, perhaps, by some miracle, Griffin could prevail against her, too.

Provided he wished to prevail.

The bank was open for business by the time Rachel gathered her thoughts and wandered back to the center of town.

Without going into the outlandish details, Rachel explained the loss of her bankbook to a sympathetic clerk. After a conference with another clerk, he issued Rachel a new account number and counted out the amount of her withdrawal.

With one hundred dollars crumpled in her hand, Rachel ventured up the street and into a dress and millinery shop. There was no time to have a gown cut and fitted, not with the party scheduled for that very night, but perhaps something readymade could be had.

The inside of the shop was small and cluttered, and Rachel was overwhelmed for a moment. What did she know about buying gowns for fancy parties? Panic nipped at the edges of her mind.

But as the proprietor approached, Rachel raised her chin. She need not, *would* not appear at that party looking like the country girl she was.

Quietly, and with dignity, Rachel explained her need for a special gown, befitting such an occasion.

The dressmaker was helpful, and she was patient. She produced garment after garment, smiling as Rachel rejected one after another. One, made of black silk and boasting a high, ruffled collar, was too dramatic and somber. Another, made of dove gray velvet, made Rachel look like a little girl dressing up in her mother's clothes.

But, at last, the right dress appeared. A simple, flowing

garment of the softest apricot lawn, it revealed the swell of Rachel's fine breasts and accentuated the trim lines of her waist.

After minor alterations had been made, and measurements taken for the dresses, skirts, and shirtwaists she wanted, Rachel paid for everything and watched in wonder as the magnificent gown was folded into a box and extended to her.

In another store, she purchased soft velvet slippers and a lacy, ivory shawl. Then, her tour complete, Rachel walked back up the hill, toward the O'Riley house.

Joanna met her at the front door, looking distraught. "Oh, Rachel—where have you been? I've been so worried!"

Rachel blushed with shame. She might have known this kind woman would miss her almost immediately, and be upset. "I'm sorry—I had some errands. . . ."

Joanna drew a deep breath and ushered Rachel through the dining room, where preparations were already being made for the party, and into the kitchen. There, Cook was grumbling over an enormous bowl of white batter.

Rachel sank into a chair and sipped the tea Joanna offered in grateful silence.

"I'm sorry, Rachel," the woman said, after a few moments, "About the party, I mean."

Rachel set her teacup down in its translucent china saucer and smiled. "Please, don't be. It is Athena's birthday and—"

At that moment, Athena swept in, resplendent in an ivory silk dressing gown embroidered with delicate pink flowers, her soft, platinum hair still rumpled, her indigo eyes bright. "It is indeed my birthday," she chimed, plunging an index finger mischievously into Cook's bowl of batter. "And I feel more like a hundred than twenty-five."

"You are twenty-seven," said Joanna, mischief sparkling in her own eyes as she smiled at Rachel.

Athena shrugged, her glance falling on the dressmaker's box leaning against the side of Rachel's chair. "Why—you've bought something of your *own!*" she cried, as though the idea was inconceivable. "What did you buy, Rachel? Let me see!"

Suddenly, Rachel was not so certain that the apricot gown was right after all. Perhaps, to this woman, it would seem unsophisticated, even childish. She blushed. "Well—"

"Oh, don't be such a little ninny!" Athena scolded good-naturedly, snatching another taste of the batter and wincing when Cook slapped her hand. "I'm not going to laugh at your little dress, Rachel."

Rachel looked to Joanna and saw a smile shining in her gentle blue eyes. Slowly, she lifted the red- and white-striped box to her lap and opened it. Then, with cautious fingers, she drew the soft, sunrise-colored creation out.

"Stand up," Joanna urged softly, "And let us see how it looks with that magnificent hair of yours."

Rachel obeyed, her throat working painfully.

"Oh," breathed Joanna, "Oh, Rachel, it is lovely!"

Athena's response rang with a petulant, fretful note. "Don't you think it's a little—well—girlish?"

Joanna was beaming at Rachel, allaying her fears of looking foolish. "Devastatingly so," she said.

"Lawn," Athena muttered, touching the fabric with fingers that trembled ever so slightly. "Yes—I think lawn is suitable for a girl your age."

Joanna's teacup rattled against its saucer with refined fury. "Do be quiet, Athena. Anyone can see that Rachel is a woman, not a girl."

Athena was frowning at the neckline of the splendid dress now, brow knitted prettily. "Are you sure you should reveal so much—bosom?"

Rachel smiled wickedly, remembering. If there was one aspect of her appearance that she could be certain Griffin approved of, it was the full roundness of her breasts. "I'm sure," she said.

The indigo eyes searched her face, and Athena's frown deepened. An instinctive knowing passed between the two women, and Rachel was glad to see some of the fetching pink color drain from Athena's complexion.

At midafternoon, the gifts began to arrive. Athena did not bother to open them, though many were gaily wrapped and ribboned. Until a parcel arrived with Griffin's name on the card, she would have no interest in birthday presents.

In the cool, dim sanction of the parlor, Athena sank into a chair. Griffin had not responded to her telegram—was he too busy with those pathetic patients of his? She had known him to miss more than one social event because some millworker had broken an arm, leg, or neck. She closed her eyes. Griffin had to come. He had to.

Through the open windows, Athena heard the rattling squeak of carriage wheels. Crossing the room swiftly, she lifted the edge of a curtain and peered out, her heart hammering in her throat.

Griffin Fletcher was striding up the walk, coatless, glowering in a way that gave Athena pause—until her eyes fell on the flat, narrow package clasped in his right hand.

She smiled to herself, scrambled into the entry hall, and wrenched open the door just as he raised one ominous fist to knock. "Griffin," she said, in a small, strangled voice.

Murderous contempt flashed in the dark eyes, and he spoke in a tone that was hardly less than savage. "Tired of Paris so soon? Or were they tired of you?"

Athena bowed her head slightly, under the incredible impact of his anger. "If we could only talk—" she faltered. "J-Just for a few minutes—"

"Let's not," he snapped.

When Athena dared to meet his gaze again, she found that it was ruthless and wounding. "Griffin, don't be stubborn—please. . . ."

His jaw tightened, and he started to speak, but before he could, Rachel came flying down the stairs, clutching her billowing apricot dress.

"Griffin!"

Incredibly, Griffin extended his arms to that bounding mannerless girl, and the rancor Athena had seen in his face was gone in an instant, replaced by a look of gentle hunger. "Hello, Sprite," he said softly, as Rachel hesitated and then flung herself into his arms.

Stunned and humiliated, Athena retreated a step.

Rachel looked up at Griffin with wide, glistening eyes, apparently forgetting the dress crushed between them. "I didn't think—" she sputtered, "I hoped—"

Griffin laughed, and one of his hands moved to caress the flushed, shining face. For one unbearable moment, Athena thought he would kiss the wretch, right then and there.

Instead, he glanced down at the soft, floaty fabric of the dress. "What's this? A sunset all stitched and hemmed?"

Rachel smiled uncertainly and whispered something, but Athena was too shaken to hear what it was. Griffin, waxing poetic? It was impossible!

Outrage climbed into Athena's throat on spiky feet—they didn't even seem to know she was there! "For heaven's sake,

Rachel," she cried, to let them take notice, "Don't hang all over the man like wisteria on a trellis!"

Rachel paled slightly, and drew back in Griffin's embrace, only to be pulled close again. His gaze swept from Rachel's face to Athena's, searing her in a flash of malicious disdain.

Athena didn't know whether to be devastated or relieved when he finally looked away. She lifted her chin. There was still the package—for all his attention to Rachel, for all his contempt, he had brought a gift. And that meant that he was merely repaying her for old injuries, that the charade would end when he was satisfied that his grievance had been avenged.

But now, unbelievably, he was extending the gift to Rachel, and his smile made him look like a besotted schoolboy.

Athena swallowed the screaming fit that burned, raw, in her throat. *Bastard,* she thought. *I'll see you crawl for this!*

Rachel's hands trembled fetchingly as she unwrapped the package, and her face glowed when the strand of precious, luminescent pearls caught the light. "Oh, Griffin . . ."

Griffin did not seem aware of Athena's presence, or her outrage. His dark eyes shone as he gently clasped the delicate necklace around Rachel's neck, beneath her hair.

Athena turned on one heel and stumbled into the desperately needed privacy of the parlor. There, looking up at the portrait that would have been her parents' wedding gift to Griffin, she wept bitter, strangled tears.

For a time, she heard their muted voices, Griffin's and Rachel's, and then, after a long interval, the closing of the front door. Athena shot out of her chair, laid both hands on the hand-painted vase that had graced the piano as long as she could remember, and flung it wildly in the direction of the fireplace.

The report of its shattering seemed to echo, chimelike, into forever and back again.

"Athena?" The voice was gentle, firm.

Athena closed her eyes. "Go away, Mama. Please go away!"

"I warned you," said Joanna, softly.

Athena whirled, wild with grief and anger and humiliation. *"He gave her the pearls!"* she shrieked.

Joanna approached, stopping just short of Athena to perch on the arm of a chair and fold her hands. "What pearls?" she asked, reasonably.

Athena's disappointment was bitter, fathomless. The pain drove her to pace frantically back and forth, along the edge of the hearth. "T-they belonged to G-Griffin's mother," she sobbed, raggedly. "H-her wedding present f-from his f-father—"

"I see."

"You *don't* see! Those pearls should have been mine. *He* should have been mine!"

There was a measure of sympathetic impatience in Joanna's answer. "You are torturing yourself needlessly, Darling. Griffin's feelings have obviously changed, and there is nothing you can do about that."

Athena was still pacing. "No! If I tell him I'm sorry—that I made a mistake—"

"Some mistakes simply can't be rectified, Athena. You've lost Griffin—you lost him a long time ago. For your own sake, accept that."

But the dreams were spinning again in Athena's mind, and she caught hold of them with both hands. Griffin loved her—he was only trying to punish her now, to hurt her the way he'd been hurt.

She smiled. Griffin had one great weakness, and no one knew better than Athena what it was or how to use it.

"Where did they go, Rachel and Griffin, I mean?" she asked, in a tone that belied the violent exchange just past.

Joanna looked alarmed—probably, she thought her daughter had gone mad. It was a long time before she answered. "To a wedding, I think. One of Griffin's friends is getting married today."

"I see," said Athena, companionably. And then she swept past her stunned mother and made her way up the stairway and into her room. She would wear the blue silk tonight, she decided. The one that André had bought for her, the one that had caused such a stir in Paris.

Fawn was afraid to go inside the church, afraid the minister would take one look at her and berate Field for choosing such a wife. Tears gathered in her eyes, making it hard to see Rachel clearly.

But Rachel took her arm. "What is it?" she whispered. "Don't you want to marry Field?"

Fawn dashed at her tears with one hand, grateful that Griffin and Field had already gone inside, that they couldn't see her crying. "What if the minister won't marry us, Rachel?" she asked, sniffling.

Rachel produced a clean handkerchief. "He's Field's uncle! And why on earth wouldn't he want to perform the ceremony?"

"Look at me!" Fawn hissed, furiously, swabbing at her face with the handkerchief.

Rachel studied her, looking honestly puzzled. "You look wonderful—except that your eyes are a little puffy."

In spite of herself, in spite of everything, Fawn laughed out loud. It was no use explaining—not to this gentle, unbiased, and absolutely wonderful idiot. She drew a deep breath. "I'm ready, then. And Rachel?"

Rachel frowned, already tugging Fawn in the direction of the church doors. "What?"

"When you come back to Providence, will you be my friend? I think I'm going to need somebody like you."

Rachel laughed, the heels of her shoes clicking merrily along the pine-board walk leading through the churchyard. "I was going to say that same thing to you, Fawn Nighthorse. I just hadn't worked up the courage yet."

At the doors, Fawn hesitated again, offering a brief, silent prayer to Field's God. *Spare him, please. Let all the hatred rest on me.*

The wedding, simple as it was, was so splendidly romantic that Rachel wept without shame. Field's back was so very straight, and he looked so proud standing there. Flashing an occasional exalted smile at his bride, he repeated his vows in a strong voice.

Fawn was clearly terrified; all the while, Rachel could see her trembling, sense her fear. But when the gentle, white-haired reverend spoke the final, binding words, Fawn Hollister cried out for joy and flung both arms around her husband's neck.

Later, when the congratulations had been made, and the four members of the wedding party had wandered outside, Fawn turned to Griffin with a look of sisterly annoyance on her upturned face.

"Did you talk Field into this?" she demanded.

Griffin laughed. "Who—me? I begged him to reconsider!"

"Liar," retorted Fawn, bright, affectionate tears shimmering in her eyes, a tiny smile curving one corner of her mouth upward.

Again, Griffin laughed. He picked Fawn up by the waist, lifted her high in the air, and then set her, stumbling, on her feet. Bending slightly, he kissed her forehead. "Be happy," he said, in a gruff voice.

"Will you unhand my wife?" Field blustered, his blue eyes luminous with happiness and laughter.

Rachel stood just a little apart, watching. Her fingers strayed to the delicate strand of pearls at her throat and softly, cautiously, she dared to hope.

Chapter Twenty-six

With a sigh, Griffin sank into the leather chair facing John O'Riley's desk. He supposed this conversation was inevitable, but he dreaded it, all the same. It would be hard to separate his feelings—loathing for Athena, abiding respect for John—but he knew he had to. John had no illusions where she was concerned, but he was her father and, quite naturally, he loved her.

"If you're going to ask what my intentions are," he said directly, "I don't have any. Not toward Athena, anyway."

There was a weariness Griffin well understood in the set of the old man's shoulders, in the depths of his wise, gentle eyes. "You were always a blunt sort, Griffin," he observed, settling into the chair behind his desk and reaching for his pipe. "It's one of the things I like best about you."

Griffin was tired, in spite of his happiness for Field and his new wife, in spite of the tender misery of being near Rachel and not being able to touch her. And the confrontation with Athena had not left him entirely untouched, either. He hated himself for letting her make him lose control like that. "There are a few things you don't like, I suspect."

"Absolutely," replied John, striking a match and holding the flame over the bowl of his pipe. Clouds of cherry-scented smoke billowed around his head. "You're stubborn, opinionated, hotheaded and not a little tyrannical. You would have been a perfect husband for my daughter."

Griffin sighed. "John—"

"Now relax. I'm not going to start pleading with you to forgive and forget—I know you can't. Don't think I could, either, if that happened to me."

"Then what is it?"

"Don't strike back at her, Griffin. Don't hurt her."

Griffin wondered if he would ever have a daughter, and love her the way this man loved his—without reserve. He hoped so. "I won't, John."

"She was in a state after you left, according to Joanna," John persisted, reasonably.

Griffin stood up suddenly, and turned his back. Thumbs hooked behind the buckle of his belt, he made a deliberate, methodical study of the ceiling. "I'm sorry," he said. "I'll avoid her from now on."

"That might not be as easy as you think," answered John O'Riley, ruefully. "My daughter has apparently decided that she wants you back. Griffin, there is no telling what she might do—turn around and look at me!"

Slowly, reluctantly, Griffin turned. "She made her choice a long time ago, John," he said, in measured tones. "As long as she leaves Rachel alone, I don't care what she does."

The old man sighed, drew on his pipe. "That is exactly my point, Griffin—Joanna and I are both worried about Rachel. She is an innocent, and if Athena levels some kind of destructive campaign at her, she could be hurt very badly."

Griffin's voice sounded hoarse in the quiet, dignified room. "Is Rachel well enough to travel?"

Grimly, Griffin thought, John nodded. "She is. But, as you know, full recovery could take a long time. From what little the young lady has confided to Joanna and me, I'd say she's been through a great deal during the past few weeks. Griffin, she simply can't tolerate very much stress."

Griffin clenched and unclenched his fists. "Go on," he rasped, impatiently.

John's voice was cautious, even. "Griffin, make certain that you understand your own feelings. Go slowly, give things time."

"Time?" he snapped. "I've been 'giving things time' for two years, John! I've been 'giving things time' since the night I found—"

"Since the night you found my daughter with another man. I know, Griffin. But even now you aren't indifferent to Athena—don't you see that?"

It was undeniable. He wanted to kill her, but he wasn't indifferent. And he knew that he should be. "I don't love her," he said, in an undertone.

"Be very certain of that before you make any binding promises to Rachel, Griffin. To hurt her thoughtlessly would be the ultimate cruelty."

Just the prospect made Griffin feel sick and shaken. "I've slept with Rachel," he confessed, for quite different reasons than he'd had in telling Jonas. "There could be a child."

There was a note of infinite weariness in John's sigh. "Griffin," he said, and the word was at once a reprimand and an absolution.

Griffin lowered his head. "The worst thing is, I'm not sure I can promise that it won't happen again."

"Try to wait—be patient. These things have a way of sorting themselves out."

"John, I just want to marry Rachel. I just want—"

"You want. Fine, Griffin—for your sake and Rachel's, I hope you do marry. But put aside what you want for a moment, and think about her. If you can't make a full commitment, you'll be cheating her."

But there was Jonas to consider, and men like Frazier. Not for the first time, Griffin wondered how much of the raging passion he felt for Rachel was really love, and how much was a need to challenge Jonas. Was he, when all was said and done, just using her?

God help me, I don't know, Griffin thought miserably. *I don't know.*

When he met John's gaze, he saw understanding in his eyes. He turned from it, and walked out of the study, into the hallway.

He would have to talk with Athena. If it killed him, he would be civil, rational—maybe even polite. That would prove to everyone, himself included, that there was nothing left of what he'd felt for her.

Instead of dragging Rachel out of this house, as every instinct warned him to do, he would remain. Suffer through the stupid party. Try to make sense of his thoughts and feelings.

As if anything in the world had made one whit of sense since the day he'd stormed into Jonas's house and laid eyes on Rachel.

With resolve, Griffin squared his shoulders and went off in search of the woman who had so nearly destroyed him.

It was odd, how quickly the romantic spell of the Hollisters' wedding wore off. Standing at her window, Rachel studied the glaring blue sky and felt uneasy again.

On the road below, a carriage clattered into view and came to a smooth stop at the O'Riley's gate. Four men scrambled out, carrying musical instruments in leather cases.

Rachel was instantly alarmed.

Dancing. There would be dancing—she should have known that, would have known it if she hadn't been so stupid. Her heart pounded at the back of her throat.

Except for a few jigs to the brisk tune of a lumberjack's fiddle, Rachel had never danced in her life. What was she going to do if Griffin didn't want to leave before that wretched party began?

What a fool she would look, while Athena swept gracefully around the room, at home in the arms of gentlemen, never missing a step or stumbling over the hem of her gown—

But then, it was as though she could see her father's face again, hear his outraged reprimand. A McKinnon didn't run scared from anything or anybody!

Slowly, Rachel raised her chin. Maybe she would look the fool, maybe people would laugh at her. But she would try—she would watch the others and she would mark what they did and then, as best she could, she would do the same.

Restless, wishing wryly that the McKinnons valued cowardice, Rachel fidgeted at the window. It was then that she saw Griffin striding around the front of the house, toward the garden.

She closed her eyes, not wanting to know what she knew, not wanting to breath or move or even be. But even with her eyes shut, she could still see with her heart, see just as clearly as if she'd been standing at the garden gate.

When Griffin entered that soft, fragrant sanction, Athena would be there.

Grasping the windowframe with both hands, Rachel forced herself to open her eyes. Life wouldn't end if Griffin changed his mind, it wouldn't. She could go on, just as she always had.

Except that her monthly hadn't come when it should have. Tears slid down her face. She still had money, she reminded herself. She still had her mother's building in Providence. . . .

Another carriage rolled in behind the first, drawn by four very familiar black horses. The door opened, and Jonas Wilkes stepped out, looking handsome in his fine clothes, smiling up at the window.

Impetuously, and against her better judgment, Rachel tugged at the sill until it gave way and squeaked upward. "Hello!" she cried, glad to see someone she knew, someone inclined to be friendly.

Comically, Jonas bowed. "Urchin!" he laughed. "You're going to fall and break your beautiful neck!"

Glad that her tears could not possibly show from such a distance, she smiled. "I'm not going to fall—I think I can fly!"

Jonas tilted his head to one side. "Never mind flying, Urchin—can you dance?"

Blushing, Rachel shook her head.

Jonas solved the problem with swift dispatch. "I'll teach you then," he promised.

Before Rachel could answer, Griffin came into view, glowering like a storm cloud, his hands on his hips. Apparently, he had already tired of the intrigue in the garden.

"What is this?" he demanded, glancing sharply from Jonas to Rachel. "The balcony scene from *Romeo and Juliet?*"

Standing behind Griffin, Athena dug her nails into the palms of her hands. What was it about this little nobody that made grown men behave like fools? Merciful heaven, Griffin was ready to fight, and Jonas looked blithely besotted.

Once, Athena thought bitterly, their boundless animosity had had its center in her.

Athena raised her chin, deliberately brushed Griffin as she passed. "Hello, Jonas," she said, summoning up the most engaging smile she possessed.

There was an acknowledgement of her beauty in Jonas's topaz eyes, but nothing else. "Athena," he said, touching the brim of his hat.

In a sidelong glance, Athena saw that Griffin was paying no attention at all to either her or Jonas—he was glaring up at Rachel. "Get down here!" he shouted, so suddenly that both Athena and Jonas flinched.

Rachel thrust out her chin and shouted back, "I will *not,* Griffin Fletcher!"

The little smile Athena scrounged from her dwindling store felt shaky on her mouth. She and Jonas could have been rolling around in the grass, naked as the day they were born, and Griffin wouldn't have noticed.

Jonas, on the other hand, seemed to be perceiving everything; his lips were taut, and his strange golden eyes were boring into Griffin's broad back.

Athena felt renewed pain. So it was true then—Jonas Wilkes had, at last, succumbed to love.

"*Rachel*," Griffin began, in a voice that would have turned Athena's bone marrow to mush, had it been directed at her. "Now!"

Rachel's head bobbed away from the window, but only for a moment. "You will not tell me what to do!" she yelled. And then a patent-toed shoe came hurtling through the still, lilac-scented air and whistled past Griffin's head. It was immediately followed by its mate.

In spite of herself, Athena felt a moment's admiration for the lumberjack's daughter. It was a pity, though, that her aim wasn't better.

Griffin was outraged; a murderous tremor moved in his powerful shoulders. "All right!" he roared. And then he bounded toward the open doors and into the house.

Athena closed her eyes, wondering why she did not feel comforted to know that the lovers were so clearly at odds.

The sound of Griffin's booted feet clamoring up the staircase gave Rachel pause. She must lock the door; she knew that she must—except that Griffin was towering just inside it before she could coerce her frozen muscles to move at all.

His jawline was taut and white with fury, and his dark eyes snapped. But suddenly, incredibly, just when Rachel was beginning to fear for her life, he began to laugh.

It was a full, rich sound, his laughter, and when it finally subsided to a lop-sided smile, Rachel was struck with the feeling that it had, somehow, been medicinal.

"I love you," he said. And then, with a courtly bow, he brought her shoes from behind his back and extended them. "Thank God, you couldn't lift the bureau."

Rachel's emotions churned inside her. "If you love me, Griffin Fletcher," she said, in a brave and dignified voice. "What were you doing in the garden with Athena?"

"Finding out that I do, indeed, love you. For a while, I wasn't sure what I was feeling, Rachel—lust, maybe. Or spite. So I decided that the only sensible thing to do was face Athena and talk to her rationally, just to see if I could."

Rachel's heart was spinning in her throat, like some jagged, spiky thing. "And?"

"And all I felt was pity."

Rachel reached out for her shoes, still suspended in Griffin's hand, and made a great business of putting one of them back onto her foot. Shame pulsed, hot, in her cheeks. "I shouldn't have asked you, Griffin. I had no right."

Griffin's hands caught her wrists gently, stayed their motion. Rachel was left to stand in an awkward one-shoe-on-one-shoe-off position. "You had every right," he said. "Now. Do you love me or not, Rachel McKinnon? You've never said, one way or the other, you know."

Rachel laughed, then flung her arms around his neck and let her face rest against the hard, reassuring expanse of his chest. "Oh, yes—yes, I do."

He placed an index finger under her chin, lifted gently. A crooked grin contrasted the dark need in his eyes. "I should have taken Becky up on her offer," he said.

Rachel frowned. "What offer?"

"She was going to give me a thousand dollars to marry you and throw in the brothel, too. Now, if I ask you to marry me and you say yes, I'll be out a perfectly good bordello."

Rachel laughed again, even though the pit of her stomach was trembling and her vision was suddenly a little blurred. "You should have held out for more—perhaps two horses and a wagon."

Griffin's eyes swept her face gently. "Is that some kind of convoluted 'yes'?"

She drew back, just slightly, in his embrace. "Was that some kind of convoluted proposal?" she countered.

He nodded solemnly, though there was a smile lurking in his dark eyes.

"Then I'm accepting. Only—"

"Only what?" he frowned.

"I want you to be sure, Griffin."

"I am sure."

But Rachel shook her head and lowered her eyes for a moment, only to have them slide, as if magnetized, back to his face. "Until now, Athena has been far away—out of your reach. Now, she's back and, well, I want you to tell me how you feel after a month of knowing that she's near again, that you could come to her if you wanted."

His hands were moving on her rib cage, just beneath her

breasts—and making it ever so hard to stick by her decision. If he drew her any closer—

But Griffin stepped back, lowered his hands to his sides. "If that's what you want, Rachel, I'll wait. But there is one thing I need to know."

"What?"

"How do you feel about Jonas Wilkes?"

The question was so bluntly put that it took Rachel aback, and the look in his eyes revealed that the answer would be important. For that reason, Rachel tried to be honest. "I like Jonas sometimes," she said. "He can be very kind, if he wants to. Most of the time, however, he is too forward."

She had not realized that Griffin's shoulders were tight with tension until she saw them slacken. "But you don't think you could love him?"

"Griffin, I love *you*."

Griffin's throat worked, and a shadow moved in his eyes, but, before he could say anything more, Joanna came into the room, looking fond and officious and harried.

"Griffin Fletcher, you shameless rounder! Leave this room before I have you horsewhipped. As for you, Miss Rachel McKinnon—it's time you were getting into that magnificent new dress of yours."

Griffin grinned, leered comically at Rachel for Joanna's benefit, and obediently left the room.

An hour later, when Rachel came down, he was waiting at the base of the stairway, looking so handsome that she was nearly overwhelmed. Had he really said he loved her, really proposed marriage? It seemed incredible.

But his eyes caressed her as she approached, and he extended his arm. "Sprite," he whispered, his smile comically fixed. "You make a month seem like a long time."

Rachel blushed, but her eyes were moving over his dark, formal clothes with frank appreciation. "You look like one of those fancy-man gamblers!" she observed, awed.

Griffin laughed out loud. "Field will appreciate that remark, Sprite. This is his wedding getup—didn't you recognize it?"

Rachel stared at him. "Griffin Fletcher, you didn't!"

He smiled suavely, as the first strains of the orchestra wafted in from the enormous dining room-turned-ballroom. "I did, though. Knocked on his hotel room door and demanded his wedding suit. He was so anxious to get rid of me that he threw it out into the hallway."

"You're lucky he didn't shoot you."

"That will happen tomorrow," Griffin replied, blithely.

Rachel's laughter died in her throat. Something *was* going to happen tomorrow—she could feel it. And she was frowning softly when Griffin escorted her into the very center of Athena's grand birthday party.

Chapter Twenty-seven

Griffin surveyed the beautifully decorated O'Riley dining room with a cynical half-smile. "It's amazing what twenty-four hours of dedicated drudgery will accomplish, isn't it?"

Rachel didn't feel very festive herself. Griffin Fletcher loved her, he even wanted to marry her. All should have been right with the world, but it wasn't. Something ominous threatened, just beyond the reach of Rachel's intuition. She looked at all the splendidly dressed men and women and thought sadly, inexplicably, that, after tomorrow, it might be a long time before they wanted to dance again.

But tomorrow belonged to itself, just as it always had, and there was no point in sacrificing this dreamlike evening to it. Raising her chin, Rachel McKinnon threw herself wholeheartedly into the celebration.

Dancing proved easy to master, for all her worry; she had only to follow Griffin's deft lead. It was very pleasurable, and there were no thoughts of an uncertain tomorrow in Rachel's mind as she whirled through waltz after waltz, feeling flushed and exhilarated and even beautiful.

There was only the slightest tension visible in Griffin's face when Jonas approached, during an interval in the music, and smiled at Rachel. Even though his golden eyes were fixed on her, his words were directed to Griffin.

"Have the good manners to dance with your hostess, Doctor," he said evenly. "If you don't, she's going to start flinging things."

Rachel wrenched her eyes from the strange hold of Jonas's and smiled up at the glowering giant beside her.

I'll be all right, she promised, without speaking at all.

Griffin's dark eyes flashed for a moment, but he'd read the message in hers, and he smiled. One of his eyebrows lifted, just slightly, however, as his gaze shifted to Jonas.

Something unrecognizable passed between the two men, chilling the fragrant warmth of the summer evening. But then Griffin squeezed Rachel's hand in an eloquent grip and walked off to seek his hostess.

There was something vaguely unnerving hiding behind the clear admiration in Jonas's face. As the music began again, he gathered Rachel into his arms, and she sensed a sort of deadly mourning in his touch.

As they danced, he spoke of ordinary things; the weather; the wild tiger lilies gracing the table, which had been pushed back against one wall; the skill of the four musicians providing the lovely melody to which they danced.

Rachel tried to be attentive, but once or twice, her gaze slipped to Griffin and Athena, who were dancing on the far side of the room. How splendid they looked together, Griffin so tall, well built, and commanding, Athena silver-haired and glowing with delight.

When Rachel returned her wandering glance to Jonas's face, she saw something there that startled her. Was it grief? Rage? She couldn't tell.

"Athena is beautiful, isn't she?" she whispered, lamely.

"Staggeringly," replied Jonas, his voice clipped and suddenly not ordinary at all. "Beware your heart, Urchin."

Rachel was flushed with a sensation of wary challenge. "What do you mean by that?"

Jonas's eyes were ferocious with that same unreadable emotion she had seen moments before. "I mean that Athena has never been refused a single desire in her life. And she wants Griffin."

As the music came to a graceful stop, Rachel stiffened. "Jonas—"

But his index finger came to rest on her lips, silencing her. "This is a dangerous game, Rachel. A very dangerous game. Just remember that I'll be here when it's over."

Rachel was still puzzling over those words when Jonas strode away. He met Griffin midway, and the two men skirted each other in an instinctive, practiced way.

There was high color in Athena's Grecian face as she

watched Jonas approach, as she listened to his whispered confidence. Then, her soft blue gown capturing the light as she moved, she took Jonas's arm and the two of them disappeared through the French doors leading out to the garden.

Rachel realized that she was staring after them and blushed with embarrassment when she turned her eyes to Griffin. Fortunately, he had been waylaid by Dr. O'Riley and was listening so intently to him that he hadn't noticed Rachel's curiosity.

When Griffin turned to her, she saw only relief in his eyes, and she relaxed a little, even though she still had unexplainable misgivings about the sudden disappearance of Jonas and Athena.

What were they talking about, out there in that rose-scented, moonlit garden? Were they, by some fantastic chance, plotting together? Rachel scolded herself. It was silly to think such a thing, and vain, too.

"Why are you smiling that way?" she asked Griffin, in an effort to shake the last vestiges of uneasiness away.

"Because you're so beautiful," he said. "Because dancing with Athena was such a deadly bore. And because I just found out I didn't kill a man."

Rachel swallowed, staring up at him now, stricken. "Kill a man?" she echoed, stupidly.

His great shoulders shifted in a confused sigh. "I don't know why I feel good to know Douglas Frazier is better, but I do. John just got word that he's conscious again."

"Conscious?" Rachel whispered. She hadn't asked anyone about Douglas Frazier since the night Griffin had somehow saved her from him, hadn't dared to wonder whether or not he still posed a danger. "Griffin, what did you do?"

"I nearly beat him to death," he answered flatly, and there was a guarded look in his eyes as he watched for her response.

Rachel was remembering Dobson, the battered lumberjack who could thank Griffin Fletcher for both his injuries and his recovery. There was a deadly, ruthless violence within this man, and the recognition of this fact had a contradictory effect on her. While she valued his strength, she found herself fearing that ungoverned rage lurking behind his brusque, if gentlemanly, manner.

To her horror, Rachel found that he had somehow followed her thoughts and anticipated the most disturbing one of all.

"You're safe with me, Sprite," he said, in a cold, measured voice.

Rachel was contrite. "I know that, Griffin," she said, and she did know it.

There was a welcome smile in his eyes now, if it didn't quite reach his mouth. "Which is not to say that there aren't areas where I find my energies a little hard to restrain. Right now, I would give anything to be alone with you."

His meaning was clear, and Rachel felt the same need he did. But a month was a tolerable length of time, and she wanted no regrets if, after that interval, he decided that it was Athena he wanted.

"You are a very forward man, Griffin Fletcher," she said, knowing full well how her eyes and body tempted him. "But you will just have to wait."

The dark eyes smoldered as they moved boldly to her breasts and back to her face. "You're the second person to give me that advice," he drawled. "And I'm notoriously bad at taking advice."

Rachel felt crimson color pounding in her face; suddenly, it was as though she was bared to him, and vulnerable, in front of all those people. To her mortification, the sensation was not altogether unwelcome, and when he grabbed her hand and dragged her out into the dimly lit hallway, she did not protest.

His mouth came down to consume hers, to consume all of her—including her worthy intentions. She trembled with an aching, unreasoning need.

The night was still and warm and bright with the light of a million stars when Griffin led her outside, around the side of the house opposite the garden, and into a small orchard of apple trees.

The blossoms had a trembling, tenuous beauty, there in the light of the moon and stars. They would be gone soon, sacrificed to the warm days of summer, but for now, they were like translucent pink silk, dipped in silver.

In the center of that magical orchard, Griffin kissed her again. And there was so much hunger in that kiss, so much commanding, irresistible hunger, that Rachel could not withstand it.

She gasped in sheer delight as his hands caressed her thinly covered breasts, making the nipples stand out, hard and pulsing, beneath the soft apricot lawn of her gown.

With a soft groan, he pressed her back against the rough bark of a gnarled, whispering tree, and held her there, his eyes moving over her in a deliciously wanton sweep.

Then, very slowly, his hands came to the daring neckline of her dress. She felt a rush of savage, reckless joy as he pulled slightly, catching both the dress and the camisole beneath it just under her breasts. She moaned as he bent his head and sampled one hard, jutting nipple with just the tip of his tongue. "Please," she whispered.

But the sweet, merciless teasing went on until it was nearly intolerable, until everything within her pleaded wordlessly for the hard pressure of his body against hers. And still, Griffin nibbled softly at the tiny protrusion.

Rachel grew wildly impatient, groaning his name, writhing with pleasure.

"Say it," he said, flicking at the pulsating nipple now with the taunting tip of his tongue.

"Oh," she groaned, in the frustration of her need.

"Say it," he repeated.

"Suck," she whispered, in delicious defeat.

Now, the full of his mouth was tugging at her, suckling her very womanhood into that single, tormented nipple. She parted her legs as his hand lifted her skirts to caress her satin-covered thighs, to explore and seek and, again, tease without mercy.

Suddenly, he stopped suckling to stand, still and commanding before her. "Undress," he said.

Rachel hesitated only for a moment, almost hating him for the way he could dominate her, overrule her decisions, make her want to plead for the touch of his hands and the fiery exploration of his tongue. She turned. "I can't manage these buttons."

Griffin's fingers were awkward as he undid them, but swift, too. He made no move to slide the dress from her shoulders, or turn her back to face him.

With a kind of shameless irritation, Rachel faced him, waited. Still, he made no move to remove the dress. His eyes, his stance, commanded that Rachel do that, that she bare herself to his gaze.

And she did. The dress drifted to the soft ground, pooled around her feet in a cloud of apricot. With trembling hands, she slid the dislodged camisole and her satiny drawers down, too.

I hate you for being able to make me do this, Griffin Fletcher, she thought, as her traitorous body throbbed under his gaze. *The strange thing is, I love you for the same reason.*

She approached him, a proud nymph clothed in moonlight, and, boldly, deftly, opened his trousers. His hard response, his hoarse, primitive cry, gave her to know that she dominated now. She commanded.

Slowly, Rachel knelt, and her teasing was as deliberate and controlled as his had been. But he had no tree to lean against, no support but the wide stance he'd taken. His breathing was harshly metered, and interspersed with soft, desperate cries.

Rachel was dizzy with desire, with triumph. "Say it," she ordered.

He moaned, savoring his resistance.

"Say it, Griffin."

He nearly shouted the word.

It was a point of honor. Rachel continued until he cried out and stiffened in violent release.

"Witch," he rasped, sinking to his knees, pressing her to the soft ground with his hands.

Again, the mysterious command had shifted. Closing her eyes, Rachel surrendered to the blazing, tender torment of his vengeance. Again and again, the passion swept her starward, to the very edge of ecstasy, and then plunged her back to earth once more.

When her release came at last, in treacherous, convulsive waves, Rachel cried out in the force of it.

Afterward, they lay still for a long time, exhausted and speechless.

"We'd better go back," Rachel whispered, when she could manage to assemble the words.

But Griffin was shaking his head. He raised himself to his knees, pulled Rachel to a sitting position. His mouth came hungrily to her breast, and Rachel held him, her fingers entwined in his dark, love-rumpled hair, as he suckled.

Jonas was grateful for the relative privacy of the O'Riley parlor. Enraged, he paced back and forth in front of the hearth, beneath the painting of Athena.

She stood just inside the closed doors, her arms folded across the blue silk temptation of her gown, her eyes following Jonas's progress with fiery impatience.

"I told you the situation was serious, didn't I, Jonas?" Athena said, in a voice quaking with humiliation and rage.

Jonas stopped his pacing abruptly, turned his unbearable anger on Athena. "Rachel wouldn't," he warned.

Athena was undaunted. "Not with you, maybe. But they're not out strolling in the moonlight and deciding the arrangement of the parlor furniture, I can tell you that!"

He wanted to die. A torrent of shattering pictures whirled in his mind, sickening him, deepening the fury that sustained him. Rachel and Griffin. The prospect was intolerable. No matter what, he could not let it happen. "Just because you do your best work on your back, Athena," he said, in a low, deadly tone, "that doesn't mean Rachel does."

Athena shrugged, and the gesture was an almost laughable contradiction to the murderous gleam in her dark blue eyes. "Believe whatever you want to, Jonas. I can't afford to delude myself any longer—something has to be done, and fast."

"Like what?" Jonas bit out.

Athena raised one golden eyebrow. "What else? We arrange the one discovery Griffin could not bear to make."

Jonas turned the idea in his mind, examining it. His anger, he discovered, had not completely displaced his reason. "No," he said, flatly.

"Why not? You could wait until she was asleep, and then we could arrange for Griffin to find you beside her—"

"You make me sick, Athena." Bile burned in Jonas's throat.

The indigo eyes flashed with stunned offense. "And you are so noble, Jonas. Are you forgetting that it practically drove him mad the first time?"

"It would push him even further now. Athena, I know you don't give a damn, but he would kill me with his bare hands. Maybe you've never seen Griffin go crazy like that, but I can assure you, it isn't a sight that inspires bravery!"

"You're afraid of him!"

"You're damned right I'm afraid of him!"

"Then you don't want Rachel as badly as you say you do."

"I want Rachel," Jonas vowed, in a rumbling, dangerous rasp. "I *love* Rachel. And even if I happened to survive your little plan, by some miracle, she would spit in my face!"

Now, it was Athena who paced. "Well, we've got to do something, Jonas. If he marries her, we're both going to be out in the proverbial cold!"

Jonas spotted a decanter of whiskey on a nearby table and poured a triple into a glass. He swilled the smooth liquor in a desperate need for its singular comfort. "He's not going to marry her," he said. "He's not going to *have* her."

Athena looked skeptical. Her beautiful features were slightly blurred now, and her dress was like a piece of moving sky. "What if he already has, Jonas? Will it matter to you that she's been with Griffin?"

"No," Jonas said. But the pain the image engendered was brutal, blinding.

Suddenly, Athena was before him, and he could see her features clearly again. "There is one other option, Jonas," she said, in a tortured whisper. "We could comfort each other."

Jonas's laugh sounded raw, tremulous, and it ached in his throat. "Comfort?" he repeated, mockingly.

Athena's hands moved to his lapels, warm and compelling; even through the fabric of his shirt, he could feel the heat of them. But he felt nothing else—he seemed to be bound by a crazy, singular fidelity of some sort. He'd learned that with Fawn Nighthorse, and he wasn't planning to test the theory again.

"You used to enjoy my company," she reminded him.

Jonas pulled free of her and refilled his glass. "You know something, Athena? You disgust me. All evening you've been telling me how badly you want to make up with Griffin, start over and all that. And here you are, offering yourself to me like some kind of Skid Road whore!"

The Frenchman's ring flashed in the light as Athena raised her hand to slap Jonas's face. He caught her wrist in a savage grasp and twisted it, pretending an interest in the diamond-and-ruby setting glistening on her finger. "You've been playing this game in France, too, haven't you, Athena?" he asked. "Well, my hat is off to this Bordeau character for having the guts to turn you out!"

Athena's round, succulent breasts were rising and falling, straining at the tenuous confines of her dress. Jonas tightened his grasp, watched with grim satisfaction as she tilted her head back, breathing in little gasps.

She hadn't changed. Her tremendous passion was ignited by Jonas's rough touch as he knew it had never been by Griffin's tender courtship. Jonas doubted seriously that Griffin had ever made love to this woman at all.

His own desire still dormant within him, Jonas slipped a hand inside her dress, grasped one plump breast, and squeezed it, hard. With his thumb, he brought the nipple to hard response.

Eyes still closed, Athena cried out softly. It was interesting, if not surprising, that she made no attempt to resist. She simply said Jonas's name, giving it the tone of a plea.

Still feeling no responding need, Jonas tore the dress, exposed her breasts to his view and that of anyone who might happen to walk through the parlor doors. He knew that that possibility would only incline Athena toward even more drastic behavior.

She opened her eyes, saw his contempt, and smiled. "You could always pretend that I'm Rachel," she said. And then she caught the front of his trousers in her hand and began to knead him, in a slow, maddening rhythm.

It was the suggestion, more than the action, that stirred uncontrollable needs in Jonas. *Rachel.*

He felt both relief and fury as his manhood exerted itself, demanding fulfillment. He'd let the game go too far; now there was no turning back.

He sank into a barrel-back chair, in front of the fireplace, and waited. Athena knelt before him and began the work for which she was most suited.

Chapter Twenty-eight

Rachel awakened late the next morning, to find the room filled to bursting with sunshine and Athena standing at the foot of her bed like a specter, staring furiously into her face.

"Cook and Mother have prepared a bath for you," she announced stiffly, her hair gleaming, like silver fire, in the bright light.

Rachel stretched, and the sensation was patiently delicious. "Thank you," she said quietly. "A bath sounds wonderful."

Athena's indigo eyes swung to the billow of apricot lawn discarded the night before. The dress was draped over the back of a nearby chair, and its very presence spoke volumes. It was sadly rumpled, if not spoiled entirely, and there were leaves and bits of faded, browning apple blossoms clinging to its folds.

Athena's chin quivered, almost imperceptibly, and her knuckles were white where they gripped the foot rail of Rachel's bed. "You and Griffin—how did you get back into the house last night, without being seen?"

Rachel sat up in bed and yawned softly. They had crept, laughing, up the stairs rising from the kitchen, but she had no intention of revealing that. It was a part of the night, a part of the magic, and, as such, a personal thing. "I don't know what you mean," she lied.

The dark blue eyes were fierce now, demanding. "You know very well what I mean! You may be fooling Mama and Papa, but I have no illusions about your wholesome, country-bred morals. Remember that, Miss McKinnon."

Rachel blushed slightly, but she felt no shame. Perhaps the lovemaking with Griffin had been ill-advised, but it had not been wrong. It could never be wrong.

"I'm sorry you don't approve, Athena," she said, tossing back the lightweight comforter and swinging herself gracefully out of bed. "But now, if you don't mind, I would like to get ready for my bath."

Athena made a soft, contemptuous sound in her throat. "Fool. Griffin is using you—you're just a joke to him."

The feeling of inexplicable dread that had been plaguing Rachel for two days was back, but it had nothing to do with Griffin, or the things Athena was saying. It did, however, bring on a dull, gnawing ache at the nape of her neck. Gathering fresh underthings and a simple cotton shirtwaist and skirt, Rachel ignored Athena, hoping that she would go away.

But Athena was following her as she moved about the room, as if prepared to pounce at any moment. Rather than feeling fear, Rachel felt a certain primitive hope that this spoiled, obnoxious woman would make a threatening gesture of some sort. It would be delightful to do battle with her, however unladylike.

"You think he loves you, don't you?" Athena went on, frantically. "You think he plans to marry you. And last night, judging by the state of your dress, you were probably rolling around on the ground with him, like some—some slut."

Rachel stopped, hairbrush in hand, and faced Athena with ferocious calm. "I know he plans to marry me," she said evenly. "He proposed."

The look on Athena's face was a stricken one, but she recovered quickly. Her beautiful shoulders, revealed by her strapless, sleeveless white eyelet gown, tensed. "I see. Well, did he tell you, Rachel, that he's been boasting about taking you? He told Jonas."

There was a taut silence, and Rachel's headache grew infinitely worse. "That's a lie."

"Believe what you like, Rachel. Or ask Jonas."

Rachel felt a dizzying nausea churn up inside her. She tried to speak, tried to deny what Athena had said, and couldn't.

Athena was flushed with bitter triumph. "He told Jonas that you were a virgin when he took you."

Rachel turned, grasped the edge of a bureau for support. In her mind, she heard Griffin's voice, heard him saying those terrible things to Field the day they'd ridden down the side of the mountain. The day she'd left Providence and Griffin had all but thrown her bodily onto the steamer.

"I didn't think she was a virgin—I succeeded—"

She shook her head mutely, but the effort was useless. The truth remained, ugly and shameful—Griffin *had* told Jonas about that night in the lumber camp, he must have. How else could Jonas have had such an intimate knowledge of what had happened?

In a frantic need for reassurance, Rachel's hand closed over the beautiful pearl necklace Griffin had given her, and the golden bracelet beside it.

But Athena was close, seeing the gesture, seeing everything. She laughed, and it was a soft, vicious sound.

"He gave you presents? Oh, Rachel, surely you don't think *that* meant anything! You innocent, don't you know that men give gifts like that in payment for services rendered? It is so much more civilized than just leaving money behind when they're through."

Hot sickness burned in Rachel's throat, and she closed her eyes against the brutal pain pulsing in every fiber of her being.

Athena saw her advantage and pressed it. "You didn't really think a man like Griffin would commit himself to someone like you, did you?" she mocked. "Merciful heavens, Griffin is a wealthy, educated man—what would he want with a timber brat?"

Rachel's knees threatened to buckle beneath her, but she used the last of her strength to make them serve her. "Get out, Athena."

Athena's footsteps were light as she crossed the room, and her voice was airy as she sang out a smug farewell. Not until the door had closed behind her did Rachel stumble back to the bed and collapse, face down, too stricken to weep.

She lay still for a long time, while scream after silent scream rang through the throbbing darkness encompassing her mind and heart. How could she have been so foolish as to believe Griffin's declarations of love, so wanton as to offer herself in the way she had?

And in return for a few promises, a string of pearls, and a bracelet!

Rachel raised herself to a sitting position, wild with the need to put this house behind her, along with all her shattered dreams. Along with Griffin Fletcher and his boasting.

If possible, she would leave Washington Territory entirely. She had money—she could take it and start over somewhere else, just as her mother had begged her to do in the first place.

Her mother. Rachel closed her heart against all that Becky McKinnon had represented, all that Griffin had assumed *she* represented as well. *He thinks I'm a whore,* she thought brokenly. *And I've given him no reason to believe otherwise.*

Forcibly, Rachel gathered her composure. There was a bath waiting downstairs, and probably a late breakfast, too. If she didn't appear soon, Joanna or Cook would come in search of her.

Unable to bear the thought of anyone finding her as she was, broken like a discarded toy, Rachel slipped into one of Athena's colorful robes and marched down the back stairway, into the kitchen.

It was later than she'd guessed; nearly two in the afternoon. Cook was nowhere in sight, and Joanna was probably in her garden, where it would be cool.

Rachel wrenched her eyes from the clock on the kitchen mantel and made her way resolutely into the little room reserved for bathing. There, she removed her robe and slipped into the now-tepid water.

Bathing was no longer a comfort or a luxury. No matter how hard she scrubbed her shame-pinkened skin, she still felt dirty.

As Rachel dried herself, an awful, mystical knowledge came to her. She had conceived a child.

Rachel tried to reason with herself. It was too early to tell, there were no signs, surely even her luck could not be so bad. But the conviction remained unshaken—Griffin Fletcher's baby was growing within her, even as she prepared to disappear from his life forever.

She felt a sort of tormented wonder as she put the robe back on, over her scoured flesh, and made her way back upstairs to the room that had been hers. There, she dressed slowly, carefully, her mind racing in converse chaos.

Rachel wept, for herself, for the baby that had been conceived in either a lumber camp or an orchard.

Where was Griffin now? Could she hope to escape this house without encountering him?

She prayed that she could.

But there was Joanna—Joanna had been so unfailingly kind. Rachel could not go without saying good-bye, but the thought of facing that perceptive woman filled her with dread. It would be impossible to lie to Joanna.

In desperation, Rachel found pen and paper and scrawled a hasty, heartfelt note of gratitude and farewell.

Half an hour later, she left the note on the entry-hall table and walked boldly out the front door, carrying nothing but a beaded handbag. Behind, in the O'Rileys' sun-brightened guest room, were the things she had cherished—the pearls, the bracelet, and the apricot gown.

The heels of her shoes made a rhythmic clicking sound as Rachel strode purposefully down the front walk, her chin held high.

Athena stood at an upstairs window, facing the street. A startled smile trembled on her lips as she watched Rachel disappear around a corner—it had been so easy. Who would have thought it would be so easy?

Reluctantly, she left the window, walked out into the hall and down, to Rachel's open door. The pearls had been left behind, along with that silly little bracelet.

Athena scooped both items up into one hand, amazed. What fun it would be to thrust these treasures back into Griffin's hands and to watch the realization that Rachel was gone spring into that impervious face of his!

She smiled. Jonas would be delighted.

Athena paused as she heard a team and carriage come to a halt in front of the house. She could not tell Jonas what she'd done, she realized suddenly—if Rachel boarded a steamer and disappeared forever, he would be outraged. And Jonas's vengeance was an eventuality that didn't bear considering.

Downstairs, the front doors were opening, closing again. She could hear the booming sound of her father's laughter, the answering, unsuspecting note of Griffin's.

Again, Athena smiled. *You haven't a great deal to laugh*

about, my dear, she thought, the jewelry Rachel had forsaken warm in the palm of her hand. *And your rage will be something to see, to remember, to savor.*

Fixing a look of gentle bewilderment on her face, Athena dropped the bracelet and pearls into the pocket of her skirt and rushed down the stairs. She was breathless when she burst into her father's study, where he and Griffin were conferring over some tedious case.

"Rachel is gone!" she gasped, wringing her hands a little, to lend the thing an air of tragedy.

Griffin sprang out of his chair and whirled, for all the world like a panther poised to pounce on some unwitting prey and tear it to shreds. The taut misery in his face was gratifying to see.

"What?" he rasped.

Athena had second thoughts about her timing then, for all the sweetness of revenge—perhaps it would have been wiser to wait a few hours and be certain that Rachel couldn't be found. "P-Perhaps she's only out somewhere, with Mother. . . ."

But Griffin's stance was ominous; he could not be reassured now, could not be stalled. Heedless of her father's presence, and the crushing strength of his hands, he clasped Athena's shoulders and shook her once, hard. "What did you say to her?" he demanded, in a bitter snarl.

Athena could only shake her head.

Griffin glared at her for one dreadful moment, then flung her away and stormed out of the study without so much as a backward glance. Athena flinched as the front door slammed.

Rachel was confused, and her head ached. It was as though her mind and heart had somehow separated themselves from her body, unable to bear the pain.

There were bells clanging, in an ear-jarring chorus of panic, but she could not be sure they were real. Nothing seemed real—not the grass beneath her feet, not the Guernsey cow grazing a few hundred feet away, not the odd haze roiling in the sky.

She stopped, wondering which direction to go. Somehow, she had wandered off the main street that would have led her down the hill and into Seattle's heart. The bank was there—she had to get to the bank and then the steamboat office.

The bank. The steamboat office. She repeated the phrases in her mind, like a litany that would save her soul, and righted her course. After several minutes, she found the road again.

People were rushing past, in buggies, on horseback, on foot. Some were going down the hill, as Rachel was, while others seemed to be fleeing up it. She thought it odd that both factions seemed equally determined.

There were more bells now, and a roaring sound rose up on the June wind to rival their tolls and clangs.

Rachel walked on.

The air was hot, and the smell of it stung her nostrils and her throat. She stumbled as a man carrying a whimpering child rushed past, nearly knocking her down.

There is a fire, she thought, mildly.

But no. It was all a part of the nightmare. Rachel raised her chin and kept going.

Vaulting over the O'Rileys' fence, Griffin saw the plume of black smoke rising against the placid blue sky and swore.

John appeared beside him, medical bag in hand, eyes trained on the dark cloud centering in the heart of Seattle. "Come on, Griffin," he said. "We'll be needed."

Griffin didn't give a damn about being needed; for the first time in his career, he turned his back on all his training and skill. Until he found Rachel, nothing else would matter.

Ignoring John, he bolted into a dead run. The distant cacophony of the firebells ringing in his ears, he raced into the O'Rileys' stables, thrust a bridle over the head of the first horse he came to, and swung onto its back.

"Griffin!" the old man roared, as he prodded the startled gelding into a run. "Griffin, stop!"

The paddock fence loomed, and Griffin urged the horse on, felt relief as it cleared the top railing and ran at full speed down the dry, rutted road.

Griffin never knew how he navigated the congested traffic clogging the street leading down toward the business district; he only knew that Rachel was not among those who scrambled up the hill, or those who scrambled down. He was in the center of things within minutes of leaving the O'Rileys'.

The Pontius Building, a two-story wooden structure, was at the heart of the disaster. Flames roared through its roof, crimson against the blue of the sky.

People milled in the streets, some captivated, others whimpering or frozen with fear. Men and boys manned a hosecart in one block, a steam-driven fire engine in the next. But the fire mocked the paltry sprays of water trickling from the hoses.

Rachel, Griffin pleaded, searching the faces in the crowd without success.

Men were prying off the clapboards edging the Pontius Building at street level now, revealing a roaring inferno in its basement. Griffin slid off the gelding's back and abandoned it.

The flames were spreading now—moving into a liquor store. The crowd surged back as the walls went up, and then the whiskey barrels stored inside. There were explosions, and showers of flaming alcohol raged like the seas of hell, carrying the fire to two nearby saloons.

It was hot—intolerably hot—and Griffin felt sweat move down his face, gather at the center of his chest, and bead on the back of his neck. Coughing, he pushed through the crowd, searching every face.

And then he saw her. She was stumbling down the plank-lined street about a hundred yards away, looking as though she hadn't even noticed the fire.

Griffin screamed her name, over the clang of bells, the shouts of panic, the deafening roar of the fire. The crowd shifted, and she was gone.

Throat raw from the thickening smoke and the incredible heat, Griffin made his way through the throng. "Please," he whispered, raising his eyes to the brassy glare of the sky.

The prayer was answered. He found Rachel huddled in an alleyway, clutching her handbag, staring at nothing. He grasped her shoulders, shook her. "Rachel!"

Slowly, she raised her eyes to his, and the look he saw there turned his blood to ice. She didn't seem to recognize him.

Frantic, he shook her again, again said her name.

But the lavender eyes were flat, dull. "They've locked the bank!" she said, incredulously.

Griffin wrenched her close and held her, tears mingling with the sweat on his face. "God," he whispered, "Oh, my God—"

There were more explosions, and men shouted in the streets. Wagon wheels hammered at the planking, and bells pealed all over the city, but Griffin Fletcher did not move. He stood still, cradling the stricken girl in his arms, battling a terror not even remotely related to the fire.

And then, incredibly, Jonas was there. He looked cool, unruffled, as though he'd been out for a quiet walk, as though Seattle wasn't in imminent danger of burning down around him. He held out Griffin's medical bag in silent challenge.

Griffin clung to Rachel, trying to ignore the bag and its attendant responsibility, Jonas, the world.

Jonas's voice was even. "Give Rachel to me, Griffin. Let me take her out of here before she's hurt."

"No." The word was a hoarse sob.

"Griffin."

Griffin shook his head, held Rachel closer.

"You took an oath," Jonas reminded him quietly.

Griffin began to come back inside himself, back to everything he believed. Slowly, he released his hold on the dazed, speechless Rachel.

Jonas drew her from him cautiously, as a man might draw meat from the paws of a lion. "I'll take care of her, Griffin. I swear that by everything our mothers meant to each other."

Griffin closed his eyes for a moment, opened them again to find that Jonas and Rachel were gone.

Medical bag in hand, Griffin reeled back into the wild confusion surrounding the fire. He had no choice but to trust Jonas—no choice. The doctor within him, for a time imprisoned in some dark part of his mind, was back in control again.

The wind was from the northeast now. The fire was sweeping toward the Commercial Mill, another business building, and the Opera House. Frantic workers were pumping water from the bay, climbing along the steaming roof of the mill with wet blankets and gunny sacks.

Griffin knelt in the river of people to tend a fireman's burned arm. "What the hell happened?" he asked, as he snapped open his bag and began work that did not require thought.

The fireman was in pain, but he was excited, too, in a ghoulish sort of way. "Somebody spilled some glue on a stove, Doc," he said. And then, incredibly, he laughed. "And the chief's away. Guess where our fire chief is, Don? He's in San Francisco, learnin' all the newest techniques."

Griffin's work was finished. "Go home," he said, standing up again, turning his burning eyes toward the wharfs. A steam engine was stationed on one dock, behind the Colman Building, but the tide was out and the pumps were drawing little more than a dribble from the bay. Worse, the hoses were too short.

Shaking his head, Griffin turned to see a firebrand carried into the sky by the shimmering heat. As if by design, it fell onto the Opera House roof and caught. There was a roar, and the Colman Building went up with a vengeance.

A woman was tugging at Griffin's shirtsleeve. "Doctor? Sir—you are a doctor, aren't you? It's my husband—"

Griffin followed her through the ever-growing crowd to find a middle-aged man slumped on the ground, against a wagon wheel. There was so much noise that, even through his stethoscope, he could hardly make out the thready beat of the man's heart.

"Mayor's takin' charge now," someone said.

Griffin stood, faced the woman. "Your husband will be all right, if you get him out of here. He's overexcited."

"He wanted to watch—"

Griffin was impatient; his eyes darted to the wagon. "I'll help him up. You get him away from here."

Dynamite was being laid under the Palace Restaurant, in the hope of creating a fire gap. The horses hitched to the couple's wagon danced in panic as the blast reverberated through the acrid, hazy air, but the woman, her husband limp on the seat beside her, brought them under control.

Griffin watched in dull amazement as the fire swept across the wreckage of the restaurant, spreading to the wharfs beside the blazing mill.

Chapter Twenty-nine

Griffin wandered for a long time, helping in the hopeless battle where he could, competently treating firemen and spectators who had succumbed to the excitement and the smoke.

A boy appeared beside him, grinning at the raging spectacle. "Ain't it somethin'?" he cried, wide-eyed. "We could see the smoke clear from Tacoma!"

"Wonderful," Griffin snapped, weak with heat exhaustion and worry over Rachel. Was she safe? Or had he subjected her to a danger far beyond that of any fire by handing her over to Jonas?

"Yes, sir!" the boy went on, undaunted by Griffin's terse reaction. "You can hear them flames snappin' and roarin' way out on the bay. We wasn't hardly out of Commencement Bay afore we could hear 'em."

Griffin drew his watch from his vest pocket and consulted it. Four o'clock, and the battle was lost.

Church bells tolled the news, as did the whistles of steamers moored along the waterfront. The incessant clang of the firebells echoed in Griffin's aching head.

The flight had begun. Business men were dragging their belongings outside, loading them into wagons. Some, having no wagons, carried cash registers in their arms, while others staggered under crates and bundles. Along the wharfs, ships accepted what merchandise they could, for safekeeping, and then moved out into deeper water as the docks themselves went up.

Hell, Griffin thought wryly. *Who would have thought hell was right here in Seattle?*

The thought led to other concerns. Were Field and his brand new bride lost in this inferno somewhere? Griffin strode in the direction of the courthouse; their hotel was just beyond it.

People were dragging beds and chamber pots and babies into the streets in the residential section, while the courthouse itself was embroiled in a modicum of orderly panic. Shackled prisoners were being brought from the basement by members of the Home Guard, and a small company of men were trying to water down the roof and the outside walls. Harried clerks fled with stacks of records, and merchant-jurors abandoned their call to scramble back to their stores and shops.

Griffin watched, without slowing his pace, as a young man climbed onto the courthouse roof and began drenching it with water from buckets hauled up by means of the halyards on the flagstaff.

Fawn was helping a blustering innkeeper carry account books and blankets to a waiting wagon when Griffin reached the small hotel.

He caught her arm. "Where's Field?"

Fawn's wide brown eyes were haunted with worry as she looked toward the furnace that was the business district. "He's down there, somewhere."

Griffin's fear for his friend sharpened his voice to a razor edge. "That idiot—what a time to save souls!"

Fawn Hollister looked as though she was going to kick him. Instead, she flung her armload of goods into the wagon and snapped, "He's helping, Griffin. Same as you were, by the looks of you."

Griffin looked down at himself then, unmoved by the soot covering his hands, his clothes, and probably his face. "I'm sorry."

There was another roar as the roof and bell tower of the Trinity Church, across from the courthouse, fell in. Countless rounds of ammunition went off when the fire spread into two nearby hardware companies, and the noise accentuated the feeling that some kind of vicious war was being fought.

Fawn's hand rose to touch his face. "I know you meant well," she said, her voice rising, somehow, over the deafening clamor.

He closed his hand over hers and shouted back, "Will you be all right?"

Fawn nodded.

The streets were choked with wagons now, as Griffin made his way back toward the fire. He looked into what must have been a thousand faces, and saw a thousand different nightmares.

The battle had moved to Yesler Way now. A bystander informed Griffin that the mayor had ordered the shacks and buildings along it to be torn down or dynamited. Even the board planks were wrenched up from the street itself.

But the early evening wind was rising, and it carried the fire across the gap and onto the Skid Road. Griffin watched helplessly as the notorious center of sin blazed, driving prostitutes and barkeepers out into the clamoring confusion.

There were more cases of heat exhaustion, more burns, more accidents caused by the crushing madness of the crowd itself. Just before eight o'clock, the crimson sun fell behind the mountains.

Above, the sky glowed hellishly, the light of the fire lending garish color to wispy clouds.

Griffin worked on, forgetting time, forgetting everything but the tasks at hand. He did not encounter either Field or John O'Riley during the hours to come, but he knew that they were nearby.

By three o'clock in the morning, the fire had consumed itself. The destruction was awesome in scope; every mill and wharf between Union and Jackson streets had been reduced to sizzling rubble, and some twenty-five city blocks lay ravaged.

Bone-weary, Griffin stumbled up the hill, toward the O'Riley house. His mind, like his heart, kept racing ahead, making the long walk all the more frustrating. Had Jonas taken Rachel there?

Griffin hoped that he had and then, conversely, hoped that he hadn't. Athena was there, and he felt certain that she'd been responsible for the frightening, almost catatonic state Rachel had been in.

He stepped up his pace.

There were whole families camped on street corners, their possessions stacked around them. Every lawn harbored a share of the homeless, and Griffin saw lean-tos built against blackened buildings and the trunks of trees.

Those most fortunate slept in tents, the others had taken refuge in crops of fern alongside the roads.

Feeling a compelling need for haste, despite his weariness, Griffin stepped over sleeping bodies to cut across a cow pasture. The field was a ragtag version of Tent Town, though here the tents were assembled from blankets or branches or even clothing.

Griffin zigzagged between the makeshift structures and took care not to walk on those who had no shelter at all.

At last, the brick house came into sight. Griffin broke into a stumbling run, drawn by the lights shining from the first-floor windows, drawn by Rachel.

The front door swung open just as Griffin reached it, and Joanna O'Riley was standing there, fully dressed, her face pale with weariness and worry. "Thank God," she sobbed, and then she flung both arms around his neck and held on as though she feared he would disappear.

Behind her loomed Field Hollister, towering like a soot covered specter in the half light of the entry hall. He nodded in greeting, but Griffin could see a muscle work spasmodically in his jaw.

"Is Rachel here?" he croaked, realizing for the first time that his voice was nearly gone.

Joanna released him and stepped back, nodding, but she wouldn't meet his eyes now.

Field had no such difficulty; his gaze flared like blue fire, scoring Griffin soul-deep. "She's in her room."

"I want to see her," whispered Griffin, starting around the soft, trembling barrier of Joanna's body.

It was Field who stopped him, pressing one hand to his chest. "You've done enough, Griffin," he said, in a terse whisper.

"But—"

Field's hand did not move, yet the pressure of it increased. "No, Griff. Fawn is with her—leave her alone."

Griffin lowered his head. Whether the ragged sobs that tore themselves from his throat, one after another, were related to Rachel or to the pounding exhaustion he felt, he never knew.

Field and Joanna clasped his arms, one on each side, and, by some unspoken agreement, led him toward the back of the house. The floors of the parlor and dining room were lined with sleeping refugees wrapped in blankets.

By the time they reached the kitchen, Griffin had recovered his composure. He drank the hot coffee Joanna provided in stony silence, then consumed two mountainous ham sandwiches.

His voice was still raw when he spoke. "Tell me, Field. Tell me why you don't want me to see Rachel."

A look passed between Field and Joanna, and Joanna left the kitchen silently.

For almost a minute, the only sound in the room was the steady *tick-tock* of the ancient clock on the mantelpiece.

"Well?" Griffin rasped finally, helping himself to another cup of coffee at the stove and then sitting down at the table again.

Field folded his arms across his chest. The fabric of his shirt was torn and stained with soot, even though his hands and face had been scrubbed to their usual wholesome shine. "Remember the night you told Jonas you'd slept with Rachel? Well, it seems that Jonas told Athena, who, of course, couldn't resist passing the word along. To say Rachel didn't take the thing well would be the understatement of this century."

Griffin groaned. "My God, she doesn't think—"

"What do you think she thinks?" Field interrupted, his whisper echoing in the large room like a pistol shot.

Griffin rolled to his feet, staggered slightly, and grasped the back of his chair. "I'll tell her—I'll explain—"

Field had not moved from his chair, but his blue eyes snapped with warning. "You'll leave her alone, Griffin. She's in shock."

"No."

"Yes," corrected Field. "Sit down before you fall on your stupid face."

Griffin sank into his chair. "If you want to fight, Field, that can be arranged."

"Right now, you couldn't best an old lady. Drink your coffee, and we'll find a place for you to sleep."

The grief, the weariness—it was all tangled within Griffin, producing a state remarkably like drunkenness. "Remember the last time we fought, Field? We were kids, rolling around in that big mud puddle in front of your father's church. Your pa and mine just stood by watching, 'til it was over. Then they dragged us out into the woods and beat the hell out of us."

Field rolled his eyes, but a grin twitched at one corner of his mouth. "I could have taken you, if you hadn't flung that muddy water in my face."

"The hell," retorted Griffin. "I had you from the first."

"What were we fighting about, anyway?"

Griffin shrugged. "Who knows?"

In spite of himself, Field laughed. "Drink your coffee," he ordered.

Calmly, Griffin complied.

It was late when he awakened the next morning; the sun was hot in his face, compelling him to open his eyes. For a moment, Griffin was confused, but then he looked down at his tattered, smoke-blackened clothes and remembered everything—the fire, the verbal round with Field, Rachel.

He sat up on John's couch and shaded his eyes against the sun and the cruel normality of the study itself. His head ached, his throat was raw, and his stomach was roiling inside him.

As if by some demonic conjury, Athena appeared before him, looking fresh and cheerful in her sprigged cambric dress. "Good morning, Griffin," she drawled.

Griffin hoisted himself to his feet. "Go to hell," he retorted, and his nausea grew measurably worse.

Athena showed no inclination to go anywhere. "Rachel is getting better," she said. "She's talking to that Fawn person, and she remembers everything. Absolutely everything. Guess who she's asking for, Griffin?"

When Griffin said nothing, Athena rushed on, savoring her triumph. "Jonas. The only person she wants to see other than that squaw or Mother is Jonas. She definitely, Griffin Fletcher, does not want to see you."

Griffin staggered to a side table, where some thoughtful soul had left towels and a basin of tepid water. He washed and dried his face and hands before he answered. "I suppose I have you to thank for that, don't I?"

Athena smiled, like a coy child. "Yes, indeed."

Griffin draped the soiled towel around his neck. "Why?"

She raised her chin, and the dark blue eyes flashed. "Because I love you."

The irony of those words sickened Griffin further. *"Because you love me,"* he repeated, in a hoarse, savage whisper. "You are sick, Athena. And your love is an honor I can do without."

"I have the right to fight for what—or whom—I want!"

Griffin shook his head in slow, purposely cruel denial. "I wouldn't wish your affections on Jonas, Athena. Your 'love' is a murderous, destructive thing."

Athena trembled. "Oh, Griffin, don't say that—"

"I haven't finished," he snarled, as John O'Riley came into the room. "If you've turned Rachel against me, Athena, I'll kill you with my bare hands!"

"Good God!" the old man cried, as his daughter whirled, in stifled hysterics, and fled the room. "Griffin, have you taken leave of your senses!"

Griffin strode past John, insane with rage. "I meant what I said!"

"Griffin!" bellowed John, from the study doorway.

But Griffin didn't stop, didn't turn back. In the middle of the stairway, he came face to face with an impervious Field Hollister.

"You can't go up there, Griffin."

"Damn it, Field—"

Field folded his arms. "I mean it, Griff. Rachel doesn't want to see you."

"Well, she's going to!" Griffin yelled, outraged and panic-stricken. "Get out of my way!"

"No, Griffin." Field's blue eyes flickering with determination, moved to someone or something just behind his friend's head. "I'm sorry."

Griffin bellowed and lunged into Field's midsection like a demented bull. Instantly, there were hands, inescapable hands, all over him.

"Watch his feet," said Field, calmly.

Griffin struggled, but even as his mind seemed to be bursting with madness and fury, he could not, would not use his feet. Not against Field. *"Damn you!"* he roared.

Unseen men subdued him, dragged him backward, down the stairs. Before he could see any of their faces, one of them pressed a treated cloth to his face. The smell was unmistakable —chloroform. He struggled, wildly, but it was too late.

There were tears—he would have sworn it—glistening on Field Hollister's face as he bent over him. "I'm sorry, Griffin."

Griffin's tongue felt thick and dry in his mouth. He battled the rising darkness in his mind, but it overtook him, crushing him into a nightmare world of nothing.

Rachel could not imagine what all the fuss was about. Now that she'd rested, she felt perfectly all right—physically, at least. Emotionally, she ached in a way that made her want to writhe.

Fawn sat on the edge of the bed, laying a cool cloth across Rachel's forehead. In the distance, there was shouting, and the sound of a violent scuffle.

Rachel noticed that Fawn closed her eyes until the disturbance passed.

"What is happening?"

Fawn frowned. "Nothing, Rachel. There are a lot of people in the house, that's all. The O'Rileys must have put up half of Seattle last night."

Rachel sat bolt upright. "Griffin—that was Griffin."

Field Hollister's bride pressed her back onto the pillows with strong brown hands. "Maybe it is Griffin, Rachel. But they won't hurt him."

Rachel turned her head away, tears brimming in her eyes. Why should she care whether they hurt Griffin or not, after the way he'd used her? But she did—she did care, and it was anguish.

"I hate him," she whispered.

Fawn's hand enclosed one of hers. "You know that isn't true, Rachel. Later, there will be time to talk, to straighten it all out. For now, you must rest."

Rachel's throat ached over a suppressed sob. "H-He bragged about me, Fawn—"

"Nonsense. I've known Griffin Fletcher most of my life; he would never do that."

"He did," Rachel insisted miserably.

Fawn was adamant. "There is some misunderstanding."

How Rachel longed to believe that there was, but she couldn't quite manage it. She'd let wishful thinking rule her life for too long as it was, and now she was in hopeless trouble. "I think there is a baby," she whispered.

"Hush," said Fawn. And then she began to sing softly, hauntingly, in a language Rachel did not understand.

Sleep came, and when Rachel awakened, the room was very dark. She thought she saw Griffin standing beside her bed, thought she heard his hoarse, gentle voice speaking to her. "I love you, Rachel McKinnon. I need you."

The dream took on further reality as he bent and kissed her cheek, his face rough against hers. Rachel felt tears gathering in her eyes, but she could not speak for fear of breaking the spell, bringing on a wakefulness that would not contain Griffin Fletcher.

It did not surprise her that he was gone again, as quickly as he'd come. Dream people did those things.

Agile in the darkness, Griffin walked back into John's study and resumed the role of prisoner. "You make one hell of a guard, Jonas," he said, stretching out on the sofa again and folding his arms.

Jonas stiffened in his chair, awakened with a start. "What—"

"Nothing," said Griffin.

But Jonas was awake now, and bent on talking. He fumbled for matches, muttered as he lit the kerosene lamp on John's desk. "How long have you been awake?" he demanded.

Griffin grinned wanly. "Long enough."

Jonas cursed roundly, then helped himself to a dose of John's best brandy. "I kept my word, Griffin," he said, after a long silence.

Griffin applauded, smiling sardonically. "A small thing, considering that you knew I'd cut your gizzard out if you didn't. Come to think of it, I might anyway."

Jonas turned his back, stared out at the darkness beyond the windows. "Will you back off for five minutes, you bastard? Sometimes I get so damned tired of this constant wrangling."

Griffin crossed his booted feet at the ankles and pretended to relax. "You're a snake, Jonas. Snakes don't get tired—they just warm their cold blood in the sun."

"We're cousins, Griffin," Jonas insisted, without turning from his post at the window. "Our mothers were the closest of sisters. What happened between us?"

"Bad blood," observed Griffin, sitting up now. "Or maybe it was that you slept with a woman you knew I loved."

Jonas turned slowly to face his cousin. "And now you've returned the favor, haven't you?"

Griffin remembered the earlier betrayal, the foolish boast that had very possibly cost him Rachel's love. "No," he said.

The need to believe him shone clear in Jonas's tortured face. Griffin saw his cousin embrace the lie, and hold it for a truth.

Chapter Thirty

By Saturday morning, things had calmed down considerably in the O'Riley household. Though Jonas and Griffin were still in evidence—Rachel avoided them both conscientiously—the refugees had gone back to whatever charred remains they could claim as their own, and the Hollisters had returned to Providence to face their flock. Athena was so subdued that she seemed absent, even when she sat across the dining-room table from Rachel or brushed past her in a corridor.

Rachel was no more gregarious herself; it seemed to her that some kind of thick batting had wrapped itself around her mind and heart, insulating her from realities with which she could not yet deal. She made no attempt to shake off this peculiar numbness, knowing that it would, all too soon, give way to the pain lying in wait.

Taking an afternoon carriage ride was Joanna's idea, and while the prospect generated neither resistance nor enthusiasm in Rachel, she agreed to go.

The weather was mild and burnished by a muted brass sun. Feathery clouds made an eiderdown tracery against the azure sky, and the bay sparkled, dappled with silver and gold. There was still a tinge of smoke in the air, mingled with the odor of charred wood.

As the carriage rattled down the hill, the full scope of the city's destruction came home to Rachel with crushing clarity. The wharfs were gnarled and blackened, or gone entirely; while the business district itself, except for a few pathetically naked brick ruins, was completely destroyed. Was it possible that she had been right in the middle of the holocaust, as Joanna said she had, and remembered nothing?

Rachel drew in her breath, and tears of shock trembled in her voice when she spoke. "Oh, Joanna—it's as though the world had ended. . . ."

Joanna's voice was gentle, wise. "Look again, Rachel."

Brow furrowed, Rachel stared out at the grim waste once more. Now, she saw what Joanna wished her to see—the tents rising from the rubble and somehow defying it; the federal and territorial flags waving beside a sooty but triumphant courthouse; the smiles of merchants who sold their goods and services from the backs of wagons and beneath canvas canopies.

"Look at Seattle," Joanna urged softly. "Look at her, scrambling back to her feet!"

Rachel's throat was unaccountably tight; and one tear slid, trickling, down her face. She dashed it away.

"Are you beaten, Rachel?" Joanna went on, a quiet challenge ringing in her words. "Or will you fight back, like Seattle?"

A ragged sob wrenched itself from her throat, but the challenge could not be ignored. All right. Her money was gone, the dress shop where she'd ordered new clothes was gone, Miss Cunningham's boardinghouse was probably gone, too, with the things she had left there. But she still had her building, and she was still a tough timber brat, bred to roll with the punches.

She raised her chin and met Joanna's gaze directly. "I'll fight," she said.

"Good," replied Joanna, her blue eyes warm on Rachel's face.

"I'm going back to Providence," Rachel announced, even though she hadn't been asked. "Yes," she added, after a short interval, for her own benefit more than Joanna's, "Yes, I'm going back."

Joanna said nothing, and she seemed to be intent on the rollicking resurrection going on all over the city. A small smile tilted the corner of her mouth upward, however, and her blue eyes were very bright.

Rachel turned her attention inward, facing facts.

As her money was gone, so was the dream of being Griffin Fletcher's wife. However, the sturdy building in Providence remained to her, as did the tiny, troublesome, and infinitely precious life nestled within her.

Life would be hard, for her and for her child, but it would be good, too. Rachel McKinnon meant to see to that, thank you very much.

A hundred misgivings sprang, tangled, into her mind. In a matter of months, her pregnancy would be visible to all and sundry, and in a town like Providence especially, that meant scandal. She would doubtlessly encounter Griffin time and time again. Wouldn't he guess that the child swelling her middle was his own?

Rachel determined to deal with that problem when she came to it. In all likelihood, by the time her condition became noticeable, Griffin would be married to Athena and totally oblivious to the proprietress of McKinnon's Rooming House.

Because all these things were churning in her mind, even after the carriage had shuddered to a stop in front of the O'Riley house and Rachel had gone into the garden to think, Jonas's appearance took her completely by surprise.

She started when she saw him, felt color surge into her face. What must he think of her, now that Griffin had boasted of possessing her so fully? "Jonas," she breathed, stricken.

He smiled, his hands resting comfortably in the pockets of his trousers, his white shirt open at the throat. His tone, when he spoke, was light, but startlingly blunt. "I trust your romance with Griffin is over?"

Rachel's color deepened, and she folded her hands in her lap, lowered her head. "Yes," she said miserably.

Boldly, Jonas sat down on the stone bench beside her. He was so close that she could smell the scent of his cologne and feel the frightening tension within him. "Rachel, perhaps it's too soon to speak, but the plain truth is, if I don't I'm going to go insane. I love you—I want you to be my wife."

The garden bench seemed to be buckling beneath them; Rachel's head spun, and her stomach knotted itself up tight. "What?" she managed, finally.

The sleeves of Jonas's shirt were rolled up nearly to his elbows; when he reached out, suddenly, and took Rachel's hand, she could see the tiny golden hairs glistening on his forearm.

"Urchin, will you look at me, please? I'm trying to declare myself here, you know, and you're not making it any easier."

There was no choice; in another moment, he would reach out, lift her chin, force her to face him. She met his eyes knowing that her own were brimming with tears. "Oh, Jonas, don't—please—don't."

The briefest pain flashed in the depths of his golden eyes. "I have to, Urchin. My options are limited, you see—either I make you mine, or I lose my mind."

Mutely, Rachel shook her head.

But Jonas stayed the motion with a grasp that bordered on pain, his fingers tight and cool on her chin. "God help me, Rachel, I know you love Griffin—I know you want him. But you must realize by now that he still belongs to Athena."

Misery swept through Rachel, just as the fire had swept through Seattle. She swallowed an involuntary cry of grief and nodded.

Jonas's hand fell away from her face, and she thought she saw her own desolation mirrored in his handsome, even features. "In spite of the things you've probably heard about me, I would be the most devoted of husbands, Rachel. I would love you, shelter you—"

A third voice broke in unexpectedly, harsh with malice. "Betray you, murder everyone and everything you hold dear."

Griffin. Rachel's heart struggled within her, like something wild caught in an inescapable trap, but she could not bring herself to look at him.

Jonas shot to his feet; out of the corner of one eye, Rachel saw his fists clench at his sides.

Griffin's voice was low, contemptuous. "Marry him, Rachel, and you marry the man who murdered your father in cold blood."

The world was reeling and tumbling around Rachel, and bile rushed, scalding, into her throat. "No!" she screamed, even as some primitive instinct hidden in the deepest recesses of her heart accepted the words as truth. She was on her feet, flailing her arms wildly, feeling her fists make contact with the hard width of a man's chest.

And Jonas's grasp was fierce on her wrists as he stayed the blows. When his face came into focus again, Rachel shuddered.

Jonas's voice rumbled, like dark, distant clouds colliding in a night sky. "He is lying, Rachel! Would I be walking around free if I'd killed a man?"

Rachel stumbled back from him, shaking her head, struggling in his grip. She felt Griffin's approach, felt the pull of him in all her senses.

He broke Jonas's hold easily, swung her up into his arms, held her close against him. He turned back toward the garden gate, still carrying Rachel, wordless with fury.

There was a soft thud; Rachel watched in horror as Griffin's features went blank, fell helplessly as he fell. She was unhurt, but Griffin lay motionless on the stone floor of that part of the garden, the back of his head bleeding slightly. Screams clustered, unuttered, in her throat, tears poured down her face.

She dropped her forehead to the dark tangle of Griffin's hair, certain that he was dead.

It was then that Jonas wrested her cruelly to her feet, one of his hands clamping over her mouth. She heard something hard fall from his other hand and clatter on the fieldstones beneath their feet. His voice was a madman's voice, rasping savagely from his throat. "Remember what I told you, Rachel? The night we went to the Opera House and then my hotel? I said that when I took you, you would be ready. Now, Urchin, whether you know it or not, you're ready!"

Terror and grief made Rachel strong; she twisted in Jonas's grasp, bit the fingers of his constricting hand until she tasted blood.

He swore hoarsely and slapped her so hard that she would have fallen if he hadn't caught her.

I must scream, she thought stupidly, but she could not make a sound; if her mind was given to calm reason, her body was stunned into a sort of hopeless paralysis.

Rachel could make no protest of any kind as Jonas dragged her out of the garden, across the lawn, and up to the door of his carriage. When he thrust her savagely inside, she fainted.

The first sensation Griffin Fletcher recognized was a pounding ache in the back of his head. He groaned, and nausea boiled into his throat.

"Lie still!" pleaded a familiar, feminine voice. "Oh, Griffin, please—don't move."

Athena. Griffin cursed and raised himself to his hands and knees, then to his feet. The familiar garden swayed around him, and it was shrouded in darkness.

It was a moment before his eyes focused on the flat, blood-splattered rock lying a yard or so away, before he remembered. When he did, he thrust Athena's hand savagely from his arm and stumbled around her, toward the stables.

The darkness began to clear away. To Griffin's great relief, he realized that it was still daylight.

Athena screamed his name, and the sound was shrill, almost angry. Griffin made his way into the barn, found a horse, saddled it. He had reached the waterfront before he remembered that Jonas had had a carriage.

The sun was high and hot, drawing sweat from the back of his neck and the space between his shoulder blades. Gulls swooped and complained against the fierce blue of the sky, steamers chugged by, their passengers gaping and pointing at the remains of Seattle.

Frantic, unable to think properly, Griffin slid from the horse's back and paced the rubble-strewn dirt that had once been a plank walkway overlooking the wharfs.

A hand caught his arm, stayed him. "Griff? What in the devil—"

Griffin whirled, ready to fight, caught himself just as the face before him came into proper focus. "Malachi," he breathed, closing his eyes.

"What is it, Griffin?" the *Merrimaker*'s captain demanded, his weathered face taut with concern. "You don't look even half right to me."

The pain in the back of Griffin's head was savage, blinding him, causing his knees to tremble beneath him. He caught himself, forced gruff, terse words of explanation past his lips.

"Where would he take the girl?" Malachi demanded, searching Griffin's face. "If it's somewhere the *Merrimaker* can follow, I swear that she will."

Mutely, Griffin nodded.

Half an hour later, the *Merrimaker* caught her share of the northbound wind and sailed away from the laboring tugs that had drawn her from the bay into the heart of Puget Sound.

Standing at the bow, his hands tight on the railing, Griffin lost track of time. But he marked the passing of West Point and Shilshole Bay, Kingston and Point No Point. The sun was raging behind the Olympic peaks when the *Merrimaker* rounded Foulweather Bluff and surged into the mouth of the Hood Canal.

The water was deep at Providence harbor, but the tide was out, so the *Merrimaker* dropped anchor almost a quarter of a mile offshore. Griffin would have swam the distance if Malachi Lindsay hadn't pointed out a better way.

After thanking his friend, Griffin climbed down a knotted rope to the twelve-foot skiff that had been lowered over the side. Three crewmen were already there, holding the boat steady.

When Griffin had taken his place beside one of four oarlocks, they pushed away from the *Merrimaker*'s creaking port side and rowed toward shore. The straining effort of the task was balm to Griffin's whirling mind.

At the wharf, he climbed the familiar wooden ladder, waved once at the already retreating crew of the skiff, and strode along the dock, toward a bevy of citizens eager for more news of the Great Fire.

Griffin ignored them, and calmly stole the schoolmaster's dapple-gray mare from in front of the general store.

The horse was slow, it seemed to him, and he was swinging from its shuddering back, in front of Jonas's palatial house, before he noticed that the animal was lathered.

He bounded up Jonas's walk, crossed the porch in long strides, kicked open both the doors. They clattered against the inside walls with a satisfying, splintering sound.

"*Jonas!*" Griffin bellowed, pausing in the marble-floored entry hall. He was about to search the rooms upstairs when Mrs. Hammond appeared, trembling, the hem of her stark white apron twisted in her hands.

"They aren't here, Dr. Fletcher. And that's the God's truth."

Griffin swayed a little, in his fury and his weariness. "Tell me," he bit out.

Mrs. Hammond's chins wobbled. "They're gone to be married. You're too late."

Griffin fought for control, attained it. They wouldn't be at Providence's one and only church, he knew that— Field could never be persuaded to perform the ceremony. That left only one possible place to look—Judge Sheridan's house on Main Street.

Seething, Griffin wheeled around, made his way back to the exhausted mare quivering at the hitching post. He remembered nothing of the ride back to town.

The door of Judge Sheridan's saltbox house stood open to the warmth of the summer evening, and the toneless complaints of Mrs. Sheridan's treasured organ greeted Griffin as he abandoned the schoolmaster's horse and vaulted over the white picket fence.

Without bothering to knock, he stormed into the close, tasseled and fringed ugliness of the judge's parlor. The justice of the peace looked up from his little black book, winced, and swallowed his opening remarks whole.

"Griffin!"

Jonas whirled, his eyes wild in the pale expanse of his face. Beside him, wearing an ill-fitting white dress that probably belonged to one of the Sheridan's four daughters, Rachel turned.

Her amethyst eyes were dilated, and her smile was warm and sleepy and confused. "You're not dead," she observed cheerfully.

Griffin's heart constricted within him. He held out his arms, and she came toward him, like a child, still smiling in that dazed, heart-wrenching way.

There was a terrible silence in the room after the tortured organ wheezed its last. Griffin drew Rachel close, scanned her widened eyes and her flushed face, and felt wild relief as he realized that she hadn't entered into this particular ritual willingly. She was drugged—probably with laudanum.

Judge Sheridan found his rumbling, politian's voice. "Now, Griffin, this is a legal ceremony—"

Now that Rachel was close, safe within the curve of his arm, Griffin's rage exploded like a volcano. "You pompous, blind old bastard, this is a circus!" he roared. "And the bride has been drugged." His gaze swung to Jonas, menacing, inviting retaliation. "Hasn't she, Cousin?"

Jonas was speechless, rigid with fury. There was high color in his face, and a hellish glitter in his eyes.

Griffin beckoned with one hand, his fingers curling back over his palm, his jaw clenched so tight that the ache ran the length of his neck and into one shoulder. "Aren't you going to reclaim your bride, Jonas?" he taunted, in low, deadly tones. "Or do you have a rock ready, for when I turn my back?"

Jonas made a chilling, guttural sound, and lunged. Prepared, Griffin thrust a mumbling Rachel behind him and waited.

But Judge Sheridan, a portly man well into his middle years, caught Jonas around the shoulders and restrained him with surprising strength. His shrewd eyes locked with Griffin's, and he uttered the first straightforward words of his long and largely incompetent career. "Your life isn't worth a fresh cow chip now, Griffin. You know that, don't you?"

Griffin's smile felt like a grimace on his aching face. "Yes, sir. I believe I do," he said, politely. "Now, if you'll excuse us—we'll skip the celebration."

Jonas yelled something obscene, and struggled furiously, hopelessly, in the Judge's grip. Mrs. Sheridan, still frozen on the organ seat, grew very pale and uttered a distracted little cry.

Griffin bowed to her, turned, lifted Rachel into his arms, and carried her out into the twilight. Jonas's bellowed threats echoed in his ears all the way to Tent Town.

He paid no attention to the frank, open-mouthed stares that greeted him as he strode through the middle of the canvas community and into the adjoining woods, still carrying the limp, befuddled Rachel.

Knowing that Judge Sheridan couldn't hold Jonas forever, he skirted the path he usually took and followed one that Billy had shown him months before. Rachel yawned and let her head rest against his shoulder.

The welcoming lights of his own house were in sight when the grim humor of the situation finally struck Griffin. He laughed uproariously as he carried Rachel across the shadowy yard, up the backsteps, and into the kitchen.

Molly was there, stirring something at the stove, her auburn hair falling in her face, her cheeks flushed. When she turned, expecting to see her son and finding Griffin there instead, Jonas's stolen bride yawning in his arms, her mouth fell open. "Saints preserve us!" she gasped, when she had recovered herself.

Gently, Griffin lowered his beloved burden into a chair. "I hope they do, Molly," he said. "We're going to need all the help we can get."

Chapter Thirty-one

Field Hollister yawned, redid the knot in his tie for the third time, and turned away from the mirror over the bedroom bureau. Fawn was sitting stiffly in the rocking chair, her hands folded in her lap.

"Wish it wasn't Sunday?" Field asked, softly.

She raised wide eyes to his face. "Don't you?" she countered.

Field sighed. "If the truth be known, Sunday has never been my favorite day." A smile played on his lips and he suppressed it, only to feel it slide into his eyes. "Yes, indeed, I started hating Sundays when I was a lad of eight. My story is a sad one."

Fawn giggled, in spite of herself. "Oh, tell me, Reverend Hollister—what is your sad story?"

He assumed the ponderous stance he'd seen his father take on what Griffin called "Brimstone Sundays," resting his hands on an imaginary pulpit. "As I was trying to say, when I was so rudely interrupted, it was a Sunday, and I was eight years old. My father was expounding on the sin of Gluttony—it was one of his favorites, you know, he rated it right up there with Debauchery and Wearing Your Underwear Backward—and it came to pass that my Aunt Gertrude was visiting. She, being a lady of some corpulence, took that sermon as a personal affront!" Field leaned forward slightly, his eyes blazing, his voice growing thunderous. "And what do you suppose came of *that*, Mrs. Hollister?"

Fawn shook her head, her eyes shining with suppressed mirth.

"Well, I'll tell you!" boomed Field, in the true tradition of his father before him. "She started shifting around in the pew beside me—hear me, for I speak but the purest truth—and her corset stays came undone. I was struck, in my innocence, wounding blows!"

Fawn was rocking back and forth now, trying to hold in her laughter.

Field went ruthlessly on. "By a wall of unleashed flesh, you ask, as you well might?" He frowned ominously. "Well, are you going to ask, or not?"

Fawn managed a nod.

He grinned, rocking back on the worn heels of his boots, waiting.

"All right!" cried his wife. "Was it a wall of unleashed flesh?"

"Of *course* not! I laughed out loud, circumstances being what they were, and my father dragged me outside, right in the middle of his discourse on Gluttony, and beat me half to death with a hymnal!"

Fawn laughed until tears rolled down her face. Then she stood up, letting her head fall against Field's chest. "I'm so scared," she whispered.

Field held her close. "Me, too," he replied.

Fifteen minutes later, he took his customary place behind the pulpit of the Providence Presbyterian Church. Word of the marriage had definitely gotten around; the faces of his parishioners were stony with outrage.

Field closed his eyes for a moment, and when he opened them again, he saw Griffin standing in the open doorway, grinning, his arms folded across his chest. He swallowed, and then proudly announced his marriage to Fawn Nighthorse.

There was an ominous silence, and then Judge Sheridan's wife, Clovis, stood up, her hands gripping the back of the pew in front of her. "Winfield Hollister, you know how the Lord feels about white men marrying Indians!"

Field saw his wife tense, lift her chin. He cleared his throat. "Enlighten me, Mrs. Sheridan. How *does* the Lord feel about that?"

Clovis bridled and turned bright red. "You've been—you've been *carrying on* with that woman for months, and we all know it! It just isn't right, that's all!"

There was a general buzz of delighted scandal now, and Field reminded himself sternly that it was Sunday, that he was a minister of the gospel. But before he could answer, his eyes were drawn back to Griffin, who was now coming up the aisle with a bulging gunny sack.

Right at the base of the pulpit, he upended the sack, and at least two dozen rocks clattered onto the board floor. Griffin bent, took a small boulder in one hand, and graciously extended it to Mrs. Sheridan.

"The honor is yours, Clovis," he said, in a pleasant voice. "Here. Cast the first stone."

Clovis sat down, her earnest face pale.

Griffin took another stone, and held it out to the storekeeper-constable. "How about you, Henry? We all know you're without sin."

Henry's handlebar mustache quivered, and he averted his eyes.

Griffin was pacing back and forth now, his face a mockery of righteous consternation. "No takers? But these are good, sturdy, *Puget Sound* rocks. They *hurt* when they make contact with flesh and bone, Brothers and Sisters—you have my professional word on that!"

Until that moment, Field had never seen an entire congregation blush in unison. But he saw it then, and it was a sight he would never forget.

Griffin, having made his point with typical directness, abandoned his bag of rocks and sat down beside Fawn to listen. He looked so dutifully attentive that Field nearly laughed aloud.

The sermon went well, and the congregation was attentive, eager to redeem itself. They sang the designated hymns with relish, and it was no surprise when four different families invited the Hollisters home for Sunday dinner.

Field declined the offers politely, remaining behind in the church even after all the others, including Fawn, had gone outside to chat under the whispering elm trees in the yard. He bent, took a stone from the burlap bag Griffin had left behind, and turned it slowly in his hand. It was rough and brown and porous, that stone, and covered with a tracery of bright green moss. Probably, it came from the banks of Billy Brady's beloved pond, hidden away in the woods beyond Tent Town.

A smile crept into Field Hollister's eyes and lingered behind a glistening blur. Griffin Fletcher had scorned organized religion for as long as he could remember, and yet, especially at times like this, it seemed to Field that no one practiced the fundamentals of the faith more assiduously.

He sat down in one of the rough-hewn pews nearest the pulpit, still turning the stone in his grasp. Griffin was an enigma, all right—causing wounds and then binding them, loving peace and then starting brawls, making his passion for Rachel McKinnon obvious to all who bothered to look, yet guarding her, sheltering her, with a tenderness Field had never seen him exhibit before.

Contrary as it might have seemed to anyone other than Field Hollister, Griffin was the most moral of men. Closing his eyes, the reverend prayed silently that his friend would not be consumed by the fires of the hell he had created with his own healing hands.

"Field?" It was Fawn, and her hand was light on his shoulder. He turned, looked up at her. It was to her credit, he thought, that she showed no reaction at all to the tears on his face.

The lingering effects of Jonas's laudanum made Rachel feel both lethargic and restless, despairing and hopeful, angry and apathetic. She tried to remember the day before, and could recall nothing beyond being dragged across the O'Rileys' lawn and thrust into Jonas's carriage.

She sighed, closed the book in her lap, and gazed at the bare hearth of the study fireplace. There were no illusions left in her mind, where Jonas Wilkes was concerned, anyway. He was obviously, for all his gentlemanly manners, just what Molly and Griffin maintained he was.

Rachel shuddered, realizing that if it hadn't been for Griffin, she would have awakened that morning to find herself in Jonas's bed, legally bound to it and to him. It was fortunate that he hadn't taken advantage of her in his carriage, or on board the steamboat that must have brought them from Seattle.

Had he?

Rachel's mind could not remember, but her body did. For reasons of his own, probably pride was among them, Jonas had not touched her.

Molly came in, carrying a tray. The teapot and translucent china cups made a comforting, tinkling sound as she set them down on the small table between Rachel's chair and the one Field Hollister usually sat in.

"Aye, and Sunday is a lonesome day," she sighed, sitting down. "'Tis good that you're here, Rachel."

Rachel smiled, reached out to pour the tea. "I was just thinking that I might have been somewhere else today, if it hadn't been for Griffin. Molly, did he really storm into a judge's house and carry me off, as you said?"

Molly sighed again, curling her small feet comfortably beneath her, sipping thoughtfully at her tea. "Aye, Rachel. It's what he told me when he came in—carrying you in his arms, he was, like you might break. 'Twas then he told me how Jonas had struck him down with a rock, and taken you away."

Rachel felt a sudden need to confide in this gentle woman, to tell her that she believed she was carrying Griffin's baby and ask her advice. But even as the wish formed itself in her heart, she knew that she could not indulge it. Molly's first loyalty was to Griffin, and she would carry the news to him immediately.

"What will happen now?"

Molly shuddered, despite the warmth of the day. "It's not like I've claim to the Sight, or anything like that, but there's trouble coming to all of us, Rachel. And soon."

Rachel thought of her mother's sturdy building and the day-to-day glimpses of Griffin Fletcher that she would catch where she could, and she mourned. "Do you think I should leave?"

"'Twas a time when I thought that would do, Rachel," Molly

said, her emerald green eyes meeting Rachel's honestly. "Now, it's too late, I'm thinking. Griffin or Jonas—most likely both of them—would only follow and drag you back. No, this thing won't end, I'm fearing, 'til one of them has you, and one of them is dead."

The pit of Rachel's stomach plummeted. "Dead?" she echoed, stunned. And then she remembered that Griffin thought her father was dead, and that she'd believed it herself, even though she couldn't bear to. Her teacup rattled dangerously in its saucer as she set it down. "If Griffin died," she whispered brokenly, "I would die, too."

The expression in Molly's eyes was unreadable, as was the tone of her voice. "And Jonas? How would you feel if he died, Rachel?"

Rachel searched her heart. "If it's true that Jonas killed my father, like Griffin said, I hope he hangs. But I wouldn't want him, or any other man, to die because of me."

Molly turned her face away suddenly, but the usual high color was gone from her skin, leaving behind a frightening pallor. "'Tis killing that weasel with my own hands I'd be, if I were strong as a man! His kind don't hang for their murders—they gloat over them and then go on as if nothing had happened!"

There was a long, tense silence before Rachel dared to speak. "Molly, do you really think there have been others?"

A tear trickled down Molly's white, tightly controlled face. "There was my Patrick—rest his fine soul—for one. We'd been living in one of the tents for more than two months when Jonas suddenly decided that we ought to have a cottage instead. Patrick was such a fine, strong worker, he said.

"Well, I didn't know it, nor did Paddy, but moving into one of those pretty little brick houses bore a frightful price. And Jonas made sure I was alone—except for Billy—when he came to collect it."

Rachel was crying now, too, because Molly was, because she understood only too well. She couldn't have said a word if her life had depended on it, but she reached out and laid her hand gently on the arm of the trembling woman beside her.

Devastatingly calm, Molly went on, and hers was the face of a woman wandering through an endless nightmare. "I tried to get away, but I couldn't. I was different from the others, though—when my Paddy came down from the mountain, I told him. He went after Jonas—in a killing rage he was—but he never got home again."

"You didn't go to the constable?" Rachel asked, trembling herself now.

Molly's laugh was bitter and hoarse. "The constable? Henry's really just a storekeeper, Rachel—and he's Jonas's friend in the bargain. I went to him, like a fool, and told him my Patrick was lying murdered somewhere."

"And he didn't do anything?"

"He did something, all right. He patted my arm and said everything would be fine. And then he went straight to Jonas."

Rachel closed her eyes, waiting, knowing that the rest of the story would be, somehow, even more terrible than what had gone before.

"I was packing my things and Billy's that night—I meant for us to be aboard the first steamboat to leave Providence, no matter where it was going."

"And Jonas came. He had two men with him, and they kicked in our door and walked into that cottage like—like the soldiers used to do in Ireland. Jonas took me again, before it was over, but that wasn't the worst part, Rachel. They beat my Billy when he tried to protect me."

Sickness rose, like acid, in Rachel's throat. "And that's why—"

"That's why his poor mind is what it is."

"H-How did you get away?"

"There was a lot of noise, and someone went and found Field Hollister. Griffin was with him when he came in, and as you can probably imagine, there was a row this town has never seen the like of. Jonas and his men *crawled* out of that cottage, Rachel, but it was too late for Billy and me, and certainly too late for Patrick.

"Jonas was questioned, but after that, the law just sort of looked the other way. So Billy and I came here to work for the doctor, and glad we were of it, too."

Rachel was too stricken to speak, and Molly was lost in memories that must have been nearly unbearable to look back upon.

They were still sitting there, shaken and silent, when Griffin came in, grumbling, and lit the kerosene lamps on the mantel.

"Good Lord," he scowled. "What's gotten into the two of you? This place is dark as a tomb."

Rachel looked up from her misery, startled to see that night had come. The tears that she had not been able to cry before came then, in a savage torrent. Her father was dead, Molly's Patrick was dead.

The knowledge was too horrible to bear.

Griffin came toward her slowly, drew her to her feet, held her. His mouth was warm at her temple, his arms strong around her, but Rachel did not feel safe. She doubted now that she ever would again.

Molly's voice was crisp, if resigned. "The fault is mine, then," she said. "May the Blessed Virgin forgive me, I've told her the truth of Jonas Wilkes."

He was angry; Rachel could feel his fury snapping between his body and her own. Still, his words sounded gentle as they passed her ear. "Please, Molly—will you get supper?"

As Molly went out, Rachel lifted her face to Griffin's. "He'll come for me, won't he? Jonas will come for me."

Griffin's eyes did not waver from hers. "Yes," he said. "I think he will. Rachel, marry me—now, tonight."

Rachel searched his face, and in that moment, she knew that Athena had lied, that he loved her, that he had not used her. She also knew that she could not say yes, even though everything within her longed to. If she did, Jonas would surely kill him.

She turned away, to hide the telling pain in her eyes. "I can't," she said.

The silence was thunderous, eternal. Griffin broke it gruffly. "Why not?"

Rachel raised her chin, reminded herself of the brutal, tragic truth. "I don't love you," she lied, praying that he would accept what she'd said without question.

But Griffin wrenched her around to face him, his dark eyes glittering, his jawline flexed. He caught her chin, hard, in his hand. "Say that again, Sprite," he commanded.

She wouldn't have been able to, had she not had a sudden vision of Griffin lying dead. Anything would be better—marrying Jonas, even being sold by Captain Frazier. "I don't love you," she repeated, in flat, steady tones.

Pain contorted his face; he closed his eyes for a moment. Rachel used that fleeting time to fight down the grief that was rising from her heart to her eyes.

He looked down at her again, as though he sensed something, but then he released his hold on her shoulders and strode out of the study. The slamming of the front door signaled an end to the deception, and Rachel sank into a chair, covering her face with both hands, and, once again, wept.

She wanted to cry forever, but there was something strong within her, something that would not give up even when that seemed to be the only sensible thing to do. Aware of a need for haste, Rachel McKinnon swallowed her grief and, once again, fled Griffin Fletcher's house.

As she stumbled through the woods, and then through Tent Town, she tried to deal with the certainty that this time, Griffin would not follow.

It was late when the front door opened, but Molly Brady heard the knob turn, then the soft click of the lock. She sat straight up in her chair, facing the study fireplace, and breathed a frantic prayer that there would be no rage this time.

Griffin came into the dimly lit room, his face haggard in the soft, flickering light. There was something broken about him, as though his spirit had been dragged out of him and beaten. His dark eyes were vacant.

Silently, Molly retracted her prayer. Even one of his uncontrollable rampages would have been preferable to this odd, animated death she saw in him now.

"Where is Rachel?" she dared.

He went to the mantel, braced himself against it with both hands, lowered his head. "Becky's."

Molly stood up. She could not risk touching him, though she longed to offer him the same comfort she would have given to Billy, had he been in need of it. "I heard it all from the hallway, Griffin," she confessed.

Griffin flinched slightly, but he made no answer.

There were tears in Molly's eyes now and in her voice, and she wasn't ashamed. "Oh, Griffin, you fool—don't you know that she was lying to you? Don't you understand what she's trying to do?"

He made a hoarse, contemptuous sound. "Oh, I think I understand that, all right."

All desire to comfort was gone now; Molly felt, in its stead, a need to hammer at that taut, impervious back with her fists. "Rachel is protecting you!"

Griffin's face was terrible when he whirled away from the

mantel, so terrible that Molly retreated a step or two, out of his reach.

"Rachel is taking up where her mother left off!" he spat. And then he brushed past his outraged, incredulous housekeeper and strode out of the study.

The heels of his boots made a hammering sound on the stairs.

Chapter Thirty-two

Rachel was a little startled when she awakened in her mother's bed that glowering Monday morning, but she recovered quickly. Today, she would dismiss the girls, the barkeeper, everyone except Mamie, the cook.

As she washed and then dressed in the worn cotton dress Molly had loaned her the day before, she made up her mind to ask for whatever profits the business might have generated in her absence. There might, with luck, be enough money to buy a few lengths of calico and poplin for dresses.

The saloon had been closed on Sunday, of course, but it was already coming to life as Rachel descended the steep wooden stairs to make her announcement.

It was more difficult than she'd expected, telling these hardened, sharp-eyed women that they would have to find employment elsewhere, but Rachel managed it with quiet dignity.

Tom Rawlins, the barkeep, burst out laughing. "Becky's kid, running a boardinghouse! If that don't tickle my whiskers!"

Rachel stood her ground, but her voice trembled a little when she spoke. "I'm glad you find it amusing, Mr. Rawlins. But the fact remains that this building and everything in it is mine now, and I have no intention of selling spirits or—or—"

One of the women, a tall, slender blonde with the face of a schoolmarm, turned a steaming coffee mug slowly between her palms and smiled. "You'd better look over the ledgers before you make too many assumptions, Miss McKinnon. Wouldn't surprise me none if you found yourself business partners with Mr Jonas Wilkes."

Rachel squared her shoulders, even though the prospect of having anything to do with that heinous man made her quake inside, and walked across the saloon floor to take the stack of black books Tom Rawlins had brought from behind the bar.

In the relative privacy of the kitchen, where Mamie was working at the stove, Rachel read the ledgers and learned the dismal truth. While the actual partnership had been dissolved, long ago, there were still outstanding debts. Sizable ones.

Mamie set a plate of scrambled eggs before her new employer, along with a cup of hot, fragrant coffee. "You owe that man plenty, from the look on your face."

Glumly, Rachel nodded. She should have been prepared for this—Jonas had mentioned a business affiliation with her mother the very day she met him—but the situation still came as a brutal shock. "I don't know much about the law, Mamie, but I think he could take the place away from me."

Mamie sat down heavily, ignoring the prostitutes as they came in and out of the kitchen, dishing up their own breakfasts, returning empty coffee mugs, plundering the pantry shelves for foods they found preferable to scrambled eggs. A long time had passed before she ventured an opinion.

"Mr. Wilkes won't stand for no boardinghouse, Rachel. Not when there isn't another saloon for miles around. His men would be unhappy about that and start looking for work elsewhere."

Rachel swallowed hard, knowing that Mamie was probably right. "My mother didn't manage her money very wisely, did she, Mamie?"

Mamie smiled, and her round, brown eyes had a faraway look to them. "I guess not. She meant to pay Mr. Wilkes off, and she gave him whatever money she could. Trouble was that one of the girls always seemed to have sick folks at home. Too, Becky was all the time giving credit to the wrong people—I don't know how many of those lumberjacks moved on without paying their bar bills."

Rachel thought of the child within her and vowed that she would solve this problem. She couldn't continue running a brothel; not even for a day could she countenance the sale of human flesh. But it appeared that she wouldn't be able to close Becky's Place without a fight.

Unexpectedly, Mamie's shiny brown hand closed, warm, over her own. "Go to Dr. Fletcher, Child. He has money, and he'd help you now—I know he would."

Hot color surged into Rachel's face and pounded at her cheekbones. "I would die first."

"Then what are you going to do? Nobody else, besides Jonas Wilkes himself, has what to loan you."

Rachel stood up slowly, wearily. She was tired—so mercilessly tired—but she was through running away. "I'm going to go to Mr. Wilkes, right now, and try to reason with him."

Incredible as it seemed, Mamie's black skin paled a little. "No! Why Becky McKinnon would haunt my nights from here on if I let you face that man alone!"

"I'm going, Mamie," Rachel said staunchly. "Don't you see? I have to!"

"Now you listen here, Child!" Mamie cried, raising her great bulk from her chair at the table and pointing one stern, black finger. "It's no secret what happened at Judge Sheridan's the other night—everybody's been talking about it since. Now, I figure that Jonas Wilkes must be madder than sin over that, and when he's mad, he's mean!"

"If he's angry with anyone, Mamie, he's angry with Griffin. Even if I'd wanted to stay and be married, which I most certainly didn't, I wouldn't have been allowed to. Blaming me makes no sense."

"Not much of what Jonas Wilkes does make sense, Rachel. Don't you go near him!"

Before Rachel could respond to that, there was a stir beyond the kitchen door, in the saloon itself. And then she knew, instinctively, that the choice had been made for her—Jonas Wilkes had spared her the journey to his house.

He roared her name.

Rachel trembled, met Mamie's startled gaze only briefly, and then turned to march into the saloon and face the dragon.

The prostitutes had fled, leaving nail files and burning cheroots and scrambled eggs behind them. Even Tom Rawlins had abandoned his post behind the long, polished bar.

But Jonas was composed, in a frightening sort of way. Rachel saw, with bitter amusement, that he had dressed with haphazard haste. He wore no suit coat, and no tie, and his shirt was open at the neck.

"What do you think you're doing?" he demanded, in a rasping undertone, his golden eyes flashing.

Rachel stood at a careful distance, aware of Mamie behind her. "What do *you* think I'm doing, Jonas?" she countered, with a lightness she didn't feel.

Jonas's booted feet were set wide apart, his fists clenched at his sides. Clearly, her attempts to stall him were going to be fruitless. "I don't pretend to know," he said. "But if you're planning to carry on the family business, I have a surprise for you—you're not."

"That is no surprise, Mr. Wilkes. If I can possibly manage it, this saloon will be a boardinghouse before the end of the week."

Something in Jonas's face relaxed; incredibly, he began to laugh. It seemed to Rachel that an eternity passed before his mirth ebbed to an amazed, disbelieving grin. "A *boarding-house?* Oh, yes, you did mention that to me once, didn't you?"

Not knowing what else to do, Rachel nodded.

Jonas looked, if anything, more dangerous than he had before. There was something about his fixed grin, his grip on the back of one of the saloon chairs, that made Rachel fear for her very life. "Where would my men take their comfort, pray tell, if this place became a boardinghouse?"

Rachel lifted her chin. "Their 'comfort' is no concern of mine, Jonas Wilkes. It's their wives and children who matter to me."

Jonas raised one golden eyebrow. "How noble. You're beginning to sound like Field Hollister, Rachel—or, even worse, Griffin."

Fury sustained Rachel, even though she wanted to run from this man and from his controlled madness. "I know what its like to live in a tent. Fleas bite you and rain drips in your face and you can't ever take a bath—"

His grin was less threatening, in spite of his words. "And you do love baths, don't you, Rachel?" Jonas paused, but went on before Rachel could voice her contempt. "Go upstairs and pack your things, Miss McKinnon. We're leaving."

Rachel shook her head. "No."

Jonas sighed, and it was a vicious sound, for all its softness. "You are a rebellious little minx, aren't you? Well, Rachel, there are certain qualities I demand in a wife, and obedience is one of them. Move!"

"I am *not* your wife, Jonas Wilkes, and I have no intention of being your wife, ever!"

Again, Jonas sighed, tilting his head back to search the ceiling as though he expected to find guidance there. Rachel was thrown off guard by this gesture, and was horrified when, with a swiftness she wouldn't have believed possible, he closed the space between them and grasped her upper arms in a painful, inescapable grasp.

Rachel tried to scream, but the sound died in her throat. She just stood there, frozen, looking up into his contorted face.

"Lesson one," he breathed savagely. And then he sat down in a chair and wrenched Rachel after him. With maniacal strength, he flung her across his knees, like a child, and began to spank her.

Outraged, Rachel struggled, and her voice came back in glass-rattling shrieks. Never, in all her life, had she ever been angrier, or more humiliated.

But Jonas was equal to the battle; he held her easily. And the palm of his hand kept coming down on her backside with ferocious, stinging regularity.

There was a loud clicking sound at one side of the room and, simultaneously, the saloon doors swung open.

Rachel looked toward the doors, probably because her fear of further humiliation was greater than her curiosity. If Griffin saw her like this, she would die.

But it was Athena Bordeau who stood in the doorway, her silvery hair bright against the threatening glower of the day. A tiny smile curved her full lips, and she removed her gloves with deft little tugs. Her blue eyes were fixed on the kitchen door, and they were sparkling with amusement.

"You'd better let the lady up, Jonas. If you don't, that negress over there is going to blow your head off."

The blows stopped, and Rachel was freed. The bright embarrassment burning in her face drained away when she scrambled to her feet and saw Mamie standing just inside the saloon, aiming a double-barrelled shotgun at Jonas's head.

He rose to his feet so suddenly that Rachel, still standing near him, was hard put to keep her footing. The look in his eyes was murderous, and his throat worked with a convulsive, stifling rage.

Undaunted, Mamie looked down the polished, blue-black barrel of that gun and met his gaze. "Get out, Wilkes. If you don't, they're gonna be scraping up your parts and pieces as far away as Wenatchee!"

Athena laughed. "I think she means it, Jonas."

With a strange dignity, considering the circumstances, Jonas

274

rolled down his sleeves and clasped his dangling cuff links into place. His gaze moved over Rachel in a possessive, scorching sweep. "You owe me a lot of money," he said, in a low, stomach-numbing tone. "One way or another, Urchin, you're going to settle the debt."

Rachel's hand, too often independent of her brain, rose to his face with a vengeance, made hard contact.

Probably conscious of Mamie's shotgun, Jonas made no move to retaliate physically, but his words were as lethal as any blow could have been. "You slapped me once before, Rachel, and it was a bad mistake even then. This time, it was disastrous."

"Get out," Rachel breathed, seething, her hands clenched so tightly that her nails were digging into the skin on her palms.

But Jonas only sighed, scanned Rachel's outraged frame speculatively, and muttered, "You have twenty-four hours, Urchin. At the end of that time, you will either be at my door, or devoutly wishing that you'd seen reason."

His meaning, veiled as it was, was crystal clear to Rachel. "And if I do 'see reason'?"

He confirmed her suspicions calmly. "Then certain people we both know and love will go right on breathing. You have one day to decide, Rachel."

Apparently tired of waiting, Mamie fired the shotgun. The mirror over the bar shattered into shards and, when the smoke cleared, Jonas was striding out of the saloon, dragging a shaken Athena along with him.

"And don't you come back here, neither!" Mamie screamed after them.

Rachel sank into a chair, flinching as her battered bottom made contact with the hard wooden seat. One by one, the prostitutes reappeared, reticules in hand, looking pale and all too aware of the dangerous climate of Becky's Place.

By the time an hour had passed, only one remained—the tall blonde who'd spoken up when Rachel had announced her intention of closing the brothel.

Her name was Elsa, and she informed Rachel placidly that she'd just as soon stay on, if it was all the same to everybody else. She'd saved a few dollars, and when Rachel saw the sense of things and went to Mr. Wilkes, Elsa allowed, she'd have Becky's Place turning a tidy profit again in no time.

Rachel listened to all this in appalled silence, sipping the brandy-laced coffee Mamie brought and wishing that she'd never heard of Providence or even Washington Territory, for that matter.

She'd been a fool to stay, to let matters come to what they had. Now she was beaten, once and for all, and there were no options left.

If she borrowed steamer fare and fled to Seattle, or points beyond, Jonas would have Griffin killed. If she stayed longer than twenty-four hours, clinging to her stupid dream of running a boardinghouse, the result would be exactly the same.

Rachel folded her arms on the table and laid her head down on them in mute despair. Griffin had proposed to her, and she knew that he loved her, but she could not turn to him either. The chances were too great that he would die suddenly, in some mysterious "accident," or just disappear entirely, as her father and Patrick Brady had.

Small, raw sobs shook Rachel's shoulders and clogged up her nose. She was going to have to present herself to Jonas within the space of one day, in unqualified surrender.

Elsa's hand came to rest cautiously on one of her shoulders. "Don't cry, Sweetie. Jonas ain't so bad, really—what's a few spankin's and a hard time in bed once in a while compared to all that money?"

Rachel cried all the harder.

Athena sat quietly in the carriage seat across from Jonas's, her hands folded in her lap. When it was safe to speak, she would know.

"Second thoughts?" she asked, five minutes later, when the easing in Jonas's anguished face told her that the time had come.

Jonas made an odd, despairing sound—it was almost like a sob. "Why did I do that?" he hissed, without looking at Athena.

"I guess you want her so badly that you can't think straight. Jonas, you can't kill Griffin—I won't allow it."

Jonas's hands moved, fingers spread apart, to run themselves through his already rumpled hair. "Relax, Sweetheart. I have no intention of killing him."

"No one would guess that!" snapped Athena, in retort. "And if you make any more scenes like the one at Becky's, you may not have a choice!"

Incredibly, Jonas laughed. "I don't know. Spanking that

saucy little dryad was almost worth dying—she deserved it so richly. Even Griffin would agree to that, I think."

Athena wanted to cry, though she didn't quite know why. "What are you going to do now, Jonas?"

He met her eyes and grinned. "Back off, of course. Apologize profusely—maybe even grovel."

Athena shook her head. "You're insane, Jonas Wilkes. Totally, unequivocally insane."

Jonas sat back in the carriage seat, sighed happily, and cupped his hands behind his head. "Yes. And I'm in august company, Mrs. Bordeau. August company indeed."

"Fool," spat Athena, glaring out at the passing countryside and the light, dismal rain that had just begun to fall.

The night passed with hellish slowness, as far as Rachel was concerned. She tossed and turned in her mother's bed, hearing the swift approach of her own doom in the steady cadence of the rain.

The sounds accompanying the dawn were no more comforting. Standing at the window, looking out at the choppy waters of the canal, Rachel listened in glum misery to the raucous calls of the gulls; the clatter of Mamie's pots and pans in the kitchen below; the lonely, distant whine of the saws in the mill at the base of the mountain.

But there were other sounds, too—sounds that didn't belong. Wagon wheels squeaking, muted curses, the steady *thwack-thwack-thwack* of a hammer.

Rachel went into the empty room next to her mother's and looked toward Providence and the harbor. But she needn't have looked so far, she discovered, for the noise was coming from the thicket of blackberries and ferns not fifty yards from where she stood.

The framework of a sizable building was going up, and Jonas Wilkes was there, directing the process.

Impulsively, Rachel wrenched at the window sill until it gave way, leaned out, and called, "What are you doing?"

Jonas smiled, doffed his rain-beaded hat in a courtly fashion. "You won't mind having a saloon next door to your boardinghouse, I hope?" he shouted back, jovially.

Rachel swallowed. "My boardinghouse?"

Jonas nodded. "It's all yours, Urchin. And, as for that little disaster yesterday, I'm sorry. For most of it anyway."

The men working among the wagons and sawhorses went about their business without taking apparent note of the conversation, though Rachel knew that they would rush to recount it, word for word, at the earliest opportunity. By the time the sun set, everyone in Providence and in the camps up the mountain would know about Jonas's Grand Gesture.

What was he up to, anyway?

Rachel's cheeks ached with color. "Which part are you apologizing for, Mr. Wilkes?" she demanded.

"The twenty-four hour ultimatum," he replied. "That was unreasonable of me."

Unreasonable. What an inadequate word that was for what he had demanded.

"And the sp—the other part?"

Jonas laughed. "I can't deny it, Urchin. I enjoyed that immensely, and I'm not sorry."

Supposing that she should have been grateful, Rachel turned crimson, stepped back, and slammed the window so hard that the glass shattered and fell, ringing like tiny bells, at her feet.

Chapter Thirty-three

The grin on Field Hollister's face was patently annoying, as far as Griffin was concerned. With a scowl, he closed his medical bag, ruffled the wheat-blond hair of his small, wide-eyed patient, and grumbled, "All right—what is it?"

Field looked at the little boy lying on a cot in the corner of the tent and smiled all the harder. "Don't mind Dr. Fletcher, Lucas," he said to the child. "He was sleeping in class when they covered bedside manner."

Lucas looked confused, but he was too sick to say much. "He give me an orange," he told Field defensively, holding up the fruit as evidence. "See?"

"I stand corrected," replied Field, as Griffin brushed past him to walk out of the tent and stand stone-still in the pouring rain. It felt good, streaming down over his face, plastering his hair to his forehead, soaking his shirt.

Field said something else to the little boy inside, and then came out to stand beside Griffin. There was no trace of the obnoxious grin in his features now, just a sad, wary look. "Influenza?" he asked, in a low voice.

Griffin nodded.

"Are there other cases?"

Griffin tipped his head back, let the rain fall full in his face for a moment. The chill of it allayed some of the deadly fatigue he'd been feeling, if not the ceaseless, raging pain. "Two," he said, softly.

Field grasped his arm and ushered him toward the large mess tent standing in the middle of the small community. "Up until now," he hissed, as they sat down at one of the long wooden tables inside to drink Chang's abominable coffee, "I would have sworn you had sense enough to come in out of the rain!"

Griffin tried for a smile, managed a grimace. "Relax, Field. Doctors don't get sick."

Overhead, the rain hammered at the taut canvas roof. "You might. Griffin, you look like hell—when was the last time you slept?"

He sipped the coffee, cursed in irritation, and reached for a crockery pitcher of cream. A generous measure turned the fierce brew to a sandalwood color and disguised its bitterness a little. "I don't sleep, Field. It's a waste of time."

"You're just going to keep moving until you collapse?" Field bit out, stirring his own coffee with such force that the spoon rattled against the sides of the enamel cup.

Griffin met the angry, turquoise eyes with a frown. "The last time I collapsed, old friend, it was because you and your cronies chloroformed me. Now, while we haven't had a chance to discuss that, the fact remains that I don't appreciate it."

Field's gaze was still direct, still full of challenge. "I didn't think you would," he said. "And I don't really care. Do you think there's going to be an epidemic?"

The coffee curdled on Griffin's tongue, and he resisted an innate need to spew it onto the sawdust floor. His aching shoulders moved in a weary shrug. "It's possible. This place breeds disease—it's a wonder there hasn't been typhoid or cholera already."

The reverend paled slightly. "Well, something has got to be done!"

Again, Griffin shrugged. "Tell that to Jonas, my friend. Those wet tents and open sewers are his province, not mine."

Exasperated, Field forced down three or four gulps of his coffee. "Maybe so, but the patients are yours, Griffin."

"You don't honestly think I ever forget that, do you?" Griffin asked evenly. "By the way, what were you grinning about, back there in the Larson's tent?"

"Rachel," Field replied, and the smile was back in his eyes again, though it looked a bit tarnished now.

The name prodded a shifting core of pain inside Griffin, lent a gruff note to his voice. "What about her?"

"I can't believe it—you really haven't heard!"

Griffin glared at his friend. *"What about her?"* he demanded.

Field laughed. "She backed Jonas Wilkes down, Griffin—with a little help from Mamie and her 'oyster gun.'"

Griffin was all attention. "What?"

"She's closed down Becky's Place, Griffin. Tomorrow it opens as McKinnon's Rooming House."

Impatient, Griffin waved away this news and insisted. "Never mind the rooming house—what's this about Jonas and Mamie and a gun?"

There was a grin—a real one—twitching at the corner of Field's mouth. "The way Mamie told it, Jonas came into that saloon roaring like a lion and demanded that Rachel pack her things and leave with him." He paused, held up both hands when he saw the fury in Griffin's face. "Now, let me finish, will you? Rachel declined, none too politely, and they had words. Griffin, she must have pushed Jonas right over the edge—he spanked her."

While the thought of Jonas touching Rachel in any way stirred murderous things inside Griffin, he couldn't help grinning at the picture that sprang into his mind. "And I thought he was all bad," he said.

Field laughed, his hands cupped around his empty coffee mug. "There's more. Mamie got out that shotgun she claims she keeps around in case any oysters decide to rush the place, and she pointed it at Jonas's head. At which time, he deemed it advisable to quit blistering Rachel. Only he didn't leave soon enough to suit Mamie, so she fired a warning shot and hit that mirror Becky had shipped in from San Francisco."

"Damn," Griffin muttered, too tired to laugh. His eyes scanned Field's face, knowing it well, seeing the serious look behind his grin. "What is it that you're not telling me?"

"Mamie got the impression that Jonas meant to kill somebody if Rachel didn't appear at his front door within twenty-four hours."

Griffin shot to his feet so quickly that the bench he'd been sitting on fell sideways, onto the sawdust floor. "Damn that son of a bitch, I'll—"

Field was shaking his head resolutely. "Sit down, Griffin. Now."

"That—"

"Listen to me! Jonas backed off, and I think you should, too. If you don't make any trouble, chances are, he won't."

Griffin barely heard his friend's reasoning. He was too busy thinking what a fool he'd made of himself, how stupid he'd been to believe Rachel when she'd said she didn't love him. Twice, her body had told him eloquently that she did.

He clasped the edges of the table with both hands and swore. Molly had been right; Rachel was trying to protect him. And he had a suspicion that she would have gone to Jonas's house if she'd had to, just to save his hide.

"You say Jonas backed down. What accounts for that?"

Field frowned. "Who knows? My guess would be that he regretted showing his true colors the way he did."

Griffin whirled suddenly, abandoning his friend, his coffee, the overturned bench. Outside, the rain was hammering at the ground, as if to wash the world clean of evils like Tent Town.

He ran, coatless, unconcerned with appearances, until he reached the locked doors of Becky's Place. Drenched to the skin, breathing hard from the exertion, he raised both fists and pounded at the doors until one of them creaked open.

And Rachel was standing there, her orchid eyes wide, her chin high.

"You lied!" he said, jubilantly. "You thought Jonas would kill me if you married me, and *you lied!*"

Her lower lip quivered. "I still believe that he would, Griffin Fletcher. And nothing on earth could make me take the chance."

He reached for her cautiously, his hands resting on her shoulders. "There's only one problem with your reasoning, Sprite. I can handle Jonas."

One tear trickled down Rachel's cheek, and she shook her head. "No. Jonas isn't straightforward like you, Griffin. He would ambush you—attack when you weren't expecting it, just like he did in Seattle, in the O'Rileys' garden."

"All right," Griffin conceded, "Maybe he would. He usually does things that way. I know this: I'd rather take my chances than live without you."

Rachel let her face rest, tear dampened, against one of his hands. "I love you, Griffin Fletcher. But I won't marry you until I know I won't end up a widow, the way Molly Brady did."

At that point in time, Griffin was willing to agree to almost anything. He sighed. "I've got to get back to my rounds, Sprite. Will you just do me one favor?"

Rachel smiled uncertainly. "What?"

"Stop worrying about what Jonas might do to me. Everything is going to be all right."

She didn't look the least bit convinced, but Griffin didn't care. She loved him, and for now, that was all that mattered. He bent, kissed her lightly, and turned to go.

Rachel caught his arm. "Griffin?"

"What?" he asked, turning back just in time to see an ominous shadow loom in her eyes and then fade away again.

Splotches of crimson gathered on her fine cheekbones, and she looked away. "It's nothing—really. C-Could you come to supper tonight, and bring Molly and Billy, too?"

Something primal and cryptic convulsed within Griffin, and he knew only that the feeling had nothing to do with anything so mundane as supper. What was that odd, writhing darkness he had seen in her eyes? "Rachel—"

But she was gone, suddenly, closing the saloon doors behind her. "Seven o'clock!" she called, through the glass and wood, a kind of stricken cheer ringing in her voice.

Griffin walked slowly back to Tent Town, oblivious to the rain, the wagons grinding through the thickening mud, and the beautiful, silvery-haired woman who watched him from the porch of Judge Sheridan's house.

Athena would have preferred to stay with Jonas, just as she had the night before, but she didn't dare. Heaven knew, if word got back to Griffin that she'd slept beneath that particular roof, any chance of reaching him would be gone.

She sighed, raising one of Clovis's gold-trimmed china teacups to her lips as she watched Griffin walking through the rain. *I love you,* she called after him, in aching silence.

But then, just as Athena was certain that she'd have to bolt from the Sheridan's porch and run after Griffin Fletcher like a hussy, Clovis appeared. As usual, she was far too observant.

"I honestly don't know what you see in that rude, tiresome young man, Athena," she piped, some private outrage snapping in her eyes. "Why, if you'd seen how he ruined poor Mr. Wilke's beautiful wedding, and the frightful thing he did in church—"

Athena's interest rose. She'd heard Jonas's grudging account of the aborted wedding ceremony, but the church episode was something new. "What happened—in church, I mean?"

Clovis shuddered at the memory. "Naturally, we were all upset that Field Hollister took an Indian for a bride—he'd gotten my Ruby's hopes up, you know—and I, for one, wanted to let him know what I thought."

"Would you believe it, Griffin Fletcher came marching up that aisle—as if he ever set foot in a church willingly—with a bundle of rocks! Mind you, he thrust one of those boulders at me and said, 'Clovis, cast the first stone.'"

Athena affected a cough, so that she could cover her mouth with one hand.

Clovis, having raised four daughters, was not fooled by the tactic. "Laugh if you will, but if there's anybody in this town more downright sinful than Griffin Fletcher, I'd like to know about it!"

"Sinful?" Athena managed, swallowing hard. "*Griffin?*"

Clovis nodded smartly. "He's been courting one of those Tent Town women, Athena. And she's Becky McKinnon's daughter in the bargain!"

He's been doing more than courting, Athena thought, and suddenly, it wasn't difficult at all to keep from smiling. In fact, she completely lost patience. "Oh, Clovis, don't be so dreary. You're just peeved because he didn't marry one of your daughters!"

Clovis flushed bright red and sputtered, "Athena, that was an impertinent thing to say! Is that the way ladies talk in France?"

Athena reminded herself that there were no hotels in Providence and softened her tone, in an attempt to mollify her hostess. "No," she said. "It's not the way ladies talk anywhere. I'm sorry."

Pleased, Clovis patted her hand. "Never you mind, dear. Never you mind. And if you want Griffin Fletcher's attentions, there is only one thing to do. We'll have a party!"

The prospect was not heartening. "Griffin hates parties," Athena mourned. *He probably couldn't be dragged away from those shabby tents, anyway,* she added in her mind.

Clovis shrugged, and once again, there was a flash of petulance in her eyes. "He hasn't attended a single one of mine," she admitted. But then her face brightened suddenly, and she chirped. "You must get sick!"

A smile curved Athena's full lips. Lord knew, pestilence was the one thing Griffin couldn't resist. "I do feel a little ill," she said.

Within thirty minutes, Athena was ensconced in Clovis's guest room bed, looking very ill indeed.

Grumbling, Griffin pulled his watch from his vest pocket and glared at it. It was nearly six-thirty, and he hadn't even had a chance to mention Rachel's supper invitation to Molly.

He squared his shoulders. Well, he would see what was wrong at the Sheridan place and then go home and change clothes. With luck, he could still be at Rachel's before seven.

The rain that had braced him before was little more than an annoyance now. Griffin strode through it, irritated, wondering which one of Clovis's daughters had eaten herself into a stupor this time.

By the time he pounded at the front door of Judge Sheridan's house, his mood was downright foul. "What is it?" he snapped, when Clovis admitted him.

Her chin quivered a little, and Griffin noted, with amusement, that she hadn't forgiven him for his last visit to this house, during Jonas's "wedding," or for the scene he'd created with the stones after Field had announced his marriage.

"Our houseguest," she said stiffly, "is suffering some affliction."

Griffin rubbed his eyes with the index finger and thumb of his left hand and sighed. "Lead the way, Clovis. I don't have all night."

The judge's wife gave him a sullen look and gestured toward the stairway. "In the guest room, *Dr.* Fletcher—where my Ruby was when His Honor had to summon you that night."

Griffin remembered, and he suppressed a grin as he moved toward the stairs. There had been a memorable fuss that snowy winter night; Clovis and the Judge had rousted him out of bed at an hour unconscionable even for a country doctor, convinced that their thirty-two-year-old "child" was dying a hideous death. In actuality, Griffin discovered, Ruby had consumed two dried apple pies all by herself and needed nothing more than a lecture and a cathartic.

He was still smiling when he rapped at the door of the upstairs bedroom.

"Come in, Doctor," said a tremulous voice—a disturbingly familiar voice.

Griffin obeyed, stopped cold when he saw Athena peering at him over the edge of a blue satin comforter. There was a decidedly healthy glint in the wide indigo eyes, and the room lacked the subtle smell that marked genuine illness.

"You," he said flatly.

Athena batted her thick eyelashes. "Well, I *am* sick, Griffin," she insisted, a sort of peevish mischief sounding in her voice.

Griffin's muscles thawed, and he stepped inside the room, placed his medical bag on a bureau, and folded his arms. "Undeniably," he agreed, making no move to approach the bed.

Her lower lip trembled, belying the bright deviltry in her eyes. "You don't believe me!" she accused.

Griffin thought of the three children in Tent Town, who might need him at any moment, and of Rachel, expecting him to share one rational, ordinary evening with her. His anger was cold and hard within him. "Of course I don't believe you. What is it that you really want, Athena?"

She sat up in bed, and the comforter made a whispering sound as it moved away from her chin to reveal her creamy white shoulders and the cleft between her breasts. "All right, I should have known I couldn't fool you. But you're so cussed, Griffin Fletcher, that I honestly didn't see how I could manage even a moment alone with you unless I was perishing from some plague!"

Mechanically, Griffin took out his watch, consulted it. Fifteen minutes—Rachel was expecting him in fifteen minutes. "I fail to see what you would want with me, Athena. If memory serves me correctly, I was always the last thing on your mind."

Athena closed her eyes, and for once, her expression looked genuine. The color drained from her face, and her lips were drawn tight across her perfect, white teeth. "Oh, Griffin, I was a fool, and I know it. Can't you please forgive me?"

Griffin sighed. "It's not a matter of forgiveness anymore, Athena—maybe it never was. I simply don't feel anything toward you."

The dark blue eyes flew open now, flashing, fierce, in the half-light of the room. Rain sheeted the windows and assaulted the roof. "Because of Rachel McKinnon!"

He took his bag into one hand again, prepared to leave. "Athena, you made your choice. You wanted Jonas. And that happened a long time before I even knew Rachel existed."

The low, even tone of Griffin's words did nothing to assuage Athena. "I *didn't* want Jonas!" she cried, in outraged frustration. "I wanted you—I wanted a husband—not some humanitarian fool who would turn his back on a timber empire to play nursemaid to a lot of ne'er-do-wells!"

The indifference Griffin felt surprised even him. He'd been mad enough to kill the night he'd come back from San Francisco, heard the gossip before he'd even walked the length of the wharf, and stormed out to Jonas's house to find Athena cavorting merrily in the wrong bed. Now, the memory stirred nothing within him—not even detached contempt.

He laughed hoarsely, at Athena, at Jonas, at himself. "You were punishing me for refusing my father's generous bequest, weren't you? You went to bed with Jonas because I wouldn't give up medicine to fall timber and squire you all over Europe on the proceeds."

Athena threw back her covers, half-hysterical in her fury. "Fool!" she shrieked. "You could have been rich!"

Griffin scanned her trembling, shapely body once, and was unmoved by its nakedness. If anything, he felt clinical boredom.

He laughed again. "Good-bye, Athena," he said. And then he turned and walked out.

Something shattered against the framework of the doorway, fell to the floor in a tinkling shower. Griffin was still laughing when he bounded out into the rain.

Chapter Thirty-four

Mary Louisa Clifford, one of the Tent Town wives, was waiting patiently, her dress and hair soaked with rain, when Griffin reached the Sheridan's front gate. "Doctor—" she began awkwardly, her hands twisting the sodden fabric of her skirts, "Doctor, it's my little girl. She's got fever so bad that she doesn't know me."

Griffin forgot Athena then, and he forgot Rachel, in the bargain. He took Mary Louisa's arm and propelled her back along the board sidewalk, toward Tent Town, shouting questions about the child's symptoms over the pounding song of the rain.

Fawn Hollister was sitting beside the little girl's cot when Griffin and Mary Louisa hurried into the tent, and the look in her brave brown eyes stopped both of them cold.

"It's too late," she said.

Mary Louisa shrieked in her grief, and the sound mobilized Griffin, thrust him toward the still, tiny form on the cot. "Do something," he hissed, even though Fawn was already moving toward the stricken woman, already drawing her into an embrace.

Griffin knelt beside the cot, laid his ear to the child's chest. No heartbeat.

He swore, tilted the little girl's head back, and bent to breathe air into her nose and mouth. Behind him, the unearthly wailing went on. And on.

Griffin pressed the tiny chest with the heel of his palm, willing the heart to beat again. For some minutes, he continued the treatment, alternating between breathing into the child's lungs and prodding her heart.

His reward was a ragged, almost inaudible gasp, a fluttering in the small, waxen face.

"What is her name?" he demanded, of the now-silent woman behind him.

"Alice," said Mary Louisa, in a raw whisper.

Griffin laid his head on Alice's chest again, heard a tremulous, thready beat. He raised his head, cautiously hopeful. "Alice!" he ordered crisply. "Listen to me! Your mama is standing here, and she wants you to come back—Alice, come back."

The child gave a small, shuddering sigh, and some of the color came back into her face. "Back—" she murmured.

"That's right," urged Griffin, more gently now. "Please—come back."

Alice's eyelids fluttered; the battle was visible in her small, pale face.

Griffin laid a hand on her forehead. "That's right," he said.

For the time being, Mary Louisa Clifford's little girl was home again. Griffin stood up, raised his eyes to the sodden, dripping roof of the tent.

Alice was by no means out of danger, and in some ways, turning to face her mother's joyous relief would be difficult. There was never any assurance of recovery, even under ideal conditions—and the conditions in that place certainly weren't ideal.

Mary Louisa was beside him, tugging at his shirtsleeve, staring in wonder at the sleeping child. "Doctor?" she pleaded.

Griffin forced himself to look at the woman. "She's still critically ill," he said. "And this tent—"

"Griffin?" Fawn interrupted, her voice small and constricted. "Griffin, she would be warm at our house."

He turned so quickly that the motion startled both women. "No," he said sharply, struggling to bring the churning emotions inside him under some kind of tenuous control. "No, Fawn—influenza is contagious. If possible, I want it confined to Tent Town."

Something moved in Fawn's throat, and her brown eyes darkened with pain. "My cottage, then. The one I lived in when—"

Wanting to spare her, Griffin looked away from her face swiftly, taking an intense interest in the smoking kerosene lamp standing on a shipping crate in the center of the tent. "Yes," he said, gruffly. "That's a good idea. If you'll go up there and get a fire going, I'll bring Alice in the buggy."

Fawn hastened to comply, while Mary Louisa searched in vain for a dry blanket in which to wrap her daughter. In the end, Griffin found his suit coat stuffed underneath his buggy seat and bundled Alice in that.

At the door of the Clifford tent, he came face to face with a pale, agitated Field. "The Robertsons are all sick, Griffin," he whispered, looking down at the tiny form in his friend's arms. "And Lucas is worse."

Griffin swore softly, thrust the child from his arms to Field's. "Take her to Jonas's cottage, Field," he said, meeting the blue gaze squarely. "Fawn is there, getting things ready."

A muscle tightened in Field's jaw, but he showed no other visible reaction to the mention of a place he had every reason to hate. "Is there anything you want me to do after that?"

Griffin was already moving around him, toward the Robertsons' tent. "Yes," he barked. "I've got some quinine at home—Molly will know where. Bring me all of it."

The situation in the next tent was grim. Mrs. Robertson was

already dead, and her four children weren't far behind. The smallest, an infant boy, had succumbed by the time Field returned with the requested quinine.

Griffin gave the other three children doses of a medicine he knew was often ineffective, swearing under his breath all the while. There was nothing to offer them, besides quinine and the relative warmth of Jonas's vacant brick cottage.

Tirelessly, Field drove back and forth between the center of Tent Town and the little house where his wife had once served Jonas Wilkes' voracious appetites, never complaining, carrying the stricken children Griffin pointed out as tenderly as if they were his own.

If Griffin had had time, he would have admired his friend for his selfless devotion to a cause that was largely hopeless.

Rachel stood at the saloon's front window, staring out at the darkness, disappointment thick in her throat and hot behind her eyes. She could not look at Mamie when the woman's gentle hand came to rest on her arm.

"You know how it is with doctors," the cook said softly. "He's probably real busy someplace."

Rachel swallowed, but the hurt was stuck fast; it wouldn't go down, and it wouldn't permit words to pass.

"You come and eat some supper now, 'fore you get peaked," urged Mamie, her voice low and motherly and unbearably gentle. "I've been keepin' everything warm."

Rachel shook her head, miserably, unwilling to leave her post at the window. "I'm not hungry," she managed, after a struggle.

"Nonsense, Child. Now, you come away from that window this instant and have some supper."

Just as Rachel was about to decline the suggestion again, she saw a dark form moving through the rain, toward the saloon. She wrenched open the doors to find Field Hollister standing on the porch, dripping wet.

"Rachel—Griffin said—"

Rachel reached out, pulled Field into the warmth of the silent saloon. "Look at you!" she cried, pulling off his drenched coat without ceremony. "You'll die of pneumonia, Field Hollister!"

"I'll get some coffee," said Mamie, hurrying away toward the kitchen.

Field ran one sleeve across his face, trying in vain to wipe away the rain. He'd been running, apparently, for his breath came in ragged gasps and his cheeks were florid. When Mamie handed him a cup of coffee, he choked on the first gulp.

Rachel was terribly frightened. "Field, please—what is it?"

Suddenly, there was a wan smile in his blue eyes. "Griffin can't come to supper," he said.

"Don't take no genius to see that," commented Mamie, in good-natured irritation. "Must be midnight by now."

Field had caught his breath, and there was no trace of a smile in his features now—just weariness and despair and some emotion Rachel didn't recognize. "There's influenza in Tent Town," he explained, at last, between cautious sips of coffee. "Griffin couldn't get away."

Rachel forgot her disappointment over the supper she and Mamie had labored over and stared up at Field. "How bad is it?"

Field's eyes were haunted. "It's very bad, Rachel. A woman and her baby are dead, and Griffin thinks there will be more gone before morning."

"I'm going over there!" Rachel cried, turning to look desperately around the room for a cloak.

But Field had set aside his coffee, and he clasped both her shoulders in firm hands. "No," he said flatly. "Griffin said you're to stay away."

Rachel twisted free. "Griffin said, Griffin said!" she mocked hotly. "Griffin Fletcher is not God, and I don't *care* what he said!"

"Well you'd better!" Field yelled back. "If you go over there, you risk coming down with influenza yourself! And if there is one thing Griffin doesn't need, it's another patient!"

Subdued, remembering the child that was, in all likelihood, growing under her heart, Rachel felt a sob rise in her throat and break free. "There must be something I can do to help."

Field nodded, making a visible effort to calm himself. "There are a couple of things. You can give us every blanket you can spare, and you can pray."

It felt good to be busy, wrenching blankets from beds and shelves, folding them, helping Mamie pare vegetables for a gigantic pot of nourishing soup. But, all the while, Rachel wished that she could be beside Griffin, helping him.

"He can't do it alone," she whispered brokenly, when Field had returned, with a wagon, and taken the blankets.

Mamie was stirring the soup, which Field had agreed to come

back for later. "Dr. Fletcher? That man is made out of granite, Child. I've seen him work for days without stopping."

Rachel was not comforted. Griffin wasn't made of stone, though he certainly gave that impression often enough, but of flesh and sinew and passion and stubbornness. She prayed that he would not collapse under the burden of his own dedication.

Mamie was determined to be cheerful. "Nothing can last forever, Rachel. This, too, shall pass."

It seemed, however, that the epidemic was going to last forever. For two solids weeks, it built toward its crisis.

In that time, Rachel retained her sanity by devouring the books Molly Brady brought to her, and sewing the clothing she needed so desperately.

One night, toward dawn, pain awakened her. It was savage, twisting in her abdomen like the blade of a knife, and she cried out in the throes of it.

There was a warm stickiness between her legs. She heard voices, and then there was another violent spasm of terrible, consuming pain, followed by a long interval of swirling nothingness.

My baby, mourned something desolate and hopeless within Rachel's heart, as still another wave of crushing pain washed over her.

Strong hands were pressing her backward, into the pillows. Mamie? She didn't know. "My baby!" she screamed, aloud.

The voice that answered her was stricken and weary and gruff. And it was Griffin's "It's all right, Sweetheart—everything is all right."

"Oh, Griffin, I—there was a baby—"

She felt his hand, gentle on her face, and heard the quiet grief in his voice. "I know. We'll talk about that another time."

There was a stinging prickle in her upper arm and then, a few minutes later, a floating, blessed relief from the pain. Strange words drifted back and forth above her, cloaked in Griffin's voice and, sometimes, Molly Brady's soft, lilting brogue. Only one of these words would stick in her mind, once the nightmare was over. It had a French sound and Rachel, half-conscious though she was, made a determined effort to remember it.

"Curettage," she said.

"Hush," replied Molly.

Jonas hated the rain. It made him feel confined, made the grim business of waiting all the more difficult to bear. It had been more than two weeks since he'd seen Rachel, and the strain was telling.

Athena's voice was peevish. "Sit *down*, Jonas. The weather is dismal enough, without you standing there at that window and brooding."

He turned, glared at the woman calmly eating biscuits and jam at his table. "Something is wrong. I can feel it."

Athena helped herself to another of Hammond's biscuits, spread a liberal helping of blackberry jam onto its porous, steaming middle. "Sure, something is wrong. There is a quarantine on. And we're losing the game, you and I."

A denial rose in Jonas's throat, concerning the game, even though he sensed the truth in her words. Before he could utter it, however, there was a persistent knocking at the front door, followed by a shrill protest from Mrs. Hammond.

Jonas closed his eyes. *Another one of Griffin's dramatic entrances,* he thought, with dread. But when he looked, Elsa Mayhugh, the best whore ever to turn a trick at Becky's Place, was standing before him, red-faced and defiant. "If you want me keepin' an eye on things," she fumed, "you'd better tell that snooty housekeeper of yours that I don't go in through *nobody's* back door!"

Jonas suppressed a laugh. "It's all right, Elsa. Sit down."

The high color that rose in Athena's beautiful, aloof face at the suggestion delighted him. Ironic, that's what it was, her not wanting to sit at the same table with Elsa Mayhugh, considering how alike the two women really were.

"Thanks," said Elsa coldly, making no move to accept the invitation. "I just came to tell you that there was some kind of trouble at Becky's early this morning. The kid woke up screamin' like a banshee, and Mamie sent me down to Tent Town to find Dr. Fletcher."

Jonas felt his stomach braid itself into an icy knot. "What happened?"

Elsa shrugged. "I listened, but they had that door tight shut, the doc and that woman that cleans his house. I didn't see nothin'."

"Then what did you hear?"

"Mostly just the kid screaming. And there was a lot of them high-falutin' doctor words, too."

"Like what?"

"Kratrog, or somethin' like that."

Jonas looked at Athena, saw his own horrified recognition

mirrored in her eyes. "Curettage?" he prompted, hoping that the trembling within him wasn't outwardly visible.

"That's it," said Elsa, pleased.

Jonas groped for the back of his chair, fell heavily into the seat. "Oh, my God," he whispered.

"I'm supposed to get ten dollars," Elsa reminded him, blithely.

Jonas was too sick to respond in any way; it was all he could do to breathe. He did, however, feel a flicker of relief when Athena paid the whore and got rid of her.

If his emotions were paralytic, Athena's were volcanic. "Curettage!" she cried.

"Please—" Jonas muttered, when he could speak. "Don't define it—I know what it means."

Athena either didn't hear him, or didn't feel inclined toward mercy. "Either Rachel miscarried," she speculated, in a furious hiss, "or Griffin Fletcher aborted his own baby!"

Jonas felt his reason give way, but he was powerless to retrieve it. "I'm going to kill him!" he said. "I swear by all that's holy, he's a dead man!"

Athena's form was a moving blur. "No! No, Jonas—I'll do anything—*anything!* But I won't be a part of murder!"

He swung at her, but she was like a mirage; he couldn't quite make contact. Then she was raising something in both hands, and there was an explosive, shattering pain in his head. He fell so slowly. It seemed like a long time before he felt the cool smoothness of the floor against his jaw.

Griffin was grateful, that grim morning, for the dogged weariness numbing his mind, dulling his emotions. Molly came into the room, handed him a welcome cup of coffee, and whispered, "How is she this morning, then?"

He could not look at the girl lying still and broken in his bed—even the pounding fatigue would not insulate him if he did. "She was pregnant," he marveled, ignoring Molly's question. "My God, she was *pregnant,* and she didn't tell me!"

Molly's hand came cautiously to rest on his forearm. "It was early. She probably didn't know, Griffin."

Griffin shook his head, still keeping his eyes fixed on the dismal, sodden view from his bedroom window. "She knew. She said 'there was a baby.'"

"Aye. Griffin, you're not thinking that the child wasn't yours, are you?"

"It was mine, all right. God, why didn't I leave her alone?"

Bless her, Molly spared him the lecture he rightly deserved. "You'll be changing nothing by torturing yourself, Griffin Fletcher. You've got your hands full enough with an epidemic and you the only real doctor for miles around."

Griffin took another sip of the strong coffee steaming in his cup. "Field wired John O'Riley last night."

"Aye, and it's a good thing, then. You'll be getting some sleep at last."

"No. Even with John's help, there won't be time. And Rachel—"

"I'll take care of Rachel," Molly said. "It's rest she's needing now, and the comfort of another woman staying near. I—"

Griffin broke in rudely, with a muttered swear word, as he caught sight of the carriage rolling to a stop on the road below. The passenger, who scrambled out and marched furiously up the front walk, was Athena.

He closed his eyes, let his forehead rest against the cool, damp windowpane. But there was no respite—Athena knocked, got past Billy without apparent difficulty, and came up the stairs in an audible, tangible rage.

Turning slowly, Griffin was prepared when she loomed in the doorway. "Get out," he said.

But her eyes were on Rachel, who slept fitfully in the big bed. "Griffin. you *monster*," she breathed. "You're not going to get away with this—I'll ruin you."

Griffin shrugged. "Ruin me."

Athena paled, and her dark blue eyes widened with disbelief. "You didn't—Griffin, tell me you didn't abort—"

"*Abort?*" the word exploded from Griffin's tongue. "Do you really think I would *abort* my own child?"

Athena raised her chin, and Griffin saw a kind of vicious relief in her face. "No," she said evenly. "I don't. But I think Judge Sheridan can be convinced that you did. And that means you'll be in jail by sundown, Griffin."

The indifference Griffin had so prized deserted him; his hands tensed, straining to close around Athena's haughty neck and crush everything within it. "You wouldn't dare," he breathed, seething.

Incredibly, Athena laughed. "Why wouldn't I? You destroyed me—now I'll destroy you. Gladly."

Trembling, Molly stepped into the short, dangerous space

294

between them. "Stop it," she hissed. "Both of you. I can testify that there was no abortion—I was there."

"No one would believe you, Molly," Athena said sweetly. "Everyone in Providence thinks you're really Griffin's little Irish bedwarmer. And that would prejudice you, wouldn't it?"

The words Griffin spoke would never be retracted, never be denied. "Do it, Athena. Have me arrested. But remember this: if it takes the rest of my life, I'll find you. And when I do, I'll kill you."

"You don't mean that," she replied blithely. Then she pulled the pearls and bracelet he'd given Rachel from her handbag and flung them at him. "Here. She'll have these to remember you by!"

A moment later, Athena was gone, in a flurry of scorn and white eyelet.

Chapter Thirty-five

Jonas opened his eyes—realized that he was lying in his own bed. The room was darkened, and at first, he couldn't be certain whether or not the night had come—it would be like Hammond to draw the drapes.

A dull ache pounded beneath the rounding of his skull, reminding him. Athena. Griffin. Rage scalded its way from his stomach to his throat, erupted in a burst of energy.

Jonas flung back the covers and sat up—only to find the motion costly. He groaned, and nausea swept through him. The pain in the top of his head was infinitely worse—what had that slut hit him with, anyway?

With slow, deliberate movements, he found trousers, a shirt, boots. The room spun around him as he struggled into them.

Rising from the edge of the bed brought on another rush of crushing pain, another wave of nausea, but Jonas's fury sustained him. He staggered to the window, thrust back the drapes, and saw that he had lost most, if not all, of the day. The rain had slackened to a misty drizzle, and twilight was settling in.

Jonas thought again of Athena, of Griffin. And he felt such hatred that he had to grasp the windowframe in both hands just to keep his footing. Rachel came into his mind, and a soft, grievous cry boiled into his throat and echoed in the stillness of the room.

Rachel. They were lying about her, they had to be lying. There had been no baby, no miscarriage, no curettage. Jonas closed his eyes, saw her rising out of the churchyard pond that day of the picnic, her silk blouse wet and translucent, leaves clinging in her hair. He'd seen her so clearly that she might as well have bared herself to him; he'd seen the fullness of her breasts, their rosy centers, even a small, diamond-shaped mark beside her nipple. And then there had been the night in Seattle, the night she'd fallen sick, and he'd undressed her tenderly, stricken by the beauty of her—

He drew a deep breath, opened his eyes. He would not, could not lose her, no matter what he had to do.

There was liquor on his bureau, and Jonas made his way to it, poured a double shot, and downed it in one scalding gulp. It braced him a little; he followed it up with another equal portion.

The bedroom door creaked on its hinges, and Hammond's shadowy bulk appeared in the opening. "Jonas, that woman is downstairs. I tried to keep her out—"

"What woman?" Jonas snapped, pouring more brandy into his glass.

"Mrs. Bordeau," replied the housekeeper. "She's bursting with some crazy idea about you and her having Griffin Fletcher arrested."

Arrested. Jonas considered that, tilted his head back, and expelled his breath in an impatient rush. "Did she happen to say for what?"

"Aborting that McKinnon girl's baby," answered Mrs. Hammond, sadly.

Jonas tensed. If that happened, the lie would be perpetuated —everyone would believe that Rachel had been pregnant. "No," he rasped. "Damn it, no! Send that—Send her up here."

"I don't think she'd come, Jonas. She's nervous as a cat as it is. Little wonder—she's the one who should be arrested, if you ask me. Why, when I found you on the floor—"

Jonas broke in crisply. "Just tell her I'll be right down."

Athena was nervous, all right. She was pacing the parlor floor like some exotic animal fresh from the wilds, and her skin was pale. She was careful, Jonas noticed, to keep a wide distance between them.

"I'm not going to let you have Griffin arrested," he said flatly.

Athena's ink-blue eyes flashed, and she came to a dead stop. "Why not? He'd be out of your way, once and for all—"

"I said no. Let it pass."

She was gaping now, her face bright with outraged color. "Jonas, that girl is lying in his house right now—in his *bed*—recovering from an illegal abortion!"

Jonas closed his eyes. He could feel the liquor mingling with the rage in his bloodstream, dulling the ceaseless ache in his skull. "No," he said, in a gruff whisper. "No."

"I can't believe you're going to let Griffin get away with this!"

Jonas's tongue was suddenly independent of his brain; he was babbling something about Griffin, something about Rachel's father, Ezra McKinnon. It was an odd feeling, not being able to comprehend his own words—something like trying to listen at a thick door.

But Athena's eyes were wide, and she was backing away from him, holding out her hands, shaking her head, muttering his name over and over again.

Steadily, slowly, Jonas walked toward her.

John O'Riley arrived aboard the *Statehood* in the early afternoon, bringing what quinine he'd been able to garner in a still-chaotic Seattle. Together, he and Griffin battled the ever-rising epidemic, seldom speaking, never looking each other squarely in the face. Griffin supposed that John didn't want to see the futility of the situation mirrored in the eyes of another doctor, anymore that he did.

There was a lull early that evening, and they ventured into the deserted mess tent, where only Chang was in evidence, to help themselves to mugs of stale, bitter coffee.

Even as they sat across from each other, in the semi-darkness of that sodden tent, John was careful not to look directly at Griffin.

"What is it?" Griffin demanded, after a long, unbearable silence.

Now, John O'Riley's weary blue eyes climbed to his face. "Griffin, Douglas Frazier died this morning."

Griffin lowered his head, pretending a compelling interest in his coffee cup. "My God."

John's voice rumbled with fond irritation. "Griffin, the man was a monster. He sold women and God knows what else—"

Griffin swallowed. "He was still a man, John. And he's still dead."

After that, there seemed to be nothing else to say. Numb, Griffin finished the terrible coffee only because it enabled him to keep moving, keep working.

He'd been expecting Providence's storekeeper-constable all day, on some subliminal level of his mind, and it came as no real surprise to him when Henry waylaid him just outside the entrance to the mess tent.

Judge Sheridan was there, too, and they were both armed. The nickle-silver barrels of their pistols caught the flickering light of the pine-pitch torches that burned on both sides of the tent's doorway.

Griffin stopped, grimly amused that they would come after an alleged abortionist with that much weaponry. *I'm danger-ous*, he thought.

Henry's mustache was quivering again, just as it had in church that Sunday, when Griffin had offered him a rock to fling at Field Hollister. "You better come quiet, Doc," he said, in a tremulous voice.

Griffin allowed his gaze to swing eloquently to the gun in Henry's hand. "I see that."

John O'Riley, who had apparently been struck speechless by the sight of Providence law in action, finally found his voice. He directed his words beyond Henry, however, to the judge. "Now, Edward, what is this about?"

Henry and the judge exchanged stricken looks, then the latter mumbled, "We sure didn't plan on your hearing about it this way, John. There's nothing for it now, though—justice must be done."

Griffin found the word "justice" inordinately funny and laughed. "It isn't justice, Judge, and you know it," he said. "Athena made that story up to avenge her wounded pride."

Sheridan's face was cold, but his eyes blazed with outrage. "Athena Bordeau is dead," he bit out. "And no one knows that better than you do, Fletcher."

John gasped, raised one hand to his chest. "No—"

Stunned to immobility himself, Griffin could make no move toward his friend. "What in the hell are you talking about?" he snapped, his eyes fixed on Sheridan's face.

"Happened a couple of hours ago, according to the undertaker," put in Henry, emboldened. "You killed her, Griffin, and you're not going to get by with murder in my town!"

Griffin could move then; he turned distractedly from Sheridan and the constable to look at John. The expression in his friend's eyes went through him like a piece of freshly forged metal.

"You said you'd kill her," the old man whispered brokenly. "That day in my study, you said you'd kill her with your bare hands—"

"Strangled her," confirmed Henry, carried away by the sudden magnitude of his office. "Her throat's plum crushed in."

"Shut up!" snapped Judge Sheridan, seeing the dangerous, stricken grief in John O'Riley's face. "We're talking about Dr. O'Riley's daughter!"

John had turned away, though; he was stumbling back inside the tent. Griffin moved to follow him, was detained by Judge Sheridan's grasp on his arm.

He wrenched free, concerned only with the blue tinge of John's lips, the gray pallor of his skin. "Damn it, let me see if he's all right!"

Henry brought the barrel of his pistol up, so that it rested flush with Griffin's midsection, pressing hard. It felt cold, even through the fabric of his shirt. "You saw to enough, Doctor. After what you did to that poor woman, I'd just as soon shoot you as say your name, so you stay right where you are!"

Griffin swore. "I didn't kill her, you wild-eyed incompetent—I've been here all day!"

"You did it, all right," insisted Henry, implacably. "We found something of yours near the body. Besides, everybody knows how she wanted you back and how you just couldn't see beyond that whelp of Becky McKinnon's—"

Griffin, swallowing the fury pounding in his throat, closed his eyes. "I didn't kill her," he repeated.

Judge Sheridan brought a small object from his pocket, extended it to Griffin. "This, among other things, leads us to believe that you did."

The pocket watch was cool against Griffin's palm, and it confirmed what some part of him had suspected all along. "This belongs to Jonas," he said, handing it back.

Henry scowled. "You expect us to believe—"

Griffin brought his own watch out of his vest pocket and dangled it, by its chain, from two fingers. It gleamed, golden, even in the torchlight. "My watch, Gentlemen," he said, and his smile felt gruesome on his face. "Look closely—it's exactly like Jonas's. And there is a reason for that."

Henry's mustache began to twitch again, up, down, sideways. "What reason?"

"'What reason?'" mocked Griffin, sardonically. "Why don't you tell him, Judge? You should remember."

Judge Sheridan looked uncertain for the first time, as far as Griffin knew, since before his election. "Jonas's mother was a twin sister to Dr. Fletcher's. Those two fine, gentle ladies always hoped that their sons would get along with each other, so they bought them duplicate watches and threw a big party to celebrate their birthdays one year."

"So?" challenged Henry, impatient with such pedantic reverie.

"So it's possible that Dr. Fletcher is telling the truth. He has his watch; it's an unusual one—the only other like it belongs to Jonas."

Henry was gravely disappointed. "It ain't so unusual!" he protested, petulantly.

Griffin opened the watchcase, pressed a small button inside it. The strains of a haunting, tremulous tune sounded. "My aunt—Jonas's mother—composed that melody," he said.

Henry sighed. "Well, there's still what Dr. O'Riley just said; he must have heard you threaten Mrs. Bordeau's life."

The judge nodded in agreement. "Mr. Wilkes was her friend—wouldn't have had any reason to want her dead."

"Did you say that? Did you say you'd kill her with your bare hands?" demanded Henry, the barrel of his pistol still nudging Griffin's solar plexus.

"Yes," Griffin replied, in an undertone.

"Then you're under arrest," said the judge, flatly.

"Just let me look in on John—please?"

Sheridan nodded sharply. "But don't try anything, Griffin. Henry would be within his rights to shoot you."

Griffin wheeled away from his captors, strode into the mess tent. John was sitting stock-still on one of the long benches, staring down at the tabletop.

Rounding the table, Griffin faced him, noted with relief that his color was better, his breathing even. "I didn't murder your daughter, John," he said.

There were tears on John O'Riley's face. "My God, I wish I could believe you, Griffin. I wish I could believe you!"

Henry and the judge would wait no longer.

"Put out your hands, Griffin," urged the latter, his voice softer now.

"Ain't we better bind his feet, too?" muttered Henry.

Judge Sheridan searched Griffin's face. "No need," he said sadly. His eyes moved to John. "I'm sorry about your daughter. Shall I send a message to your wife?"

John shook his head slowly, and his eyes looked sightless, glazed. "I'll let Joanna know myself," he said.

Rachel sat up in the big bed, tried to scan Molly Brady's pale, averted face. "What is it?" she demanded, in a broken whisper.

"It's Athena Bordeau," Molly answered, facing her patient squarely as she laid a tray of hot food in her lap. "Eat now."

But Rachel felt no interest in the nourishing supper she'd so longed for only moments ago. "What about Athena?" she pressed, shaken by the fierce, distracted green of Molly's eyes.

"She's dead," Molly whispered. "And they've arrested Dr. Fletcher for murdering her."

The tray and its contents clattered to the floor as Rachel thrust away her covers and scrambled out of bed. *"No!"*

Sniffling, Molly Brady knelt to gather bits of broken crockery, a buttered biscuit, a pork chop. "Now look and see what you've done, Rachel McKinnon. All your nice supper, and the best china—"

Rachel's voice was high and thin with stunned impatience. "How can you go on about china when Griffin is in so much trouble!"

Molly looked up, and there were tears pouring down her face. "Oh, Rachel," she sobbed, "He said he'd kill her! With my own ears, in this very room, I heard him make that vow!"

Rachel's knees were weak and wobbling beneath her but she had no intention of crawling back into bed and meekly accepting something that couldn't possibly be true. "Where are my clothes—I'm going to him—"

Molly dropped the litter she'd been gathering and shot to her feet. "You'll be going nowhere, Miss Rachel McKinnon! My Billy's gone for Field Hollister—it's him the doctor needs now, not you!"

Rachel wove her way around Molly, stopping to rest once against the wall. "I'll find a stupid dress myself!" she screamed.

But Molly Brady had not been ill, and she was not in a weakened condition, like Rachel. Taking care to avoid the china shattered on the floor, she grabbed her charge and propelled her back to the bed.

"And what help will you be to that man if you're dead of the bleeding?" demanded Griffin's housekeeper savagely, her hands on her narrow little hips, her eyes bright with tears and determination.

Now, it was Rachel who wept. "He wouldn't—oh, Molly, he *wouldn't*—"

Molly's eyes were distant now, emerald in their fierceness. "She's destroyed him, sure as I'll draw my next breath."

Before Rachel could manage a reply, there were sounds from the entry hall below, followed by quick, light footsteps on the stairs. Fawn Hollister came into the room, brown eyes desolate, and gravitated toward the bed. Reaching it, she sat down on its edge and, without ceremony, wrapped her arms around the shuddering Rachel.

"Field is with him," she said softly. "Field is there."

Rachel swallowed a fresh spate of tears. "I think Molly believes Griffin's guilty."

Fawn's brown eyes rose to meet Molly's, but there was no accusation in her gaze, and no anger. "Molly is wrong, then," she said.

Molly turned, went to stand at the black, uncurtained expanse of Griffin's window. "I pray that I am," she said, in a small, hopeless voice. "I pray that I am."

A moment later, she gathered up the tray and its scattered contents and left the room.

"Jonas," Rachel said, her forehead resting on Fawn Hollister's small, strong shoulder. "Jonas killed her."

"Probably," agreed Fawn, and there was no more hope in her voice than Rachel had heard in Molly's. "Nothing on earth could make him admit it, though. Nothing."

"But Griffin could hang!"

"We'll think of something," Fawn promised, pressing Rachel gently back onto her pillows. "But you must be strong, if you're going to help. Sleep now, and we'll make plans in the morning."

Rachel could not sleep, but for the sake of her friend, she pretended to. And as she lay still in that darkened room, alone, a plan began to form in her mind. It was wild and it was desperate, but it had one distinct virtue—it was the only way Rachel could think of to save Griffin.

Griffin Fletcher stood gripping the bars of his cell, tracing a pattern in the sawdust floor with the toe of his right boot. The door leading from the jail's solitary cell to Henry's dry goods store swung open, and Field was there, beyond the bars, looking grim and frightened and sick.

"You were in Tent Town when it happened!" he barked, without preamble. "Weren't you?"

"Of course I was," Griffin snapped back. Then, gruffly, he added, "I didn't do it, Field."

For the first time that Griffin knew of, Field swore roundly. "I know that—it's just that Henry and the judge and a lot of other people around here would just as soon see you hang as anybody! Damn it, Griffin, why do you have to go around making enemies all the time, anyway?"

"Habit," said Griffin, with a shrug and a rueful grin.

Before Field could retort, the door opened again. This time, the visitor was Jonas.

There was a look in his cousin's eyes, a quality in the set of his face, that made Griffin feel fear—not for himself, but for Rachel. Deliberately, he kept his voice light, even. "Don't tell me, Jonas—let me guess. You came to bail me out."

Jonas laughed, and the sound was disjointed somehow. Griffin's fear deepened, and so did his determination to hide it.

"I wouldn't think of impeding justice," Jonas said. But then his eyes fell to the design Griffin was tracing in the sawdust on the floor, and a horrible spasm moved in his cherubic face. "The scar," he whispered, brokenly. "The scar."

And then he turned and bolted out of the quarters reserved for Providence's rare transgressors, leaving the door to gape open behind him.

"What the—" began Field, staring after Jonas.

But Griffin knew. He looked down at the tracing he'd made on the floor and groaned. It was a diamond shape.

Unwittingly, he had confirmed something that Jonas couldn't bear to know.

Chapter Thirty-six

Fawn's brown eyes widened as she watched Rachel scrambling into a simple calico dress. "You must be out of your mind, Rachel McKinnon!" she announced bluntly. "Jonas would never fall for a trick like that!"

Rachel fought down a rush of lingering weakness and forced herself to be strong. "Can you think of anything better?" she challenged, wrenching the now-scruffy kid leather shoes she'd bought in Seattle onto her feet.

The beautiful Indian woman lowered her head. "No," she admitted. But when her eyes came back to Rachel's face, they were filled with foreboding. "I don't think you really understand Jonas Wilkes, Rachel. But I do, and I can tell you that the man is vicious even under the most ideal conditions. It's obvious, considering what he did to Athena, that he has already passed the point where reason gives way to madness!"

Rachel turned away, to stand before Griffin's mirror and brush her hair in fierce, determined strokes. "I don't care how dangerous he is, Fawn. I won't stand by and see Griffin hanged for something Jonas did!"

"He's *mad*, Rachel."

Grimly, Rachel nodded. "I'm depending on that," she said.

Fawn sighed furiously, but her reluctance was insignificant. It was clear that she planned to help.

Judge Edward Sheridan reviewed the case of Athena Bordeau's murder over and over in his mind. God knew, after what that woman had done two years before, it was a wonder that she hadn't turned up dead sooner.

Sheridan settled back in his desk chair, lit his pipe, drew thoughtfully on the cherry-scented smoke. He'd seen Griffin Fletcher that night, and been awed by the cold, murderous rage in his eyes, in the taut set of his shoulders. He'd stood at Becky McKinnon's bar, Griffin had, swilling more whiskey than any man had a right to consume and still stand.

304

Griffin hadn't talked about finding his fiancée in Jonas Wilkes' bed, but then he never talked about much of anything unless he was pressed. No, he'd just stood there, trying to exhaust the whiskey supply, and whatever demons had possessed him had been silent ones. It must have been hell, Sheridan thought, knowing a thing like that, knowing that the whole town probably knew it, too.

Clovis came into the Judge's study, her face avid, for all its aversion to the crime committed the night before. She put a shot of brandy into a coffee mug, poured the steaming brew in after it. "Louisa Griffin Fletcher would roll over in her grave if she knew what's happened," she said, with a kind of horrified relish. "When is the trial to be held, Edward?"

The Judge reached out for his coffee, stirred sugar into it with irritated vigor. "I think you would like to see young Fletcher hung by sunset at the latest, wouldn't you, my dear?" he bit out.

"He murdered dear Athena!"

"Dear Athena," mocked the Judge, with gruff scorn. Then, after a reflective silence, he said. "You know, Clovis, that young man is brash and ill-mannered and generally obnoxious, and I don't like him one bit better than you do. But I don't think he killed that woman."

The very prospect of Griffin Fletcher's innocence had an alarming effect on Mrs. Sheridan. She sank into a chair, pale, and her eyes were suddenly too bright. "Of course he did, Edward! Why, after that scandal two years ago—"

"Exactly," breathed the Judge. "It was two years ago. Why did he wait so long? Why didn't he murder Wilkes and the woman then and there? A lot of men would have, you know.

"That bothers me, Clovis—that and a few other things. Like the watch, and the fact that the body was found in the woods between Tent Town and the Fletcher house. Seems too easy. Griffin Fletcher is a smart man, Clovis, and he's in love with that McKinnon girl. If he was going to kill Athena, why would he leave so many clues?"

"Edward, really! You're just defending that wastrel because you were so smitten with Louisa!"

Louisa. The name still ached in a darkened, benumbed corner of the Judge's heart. "Mike and Louisa Fletcher were friends of mine, Clovis, and I'll be damned if I'll railroad their son just because he annoys the hell out of me—or because he nettles you, for that matter."

Clovis's voice was a petulant whine. "He's guilty as sin, Edward Sheridan!"

The Judge relit his pipe. "Maybe. And maybe not. But he isn't going to hang if he didn't kill that woman, Clovis, and you and the rest of Providence had best be about accepting that." He sighed. "Now, leave me alone. I've got to think."

Judge Edward Sheridan was still thinking at seven that evening, when Clovis burst into his study to announce that Mr. Wilkes's housekeeper, Mrs. Hammond, was waiting anxiously in the parlor to see him.

Fawn gasped when she saw the dress. "Where did you get that?"

Rachel turned the finely tailored white gown in her hands, thought she could feel Athena's terror in its very folds. "Mamie got it from the undertaker somehow. I've sent the message to Jonas, too—so everything is ready."

"If Jonas doesn't kill us," Mrs. Hollister breathed, "Griffin and Field will. Lord in heaven, Rachel, you're mad as Mr. Wilkes himself!"

Rachel had spent the day constructing a dummy of bedsheets and feathers purloined from several pillows. Now, calmly, she began to clothe the crude manikin in Athena's gown. "Billy checked," she said, as if Fawn hadn't spoken at all. "There are no men around Jonas's barn—I suppose most of them are down with the influenza. He's going to put this in place for me, and then, when it gets really dark—"

Fawn's gaze shifted to the window, The rain had stopped; but the sky was overcast all the same, and the night would come sooner because of that. She stood up, smoothed her calico skirts. "I'll do what you asked me to," she said. "But there is something else I have to do first."

"Don't you tell!" warned Rachel, in a terse whisper.

As she walked out of the bedroom, Fawn Hollister made no promises, one way or the other.

Jonas stood still at the upstairs window, looking out over the grim aftermath of the rain, the note crumpled in his hand. Did Rachel think he was a fool? he wondered, with savage calmness. Did she really believe that he would walk blithely into whatever trap she was laying?

He let his head rest against the cool dampness of the window, closed his eyes. There were no illusions now; he knew that

306

Rachel had betrayed him with Griffin, knew that he could not allow her to live.

In his mind, he saw Griffin Fletcher drawing that diamond symbol in the sawdust of the jailhouse floor, pretending not to know what he was doing. But he'd been taunting him all the same—proving that he had, after all, been the first to possess Rachel.

A guttural cry rose in Jonas's throat, tore itself free. He'd loved her so much, loved her against reason, loved her against his own will. And she'd lain with Griffin.

As Jonas waited, he was certain that he couldn't bear the knowledge.

Griffin paced the sawdust floor in volcanic desperation. As he moved, he allowed the nonsensical prayers hammering in his heart to take shape in his mind, as words.

All the while, he despaired. It wasn't likely that Field's God would be inclined to listen to him. After all, this was the second or third prayer he'd ever consciously offered—and he hadn't exactly lived the faith.

He remembered the first time he'd directed a word deliberately to heaven—it had been in Seattle, just after the fire had broken out, when he was searching for Rachel. "Please," had been all he could manage then, and his entreaty was hardly more articulate now.

Still, that one-word supplication had been answered then, hadn't it? He'd found Rachel.

Desperately, Griffin Fletcher clung to that. God would hear him—for Rachel's sake.

The opening of the outer door startled him, drew him to a sudden, stomach-twisting halt. Field came in, looking both worried and relieved, and Judge Sheridan was behind him.

Griffin was afraid to hope, afraid to speak.

But Judge Sheridan had keys. With maddening slowness, he was unlocking the cell door. "You're free, Griffin," he said. "Eliza Hammond saw Jonas kill the woman. Henry's gone out to arrest him now."

Griffin was feeling a number of things—relief, urgency, rage. And the look on Field's face made him uneasy on some deep, intuitive level.

"Field, what is it?" he rasped, bolting out of the confining cell, pulling on his suit coat.

"There was a note," Field said. "There was a note on my

307

kitchen table when I went to look in on Fawn. Griffin, she and Rachel are on their way to Jonas's, if they're not there already."

Griffin broke into a dead run, a swearword rattling in his throat. "What in the hell are you doing here, then?" he demanded, in front of the store, as he and Field and Judge Sheridan climbed onto waiting horses.

Field offered no reply.

It was dark in Jonas's barn; Rachel hadn't dared to light even one lantern. Swallowing her fear, she waited, a stack of baled hay scratching at her back.

The dummy was in place, Fawn was surely at her post at the back door of the barn, everything would happen just as it was supposed to. It simply had to.

In the many stalls, horses nickered uneasily, invisible in the thick darkness. But a buggy was hitched and ready to go, and that meant that Jonas had believed her note, believed that she wanted to run away with him.

Rachel closed her eyes, listening to the rapid, hard beat of her own heart.

And then, suddenly, there was lantern light glowing in the front entrance to the barn, casting ghostly shadows on everything within a radius of several yards. "Rachel?"

She swallowed. "I'm here, Jonas."

He approached, holding the lantern aloft, and even in its flickering light, she could see the strange, frightening contortion of his features. "You've had a change of heart," he said, in an odd, chantlike voice.

Rachel lifted her chin. "Yes. G-Griffin is a murderer—I made a mistake."

Jonas drew nearer, and though he walked upright, he seemed to be crouching, like a wild beast poised to pounce. Rachel swallowed a scream as his hand flashed out, clasped the bodice of her calico dress, and tore the fabric away.

Idly, his finger traced the tiny birthmark beside her left nipple, his eyes consumed her naked breasts in their golden fire. Rachel closed her eyes, resisting a reflexive need to cover herself.

"You're a liar, Rachel," Jonas said, in a companionable tone. The topaz eyes moved languidly to her face. "I would have been the most adoring of husbands—that's the irony of it. But you wanted Griffin."

Rachel stood still, mute with terror. *Now, Fawn,* she pleaded silently. *Please—now!*

But Jonas's madness seemed to allow him to view her thoughts as easily as her bared breasts. "Fawn isn't going to help you, Rachel. She's bound and gagged at this moment, in my kitchen. I didn't have time to kill her, but of course, I will."

Slowly, Rachel raised her arms to hide her naked chest. She'd gambled, and she'd lost. Worse, Griffin and Fawn would lose, too.

"What about my father?" she whispered. "And Molly Brady's husband?"

Jonas arched one eyebrow. "They were in my way."

Sickened, Rachel closed her eyes, opened them again.

There was a creak at the back of the barn, and Jonas whirled, the lantern swinging dangerously in his hand. "Who's there?" he yelled.

The horses hitched to the waiting buggy were spooked by the sound; they broke into a frantic run, dragging the buggy toward the half-open doors of the barn.

There was a loud, splintering sound as the buggy was caught between the doors, and the horses screamed in panic. Inside the buggy itself, the dummy bounced around like some kind of nightmare specter, horrifying in its limbless motion.

Rachel's heart clamored into her throat, lodged there in very real terror. For a moment, she actually believed that Athena had returned to take her own vengeance.

Jonas's throat worked convulsively as he stared at the effigy of his guilt, and then he screamed and flung the lantern in his hand. There was a *whoosh,* followed by a roar as the straw on the barn floor went up in flames, and then the buggy.

Beyond the barn doors, the trapped horses shrieked and struggled in renewed terror, and the animals inside the stalls were raising havoc, kicking at the sides of their stalls, neighing over the rising roar of the flames.

Rachel stared, her breath still in her lungs. Jonas stood frozen, gazing sightlessly at the burning buggy.

We'll burn to death, Rachel thought. But she still could not move.

There were voices outside the barn—shouted orders, swear-words. And then the doors were opening, and the blazing buggy was being dragged outside.

Griffin and Field burst in through the doorway, skirting the inferno that nearly blocked their way.

Griffin dragged Rachel to the door and thrust her out, into the cool sanction of the night, before he went racing back inside. She was huddling beside a towering madrona tree when Field led a stumbling, witless Jonas to safety and went back to help Griffin.

The shrieks of the horses rang with terror and pain. Only three had been led from the barn when Field and Griffin were forced to flee themselves.

The wooden roof was a sheet of leaping orange and yellow flames now, and the fire danced in the windows.

Suddenly, Jonas screamed Rachel's name and bounded past Griffin and Field and through the glowing, crimson doorway of the barn. At the same moment, a portly man came from the direction of the main house, half-supporting a dazed, stumbling Fawn.

Jonas staggered out of the inferno, his clothes and hair afire. He was still screaming Rachel's name when Griffin and Field tackled him, rolling him on the ground to extinguish the flames.

Firebrands from the barn exploded into the night sky, landing as far away as the roof of Jonas's palatial house.

Rachel stood still, stricken, until Griffin looked up from Jonas's prone, charred figure and gestured with one hand.

She stumbled across the short distance, knelt on the ground beside Jonas as Field rushed off to meet his wife.

"Oh, Jonas—" Rachel whispered, looking down at him. He was hideously burned, but he seemed to be beyond pain.

"Rachel," he said. "I'm sorry."

And then he was dead.

Griffin pulled off his coat, laid it gently over his cousin's still, disfigured face. "God," he said. "Oh, dear God."

And Rachel was not surprised to see that there were tears glistening on his face. She rose, moved to Griffin's side, let go—for the first time—of the torn bodice of her dress, and drew him into her arms.

"It's over now," she whispered. "It's over."

Griffin's ragged sob was almost inaudible over the crackling roar of the fire. "He thought you were inside—"

"Yes," she said, because there was nothing else to say.

Field appeared, his face, like Griffin's, masked in soot. He gave Rachel his coat, and gently pulled his stricken friend to his feet.

Molly came and led Rachel away, too.

"You were here all the time," Rachel whispered, seeing

Molly's torn, sooty skirts and disheveled hair. "It was you that made the back door of the barn creak like that—"

"Aye," replied Molly. "And it was myself that put the figure of Athena into the buggy seat, too. I heard you and Fawn plotting this, and I followed along to do what I could." At a good distance from the blazing barn, she stopped cold, and her green eyes came, fierce, to Rachel's face. "I wouldn't be in your shoes for anything, Miss Rachel McKinnon, when the Doctor hears the whole of this! An effigy in a white dress!" Molly paused to shake her head in furious wonder.

Rachel lowered her eyes; it was true that the night hadn't gone according to plan. The dummy was supposed to fall, swinging, from the barn rafters, while Fawn called Jonas's name in a ghostly voice. And Jonas was only supposed to confess to the murder, not die.

"He admitted killing my father, Molly. And Patrick."

Molly was livid. "And it's God's own miracle that he didn't kill you—and Field Hollister's brand new bride in the bargain!"

Rachel looked up, sought Griffin with her eyes, needing the sight of him. He was leaning against a tree, not far away, and his shoulders were moving beneath the smudged fabric of his shirt. Field stood, silent and supportive, beside him.

The month to come was a grim one.

There were more funerals, Athena's, and then Jonas's. Intermittently, victims of the raging epidemic of influenza were buried, too.

There was no time to talk, and certainly no time to make lasting plans. Griffin's practice consumed every moment, and Rachel followed him doggedly from one tent to another, ignoring his terse orders that she go home, offering what comfort she could to his patients and to John O'Riley's.

Finally, the sickness ebbed away.

The morning of July twentieth dawned bright and clear, and Rachel knew, without being told, that it would be a momentous day.

There were two sealed jars of cinnamon pears on the kitchen table, along with a small package marked with Rachel's name. She opened the parcel and smiled at the contents; clearly, this gift, like the ruby red pears, was from Joanna.

Griffin was in the back yard, the sleeves of his shirt rolled up to his elbows, industriously digging a hole.

"What are you doing?" demanded Rachel, from the steps.

311

He grinned and then, with a flourish, set a seedling tree into the pit he'd dug. "Planting my wedding present from Joanna O'Riley. Now why would she give me a pear tree?"

Rachel arched one eyebrow. "Now, why would you get a wedding present?" she countered. "Is there something I don't know, Griffin Fletcher?"

Griffin laughed. "Sprite, there are a lot of things you don't know—like how to handle that mountain full of timber you inherited from my cousin."

She lifted her chin. "I'll learn," she said. "And Tent Town is going to be rebuilt, too—with cabins."

Griffin's eyes were bright with love and humor as he began shoveling dirt onto the roots of the infant tree. "My future wife, the timber baroness and crusading reformer."

Rachel came to stand before him, looking up into his face. "Just how far in the future am I, Griffin?"

"How does five minutes sound? That's how long it will take to get to Field's church."

Rachel flung her arms around his neck and held on, laughing up at the sky.

An hour later, as they drove away from the church in Griffin's buggy, he grinned down at her. "Well, Mrs. Fletcher, now we can enjoy something new—making love in a real bed."

Rachel smiled and, once again, opened the little package Joanna O'Riley had sent. She took two handfuls of the tiny bits of paper inside and flung them into the wind, where they billowed and swirled like snow.

Rachel Fletcher clasped her hands and looked back at the paper-strewn road. *That* would keep the devil busy, and Griffin was turning lots of corners.

LINDA LAEL MILLER

POCKET STAR BOOKS
PROUDLY PRESENTS

MY OUTLAW
LINDA LAEL MILLER

Coming
mid-April from
Pocket Star Books

The following is a preview of
My Outlaw . . .

PROLOGUE

Redemption, Nevada, 1974

Keighly Barrow was precisely seven years old the first time she saw Darby Elder's image reflected in the dark, wavy mirror of the old ballroom in her grandmother's house, though she didn't know his name then. She was startled by this encounter, being a practical child, but not really frightened.

It was her birthday and there had been a family party, with numerous cousins, colorful balloons, and piles of presents, and an enormous cake in the shape of a teddy bear. Keighly was dressed all in ruffles, her long, fair hair brushed to a high shine and held back from her face by a wide satin band. Her favorite gift, a doll that talked when the string in its stomach was pulled, was clasped in her arms.

The other kids thought the ballroom was spooky, with its shrouded furniture, its looming chandeliers, its silent harp, and ancient, shadowy mirrors. Though the echoing chamber was as clean as the rest of the house, it was private, closed off, as if in sacred tribute to someone or something long gone.

Keighly loved the place, perhaps for the very reasons her cousins did not, and used it as a refuge when she needed a few minutes to herself.

Now, hazel eyes wide, Keighly slipped off the needlepoint seat of the piano bench and approached the mirrored wall. The boy gaped at her, as if through a giant window, pale under his freckles.

Behind him, Keighly saw a large room with a sawdust floor, a long bar, an old piano. Women in gaudy low-cut dresses strolled between tables full of cowboys. It was like something out of a western movie, except that the people were far more untidy, and there was no soundtrack.

The boy looked back once, quickly, as if to see if anyone else had noticed Keighly, then turned narrowed eyes back to her. He was about her age, she supposed, and just a little taller. His clothes were odd—he wore knee-length pants made of some rough fabric, dark stockings, scuffed black boots with broken laces, and a loose dirty cotton shirt. He had rumpled brown hair and light amber eyes that seemed to sparkle with mischief, even though his expression was solemn just now, and more than a little wary.

Keighly smiled, in spite of the queer, jiggly feeling in the pit of her stomach. "Hello," she said.

He frowned and his mouth moved in silent response. Tentatively, he raised one grubby hand to the glass. She laid her fingers and palm to his, but felt only the cool smoothness of the mirror against her flesh. A vast sadness overtook her, one she was not capable of understanding, for all that she was one of the brightest children in her school.

They stood like that for a while—Keighly wasn't sure how long—and then, in an instant, the vision vanished. The only reflection Keighly saw was her own, along with the harp that had belonged to her grandmother's sister, and all the ghostly furniture.

Keighly was a relatively happy child, the only offspring of intelligent parents who loved her if not each other, and it was, after all, her birthday, an occasion surpassed, in the Barrow family, only by Christmas. Still, she felt an odd, piercing disappointment because the boy was gone. She had no doubt that what she had seen was real.

That night, because her parents were out with friends, it was Keighly's grandmother who came to her room to tuck her into bed. Audrey Barrow was an impressive woman; until her retirement only a year before, she had been a practicing attorney. She had masses of red hair, streaked with gray and always worn in a loose bun at the back of her head, and her eyes were exactly the same shade of hazel as Keighly's own.

They were "kindred spirits," her grandmother liked to say, cut from the same cloth.

"The mirror in the ballroom is magic," Keighly announced. With Gram, you just said what you wanted to say, straight out. If you didn't, she'd tell you to speak up and stop beating around the bush.

Gram arched one eyebrow. There were age spots on her skin, and she was pretty wrinkled, but to Keighly she was beautiful. "How so?" she asked.

"I saw a boy in there. And dancing girls. And cowboys."

"Hmmm," said Gram.

"This isn't a story, either," Keighly pointed out, braced for opposition.

"I didn't say it was," replied Gram. She'd come to the house some forty years before, as a bride, according to Keighly's dad. The ballroom had still been in use then, and Gram had danced there, in her wedding dress, with her handsome young husband. Keighly had seen pictures of the celebration, in one of the many photo albums lining the shelves in the study.

"But you didn't say it wasn't a story, either," Keighly replied. She had, after all, been born into a family of lawyers; her mother was an assistant district attorney in Los Angeles, and her dad, the youngest of Gram's four children, had just been made a partner in a large firm specializing in real estate.

Gram smiled, perhaps a bit wistfully. "No," she

to the glass, bolted to a nearby table, and returned with an old-fashioned slate and a piece of chalk. Hastily, he wrote *Y B R A D,* all the letters facing firmly in the wrong direction.

Keighly was puzzled at first, but she quickly translated. Darby.

His name was Darby.

The knowledge filled her with a strange, heady joy.

She saw him often after that—almost every day, in fact. Sometimes, to Keighly's alarm, the view was one-sided. Darby would be there, plain as could be, playing cards with women who wore sleazy dresses and funny makeup, or raking the sawdust floor, or wiping down the long bar, but if his gaze strayed toward the mirror, the blank expression in his eyes made it clear that he did not see Keighly at all.

She did not like the feeling of being invisible, especially to Darby Elder. It was almost as though she didn't exist, as if he couldn't see her.

That, Keighly told herself firmly, and repeatedly, was nothing but nonsense. Still, it was during that hot, sleepy, slow-moving summer that she first experienced the sensation that would plague her well into adulthood—a disturbing feeling that she was somehow insubstantial, unreal, a mere projection of another, better, stronger Keighly.

Keighly, though troubled, did not confide further

in her grandmother or, for that matter, in anyone else. Nor did she mention the boy in the mirror.

That fall, her parents decided to get a divorce. Keighly's mother moved to Paris, to work for a multinational firm, and her father went to Oregon, where he practiced law out of a storefront and lived with a woman named Rainbow, who told fortunes and had four children by a previous marriage.

Keighly was sent to a fancy boarding school in New England, far from her friends and cousins in Los Angeles, and she was suddenly, utterly miserable. The awful feeling that she had no more reality, no more substance, than a shadow wavering on wind-roughened waters went bone-deep and took permanent hold.

When the holidays approached, Keighly refused separate invitations from both her parents and declared that she wanted to go to her grandmother in Redemption instead. A compromise was reached: She spent Thanksgiving in New York, with her mother and an aunt and uncle, and flew to Nevada for Christmas, there to be joined by her father and Rainbow and the kids.

Her grandmother met her plane in Las Vegas, alone, and drove her home to Redemption. Her dad wasn't coming after all, Gram explained carefully, when they stopped for hamburgers and french fries along the way. Rainbow suffered from migraines, and needed to lie in a dark room for a few days.

conceded, smoothing the lace-trimmed, pink-and-white gingham coverlet on Keighly's bed. "I didn't." She paused, sighed softly. "I've caught glimpses of things in that mirror myself over the years—just out of the corner of one eye, you understand. It always happened so quickly that I thought it was only my imagination."

"I saw a saloon," Keighly confided. "Like the ones on TV, but dirtier."

Gram hardly batted an eyelash at this news. "This house was built on the site of an establishment called the Blue Garter, according to my research. The ballroom was part of the original building."

Keighly yawned, snuggling down deeper into her pillows, weary from the long, happy day. It was tacitly agreed that what she had seen in the mirror that afternoon would be their secret, hers and Gram's. Both Keighly's mother and father thought she had too much imagination and implied, sometimes, that she used it to liven up the truth.

The following year, Keighly spent the summer with her grandmother, because both her parents were tied up with important cases. As soon as her bags were unpacked and she'd changed into jeans and a T-shirt, Keighly wrote her name on a sheet of paper, backward, and rushed to the ballroom.

The sturdy, raggedy boy appeared almost immediately, as though he'd been waiting for her. He squinted at the tidy letters on the page Keighly held

Keighly didn't let on that she was relieved by the change in plans, but she guessed her grandmother knew. Gram didn't miss very much.

When they arrived at the house Keighly now thought of as home, she found a fourteen-foot blue spruce waiting in the ballroom, still clad in the damp, fragrant chill of the high mountains from which it had come. The handyman, Mr. Kingsley, had strung thousands of tiny fairy lights through its lush branches, but the job of bedecking the tree with priceless ornaments, made and collected over generations, had been saved until Keighly could be there to help.

The following evening, when supper was over and the decorating had been done, Gram teetering atop a high stepladder to do her part, Keighly sat alone in the dark ballroom, gazing at the twinkling lights and shimmering decorations and indulging in a sort of broken-hearted admiration. She would have liked to live in Redemption with Gram until she grew up, but the older woman's health was declining, and there were days when her arthritis kept her in bed.

Nobody seemed to take Keighly's suggestions that she might be helpful, even if she was almost nine years old, very seriously, so she finally stopped making them.

She was reflecting on the fact that she didn't really belong anywhere, and was feeling more transparent than ever, when she saw him, just at the edge of her vision. She turned her head quickly, her heart giving a lurch and then swelling with anticipation and relief. Darby was there, gazing in wonder from her to the tree and back again.

He'd grown taller. His hair was longer and somewhat shaggy, and there was an angry scrape on his left cheek.

He mouthed her name; she felt his soul tug at hers.

Keighly rose from her chair, crossed the room, and pressed her forehead against the glass, as if to will herself through it, so strong was the pull between them. She laid her hands flat on the mirror's cold surface, barely able to keep herself from squeezing her fingers into fists and pounding at the barrier that separated her from Darby, who did the same. There was no mockery in his motions; only a certain awkward tenderness.

"Darby," Keighly whispered. "Oh, Darby—the world's fallen apart and I'm only a pretend girl— I'm not real at all." She talked on and on, emptying her heart, never moving, and felt better for having said it all when the emotional storm was over. Even though Darby couldn't hear her, he seemed to understand, to know how sad she felt, and how lonely.

Most important of all, she knew he cared.

They stood like that, touching and yet not touching, for a long time. Then, when Gram came in and flipped on the overhead light, Darby vanished in an instant.

Keighly turned, blinking, half-blinded by the sudden illumination and by her tears. Her grandmother hurried over and drew her tightly into her arms, kissing the top of her head.

"Oh, sweetheart," Gram whispered. "Sweetheart. I'm so sorry, about everything."

Gram didn't ask why Keighly had been leaning against the mirror and crying—she had her own theories, of course—and Keighly didn't attempt to explain, then or ever. It was too private and too precious a thing to share, even with Gram.

Over the coming years, Keighly visited her grandmother whenever she could, and as she grew older, she began to dream vivid, dizzying, breathless dreams about Darby, whether she was in Redemption or far away, but to her sorrow she saw his image in the mirror less and less often.

When Keighly was twenty, and in art school, her mother was killed in a car crash in Europe. Her father died, only a year later, after a bout of flu, and then, six months after that, her grandmother passed on, too. The house in Redemption was closed, pending settlement of a large and complicated estate.

The mirror became only a mirror, something dark and empty, in a house far away. And Keighly, living in L.A., engaged to a man she should have loved, but didn't, did her best to forget Darby Elder, and all she'd felt for him.

Still, he called to her, waking and sleeping, working or playing, and the longer Keighly stayed away from Redemption, the more ethereal she felt.

Look for
MY OUTLAW
Wherever Paperback Books
Are Sold
Coming mid-April
from Pocket Star Books

Pocket Books celebrates Linda Lael Miller's new paperback with a $1.00 rebate

OFFICIAL MAIL-IN OFFER FORM

To receive your $1.00 REBATE CHECK by mail,
just follow these simple rules:

- Purchase the paperback edition of Linda Lael Miller's **MY OUTLAW** by July 31, 1997.

- Mail this official form (no photocopies accepted), proof of purchase (the back page from the book that says "proof of purchase"), and the original store cash register receipt, dated on or before July 31, 1997, with the purchase price of **MY OUTLAW** circled.

All requests must be received by August 7, 1997. This offer is valid in the United States and Canada only. Limit one (1) rebate request per address or household. You must purchase a paperback copy of Linda Lael Miller's **MY OUTLAW** in order to qualify for a rebate, and cash register receipt must show the purchase price and date of purchase. Requests for rebates from groups, clubs or organizations will not be honored. Void where prohibited, taxed, or restricted. Allow 8 weeks for delivery of rebate check. Not responsible for lost, late, postage due or misdirected responses. Requests not complying with all offer requirements will not be honored. Any fraudulent submission will be prosecuted to the fullest extent permitted by law.

Print your full address clearly for proper delivery of your rebate:

Name_____

Address_____Apt #_____

City_____ State_____ Zip_____

Mail this completed form to:
Linda Lael Miller's **MY OUTLAW** $1.00 Rebate
P.O. Box 9266 (Dept. 5)
Bridgeport, NJ 08014-9266

In Canada mail to:
Linda Lael Miller's **MY OUTLAW** $1.00 (Can.) Rebate
Distican 35 Fulton Way
Richmond Hill, Ont L4B 2N4